NAN

Doctor and author Robin Cook is widely credited with introducing the word 'medical' to the thriller genre, and over twenty years after the publication of his breakthrough novel *Coma*, he continues to dominate the category he created. Cook has successfully combined medical fact with fiction to produce over twenty-eight international bestsellers, including *Outbreak* (1987), *Terminal* (1993), *Contagion* (1996), *Intervention* (2009) and, most recently, *Death Benefit* (2011).

www.robincookmd.com

'Forensic pathologists and doctors-turned-detectives do battle against epidemics, lethal illness and drug-related deaths, the causes of which are far from natural . . . you'll find yourself completely hooked'

Daily Mail

'Likeable heroes, a compelling medical mystery and growing suspense – the result is a highly entertaining read. Commercial fiction, at its best, is pure entertainment. But Cook, like Michael Crichton, offers readers a smart dissection of contemporary issues that affect us all'

USA Today

'Robin Cook virtually invented the medical thriller in the 1970s with *Coma*, which was turned into a film. He followed that with a further 28 medical thrillers, most of which were bestsellers'　　*Guardian*

'Gripping . . . terrifying'　　*New York Times*

'Strikes a deafening chord of terror'　　*Washington Post*

'Holds yo　　*Larry King*

Also by Robin Cook

ROBIN COOK

NANO

PAN BOOKS

First published 2012 by G. P. Putnam's Sons,
a member of Penguin Group (USA) Inc., New York

First published in Great Britain 2013 by Macmillan

This edition first published 2013 by Pan Books
an imprint of Pan Macmillan, a division of Macmillan Publishers Limited
Pan Macmillan, 20 New Wharf Road, London N1 9RR
Basingstoke and Oxford
Associated companies throughout the world
www.panmacmillan.com

ISBN 978-1-4472-2988-9

1 3 5 7 9 8 6 4 2

A CIP catalogue record for this book is available from the British Library.

Printed and bound by CPI Group (UK) Ltd, Croydon, CR0 4YY

Visit **www.panmacmillan.com** to read more about all our books
and to buy them. You will also find features, author interviews and
news of any author events, and you can sign up for e-newsletters
so that you're always first to hear about our new releases.

NANO *is dedicated both to the promise nanotechnology brings to medicine and to the hope that any downside will be minimal.*

PREFACE

Smallness has been a most unappreciated attribute. We're always implored to think "big," and never "small." But now smallness sits at the convergence of chemistry, physics, and biology at a place called nanotechnology, which is transforming the world of scientific research and development and which is going to have an enormous impact on medicine. Despite its emergence only at the end of the last century, nanotechnology is already a multibillion-dollar phenomenon, with more commercial applications arriving on the scene at an ever increasing pace.

In the nanotechnology arena, small is very small indeed. The basic unit of length is the nanometer: one-billionth of a meter. Consider that if a marble were to represent a nanometer, then the entire earth would represent a meter. A hydrogen atom is approximately a tenth of a nanometer in diameter; a DNA molecule is 2 to 3 nanometers thick. Among living organisms, viruses range from 20 to 400 nanometers; bacteria are larger. Salmonella, the cause of typhoid fever and 90 percent of cases of food poisoning worldwide, is on the order of 2,500 nanometers in length and about 500 nanometers in width, with a narrow tail-like flagellum, also 500 nanometers long. The cells making up the human body are larger, with the disc-shaped red blood cell coming in at a diameter of around 7,000 nanometers, while white blood cells are 10,000 nanometers plus.

This nano netherworld is governed more by quantum mechanics than by the laws of macro-chemistry and physics such that bonds, forces, and fields prevail over mass, gravity, and inertia. And the power of these bonds, forces, and fields is stupendous, representing the potential energy locked away from the cataclysms of billions of celestial supernova explosions that have occurred over the life span of the universe.

Within the microcosm of nano-sized constructs of individual atoms and molecules, surface phenomena assume particular importance because the ratio of surface area to volume increases dramatically, essentially exposing their negatively charged electron fields and thereby their characteristics. For example, in the nano realm, gold is not the color of gold, nor is it inert. More important for nanotechnology is the element, carbon, the basic building block of life, already known to be versatile in forming both diamond and graphite. In the nanotechnology domain, carbon atoms have recently been found to form other astonishing and marvelous nano-sized structures when subjected to equivalent violent conditions that exist in the interior of red giant stars. These structures, called fullerenes, include sixty-carbon-atom buckyball spheres 1 nanometer in diameter, and even more important for nanotechnology, nanotubes of varying length and structure 1.3 nanometers in diameter. These surprising constructs have unique physical characteristics—amazing strength, lightness, stability, and conductivity, and will assume increasing importance as nanotechnology surges ahead.

In nanotechnology there exists a world of possibility but also of potential threat. Not even the experts know of the environmental or health effects of nanoparticles. For example, it has been noted that concretions of carbon nanotubes, something they tend to do, resemble the microscopic structure of asbestos with its known carcinogenic tendency. The fact that nanoparticles penetrate the human body, even the brain, is a known fact. How damaging this could be is totally unknown.

The second threat of nanotechnology is based on its immediate commercial success. In a very real sense, no one is guarding the multibillion-

dollar R&D hen house. There is no oversight, like there had been with recombinant DNA research, on the potential negative impact of nanoparticles. Nanotechnology research is being done in thousands of private laboratories, each racing ahead willy-nilly to be the first to secure valuable patents in a competitive environment where secrecy is paramount and the risks are minimized or ignored.

PROLOGUE

The cyclist decided to go for a relaxing ride—the real training would resume on Tuesday, after he underwent more medical tests. The trainers had said it was okay for him to take his bike out to work off some of the stiffness he had built up the previous day, but insisted he shouldn't push himself too hard. They had also made sure he was wearing the usual sensors for heart rate, breathing rate, and oxygen partial pressure, as well as the GPS device so that he could be appropriately monitored.

The route he was provided went north of Boulder to Carter Lake and back. The total trip was more than seventy-five miles, but there wasn't much change in elevation along the way. If he and the others expected to compete at the level intended, they would have to be able to cycle seventy-five miles of predominantly flat terrain without breaking a sweat.

After a few miles, the cyclist felt bored and restless. He knew he was supposed to take it easy, but his body felt so good, it was as if he were flying over the pavement. His legs were stronger than they'd ever been, and not only was he not out of breath, his breathing was shallow and easy like he was strolling in a park. It was a lovely spring day, and he welcomed the warmth of the sun on his back. Despite warnings to the contrary, he was ready to push himself. Why shouldn't he take advantage of feeling this good? Perhaps they'd punish him in some form or fashion, but the cyclist was confident they wouldn't follow through on any of the threats they made to hurt his family back home. Those sanctions were reserved for trying to escape, not for pushing oneself too hard during a workout. In fact, he thought he might even be rewarded for making such obvious progress in his conditioning.

What the hell? the man thought, and he started to race hard, pumping his legs, picking up speed, crouching flat against the handlebars to reduce the wind resistance. He'd been cycling for only about a year, but he doubted there was anyone in the world who could do this better. Wasn't his country about to demonstrate to the world that they could compete on a world-class level and in all endurance-based sporting endeavors?

The route had one climb of any significance, and the cyclist attacked it hard, initially holding his breath. He didn't slow down at all, taking the paved road as if it were flat, rather than a 6 percent incline. He was really racing now, flying, exhilarated, when, suddenly, halfway up the hill, he couldn't breathe and there was a sharp, stabbing pain in his chest and another in his left upper abdomen. The cyclist's hand went to his throat as he felt his airway contract. He tried to brake, but lost control and the bike veered right, hit the slight curb, and threw the cyclist hard into a downward-sloping shoulder that was half grass, half gravel. He landed awkwardly and bumped and rolled before coming to a stop. His arms and legs were scraped and cut, but that didn't matter because, try as he might, he couldn't catch his breath. It was as if he had breathed out but couldn't breathe in. On top of that, he was perspiring crazily, his heart was beating at an impossible rate, and the pain was unrelenting. The man hovered on the brink of unconsciousness, unable to get up or even move.

He had no idea how long he had been lying there, his body motionless on the outside but spiraling out of control within, like a runaway nuclear reactor. After a time—ten, thirty minutes?—he was aware of figures standing around him. Three or four people were talking at once and a hand grabbed his wrist. The man was aware that these were countrymen—he was in the United States but these people were Chinese, like him. They were part of the team. He felt his body being lifted roughly from the road and laid on a hard surface, and then a different kind of motion. The last sensation he had before finally falling unconscious was of being driven, presumably back to home base.

THE TECHNICIAN IN THE VAN switched off the GPS device. It had worked—the combined tracker and vital-signs register had sounded the alarm, and the team knew at once that number five was in distress and where he was located. He had been easy to find off the public road, and luckily no one had seen him fall or stopped to help him. The crash had taken him clear of the road and down a small embankment where he wasn't visible to passersby. The doctor in charge had been grateful for that.

Now the subject was displaying a highly unusual assortment of signs, but nothing they hadn't seen before. The GPS showed what speed he had been going—much too fast for that phase of the training cycle. It looked as if they were losing him, but the doctor knew a fresh batch of subjects were conveniently scheduled to arrive that very day. On the other hand, it was a shame; this one showed some promise, as he had been an athlete before getting in trouble with the law.

Within twenty minutes they had reached their destination. The van backed into a loading dock where another medical team was waiting, and they transferred the cyclist into a windowless room full of emergency medical equipment. As he lay unconscious on a gurney, one orderly cut away the man's cycling gear while another wheeled over what resembled a dialysis machine. By the time it was hooked up, the EEG monitor showed that there was no brain function, but that was of secondary importance—they had to make sure that the heart kept working so that they could recycle the blood and figure out exactly what had gone wrong, even though they had a pretty good idea.

A half hour later, the cyclist was technically dead, but his breathing and heart and vital functions were being maintained mechanically. His body would most likely be worked up and kept with the others in this state for as long as it was useful. The man's blood was running through a system that centrifuged it in 100 cc samples, separating out the usual components and the additives before reintroducing the cells and the plasma back into his artificially maintained circulation.

A surgical team entered the room, gloved and gowned as if for a regular operative procedure. The only difference was that none of the team was terribly concerned with sterility, and the scrub had been perfunctory at best. Without ceremony, a splenectomy was performed on the dead man and a lung sample was taken. Both the spleen and the lung sample were immediately sectioned and examined in the same room by one of the senior scientists on the staff. Under the high-powered microscope, he could see what he knew would be there, a profusion of microscopic, sapphire-blue spheres blocking the capillaries. The scientist checked his watch. He knew the boss was out of the country, but he'd need to hear about this right away.

1.

The woman is desperate and defenseless. A large man is sitting on her chest, restraining her, his head turned while watching the other end of a long room. The man's blocking her view, but she knows that whatever's going on is bad. She senses that someone she knows and cares for is going to die. As she struggles with the weight on top of her, she looks at up at her tormentor's face. He's a man she knew at one of the foster homes and institutions in which she was raised, a man who got too close. She looks away and then back at him. Now he's another man, her uncle, the worst of the men who have affected her life, and he's holding the video camera she came to hate.

The uncle she so despises says something in Albanian to a colleague who is somewhere in the room. It's a language she recognizes but no longer understands. The look on his face, with its cruel smile, is that of a predator, with her being the prey. Enjoying his victim's terror, he speaks again, but now in English. "Do it!" he snarls to his compatriot. "Shoot him!" The woman lifts and twists her head unnaturally to get a view. A hooded man is tied to a chair with duct tape. He jerks back and forth as he tries to free an arm or a leg, like a desperate insect caught in a spiderweb. The other man has a gun. He's walking around the chair, shouting in Albanian, lunging forward with the gun outstretched, poking the bound man, teasing him as a cat teases a captured mouse. With his free hand the armed man reaches over and tears off the hood and then looks back toward his partner. The woman recognizes the bound victim. It is a former medical school classmate named Will. And now she can see the gunman and recognizes him as well. It's her father. He sees her and turns back toward Will, and as she fills the world with a screamed "No!" he shoots the prisoner in the head.

Just as suddenly as it appeared, the weight left her chest. The heavy, molecular immunology textbook that she had been reading thudded to the floor. The woman sat up from the sofa, momentarily disoriented, sweating, shivering in the coolness of her apartment's living room. She became aware of an unfamiliar sound, not screams or gunfire, but a penetrating ring. It was her doorbell, which had been pressed possibly twice in the eighteen months she'd been living there.

Still confused, the woman unsteadily got to her feet and walked to the narrow entryway of her apartment. Who on earth could be ringing her doorbell? Looking through the peephole, she recognized her visitor. She turned and leaned her back against the door, stunned anew. The doorbell's raucous sound echoed around her mostly empty apartment, seeming louder than it actually was, but as she recovered from the anxiety and tension of the nightmare, it was easier to bear. She fortified herself with a deep breath as her visitor gave up on the doorbell and loudly knocked three times in quick succession. He always was very persistent. With a sigh, she turned and opened both locks on her door and pulled it open.

"Pia!" said George Wilson. "You're home. Terrific! How are you?" His lips were pulled back in an uncertain smile as he vainly tried to look her in the eye and gauge her reaction to his unexpected appearance on her doorstep. Then his line of sight went south, taking in her nearly naked body, and his smile broadened. At least the sight of her was welcoming. To him she was as alluring as she'd always been. He held a sad-looking bunch of roses.

"George, what the hell are you doing here?" demanded Pia Grazdani, pronouncing each word separately, uninterested in hiding her intense irritation. Her hands were jammed down on her hips with her jaw jutting forward, lips pressed together. Only when she followed George's gaze did she remember she was dressed in only a sports bra and panties, exposed to the apartment-complex's hallway, where some of the neighbors' children were playing. At her feet and extending over to the couch where she had fallen asleep was a trail of running gear: shoes, ankle-high socks, a white sweatshirt, running shirt and shorts, and a small backpack. On the coffee table was an iPod with earphones.

"You better come in," she said with uncamouflaged resignation, backing into the sparsely but tastefully furnished room. "What are the flowers for?" Her tone reflected her exasperation.

"What do you think? It's April twenty-first. It's your birthday. Happy birthday, Pia." George smiled, then shrugged defensively and busied himself by shutting the door behind him. He stood his roller bag up on its end and telescoped the handle.

"Oh," Pia said simply. "It's my birthday?" Pia was aware of the date, but had done nothing to acknowledge it. She retreated back into the interior of the apartment, picking up her running gear as she went.

George took in the lovely swell of Pia's derriere, appreciating that her figure was just as stunning in reality as it had been in his imagination over the far too many months since he'd last seen her. He watched as she quickly pulled on the clothes she'd rescued from the floor. When she plopped down on the sofa, clutching her knees to her chest with her bare feet poised on the coffee table's edge, she looked across the room at him. It was painfully clear she was less than thrilled about his surprise visit. George's eyes swept the apartment. It was of generous size, sparsely appointed with what appeared to be new, nondescript furniture. To George it looked as if no one lived there. There were no knickknacks, no photos, just a stack of medical textbooks on an otherwise empty dining-room table.

"Nice place," George said, wanting to be positive. He was nervous but determined. After months of calling Pia and leaving unreturned voice messages and sending countless pleading emails and texts with barely a reply, George had talked himself into coming out to see Pia, using her birthday as the excuse for a surprise visit.

Since they had last seen each other almost twenty-four months previously in New York, George had tried to change his persona, even dating a couple of attractive and personable women at the UCLA Medical Center, where he was a second-year resident in radiology. George thought he was stronger now, but now that he was in Pia's company, he realized he was no less in love with her, if that was what it was. Love sounded better than obsession. His attraction for her had become part of his life and would probably remain so, as simple as that. It was as if he were addicted. Ultimately George didn't totally understand his own behavior, he just accepted it.

George approached the couch, trying to to make eye contact. As usual, Pia looked away. George was able to take that in stride. Over four years of medical school he'd grown accustomed to her inability to make eye contact. George had also done a lot of reading about reactive attachment disorder and post-traumatic stress disorder since he and Pia had graduated and parted ways. Earlier in their relationship, at Pia's suggestion, George had contacted her former social worker, Sheila Brown, who had hinted without exactly saying that Pia was contending with these disorders. For George, knowledge was power, and the doctor in him wanted to help Pia and cure her, or so he had told himself. Such information was a great source of support for him and allowed him over the years to medicalize her inability to reciprocate his passion. This way he could weather what others might have found challenging, even devastating, to their self-esteem.

Reaching the coffee table, George held out the flowers. Pia sighed, and as her shoulders sank, George's heart fell with them. He'd hoped for a much more propitious reception.

"Happy birthday . . ."

"George, you know I don't care about my birthday," Pia commented, keeping her arms clasped together around her knees. "And that happens to be the sorriest-looking bouquet I've seen in a long time." Her voice had lost a degree of its hardness.

George glanced at the flowers. She was right. The blossoms were all wilted. He laughed at the flowers and at himself. "They have had a hard journey. I bought them at the L.A. airport on a whim; we had a middle seat on the red-eye to Denver, jammed between two people who must weigh three hundred pounds each. I held them the whole time, unwilling to consign them to the overhead bin. Then we stood all the way from Denver on a bus for ninety minutes before catching a cab here to your apartment."

"Why didn't you run the idea of coming here by me first?" Pia asked, shaking her head in disbelief that George would fly all the way from L.A. on a whim, trusting she'd be receptive. It was something she would never do in a million years.

"I couldn't run the idea by you. You haven't been answering voice mail, email, or texts. For all I knew, you'd been kidnapped again."

"Let's not be overly melodramatic," Pia said as a chill descended her spine. She recoiled at George's comment as if he had slapped her. Since the episode of having been kidnapped back in New York as the culmination of a series of tragic events, she had tried to suppress the whole experience, but it still consumed her, as attested to by the nightmare from which George had just rescued her.

"Okay," Pia said with another sigh, noisily letting air escape from her lungs like a deflating balloon. "I guess you're right, I have been out of touch, but not deliberately. I mean I haven't been ignoring you specifically. I've been so busy, I've been ignoring everyone and everything."

Pia gathered her thoughts as the shock of seeing George and the anxiety of her nightmare abated. "Listen, I don't mean to be an ass. I had a hard night. I worked till six this morning, and instead of sleeping when I got back, I went for a run. After that I tried to read. This isn't a great time for me to have company." Pia sighed again. The reality of having to deal with George was sinking in.

The more her mind cleared, the more she realized that George's sudden appearance was probably her fault, and not just because she had been ignoring his persistent attempts to reconnect. The problem really stemmed from what she had said to him, standing in a hospital room in New York two years before, at the very end of the events surrounding her kidnapping. She knew she'd encouraged him more than she should have. She'd talked to him about love, how she didn't know what love meant and how she wanted to change and be more like George, who she knew loved her, as evidenced by his steadfast personal generosity, which he had showered on her, despite little encouragement from her.

At the time, Pia and George had been speaking in the presence of their fellow medical student, Will McKinley, who was lying in a hospital bed, surrounded by monitors, stuck full of tubes and barely clinging to life. He'd been shot in the head, just like he had in Pia's nightmare, and left for dead by Pia's kidnappers, the men who wanted Pia and, secondarily, George to stop investigating the death of Pia's mentor, Tobias Rothman, a death Pia had eventually proved to be murder. Pia felt another chill creep through her body. Thinking about the whole horrid affair and Will's shooting was something she doubted she'd ever be able to come to terms with.

"Have you heard anything new about Will?" Pia asked, hoping for some good news since she assumed George was more in contact with their previous classmates than she.

"Last I heard, things were pretty much the same. That was a few weeks ago. Antibiotics still haven't been able to rid him of infection. Nor have multiple surgical debridements."

Pia nodded. This much she knew. The persistent osteomyelitis in Will's skull where the bullet had entered had proved to be resistant to all antibiotics. Of course she knew: Will's continuing health problems were in large part why she was in Boulder, Colorado.

"I'll put these in some water," said George, eager for something to do. "Maybe they'll perk up." He found a small kitchen off the living room and started looking for something for the flowers. Like the rest of the apartment, the kitchen looked barely lived in. The fridge was empty other than for some energy drinks and a couple of prepacked sandwiches. He picked one up and saw the "best by" date was more than three weeks in the past.

"How about we go out and get some lunch?" asked George, who had not eaten since the day before and was ravenously hungry. He received no reply as he continued looking into cupboards for something akin to a vase. He found water glasses, but they were far too small. Finally he laid the stems in the sink and looked at them wanly. He himself didn't feel much better than they looked.

"Listen, George, I'm sorry I didn't respond to your messages over the last couple of months or so." Pia had gotten up from the couch and was now standing in the doorway of the cramped kitchen.

George wanted to comment that she hadn't responded to any of his messages for more than two months, but he bit his tongue. He tried to look her in the eye, but as usual she resisted. George wondered if Pia had tried to change, as she had promised back in Will McKinley's hospital room. Would she ever be able to speak from the heart, or was she always going to keep a wall between them, fearful he might betray her? George knew what kept her from opening up. Her childhood in foster care from age six until age eighteen had been one of ongoing abuse and betrayal, sucking all the love out of her. She had learned to survive by going inward, not trusting anyone.

"I know what I said in Will's hospital room," Pia continued. "I've tried to change, to be open to love, but I just don't seem to be able to do it."

George wondered, as he had so often, if Pia could read his thoughts. But what was encouraging was that he also thought she looked convincingly pained. If it were true, he thought of it as progress of sorts. It certainly wasn't bringing them together, but at least it might be a few steps in that direction.

"My father suddenly reappearing like he did, saving my life at the eleventh hour, I suppose I should have been more thankful, but it was difficult. After abandoning me to foster care and all the pain that caused, he thought he could just march back into my life. He said he wanted us to be a family, as if that were possible. I had to get away from New York and from him and you didn't help."

George looked at his shoes. He recalled the uncomfortable meeting he had had with Burim Graziani, born Grazdani, Pia's father, without telling Pia beforehand, much less asking her permission. By that time Pia had refused to talk about her kidnapping to George or to anyone, and George had been questioned for days by the police. What did he know about the deaths of Pia's boss, the renowned researcher Dr. Tobias Rothman, and his associate, Dr. Yamamoto? What had happened when Pia was abducted in the street and Will McKinley shot, events he had witnessed? Did he know where Pia had been held, and how she escaped? Had he ever heard of Edmund Mathews and Russell Lefevre, two bankers whose deaths were thought to be linked to Rothman's? In truth, George knew very little, and when Burim called him, saying he was Pia's father who had changed his family name after giving Pia up to foster care, and asked to meet, it was a bolt from the clear blue sky. Unfortunately George had thought he could help.

When they met, despite George's unfamiliarity with life's unpleasant underside, he recognized in Burim Grazdani, he couldn't adjust to Graziani, a very dangerous man. George had left their meeting in a café shaken up, but he had agreed to try to intercede be-

tween Burim and Pia. Once again his urge to try to help had got
the better of him. When Pia had learned of the meeting she'd become enraged, screaming at George to stay out of her life, saying
that this man who said he was her father was dead to her. It was
one of the last times George had seen Pia before he left for Los
Angeles and she had left for a supposed long sojourn on a beach
somewhere, a trip Pia had never talked about to him before coming
to L.A. herself.

"I understand you wanted to get away from New York, and maybe
it was best for you," said George, even though he regretted her
leaving terribly. "I understand your sudden career confusion and
wanting to put off your internal medicine residency and getting a
PhD because of Rothman's death. I understand all that. But Boulder! Why Boulder . . . ?"

"I love it here, George. I love the air. I love my work. I love the
mountains. I've become a health nut. I started running, mountain
biking, even skiing."

As Pia carried on about Boulder and exactly what she was doing
in her current work, George stopped listening. He didn't care about
Boulder; what he really wanted to know was why she had not ended
up in L.A., where Pia had said she was going before they had fallen
out over her father. The fact that Pia had told him she was going to
L.A. to do research for several years was the one and only reason he
had turned down the residency at Columbia Medical Center and
gone to Los Angeles himself. As he might have predicted, without
Pia there, he was not fond of L.A. Pia was still talking.

". . . and another reason I came here to Boulder was because of
Will McKinley's osteomyelitis infection in his skull. If you haven't
guessed, I feel overwhelmingly guilty about his condition. Indi-
rectly, I was responsible. My hope is that we can use nanotechnology
in the form of a microbivore-based antibacterial treatment on him.
We've got them here at Nano, and they work. What is needed at this
point is FDA approval, which is what we're going to be working for

as soon as we finish preliminary safety studies. Ever since I've been here I've been working with these microbivores. They are amazing."

"Microbivores? You'll need to fill me in a little."

"George, you weren't listening. Didn't you hear what I was just telling you about what I've been doing here for eighteen months?"

"My mind wandered a bit," George admitted. His uncertain smile returned. The hoped-for rapprochement with Pia was testing his less-than-perfect diplomatic skills.

"I'm not supposed to be talking about what we are doing before all the patents are formalized, but what the hell. I haven't breathed a word to anyone. I trust you will keep what I say under your hat."

"No problem," George assured her. He wanted to encourage her. Counting on his confidence was a suggestion of intimacy, for which George hungered.

"It's going to be a new type of antisepsis," Pia continued. "The antibiotic era of fighting bacteria is near its end. I mean, bacteria are developing resistance faster than new antibiotics can be found. The hope is that medical nanotechnology will come to the rescue and provide rapid cures, particularly for sepsis. Specifically, I'm convinced it could cure Will's osteomyelitis."

"How will nanotechnology help Will?"

"As I said: by using the microscopic nanorobots called, appropriately enough, microbivores, which I've been working with for almost two years. They are much smaller than red blood cells, and they eat bacteria and other microorganisms when introduced into the bloodstream of a living animal. They'll even be able to be programmed to seek out, eat, and digest infectious proteins like prions or the tau proteins associated with Alzheimer's disease, which antibiotics are useless against."

"I'm sorry to have to admit this, but my knowledge of nanomedicine isn't the greatest. I mean, I know how it has contributed to sun screens, but that's about it."

"Well, you are going to have to catch up or you're going to be left behind. Medical nanotechnology is the future. It's going to totally change medicine, probably as much as regenerative stem cell technology. Between the two, five or ten years from now, the practice of medicine is going to be completely different."

"Microbivores coursing around in the body eating up bacteria. Sounds like that old science-fiction movie *Fantastic Voyage*."

"I guess. I never saw it. But this is not science fiction."

"And they are smaller than a red blood cell?"

"Absolutely. The ones I'm working on are ovoid, with their long axis about three micrometers long, which is six times smaller than the width of a human hair."

"I'm telling you: this sounds like science fiction."

"They're real. I'm working with them every day."

"So, what about L.A.?"

Pia cocked her head to the side and regarded George questioningly. "What do you mean, 'what about L.A.?'" To her, George's comment was a total non sequitur.

"I thought you were going to L.A. to do research. You never mentioned Boulder . . ."

"Well, there was a brief period when I thought I was going to go to L.A. I had found out there was a nanotechnology company in L.A. that was interested in microbivores, but their program is still in the design stage. I applied for a research position, but then I was contacted by a head-hunter who sought me out for the company here in Boulder called Nano, which has far outpaced its competitors in molecular manufacturing."

"You've lost me again. What's molecular manufacturing?"

"It's building nano-sized devices essentially atom by atom, molecule by molecule. It is the key to making these nanorobots. The head-hunter told me that Nano had already built some microbivore prototypes and had begun testing them in vivo. At that point it

was a no brainer for me. You'll have to see scanning electron microscope images we have of these things. They'll blow you away. Truly.
They are incredible."

"My mind is ready to be blown!" George said, looking at Pia, who
returned his stare with more eye contact than usual. He could tell
her formidable mind was in high gear. As so often happened, he
worried that she could read his mind and realize how little he knew
about what she was so passionate about and, if she could, the progress they seemed to be making reconnecting on a personal level
would evaporate.

"I guess I'm going to learn a lot about nanotechnology."

"Wait a second," Pia commented. "George, you didn't move to
L.A. because I—"

"No, no, of course not." George desperately wanted to change
this particular subject. He *had* moved to L.A. because of Pia for
sure, but at the moment he didn't want to admit it and look weak.
He knew Pia hated when he seemed weak and apologetic. "This
work with microbivores must be fascinating," he continued lamely.
"Will you be able to show me what you are doing? I'd love to check
it out."

Pia continued to regard George with an intensity that made him
look away.

"I really am starved," George said, needing to say something. He
rubbed his hands together nervously and changed the subject. "What
about some lunch? You must be hungry yourself."

Pia glanced over at George's roller bag, then back to George.
"Where are you intending to stay?"

"Actually, I was hoping . . . " George said, smiling his broadest,
albeit insincere smile. It had worked in the past with other women,
but he feared it was wasted on Pia.

Pia closed her eyes for a moment and shook her head almost
imperceptibly. "How long are you intending to stay in Boulder?"

"Not long," George added hopefully. "I only got a couple of days free. I told my chief it was a family emergency. I have to go back on Tuesday. I'm hoping to talk you into reciprocating and coming out to L.A. sometime soon."

"Okay, we'll talk about that later. Lunch? Sure, but it'll have to be fast. Then how about we head out to where I work. I can show you some of what I've been doing. The fact is, I've got a couple of experiments running I need to check on within the hour."

"Sounds good," said George. He brightened. It seemed like progress, of a sort.

2.

Zachary Berman was happiest when he was flying, and preferably, as he was now, on the Gulfstream jet owned by Nano, LLC, of which he was the majority stockholder, president, and CEO. He loved the feeling of time being suspended as the plane sped on toward its destination at 51,000 feet, currently far above the seemingly limitless expanse of the Pacific Ocean, heading for the North American continent. However hectic and stressful his life was on the ground, in the air he felt detached, safe, maybe even invincible. The plane had communications that rivaled those of Air Force One, but by turning them off, he had plenty of time to plan, strategize, and gloat about Nano's progress, especially on a long flight like this one: Beijing to Boulder, more than six thousand miles as the crow flies. Of course Zach, as most people called him, knew that his plane's journey would be less than that, due to the plane's polar route and the oblate shape of the earth.

As far as Zach was concerned, the trip had been a great success to the point of bringing a smile to his face. Putting his work aside, he lowered the back of his chair and raised the footrest, turning the seat into a comfortable lounger. Cradled in the hand-selected, hand-stitched Moroccan leather, he thought about Nano's spreadsheets and capital needs. A smile appeared on his stubble encrusted, masculine face. For the moment things seemed to be going swimmingly. He even allowed himself to doze.

About an hour later, as Berman nursed the dregs of what would be his last single-malt scotch of the trip and with the back of his chair in the upright position, he idly looked out of the plane's small window. His mind turned as it often did to his father and to the question of what he would have made of his son's enormous recent success and flying home from a business trip to China in a sumptuous private jet that was, for all practical purposes, his. Every day as he looked in the mirror to shave, Zachary flinched at his progressive resemblance to his late father, Eli, especially now that Zach was closing in on fifty.

This was one reason he kept his thick, slightly salt-and-pepper hair considerably longer than his father's closely cropped style. Zachary's expensive cut would have made the older man blanch. Growing up in a middle-class home in a strongly blue-collar neighborhood in Palisades Park, New Jersey, Zachary often saw flecks of paint in his dad's hair, an occupational hazard for a painting contractor, and he wondered why his father took so little interest in his appearance and what it implied. When Zach worked summers for his dad, from the time he was fourteen through college and grad school, he always wore a baseball cap as protection against such paint splatters. He'd worried their presence would mark him as a mere day laborer. From an early age, Zach had set his sights high.

A more profound disconnect between father and son was over what Zachary saw as Eli's contentment and fundamental lack of ambition. Even as Zachary excelled at Yale as an undergraduate and at Harvard Law School, Eli plodded along in the paint business without any concern to make it grow. Still, his father felt entitled to de-

ride his son's inability to play baseball as well as he had, and had
railed at his decision not to go into medicine as Eli had so vociferously voiced.

As the years passed, Eli's contempt for his son's career choices
only increased as Zachary abruptly abandoned his rather well-paid
corporate law job in Manhattan to enter the financial world, and
then, after ten years, quit his extremely lucrative job as an analyst
on Wall Street. Zachary had tried to explain to an uncomprehend-
ing Eli that he had become bored and thought of Wall Street as a big
con, believing there was much better money to be made and certainly more satisfaction in actually creating something, not just
playing around with paper, betting on a rigged market with other
people's money.

Zachary's watch sounded a single soft chime, reminding him of
the time and hence the proximity of their destination, and he swiveled in his seat to face the back of the plane. Halfway down sat
Berman's private assistant cum secretary, Whitney Jones. She looked
right at Berman, ready for his instruction. In one of her straight-line
Chanel suits, she was exquisite. Her black hair was pulled back
from her face to show off her striking features, which combined the
best of her African American father and Singaporean Chinese
mother. For Zach, seeing her profile never failed to remind him of
the famous bust of Nefertiti housed in the Neues Museum in Berlin.
Berman merely tipped his head very slightly, and Jones, ever attentive, unclipped her seat belt. With an equivalent return nod, she
stood. From previous instructions, she knew it was time to wake up
their guests.

Confident that everything was being taken care of, Berman
turned his attention back to the view and to his reverie. "A day's
hard work is its own reward," Eli Berman had probably said once a
week over the course of his whole adult life. He was distressed that
his son couldn't seem to settle on anything and failed to appreciate

what Eli had learned in the decades he had given to his paint business. Berman smiled. He far preferred being at 51,000 feet in a Gulfstream jet to any satisfaction gained from a day's manual labor.

Zachary absentmindedly played with his wedding band. The coming weeks were vitally important to his enterprise and billions of dollars were at stake, yet his wife and children, who should have been more involved in his triumph, were in New York City, barely aware of Zachary's work and the role he was playing in the fantastic evolution of nanotechnology. Zachary had wanted children, or so he thought, but he found domestic life as humdrum as he'd found corporate law. Ever since he'd been a child he'd been addicted to challenge and creativity. He couldn't stand status quo and predictability. He'd broken his wedding vows many times, even with Whitney Jones on a few occasions, and he'd come to think of his own family with little sentiment above and beyond the need to provide for them in an appropriate manner.

"Work is its own reward," Zachary silently mouthed contemptuously. It had been another, similar one of his father's dictums. "Somebody should have told that to Jonathan," Zach added. Jonathan had been Zachary's beloved younger brother, the one who could play baseball, and Eli's obvious favorite, who had died in agony from bone cancer, the failed treatment proving to be even worse torture than the disease.

"No, Dad, the reward is whatever you can take, whenever you can."

Zachary changed when Jonathan died. He'd always pushed himself, but after his brother's demise he had become supercharged, and had started to be reckless. He left Wall Street when Jonathan had been diagnosed, and Zachary helped Jonathan run their father's firm while Jonathan was being treated.

Unfortunately Jonathan's aggressive cancer was not to be denied, and he died within four months. As if from a broken heart, Eli, who had developed rapid onset dementia, followed quickly, leaving Zachary, a cynical and ambitious man, in charge of a moderately successful company that was poking along with seemingly little upside.

As a gesture of respect to his brother and his father, Zachary gave himself six months to make something of Berman Painting and Contracting, taking on the challenge at sixty miles per hour. He cut prices aggressively, hired more crews, and immersed himself in the details of the business, looking for some angle that might persuade him that it was worth his time. When Zachary found an article about the possible uses of nanotechnology in paint he almost didn't bother to read it. Paint was paint was paint. What relevance could it have for him when he was busting a gut trying to establish a foothold over the competition in northern New Jersey?

But Zach did read the article, particularly a section about research into the use of carbon nanotubes in paint that could block cell phone signals in a concert hall. He read the piece again and quickly went on to read all he could find on nanotechnology. Zach was convinced this was fertile ground that was virtually unexplored and certainly underexploited. There was so much about nanotechnology that he didn't understand, but the potential was obvious, exciting, and challenging. In college he'd steered clear of chemistry, math, physics, and even biology. He now regretted it. He had a lot to learn, and he applied himself with the zeal of a starving man having stumbled into a grocery store.

Within weeks, he had sold the business at a healthy profit and given all the proceeds to Jonathan's widow, and with that he felt he had fulfilled his obligation to his brother's family. When his mother was diagnosed with Alzheimer's some months later, and Zachary realized nanotechnology might possibly offer some hope, he felt thoroughly vindicated. Suddenly he was consumed by the promise of nanotechnology in the medical realm. What if he could cure bone cancer as a fitting tribute to his late brother? And what about his mother? Could he help her? Why not? With nanotechnology the sky was the limit.

Zachary felt a light pressure on his arm. It was Whitney. As she leaned in to whisper, Zachary smelled the fetching perfume she wore as well as her personal pheromones, and the scents conjured up a brief but welcome image of her long, toned body stretched out on a bed.

"They're all set," Whitney whispered. "We're landing in forty-five minutes."

Zachary nodded and stood up and stretched his arms, shoulders, and legs. His clothes—black T-shirt and blue jeans—fit tightly over a muscular body. Zachary was health conscious, particularly after Jonathan's sudden illness and demise and his parents' dementia. Even when he was busy, which he always was, he found time to work out and eat healthfully.

Berman freely admitted he'd become something of a hypochondriac, and he regularly took advantage of the fact that Nano employed a number of doctors. What consumed Zachary was the fear that he would suffer the same Alzheimer's dementia he witnessed in both his parents as they descended relentlessly into total helplessness. Hoping to reassure himself, he had himself tested for the apolipoprotein E4 gene associated with an increased risk of the disease. To his horror, the test had the opposite effect. He'd learned that he was homozygous for the gene, a factor that increased his risk, as did the fact that both his parents had had it. For Zach, his interest in medical nanotechnology became a personal obsession.

"Time for our little speech," said Zachary, and he followed Whitney toward the rear of the plane. Seated in leather armchairs similar to his were three Chinese men attired in carefully tailored Western-style suits. In a jump seat in the very rear of the plane was a large and serious-looking Caucasian man whose bulky jacket concealed a variety of airplane-safe weapons: a Taser, knives, and a rubber truncheon. He had never had cause to use any of these on a trip such as

this because the main cargo was very secure. Four figures in shape-
less brown jumpsuits slumped in the facing banquettes. The plane's
manufacturers may have designed the seats and table for a card game
or a meal on a long flight, but Zachary had found the arrangement
perfect for his purposes. The four, three men and a woman, were
shackled together and chained to the table. They were unconscious,
having been tranquilized when they had reached altitude.

Berman and Jones stood side by side. Zachary spoke and Whitney
translated into her perfect Mandarin for their Chinese guests. Her
fluency in the language was one of the reasons she was paid more
than a million dollars a year.

"We will be landing at our destination shortly," Berman said.
"Please follow our representative into the vehicle that will meet the
plane. We will proceed directly to the research plant, where you
will be staying in very comfortable accommodations. Our luggage
will follow us to the facility." Berman motioned to the four passengers with his head, including them as part of the plane's designated
cargo.

"We are entering a very exciting phase of our partnership. As
we advance together toward our common goal we must focus on the
end objective that we have all identified, toward which we have
been working so hard." Berman paused and waited for Jones to finish. He finished in Mandarin.

"Welcome to Nano."

The men nodded and muttered a greeting of their own. They
seemed nervous, aware of the responsibility the secret branch of
their government had placed upon them.

Berman resumed his seat, steepled his fingers together, leaned
back in his chair, and closed his eyes. For the last few minutes of the
trip home, he wanted to think of the best reason he could for getting
back to Boulder. On the trip out to China and even as he was con-
ducting his vital business, his mind had been preoccupied by the
same thoughts . . . Pia Grazdani.

3.

"So the company you work for is called Nano. What's the main guy's name again?" George shouted to make himself heard above the sound of the wind and raspy growl of the VW's engine. It was a fire-engine red VW GTI. He didn't even know Pia could drive, let alone like this. He gripped the edges of his bucket seat and nervously watched the winding road as Pia slalomed along.

Every time they turned, he reflexively pressed his left foot against the floor pan as if he could influence what the car might do with an imaginary foot brake. The last thing he wanted was for the vehicle to spin out on one of the hairpin turns. They were heading up into the foothills of the Rocky Mountains that cascaded down onto Boulder like an angry sea. The aspens were still leafless despite the fact that it was almost May, and their spidery branches, in contrast to the dark evergreens, looked yellow. On straightaways, where he felt he could release his life-or-death grip on the seat, George wrapped his arms around himself. Coming from Los Angeles, he thought the place was damned cold. Pia seemed immune. She was still dressed in her jogging clothes and a sweatshirt thrown over her shoulders.

"Berman. Zachary Berman," Pia yelled back. The car's windows were down, and the wind was whipping around her jet-black, nearly

shoulder-length hair. She was wearing a pair of cycling sunglasses
that curved around the side of her head. When George hazarded a
glance in her direction, he saw a distorted reflected image of himself.
His hair was standing on end and his face was twisted horizontally.

"What's he like?"

"I don't know much about him," said Pia, telling a white lie. Despite what she wasn't telling George, Pia didn't know a huge amount
about Berman above and beyond what was in the press. He was
a kind of international playboy in the mold of a few other more famous, relatively young, highly successful business entrepreneurs
such as Richard Branson and Larry Ellison. But she did know that
although he was married with kids, it was, in his words, an open
marriage.

The reality was that Zachary Berman had happened upon Pia in
one of Nano's several cafeterias and was actively pursuing her. At
first Pia had allowed herself to have a few casual dates with the man
because she was truly impressed with what he was accomplishing in
nanotechnology and the promise he represented in medical nanotechnology. But when he started to get personal, and she learned
about the Berman family in New York, she put an end to it, to Zachary's chagrin.

Then it became a problem. As a man unaccustomed to hearing
the word *no* from a woman, he'd become a pest, as far as Pia was
concerned. Even if he hadn't been married, she wouldn't have been
all that interested in any kind of a relationship. She was in Boulder
to work and recover from the emotional trauma she'd experienced
in New York City. Besides, she didn't even know if she was capable
of a relationship even if he was not the driven, selfish man she
thought he was. Over the years, Pia had become quite knowledgeable about her social limitations.

"Is he single?" George continued.

"No, he's married with two kids," Pia shouted back without elaboration, hoping the topic would end there. She didn't want to trouble George with the information that Berman was attracted to her and that his attentions had gotten to the point of being bothersome. Also in the back of her mind was the gnawing discomfort that Berman was due back that very day from an important business trip that had thankfully taken him away for almost two weeks.

"How old is he?" George persisted.

"Late forties, something like that." Pia clenched her teeth. George could be tedious about such things.

"I think I saw a picture of him," George said. "It was in *People* magazine, taken at the last Cannes Film Festival. He has one of those big yachts."

"Really?" Pia responded vaguely, as if she weren't interested, and she wasn't.

"Was he involved when the company, as you said, gave you this car?"

Pia massaged the leather steering wheel. She didn't like where the conversation was going but didn't know how to prevent it, short of saying she didn't want to talk about Zachary Berman, which would have conveyed the message she was trying to avoid. George was behaving exactly as she remembered he did—he was always full of questions that probed her private life. He had fussed around Pia's apartment for twenty minutes before she could get him to leave, with his litany of questions about whether or not she was looking after herself properly with no appropriate food in her refrigerator, suggesting that perhaps she wasn't actually living there. Pia knew George was trying to find out if Pia was seeing someone.

"Actually, he was involved. He had found out that I had been cycling to work and wanted me to have one of the company cars. He said it was too dangerous on the mountain roads, especially at night when I have to go in to check on some of my experiments."

"It looks brand new," George said, glancing around the interior.

"Guess I got lucky," Pia responded, looking over at George. George was annoying her, but maybe his showing up like this might actually serve a positive purpose. Perhaps it was a way to discourage Berman from pestering her.

"Pia!" George yelled.

She looked back at the road and something flashed in front of the car. There was a dull thump.

"We hit something," said George, and he turned around to look behind. Pia slowed the car, stopped, and flipped into reverse. She then backed up the road faster than George would have preferred. Pia stopped and jumped out of the car, the engine still running. Before George could get out, she came around to his side of the car, holding something in her hand. George got to his feet to see what it was.

"It's a prairie dog," she said. "Must have barely clipped it; at least I hope that was the case. It's alive, I think. Damn, I hate this kind of thing."

Pia cradled a small fur ball in her two hands. George could see a creature like a fat squirrel. It didn't look like it was moving too much.

"They're all over the place farther down the mountain," said Pia. "What are you doing up here, little guy?" Her voice was quiet and kind, and awakened in George a confusion he'd harbored about Pia. He knew she could be remarkably dismissive of people, himself included, as if she thought others had no feelings. But with animals, she couldn't be more caring. In physiology lab during the first year of medical school, Pia had refused to take any part in elaborate experiments using dogs, because the animals were euthanized at the end. Even stray cats around the med school dorm never failed to get her attention in some form or another.

"Here, you take him!" *That was more like Pia*, George thought. She handed him the small, still-warm bundle. "There's a vet in town that's open on weekends. We're making an emergency detour."

George held the animal as they drove in silence back into Boulder proper. George thought the creature was dead, but Pia intently stared ahead, a woman on a mission. Over the next half hour, they visited the vet clinic and determined that, yes, the animal was dead, most likely of a broken neck. Pia was as upset as George had ever seen her, her eyes even watery. For George that was definitely a first.

Leaving the vet, George was pleased when Pia pulled into a nearby Burger King. They didn't talk until they'd gotten their food.

"Sorry about the little guy," George offered to break the silence.

"Thank you," Pia said. She took a fortifying breath. "It's the second time it's happened. The last time I had trouble sleeping for days."

Wanting to change the subject, George said, "Back at your apartment, when you were explaining that Will's infection influenced your coming here to investigate nanotechnology as a possible cure, it reminded me of Rothman, and his death. I know you didn't want to talk about it back then, but I'd love to know what really happened. I know those finance guys in Connecticut were involved, but who actually did the killing? Do you know?"

Pia put down her burger and stared hard at George with dark pupils so huge that George thought he could drown in them. Her full lips narrowed. She looked as if she were about to combust. George put down his burger, afraid of what was coming. He leaned back in his chair to create a little distance.

"I've said this once and I'm not going to say it again," Pia hissed, leaning forward with narrowed eyes. "Time is not going to change the way I feel. I'm not going to talk with you or anyone else about Rothman's death. Not now, not ever! Just understand that the people who ordered it are gone. That's enough. Although I know it was done with polonium-210, I don't know exactly how it was carried out, nor exactly who did it, but I do know that if I talk about it, I will be killed. And if I were to tell you what I do know, you'd be killed."

"Okay, okay!" George managed. He could see fire in Pia's eyes. "I won't ask again."

Pia's face relaxed. She did know that Rothman's and his colleague's murders were carried out by an Albanian gang that was a rival to one in which her long-estranged father was a high-ranking member. What she had been told was that if she talked about what little she knew, it would not only lead to her and George's deaths, but would excite a blood feud between the two rival gangs, with scores of people probably ending up in the ground. It was a lose-lose situation and a responsibility that Pia could not bear.

Pia and George finished their lunch in silence. It wasn't until they drove within sight of Nano, LLC that they talked.

"This place is impressive," George said, gazing at the institution as they pulled up to a vehicular gate. The landscaped complex was far larger than he would have imagined, comprising multiple modern buildings, some as high as five stories tall, that stretched off into dense clumps of huge evergreen trees. The whole area was surrounded by a towering chain-link fence topped with razor-encrusted concertina wire. It appeared more like a military base than a commercial establishment. "Looks like they take security very seriously here." The people inside the booth were all dressed in smart, military-style uniforms.

"You got that right. As fast as nanotechnology is expanding, the competition is fierce and contentious. Nano has its own legal department with a number of very busy patent attorneys." Pia waited as one of the security men slid open a door and stepped out of the booth.

Pia handed over her identification, which the guard examined carefully. He then looked over at George expectantly.

"He's with me," Pia said. "He's a guest of mine."

"You'll have to head over to the central security office and talk to a supervisor," the guard said. His tone wasn't friendly, but it wasn't unfriendly, either; just professional.

As the gate lifted and Pia drove forward, she said, "I've never brought a visitor here. It's not really encouraged."

"Is it going to be a problem?"

"Let's see what they say at the central office. I can't imagine they're not going to let you come in, at least to the building where I work. I see FedEx people and the like there every day, so it is not as if it is off-limits to outsiders."

"Maybe you should go in alone and do your thing. I could always just hang out in the car beyond the fence until you're finished."

"Oh, come on, George. Nothing ventured, nothing gained."

George fought back the timidity that overtook him whenever Pia was taking him somewhere he thought he wouldn't be welcome. In medical school she'd come close to getting them both kicked out when she became hell-bent on investigating the deaths in the laboratory where she was doing an elective, despite the administration's very specific warnings against it. But this was a scientific lab. What would they have to hide from him? He was a radiology resident, for chrissake.

In the ultramodern, spacious lobby, Pia went directly to the security office and asked for a supervisor. As they waited, they looked at the banks of closed-circuit monitors watched by attentive staff. Scenes of labs, corridors, and common areas throughout the complex changed rapidly on the screens.

When the supervisor appeared, she examined George's driver's license and hospital ID, interviewed him briefly, had him sit in front of an iris-recognition recorder, then wordlessly disappeared back into the bowels of the department. After more than twenty minutes, she emerged, handed George's IDs back to him, and then gave Pia his pass.

"He's your responsibility while he visits here," she said matter-of-factly.

"Let's go, we're all set," Pia said.

"What do you think took so long?" George asked as he followed Pia back out into the lobby.

"I'm sure they ran a background check on you. They must be re-lieved you're a radiology resident at UCLA, since there's little chance of your being some kind of industrial spy. My sense is that's what they're paranoid about."

Before accessing the elevators, Pia and George had to swipe their passes and then peer through the iris scanner. Green lights showed all was in order. George had seen security like this before, but only in movies.

"So what's in this building besides your lab?" George asked as the elevator rose to the fourth floor.

"This building houses all the general biology laboratories. There's a lot of biology research going on because the powers that be at Nano are convinced that the real future of nanotechnology is going to be in medicine."

"The complex is huge. What goes on in all the other buildings?"

"I haven't the faintest idea," Pia said.

"You're not curious?"

"Somewhat, I suppose. But not really. Most current nanotech-nology applications are concerned with paints, lightweight mate-rials, energy generation and storage, fabrics, and informational technology—nonmedical uses like that, which doesn't interest me in the slightest. I do know that Nano has some medical diagnostic products on the market, like sensors and DNA arrays for in vitro testing and sequencing. That I would find more interesting, but not the other commercial stuff. All I'm really interested in is their nanorobot microbivores, the ones I'm working with."

The elevator stopped and the doors silently opened into a blind-ingly white, fluorescent-lit corridor. Pia strode off with George tag-ging along behind, squinting. He moved his sunglasses down from their perch on top of his head to shield his eyes.

"As I mentioned back at the apartment," Pia continued, "Nano has made major strides in molecular manufacturing so they can build complex devices here atom by atom, such as the microbivores."

All of a sudden Pia stopped, and George stopped, too. "Does it sound like I'm giving you a lecture? Maybe you don't want to hear all this. You can just tell me to shut up. I'm really excited about what I'm doing here. I might have come to Colorado mainly to get away from New York and my father, to deal with my guilt about Will, and to clear my mind career-wise, but work here has taken me over. I find it as engaging as what I had been doing back with Rothman before he died."

"I want to hear about it," George said, eager to keep Pia talking. "Really, I do."

"Are you sure?"

"I'm sure."

"Okay, because I think you're going to be intrigued, provided you listen instead of zoning out like you did in the apartment."

"I'm listening!"

Pia started walking again, gesturing with her hands as if she were fully Italian rather than just half. George followed, keeping up with her, watching. In truth he was only half-interested in the details of what she was saying. The other half was just enjoying her company, her excitement, and her remarkable physiognomy, with her almond-shaped eyes; incredibly long, dark eyelashes; delicately sculpted nose; and absolutely flawless skin. George would be happy to follow her anywhere. He was a basket case, but so be it, even if he had little understanding of why.

Pia took George at his word and kept talking: "Each individual microbivore has more than six hundred billion atoms arranged in its elaborate structure. It's actually a bit more than six hundred billion, but what's a few billion here or there?" She laughed at her own humor. "They are tiny, functioning robots with movable arms that seek out and grab pathogenic microbes and guide them into a digestion chamber, where they're eliminated. It's incredible. Okay, here we are."

Pia stopped in front of a blank door protected by another iris scanner. She positioned herself, mostly her head, so that the sensor could scan her iris. A light over the door clicked green. George was about to follow suit when she restrained him. "You don't have to do anything. This scanner is just to get the door open."

Once inside, George immediately thought of Professor Rothman's lab back at Columbia, but this was larger and more modern. He heard the familiar low hum from the vent hoods and from the array of medical machinery dotted around the room.

"Impressive," George said.

"It is. My boss keeps telling me there's fifty million dollars' worth of equipment in this lab alone."

"Your boss, this Zachary Berman guy?"

"No, he's the big boss. My direct boss is a woman named Mariel Spallek, who's not my favorite person in the world." Pia didn't elaborate. She put down her backpack, picked up a ledger, and moved over to a central display console with readouts from all the biotech equipment. With a pencil Pia ticked off some boxes in the ledger and wrote in others.

"Everything okay?"

"Looks that way. My iPhone would have alerted me if something was amiss. But things are looking good. Until this series of experiments, we'd been having biocompatibility issues with the microbivores. Back when we first introduced them into our animal models, we were surprised to see some allergic reactions. Not a lot, but enough to be troublesome. When it comes to the mammals, especially the primates and humans, there cannot be any reaction. Initially we found that our subjects' immune system could occasionally treat the microbivores as foreign invaders, which, of course, they are. Why we were surprised is because the surface of the microbivores is of diamondoid carbon, which is about as nonreactive and as smooth as can be. Are you following me?"

"Yes, sure," George said almost too quickly. Nonetheless, Pia kept talking.

"What we deduced was that some molecules had adhered to the microbivore's surface despite its presumed nonreactivity, leading to some level of immune response. I assume you remember all this from immunology in med school. Do you?"

"Oh, yeah. Of course!" George said, hoping to hide the fact that he remembered little of what Pia was talking about. Pia's retention of such minutiae always impressed him. Whenever she spoke about science, her face radiated a kind of passion. She also had no trouble maintaining eye contact, which she could not do in general conversation, especially conversation involving anything personal, like emotions.

George nodded enthusiastically. He tried to think of an intelligent question, which wasn't easy as close as they were standing together. He could smell her wonderful aroma. It was erotically intoxicating thanks to his memory of the few times they had had sex. "What kind of animals are you using as subjects for these studies?" he managed, even though his voice cracked.

"A type of roundworm, but we will soon be moving to mammals, provided these subjects show no immune response, which so far seems to be the case. I'm not looking forward to working with mammals, as you can well imagine. I'm sure you remember my feelings about that."

George nodded again, knowingly.

"If and when you get to injecting these microbivores into human subjects—into Will McKinley, for instance—how many microbivores would be involved?"

"Somewhere in the neighborhood of a hundred billion, about the same number of stars in the Milky Way."

George whistled. "How big a bolus would that be?"

"It wouldn't be big at all. About one cubic centimeter diluted in about five ccs of saline. It gives you another appreciation of how small these things are. Each one is less than half the size of a red blood cell."

"So this is what you have been working on for the last eighteen months, the biocompatibility of these microbivores?"

"Yes. It's the main thing I have been doing, and we're making progress. There was a breakthrough of sorts when I suggested that some oligosaccharide polymers be incorporated into the microbivore's diamondoid surface."

George couldn't keep himself from wincing at this comment. Pia was talking way over his head. He vaguely remembered the word *oligosaccharide* from first-year biochemistry—something about complex sugars—but that was about all. To divert attention from his ignorance, he quickly said, "You mentioned back in the apartment having some scanning electron microscope images of these microbivores. Can I see them so that I have an idea of what we're talking about?"

"Good idea," Pia said with enthusiasm. She led George to a nearby computer terminal, and with a few clicks she brought up an image. She stood aside and proudly gestured toward the screen. The image was in black-and-white, showing multiple, dark, shiny microbivores in the presence of a larger donut-shaped object. Pia pointed toward the object. "That's a red blood cell. The rest are the microbivores."

George stepped closer for a good view. What he saw amazed him. "They look like spaceships with a big mouth."

"I never thought of it that way, but I see your point."

"What are all these circular objects arranged around the hull?"

"Those are the sensors that detect the targeted microorganism or protein, as the case may be. They also contain reversal binding sites to cause the target to stick. The very tiny circles surrounding each sensor are the grapplers that come out to move the target along the microbivore in a kind of bucket-brigade fashion before pulling it into the digestion chamber."

"Is that what this hole is?"

"That's right. Once the target has been swallowed, so to speak, it is enzymatically digested into harmless by-products, which are then pushed back out into the bloodstream."

"And this whole thing is six times smaller than the width of a human hair? It seems incredible."

"It's got to be that small to get through the smallest capillary, which is about four microns in diameter."

George straightened up and looked at Pia. She was still doing well with maintaining eye contact with him. "How does this miniature robot know what to do and when to do it?"

"It has an onboard computer," Pia said. "Thanks to nano circuitry and nano transistors, it has a computer with five million bits of code, twenty percent more than the Cassini spacecraft had in its onboard computer on its mission to Saturn."

"It's all hard to believe," George said, and he meant it.

"Welcome to the future. When we get back to my apartment I'll give you an article on microbivores written more than a decade ago by a futurist named Robert Freitas. He predicted all this back when molecular manufacturing was nothing but a pipe dream. It's pretty exhaustive."

"I bet that's fun reading," George said, unable to resist a bit of sarcasm. Luckily it went over Pia's head, as she had returned her attention back to the microbivores image. From her expression and posture, he could tell how proud she was about what she was doing.

"I think you'll find it fascinating."

"So doing this is what the head-hunters brought you out here to Boulder for?"

"No. What brought me out here was that the CEO, Berman, had read about Rothman's work on salmonella that I was involved with. You see, from an operational standpoint, microbivores are having a problem with bacteria that have a flagellum. You know, little whip-like tails, like salmonella has. When the microbivores ingest a salmonella, the flagellum doesn't get into the digestion chamber but rather gets detached and floats off, and the flagellum can cause as much immunologic havoc as the intact bacteria. With my experience with salmonella in Rothman's lab, they thought maybe I could help with this problem."

"Were you able to help?"

"Well, I've been thinking about it and have done some work toward a solution. I do have an idea of how to solve it, but when I learned of the biocompatibility issue, I got more interested in that. The flagellum problem is mechanical, the biocompatibility is more intellectual. I find it more of a challenge."

As Pia talked, George couldn't help but ruminate again of how he had ended up at UCLA.

"When did Nano actually make you the offer?"

"The offer? I don't know, late June, I guess, just before graduation? Why are you asking about that again?"

George's frustration surged again—again being reminded that his whole move to Los Angeles had been a wild-goose chase. He should have stayed in New York. Luckily, before he could say anything, his attention was diverted. The door to the lab swung open, and a woman in a lab coat strode into the room. George regarded her. She was striking, athletic-looking, and taller than Pia, with light blond hair pulled back into a tight ponytail. She had a decidedly imperious air, and her demeanor was not friendly as she looked first at Pia, then at George, and back to Pia. The blond woman referred to a clipboard she was carrying. George felt immediately uncomfortable.

"This is Mr. Wilson?"

"Yes, Mariel. Dr. Wilson, actually," Pia said.

George stepped forward and stretched out a hand. "Nice to meet you. George Wilson." He assumed this had to be the boss Pia had mentioned.

The woman merely nodded, and George withdrew his hand.

"Mr. Berman is on his way back. He may even have landed. He

doesn't like visitors to Nano, which is why they are not encouraged. I thought you understood this. I would hazard to guess that he will be especially displeased about young men coming to visit you, Pia. We are counting on your being productive here at Nano. You were recruited for very specific reasons."

George looked over at Pia. What did she mean by that?

"George and I were med students together in New York. He's a resident at UCLA, and he's staying with me as a houseguest for a couple of days. I can't imagine Mr. Berman would find that irregular in the slightest. It is not going to have any effect on my productivity."

Houseguest? thought George. That was the first encouraging news about where he was going to stay, but he kept quiet. Tension sparked between these two women, and it was obviously related to Berman and Pia. Perhaps his intuition and vague fears had been justified, knowing what he did about Zachary Berman. Too often George had seen how a lot of men reacted to Pia, himself included. And a brand-new VW sports car seemed a bit beyond the pale for any casual boss-employee relationship.

"What exactly is Mr. Wilson doing here in the lab?"

"I'm just checking on several of my biocompatibility experiments that I started last night," Pia said. "I just wanted to be sure they were running properly. I knew it would be quick. He's merely accompanying me. We're almost done."

Mariel Spallek glanced at George and gave him a look that made the discomfort all the more intense. The situation reminded him that there was an unfortunate history of Pia's ability to get him into trouble.

"I'll be sure to let Mr. Berman know you're around." Mariel looked over at Pia as she left, but George wondered if she meant him.

"What was that about?" George questioned. "Or shouldn't I ask? She seemed to be implying something about you and Berman or am I reading more into it than I should?"

"It's probably better that you don't ask," Pia said without elaboration. She was pleased. Now she was certain that Berman would hear that she had a gentleman visitor. Perhaps, as she had hoped, it would cool Berman's ardor. As far as what George might be thinking subsequent to this episode with Mariel, the issue didn't even enter her mind.

4.

NANO, LLC, BOULDER, COLORADO
SUNDAY, APRIL 21, 2013, 2:45 P.M.

The pleasant sense of calm that Zachary Berman had felt during
the plane flight had dissipated completely. It wasn't that there'd
been any hitch in the arrival and delivery, and everything had run
smoothly at the general aviation terminal at the airport. The dignitaries were driven in one of Nano's Suburbans to company head-
quarters, where they would be set up in their accommodations. The
involuntary guests were discreetly carted off the plane by means of
a catering truck and were also at Nano, in less comfortable surroundings than their compatriots. Berman impatiently demanded that his
driver get him to his office as soon as possible. Berman's unofficial
arrangement with the airport allowed him easy access to all areas,
and his car was able to take him right off the tarmac and out onto
the airport's perimeter road.

With Whitney Jones trailing behind him in a separate limo, Berman entered the Nano facility through an unmarked private vehicular entrance. Once at the proper building, an inconspicuous outer
door opened into a compact lobby, where two armed guards stood
at an inner door, on either side of the iris scanner that everyone, Berman included, had to negotiate before gaining access to the core of

the facility. Passing through the scanner and hustling along, Berman reached his office to find Mariel Spallek waiting for him.

"How was the flight?" asked Mariel.

"Who's the guy with Pia?" Berman demanded, ignoring the question.

Mariel knew Zachary would latch on to that part of the email message she had sent as Berman drove in. He wouldn't tell her about the status of the four new subjects; he would neglect to bring her up to date on the state of the financing negotiations; he wouldn't ask her about progress in the multiple trials that were going on in the private and the public areas of the facility; he would want to know about Pia and the young man who had accompanied her here to Nano.

"His name is George Wilson and he's a radiology resident at UCLA. He checked out."

"What's he doing here?" Mariel could tell that Zachary was trying to be calm, but he was failing miserably. He was like a lion in heat. He picked up memos and reports from his desk, feigning interest in them, but his eyes were elsewhere, darting across his desk and back. This piece of news about George Wilson was driving him crazy, and a part of Mariel relished his discomfort. She didn't know the nature of Pia and George's relationship, but she didn't mention that. She was content to allow Zachary to think the worst.

"She said he was visiting for a few days. They were classmates at Columbia Medical School. The background check we ran on Pia before we hired her mentioned him; they had been friends for the duration of the four years. The exact nature of the friendship had not been mentioned. What had been mentioned was that he had been involved in that kidnapping business."

"Right, I remember. He was the guy who was supposed to get shot."

"That's right," said Mariel. "He certainly seems to be a lucky young man."

Berman looked up and fixed Mariel with a stare. Was she messing with him? He knew that Mariel was fully aware of his unrequited interest in Pia, and he knew with ever greater certainty that his brief affair with Mariel had been a mistake, a big mistake. She had latched on to him like a limpet and had taken some shaking off, despite the chasm in status between the two of them at work. Mariel had been spurned, but he was certain she was hoping that passion would be rekindled, and if so, she would come back to him in a second.

Berman would have liked nothing more than to fire Mariel so he wouldn't have to be continually reminded of his mistake, but no one knew more about Nano's medical nanotechnology program than she did. The sum total of everything she knew about Berman and Nano could be dangerous to him, so he was constantly walking a tightrope with her. Perhaps one day he'd jump off, but not today. Berman wondered why Mariel couldn't be as mature as Whitney Jones. Whitney knew the working relationship they had was too important to jeopardize over something as frivolous as a few rolls in the hay.

"Do you want to go and see her?" Mariel broke the uncomfortable silence. "When I left her, which wasn't that long ago, she was in the lab with the young man checking on some of her experiments. Perhaps she is still there."

"How are those experiments going?" Zach was well aware of what Pia was doing and was impressed, which only fanned his desire. She was erotically gorgeous and smart, both qualities Zach found irresistible, especially in the same person.

"Seems they're going well. So far no suggestion of any immune response. But they are not over."

"Right," Zachary said. He got to his feet. "I need to talk to her about the flagellum issue. Now that she's been making such progress on the biocompatibility problem, she needs to get cracking on what she was initially hired for."

"Of course," said Mariel, backing away to let the onrushing Berman past. She knew the real reason he wanted to get down to

Pia's lab, and she set off slowly behind her boss, letting him charge ahead. In his eagerness he was soon out of sight. "Men, they are so predictable," she muttered disparagingly.

When she got back to the lab where Pia worked, she found Berman standing alone in the center of the room, holding a file.

"She left," he said. "What does this mean?" Berman handed the file to Mariel. She was well aware of Pia's ongoing experiments—she had helped to design the protocol herself for most of them.

"It is a summary to date of what is currently running. As you can see, everything is negative for any suggestion of an immune reaction, which is encouraging. The new microbivore design with the polyethylene glycol molecules incorporated into the outer shell apparently is a stroke of genius. Obviously, Pia was right, and I think we should use it you know where."

Mariel might not have been the easiest person to get along with, but she was honest to a fault. She disliked Pia not only because of Pia's signature aloofness but also because Berman was so obviously physically attracted to her and not to Mariel. She also knew that Berman's ardor was fueled by Pia's rejection of him, meaning he wanted what he couldn't have. Although Pia was a reminder to Mariel that Zach had rejected her, she was able to give Pia credit for her intelligence.

"If these positive results continue," Berman said, "I think we can start considering moving to mammals for safety studies."

Mariel studied Berman's face. It appeared as though he had forgotten momentarily about Pia. She recognized his expression—he had it every time they made a step toward the major breakthrough they sought. The look on Berman's face suggested more to Mariel than just excited anticipation of a seriously profitable business accomplishment, it was almost yearning.

5.

Pia sat on her couch, going over a copy of the same results Mariel and Berman had just seen while George took a shower. The results were certainly favorable, enough so that she anticipated she'd soon be encouraged if not forced to return to the flagellum conundrum, and her mind wandered to it. Her intuition told her that it was not going to be as easy to solve as the biocompatibility problem. As she had explained to George, the flagellum issue was more of a mechanical problem, and she thought the solution would have to be mechanical, too. Pia had developed a clear picture in her mind of the battle that would take place in the body between the bacteria and her beloved nanorobots.

"What's the figure again, ten to the minus nine?" George's question disturbed Pia's concentration. George might as well have clashed cymbals together, and Pia literally jumped at the intrusion. In the eighteen months she'd been in Boulder, Pia had never had company in her apartment.

Pia shot a quick glance over to see George standing in the doorway, loosely wrapped in her only large bath towel. She'd put out a hand towel, of which she had several, and apparently it wasn't adequate. Pia had a thing about her space and her stuff. In foster care she'd always had to fight for both.

"A nanometer is what size?" George continued.

"Yes, that's right, a billionth of a meter," Pia responded. She closed her eyes and counted to ten. She found the towel issue irritating; she was irritated he was there at all. What the hell was she going to do with him until Tuesday?

"I was really blown away when you described the relationship of a nanometer to a meter being the equivalent of a marble to the size of the earth. And when you said human fingernails grow at a rate of a nanometer a second. I really have an appreciation of how small a nanometer really is."

"I'm glad," Pia said with a hint of sarcasm that was lost on George.

"Before today I really didn't know anything about nanotechnology. And you say in a few years, fifteen percent of everything manufactured will use nanotechnology in some form or fashion?"

"Maybe within three years. In 2011 nanotechnology had already spiked to over fifty billion dollars a year worldwide. Now it is around seventy billion."

"And who's regulating it?"

Pia drummed her fingers absently on the arm of the couch. Social and political issues about nanotechnology didn't interest her. For her it was all science, extraordinarily promising science.

"I don't know, George. I don't think there's any real regulation. I mean, who cares whether tennis racket frames are lighter and stronger. I certainly don't."

"I'm thinking more about those nanoparticles you mentioned in the car on the way back from Nano: the buckyballs and nanotubes. As small as they are, I imagine they'd be absorbed through the lungs, maybe even through the skin. Seems to me that health and environmental issues should be considered, especially if they are as stable as you described."

"You're probably right," Pia conceded, but her mind was already back on the flagellum issue. A mechanical solution was beginning to germinate in her mind.

"And the microbivores that you are working with. Are they safe do you think?"

Pia rolled her eyes as her incipient creative thoughts fled from her consciousness under George's persistent questioning. "Proving microbivores safe is what I've been doing for the last eighteen months."

"Not really. So far you're just making sure they are immunologically inert. That doesn't mean they are safe, necessarily. What if they begin doing something you don't expect, like chewing through capillaries or eating red blood cells? I mean, the way you have described these things, they might turn out to be insatiable, miniature great white sharks." George chuckled at what he thought was a humorous metaphor. He vigorously dried his hair, pretending to be unaware of his nakedness.

"As I already told you, they will be specifically targeted to bacteria, viruses, fungi, and hopefully bad proteins. They are not going to go wild. Each microbivore has multiple backup systems like a jet plane, and they can be turned on and turned off from outside the body using ultrasound signals. You have an overactive imagination. You've seen too many bad disaster movies."

"What about these buckyballs and nanotubes just wafting out of Nano's labs and floating off with the wind. Has anybody thought of that?"

"All the labs at Nano involved with medical nanotechnology are the equivalent of level-three biosafety labs, the same as those at Columbia when we were working with the salmonella grown in space. Actually the equipment here is newer than what we had at Columbia. Look, we are at the beginning of safety studies for microbivores, and they are going to be exhaustive. Otherwise, we won't get FDA approval. Rest assured, when microbivores are made available as a treatment, they will have been proven beyond any doubt to be perfectly safe."

Pia's mention of the lab at Columbia did little to reassure George. Pia's mentor had died as a result of radiation poisoning in his level-three lab. In George's mind, labs doing cutting-edge research were dangerous. He watched as Pia returned her attention to the papers she was holding. It was amazing to him that she could look so good despite still being dressed in her jogging clothes with her hair having been blown around in the car. For the first time, he noticed that she had cut off a few inches. As he stood there admiring her, he could barely stand being so close and not touching her. Just when he was considering walking over to the couch, Pia's iPhone buzzed, claiming her attention and yanking George back to reality.

"Why don't you finish up in the bathroom and get dressed," said Pia without looking up. It was yet another text message from Zachary Berman. "I want to shower, too, and change out of my running gear." Berman had already sent three messages in the last twenty minutes, each a permutation of the other, asking her to call ASAP. Pia sighed. George's presence was not going to deter Berman as she'd hoped but rather inflame him. Each text message was progressively more demanding.

Pia regretted anew having those few dinners with Berman. She should have known better because she had heard rumors about his reputation and that he was married. She thought the rumors were sour grapes on behalf of some women who saw him as a spectacular catch. Dining with him several times, she had enjoyed herself. He had been all business, talking about his wish to succeed with medical nanotechnology and its promise of dealing with cancer and Alzheimer's disease. Although he didn't elaborate, nor did Pia question, he alluded to the fact that his interests had sprung from personal experience.

During those first casual dinners, Pia thought he seemed different from other men she'd had to deal with. There had been no come-on whatsoever. The closest he'd come to anything personal was to talk about her interest in research and how appreciative he was that she had been willing to put off her residency training and getting her PhD to come to Boulder and help with their microbivores program, which he thought was going to put Nano on the map.

A couple of more friendly dinners followed, but then, out of the blue, the presents started coming. First flowers, then expensive wine, chocolates and jewelry, culminating in the car. Other than the flowers, which couldn't be returned, the only gift Pia kept was the VW she'd talked herself into accepting, and even that, she recognized, would have to go. The last time they had met privately, Pia had to fend off her boss, who told her how smitten he was with her, after trying to push his way into her apartment. Pia had managed to extricate herself without having to resort to her expertise in martial arts.

She was more than adept at tae kwon do, which she had learned at the Hudson Valley Academy for Girls, a derelict institution where she had been incarcerated in the name of foster care. That last evening with Berman, she was proud of the way she'd handled the situation while leaving her inebriated boss's dignity intact. That had been a week before he had left on his trip to China, and now he was back, trying to contact her, whether she had a gentleman visitor or not.

"What do you want to do this afternoon?"

"I was going to take a nap," Pia said. She was suddenly exhausted after her near all-nighter that had only ended that morning. She resolved to ignore Berman's text, as she had the three previous ones. Pia was sure Berman wanted to quiz her about George. And she knew George was dying to ask her more about Berman. Perhaps it was best to let them both think what they wanted, and allow both of their imaginations to run wild. And a couple of hours' sleep really would do her a world of good and give her a bit of perspective. Sunday was a day that was meant to be taken a little easy.

6.

The man had been in this strange place only a few hours when he was hauled out of a deep sleep, given athletic gear to put on, and led to the room he was standing in now. A countryman of his, but not one who had accompanied the four of them on the plane ride, was reassuring him that everything was fine; they just needed him to run a couple of tests on a stationary bicycle. The man in the suit seemed friendly enough but didn't offer any explanations of where they were. His accent suggested he was from a different province from his own.

The cyclist looked around the brightly lit room, at the bike, and at the shelves lined with banks of equipment with flashing lights. Where he was exactly, he had no idea. All he knew is that it was somewhere in the United States. Four Westerners in medical scrubs, hoods, and face masks stood around checking the equipment. They looked like the man who had given the four of them an injection soon after they arrived. One of the masked figures said something, and it was time to get on the bike.

"WE HAVE THE BIKE set to the same parameters as this morning's ride," a Westerner said.

"That's right. This is the control. We need to see if this morning's incident was an anomaly or whether there is a systemic issue," said another. He was the leader, so he indicated to the Chinese official that it was time to start. Through a translator, the official explained to the cyclist that he would feel the bike speed up and slow down and he had to keep up with it, that was all. They were monitoring the effects of the exercise on his body.

"Tell him he has nothing to worry about," the leader said, and one of the other masked figures in the room shot him a look.

"Let's hope not," the leader said under his breath.

The cyclist started pedaling. He had noticed that the bike's rear wheel was encased in equipment, and now he knew why. The machine was speeding up and he exerted himself to keep up with it. He had cycled before, but this seemed easier than he remembered. If this was to be the extent of the work they were going to have to do, he could cope with it easily. He wasn't out of breath in the slightest.

"Okay, where are we on the run?" the leader asked after a few minutes.

"Coming up to the crisis point." The translator had been asked to leave the room before the test began. The cyclist's vital signs looked good. Perhaps this morning was just an accident, after all.

What the cyclist was feeling was something close to exhilaration. He willed the machine to test him harder—this was too easy! He looked at the faces of the people watching him and was glad to see they looked pleased. He would surely have a good chance of freedom if he gave these people what they wanted.

As the resistance increased, the cyclist pushed even harder—he felt free, almost, until in an instant he felt as if a hand were clamped around his throat. He yelled out and pawed at the oxygen mask he was wearing.

The medics and technicians all started yelling at once. The vital signs were way off—it looked as if the man's heart had failed. The leader observed the chaos playing out in front of him but made no effort to intervene. It was the same event. He was already thinking what he was going to tell his boss. The event that morning had not been an anomaly. It was a real problem that would have to be addressed.

7.

The woman drinking her tea had no idea who he was. He knew it, and it no longer surprised him or even upset him very much. *If there is a Creator*, the man thought, *he has a very bleak sense of humor.* This was not the way human beings should back out of life.

He had gotten used to the procedure he went through before he saw her, but the necessity for it still eluded him. While he waited in the lounge of the assisted-living home, a young male nurse made preparations for the visit, tidying the woman's room, making sure she was comfortable and properly dressed, and making two cups of the wretched tea, one of which would sit on its coaster by his chair, untouched. *What did all this matter?* the man thought. *I don't much care how she looks, and if there's any embarrassment, she won't remember anyway.*

Zachary Berman looked at his mother, who was staring out of the ground-floor window of her one-room home. There was a tree outside with a bird feeder, and at the best times of year, she sat here all day and watched the birds fly up and feed and squabble over where they would stand on their perches. She put the teacup back on the saucer and looked at her son. Zachary reached behind him and took a picture frame off the bureau that had stood in their New Jersey home for years. It was too big for this room, but Zachary thought it was a good idea to have as many reminders of home as possible. That was before she was completely lost to the world.

The frame held ten small pictures. There was one of his mom and dad on their wedding day; of Zachary and Jonathan as kids; of the next generation of couples and their own children. Zachary held the frame out to his mother and pointed out a picture of his brother.

"This is Jonathan, Susan. Do you remember Jonathan? He was about ten when this picture was taken. I remember that day very well."

"Why do you remember?" she asked. Zachary no longer maintained that Susan was his mother, or Eli his father, as both these notions upset her terribly. Eli was someone she obviously guarded somewhere safe in her mind.

"I remember it because I took the photograph. We went up to the Poconos in the spring to look at a camp. I borrowed the camera and took the picture. See how he's smiling? Jonathan always loved that picture, it was his favorite."

"How do you know it was his favorite?"

"He told me, Susan."

"What time is it?"

"It's after seven, why?"

"Well, what day is it, dammit?"

"It's Sunday, Susan."

"My program's coming on. At seven." Susan resumed her watch of the darkened inner courtyard. "I better not miss it."

The nurse appeared at the door. "How does she seem?" he asked.

"She's the same as she was several weeks ago, or so she seems to me. Have you noticed any change?"

"She's getting very agitated, and more frequently," the nurse said. "There's a show on TV she's fixated on seeing, but we can't figure out what it is. You know she tried to get out through the fire escape last week. It's such a shame there's nothing we can really do for her."

Berman was surprised at the young man's candor, but he was right. Alzheimer's had a death grip on his mother and her brain was wasting away, and with it her personality, everything that made her Susan Berman. To all intents and purposes, that person had been erased and replaced by this horribly reduced version of her, one who would soon lose the ability to control any bodily functions as the brain proceeded to shut down completely. His mother was now less functional than a small child, but that wasn't precisely the right analogy for her. Berman thought she was less capable than even that.

Thanks to his extensive research, Berman knew what was happening to his mother. Her brain was a collection of neurons or nerve cells that passed information from one to another. Thoughts, ideas, memories, such as the ability to recognize her surviving son—all these could be described by chemical or electrical interactions among nerve cells. In some people like Susan, these interactions started to become interrupted, blocked by abnormalities called amyloid plaques, made up of a protein called beta-amyloid, or by neurofibrillary tangles, also caused by misplaced proteins called tau. In each case, the hard proteins built up to such a degree that they blocked neuron transmission, killing the brain one neuron at a time. When tau proteins performed their proper function, they physically assisted in the feeding and maintenance of the neuron, but under certain conditions, the tau came together like strands of thread, to disrupt and destroy the microtubules that made up the structure of the neuron.

Berman shuddered, unable to avoid the horror of imagining himself sitting where his mother was now. Although the home was clean and well run, it still reeked of old, incapacitated people, of urine and God knows what else. He hated to see his mother like this and hated to be in such a depressing place, but still he came, despite his mother's not recognizing him or even remembering he'd been there.

As he watched his mother, he felt a rising sense of anxiety that he had to speed up the work with the microbivores. They had to be available if and when he started a downhill course, maybe even before that happened. Each day when he couldn't remember some fact or figure, he worried that it was starting. A few hours earlier, while he was on the plane, he couldn't remember the name of his favorite movie actor. It hadn't been until he'd gotten back to his office at Nano that the name Tom Hanks came to him out of the blue and relieved his anxiety.

Berman believed that the microbivores were going to be the answer since they had the theoretical ability to work within the brain, identifying and destroying rogue tau proteins and beta-amyloidal plaque. But if his team followed the typical development path, they were looking at years of work and a huge amount of fund-raising that had been taxing his creativity. But now he had a source. He just had to make sure the spigot stayed open, meaning he needed results.

"Who are you?" Susan suddenly challenged. "What are you doing in my room? Get out of here." Her voice had risen to a shout, bringing the nurse in at a run.

Zachary said nothing during this short tirade. It had happened in the past, and nothing he had said on those occasions comforted her. She needed the nurse, whom she recognized on some level. He quieted her down, and she went back to watching the birds.

After his initial success in nonmedical nanotechnology, Berman had invested heavily and hired the best minds he could afford to move the company into the medical realm, particularly after the breakthroughs they'd managed in molecular manufacturing. It had been Berman's idea to mimic the way living cells used ribosomes to manufacture proteins that had put Nano way ahead of the competition in the molecular manufacturing nanorobot arena. With his continued urging, the first product of this method was the Nano microbivore, which had been theoretically designed more than a decade previously.

At the same time the microbivore molecular manufacturing project was under way, Berman launched a private investigation of Alzheimer's disease. More than a few of the scientists Berman had hired at Nano were working on diagnostic tests for Alzheimer's with the idea that the earlier the protein buildup could be detected, the better chance doctors had of slowing the spread of the disease. It stood to reason. It was around that time that Berman had allowed himself to be secretly tested for the predictive gene, which only served to heighten his general anxiety.

As the light began to fade outside the window of his mother's room, Berman slowly got to his feet. He truly hated coming to visit her. In a strange way he thought it was disrespectful to her as a person. Inwardly he suspected that if she knew how she was going to end up, she'd be the first to tell him not to come but rather to remember how she had been as a loving mother.

Without trying to say good-bye, Zachary descended the long hall toward the lobby of the facility, breathing shallowly to avoid the smell. He was disgusted, and hated himself for it, knowing as he did how tenuous the threads of nerve fibers were that separated his mental state from that of his mother's.

Berman emerged into the gathering gloom as the sun had settled behind the mountains to the west. Darkness fell rather quickly as he walked across the lawn and the parking area on his way to his Aston Martin.

With the engine purring under the hood, Berman checked his watch again. It was time to go back to the lab and find out what it was that Stevens, the investigative leader on the Chinese study, who had texted him yet again, wanted to talk to him about so urgently. It sounded ominous, and Berman did not like surprises. Pulling out onto the road, Berman laid a strip of rubber as a defiant adolescent gesture.

8.

George stirred from his place on Pia's lumpy couch and felt his back complain. After settling in for the night, he'd woken every half hour or so and tried to get comfortable, but with little success. He sensed he wasn't going back to sleep. He checked his watch, and it was early in the morning for Colorado but even earlier by his body clock, which was on Pacific time. It took George a second to realize where he was. Then he heard the shower come on, so Pia was obviously awake and getting ready for the start of her workweek. He thought about going into the bathroom and getting into a conversation with her while she showered, but he chickened out. He guessed she would think of it as an intrusion, not as an endearment. After not inviting him into her bedroom the previous evening, she had made it obvious that she wanted to maintain her space. He lay back down.

George's visit was hardly going as he had intended, or hoped. He understood he had shown up unannounced and uninvited, but he had expected Pia to be more welcoming. Although she had allowed him to stay in the apartment, for much of the previous evening she had acted as if he weren't there. Her nap had turned into a three-hour epic. It had gone on for so long that George started to wonder if she was done for the night. Since he'd come without much forethought, he'd brought nothing to read. Pia didn't have a TV, or even a radio, so he listened to music on his iPod and flipped through some of the immunology textbooks piled on her dining-room table, hardly recommended pleasure reading.

Pia finally had surfaced in her bathrobe at eight, just after the sun had set, like some sort of vampire, or so George had thought, irritably. She clearly wasn't in the best of moods or primed for conversation. This apparent depressive behavior caused George's concern for her that had started in Los Angeles to ratchet upward. So far her actions there in Boulder weren't doing much to alleviate his worries.

George couldn't help but wonder about the simple necessities of life that Pia was obviously neglecting: there was the almost-empty fridge and a lack of personal possessions in her apartment. Pia always acted as if she were just passing through, but there was less of Pia's stuff here in Boulder than an overnight traveler would bring to a hotel room. And then there was the situation with Zachary Berman, who his intuition was telling him was not as copacetic as Pia seemed to want him to believe. The last thing George wanted to do was fuss over Pia or nag her, because he knew she'd push back big time, but he wanted to show that he was thinking about her well-being without irritating her. The question was how to do it.

Pia had suddenly appeared from her nap and had gone into the kitchen. George had followed her, leaning on the countertop as she got out some green tea from a cupboard and put on the kettle to boil. As the water heated, she looked over at George. To George she appeared both sleepy and defiant at the same time.

"So, George. I sense from your silence and expression that you're building up to one of your speeches."

George had blushed. He truly had come to believe she could read his mind. "Well . . ." he began uncertainly. "You don't have to be a rocket scientist to see that you haven't really established any roots here."

"What's that supposed to mean?"

"Just look around this apartment!" George had said, sweeping his hand around the room. "The place is like a hotel room. Maybe that's being too generous. Even hotel rooms have more pictures. Come on, Pia. I'm worried about you. It's been two years since all that trauma you suffered, and you're out here incommunicado, keeping yourself pretty much cut off from the rest of the world. That ain't healthy."

"I've never been a great fan of the rest of the world."

"Okay, cut off from me, then."

"George, I'm fine." Pia had poured hot water into a cup with the green tea but failed to find a second cup. If it bothered her, she didn't show it.

"I understand you're okay at Nano," George had continued, "and you're really happy with your work, but what's with this Berman guy?"

"What do you mean 'with' this Berman guy? I'm not 'with' this Berman guy. He's my boss's boss. And, yes, I'm okay at Nano. The work is great. You don't need to think about me like I can't take care of myself, really! It's demeaning, if you want to know the truth."

"I don't mean for it to be demeaning. I think of it more as caring."

Pia had ended the conversation by merely saying: "Let's talk about something else."

Later Pia had resisted George's offer to take her out to dinner for her birthday, saying she didn't want to get dressed, but agreed to drive to the grocery store to buy some food for dinner. Still in her bathrobe, she had stayed in the car while George had run in for the fixings for a simple pasta and salad. Back at the apartment, he did the preparation while she busied herself doing a load of laundry in the basement. The dinner had been pleasant enough, but Pia had kept the conversation away from herself, asking George about Los Angeles and what he was doing in his residency. Pia had turned in for the night after finding a sheet and a blanket for George. George had hoped for some sign of intimacy but there hadn't been any, and as he lay on Pia's couch before falling asleep, he had wondered whether he'd ever be able to reach her.

When George heard the shower go off, he debated what to do. Since he couldn't decide, he did nothing. He just pretended to be asleep, curious as to what she would do. In his imagination he could see her come out and look at him longingly before coming over to wake him gently. She might even lie down with him for a moment or two, celebrating the fact that in the past they had made love on maybe a half dozen occasions.

George heard the door to the bedroom open quietly. A moment later it closed just as quietly. For a few minutes there was an uneasy silence as George, in his mind's eye, could see her approaching the couch. At any moment, he was expecting to feel her touch and he reflexively tensed. But the touch never happened. The next thing he heard was the apartment door opening and then closing.

With a certain amount of pained disbelief, George sat up and looked over at the closed apartment door. She was gone. Leaping up, George flew to the window, glancing out just in time to see Pia climb into the VW. Unfortunately George was naked, so the idea of waving her down had little appeal. A second later his options evaporated, as Pia motored out of the parking lot and sped off into the early morning.

Letting the venetian blinds fall back into place, George turned and scanned the room. He was stranded. "Jesus Christ!" he murmured dejectedly. The day stretched out in front of him, completely empty.

9.

As a hyperactive, extraordinarily competitive man, Zachary Berman needed little sleep. Sometimes after four hours, but usually after five or six, he woke up and was out of bed. For him there was no lying around, not ever. After some fruit, he was on the exercise bike, watching Bloomberg financial news. Then it was into the office at Nano usually well before anyone else, except for Mariel. She was the institution's primary workaholic. Sitting at his desk on this particular morning, he wasn't in the best of moods. Besides his mother's condition, there were several other bothersome items on his mind.

After leaving his mother's assisted-living facility, Berman had driven directly back to Nano to meet with his senior scientist, Allan Stevens, and had been briefed on the fate of the second cyclist, subject number 5. Berman had been furious that the team had allowed the first subject to overexert himself on his ride outside the facility in such a way as to cause his death, but Stevens had defended his people, saying that his instructions had been very specific and it was the cyclist who had chosen to ignore them. When they repeated the run and proved they had an issue with the program, and not the riders, Berman asked that a detailed report on the incidents be on his desk within twenty-four hours. He wanted to know how these deaths differed from, or was similar to, any of the others the program had experienced.

"What are your thoughts on what happened on a cellular level?" Berman had asked Stevens before they split up.

"We're not certain," Stevens had admitted. "Light microscopic evidence shows congestive blockage in the spleen and the lungs in both men."

"And the cause?"

"We're assuming it's immunologic again."

"Are we taking advantage of what we have learned recently with the microbivores?"

"We have a new crop being delivered today, so the answer is most definitely. The new subjects will be infused with the new agents."

"It's ironic. We thought that the endurance program was going to help the microbivores program, not vice versa."

"It is ironic," Stevens had agreed.

After going through most of the snail mail that had accumulated during his trip to Beijing, Berman leaned back in his ergonomic executive chair and stared out at the mountain scenery with unseeing eyes. He was thinking of what to say to his recently arrived guests, thankfully none of whom had witnessed the setback. It was implicit in the arrangement that the subjects of the testing program were expendable, but clearly deaths meant that something had not gone according to plan. He decided it would be counterproductive to tell them. Berman knew the current dignitaries would be severely jet-lagged on their first day in the United States. Everyone knew that flying east was harder than flying west, and there was no need to get them perturbed on top of that. Instead Berman composed a text to Whitney, asking her to arrange a lunch for the visiting dignitaries in Nano's executive dining room, which he would attend, along with a few senior staff. She should also inform them that for the evening they would be at their leisure. Berman wanted the evening kept free for a more interesting purpose.

Berman quickly typed out another text, this one to Mariel, that said simply: "Come see me!" Berman was confident Mariel would be somewhere in the bio labs, as she always was. Whitney Jones he didn't expect would show her face for at least another hour.

Precisely three minutes later, Mariel arrived in his office. She was one of only three people with access through the iris scanner outside his suite. The other two were Berman himself and Whitney Jones.

"We lost another rider yesterday," said Berman. "That's two in the same day."

"I know. It's unfortunate." Mariel sat in one of the two chairs facing Berman's desk. She crossed her legs. She wore slacks as she always did, and a silk blouse under her immaculate and heavily starched white lab coat.

"The first rider disobeyed the protocol, although he should never have been allowed out by himself so soon after getting the treatment. Looking on the good side, we'll have more data on tolerances, which will be very useful. What these incidents prove is that the system works as well as or better than we imagined. Perhaps it's the body that needs to adapt, like high-altitude mountain climbing."

"Do we know exactly what happened?"

"Stevens thinks it was an autoimmune reaction due to or on top of a hypermetabolic state. We'll know more when the report is in later today. We've got the team concentrating on finding out."

"I'll be interested to hear the details."

There was an awkward pause in the conversation. Mariel noticed that Berman was looking at his computer screen and not at her. She had no idea why she had been summoned, but she needed to get back to work. Mariel couldn't imagine that he'd called her to his office about the second cyclist's death, since she knew he'd already gone over it at length with Allan Stevens. After a beat she said: "Do you need me for something in particular?"

"Huh?" Berman said, as if he'd totally forgotten about Mariel's presence.

"I was asking if there was something you wanted to talk to me about. Otherwise I need to get back to the lab."

Berman ran a nervous hand through his hair and glanced back at his monitor screen for a moment before refocusing on Mariel.

"Actually, there are a couple of things I want you to do for me. First off, I want to know what else you know about this man visiting Pia. What is his name again?"

"George Wilson. I already told you what I know. He went to medical school with her. "

"Were they lovers? Are they now?"

Mariel felt that same tinge of schadenfreude she'd experienced the day before. Obviously for Zachary the continued presence of Pia's guest was akin to sprinkling salt into an open sore. He deserved to squirm after dumping her once he'd gotten what he wanted from her. She knew Berman was the kind of man who wanted mostly what he couldn't have. For him it was the chase and numbers that mattered, nothing personal.

"There was no mention of the character of their relationship according to the background check," Mariel said. She would have liked to suggest otherwise, but she couldn't. It wasn't her nature to lie. "All I know is what I told you yesterday. They were classmates in medical school. He was involved to a degree in the kidnapping episode. Which I also mentioned yesterday."

"He's a second-year radiology resident at UCLA?"

"That's what the background check revealed."

"What's he look like?"

Mariel shrugged. "Describing men is not one of my strong suits. He looks like what he is: a young doctor in training."

"Would you say he's good-looking?"

Mariel shrugged again. "I suppose in a stereotypical way. About six feet or thereabouts. Sandy blond hair. Reasonably athletic figure. He's neither fat nor skinny."

"Did you find him attractive?"

"He's not my type, Zachary. It never crossed my mind one way or the other."

Mariel's tone and the use of Berman's first name caught his attention. It reminded him of another of her characteristics that rubbed him the wrong way. Often he had the sense she was reprimanding him, even in intimate circumstances, hardly a turn-on. It had been one of the reasons he'd dumped her when he did. With her, everything was mechanical, even lovemaking.

"Well, I think I should meet the guy, find out if he's here just because of Pia or because of Nano."

"The background check didn't come up with any ties to industry, other than his being a radiology resident."

"Radiology, just like medicine in general, is going to benefit big-time from nanotechnology," Berman said. "But I agree with you. The chances that he is an industrial spy are minimal. However, I want to meet him. I'd like you to get Pia to bring him to dinner tonight at my house. Make sure she understands it is a command performance. She had refused an invite on her own, but I think she will come accompanied."

Mariel swallowed hard. She was shocked. A minute earlier she was enjoying Berman's undoubtedly jealous response to Pia's guest, and now he was inviting the man and Pia to his home, a place where Mariel had never been invited.

"Tell her that she and her houseguest should arrive at eight," Berman continued. "But make sure she realizes it is a social event. Tell her it has to be tonight, because the rest of the week I'm going to be busy charming the socks off our important Chinese visitors."

Mariel got to her feet, clutching her clipboard against her chest. She looked Berman right in the eye but didn't say anything. She knew Berman was taking advantage of her and deliberately humiliating her. Here she was, one of the principal people of Nano and key to its biomedical R&D program, and he was treating her like a gofer, asking her to arrange some weird, sick rendezvous. From sore experience she knew what Berman really wanted.

Without another word Mariel headed for the exit. Before she got there, Berman called out to her, and she stopped without turning around.

"So you'll pitch it like I described, okay? A social event among friends. And it has to be tonight."

Mariel hesitated, thought about turning around and telling Berman to do his own personal errands, but she didn't. Despite his behavior toward her, she was still enamored of the man. Instead she shifted her resentment and spite to Pia, the bitch.

10.

George whistled and shook his head in disbelief as he and Pia sat in her car in the cobblestoned turnaround of Berman's imposing post-and-beam timber home.

"What a house! It looks more like a hotel than a private home. This nanotechnology stuff must really pay off."

All that day while Pia was off at work, George busied himself on the Net, reading about nanotechnology in general and microbivores in particular. He'd become something of an armchair expert. He'd even made it a point to read the article by Robert Freitas that Pia had suggested he'd find interesting.

"It's such a waste since his family isn't even here," Pia said. She was as impressed as George, especially with all the rough-hewn masonry and soaring gables. Set at the top of a wide stone staircase, it dominated the environs like a medieval castle.

"Were you surprised at the invitation?" George asked. He had been nonplussed to have been specifically included. He had no sense of what role Berman played in Pia's life, and no idea what to expect. The one thing he knew for certain, if push came to shove, there was no way he could compete on a level playing field with a man with his resources.

"I was more than surprised. I was shocked," Pia admitted. It was the last thing she'd expected, especially since she'd ignored Berman's increasingly insistent texts the day before. All day she had worried that Berman would suddenly appear in her lab and there'd be a confrontation. But it hadn't happened. In fact Pia hadn't seen him all day. When she'd asked, she was told that he was involved with a luncheon for a newly arrived contingent of Chinese guests.

"I tried to beg off at first," Pia continued, "but Mariel was adamant about the invitation, and she was an absolute bear all day, like she's never been with me. It was as if I had screwed up some experiment, which I haven't. She reminded me at least ten times not to forget about tonight. She was very curious about you as well. 'Is your friend enjoying his stay?' 'Does he like your apartment?' 'Don't forget that Mr. Berman wants to meet him. . . .'"

"And you don't know why he wants me to be here? I feel a little nervous."

"No, George, I have no idea why he wants us here. But I tell you, I'm glad you are with me. If you weren't, I wouldn't come within a mile of this place."

"Why do you say that?"

"I didn't mention it because I was afraid you'd get upset, but there was a bit of a come-on between us before Berman left on his most recent trip. It happened after a perfectly innocent dinner. Let me put it this way: Berman and I shared a few meals that were all business. Then it suddenly changed, and not from anything I did. I resolved I never was going to be alone with him again, pure and simple. I mean I still respect him for the visionary entrepreneur he is and what he's accomplished in nanotechnology, but I didn't come out to Boulder for a relationship with anyone, and certainly not with a married man."

George nodded. He'd expected there had been something between Pia and Berman, what with the car and Mariel's strange

comments. He appreciated Pia's candor but couldn't help but wonder if she was telling him the whole truth.

"So," Pia continued, "I'm glad you are here because I've wanted to
see this place. I've heard about it around the proverbial watercooler,
but never imagined I'd get to see it. I might not want a relationship
with the guy, but he does interest me. He's unique, and a major
contributor to medical science, like Rothman was, just not in the
same way."

George smiled inwardly. Pia saying she was glad he was there was
more than justification for his trip to Colorado. Maybe it had actually been a good idea. Earlier that morning, when Pia left the apartment without a word, he had despaired that it hadn't been, especially
when she reappeared late that afternoon without apology or even a
word of explanation.

"Come on!" Pia said suddenly. "Let's get out of the car. He knows
we're here, he let us in the gate ten minutes ago. Just try and relax
and enjoy yourself. You're good at small talk, which I'm not. And
you've been saying you wanted to go out for dinner."

Pia climbed out of the VW and George followed, clutching the
bottle of wine he had brought as a gift. George had spent ten minutes looking at the reds at the nearest liquor store before dropping
almost $100 on a bottle of Sonoma Syrah, money he could little
afford.

As George neared the top of the stairs a few steps behind Pia, he
saw that Berman had already opened the enormous, oversize wooden
entrance door and was standing on the threshold. He was dressed in
a snugfitting Italian gray herringbone silk jacket over a silk mock
turtleneck. From the bulges in the right spots, George guessed he
was a weight lifter. George's confidence sagged. The man was not
only rich but good-looking to boot.

"Dr. Wilson, I presume," said Berman when George and Pia arrived at the level of the entrance. Berman examined George as if he
were inspecting livestock. Or at least that was how George felt,

dressed as he was in jeans and a comparatively dorky flannel shirt. Berman had a fixed smile on his face that looked to George more cruel than sincere.

"That's me. Nice to meet you. Er, I bought this . . ." George thrust the bottle of wine in its silver gift paper toward Berman, who nodded. The men shook hands, and Berman guided him into his house, redirecting his attention toward Pia.

"You haven't been here, Pia?"

"I have not," she answered, recognizing his comment as a mere figure of speech. He knew full well she'd never been there. If she was hoping for sincerity, it wasn't a good way to begin the evening. She was already surprised he'd directed his first comments to George. "It's quite a home."

Berman chastely touched both his cheeks against Pia's, European style, before directing her inside the house after George.

Pia was not often impressed by material trappings, but even she could tell this was an extraordinary place. The front door opened into an atrium, whose ceiling extended up two stories to the underside of a pitched gable. Between the exposed beams was adobe-colored plaster. The living room, which was more expansive, with even higher ceilings, was spanned and crisscrossed by giant, hand-hewn beams, which Berman said came all the way from Montana.

By the time they walked into the center of the living room, Pia counted three substantial fireplaces, all ablaze with six-foot logs. The furniture was likewise oversize and upholstered in burgundy-colored leather. Ample fur throws and pillows were haphazardly but invitingly distributed. The wall without a fireplace was all glass, rising three stories to the massive central gable of the roof. Off to the side was a state-of-the-art entertainment system. Classical music hovered in the room more as a hint than as an intrusion. It was impossible to tell exactly where the sound was coming from.

Berman led them outside to the deck, which extended the entire rear of the house, commanding a view to the west of the Flathead

Mountains, swathed in moonlight. Berman offered his guests seats in large wooden rockers, and a server appeared at once to take a drinks order. George saw that Berman had set down the bottle of wine he had brought in an inconspicuous place.

"You know Miss Jones already, Pia," Berman said when Whitney appeared, as if on cue. Like Berman, she was dressed in elegant simplicity, her hair drawn back from her face and gathered in a bun without a single strand misbehaving. Her shapely and toned physique was in ample display.

George jumped up to be introduced. The deck was dimly lit but George could see how stunning this woman was. He was pleased— Berman had an impressive girlfriend.

"Miss Jones is my valued assistant. This is Dr. Wilson, who has come with Pia. I asked Miss Jones to join us to even up the numbers."

So much for having a girlfriend, George lamented silently.

"Welcome to Boulder," said Whitney to George. She came around and sat to George's right; Pia and then Berman were to his left. Berman adjusted his seat closer to Pia and started talking to her. George took a deep draft of the vodka tonic that had just been brought to him. He felt he was going to need some alcohol to get through the evening.

"Thank you," said George to Whitney, who crossed her legs, leaning into George's space with both her person and her strong perfume. He strained to hear what Berman was talking to Pia about, but Berman was talking in low tones. Almost immediately he sensed Pia stiffen.

"So, Dr. Wilson, how do you like Los Angeles?"

In spite of his interest in what Pia and Berman were talking about, George found himself progressively pulled into conversation with Whitney Jones without a lot of effort. Her décolletage played a role, but more important from George's perspective, she was interested in what he had to say and was interesting in return. Answering George's numerous questions about Nano, she had reams of data at her fingertips. As absorbed as he was, George was unaware that his glass was being discreetly refilled, and was sorry when Ms. Jones excused herself to go check on the progress of dinner.

At that cue, Berman stood and walked over to the timber rail of his deck and looked out. "Not quite like Los Angeles, Dr. Wilson."

"No, it's not," George said, casting a quick glance in Pia's direction. She responded by rolling her eyes, which he had no way to interpret.

"Do you think it's a good place to train in radiology?" Berman asked.

"The training is top notch," George said. "But I'm not so sure the city is my cup of tea."

"Maybe you should think about coming here to Boulder," Berman said, still seemingly transfixed by the mountain scenery. "The University of Colorado has a superb program."

"It's a very attractive environment." George looked back at Pia and silently mouthed "What?" Pia merely shook her head.

"I tried to get Pia to talk to me about her ordeal when she was kidnapped," Berman said, before turning back to look directly at George. "She's not interested in talking about it. I know you were involved, what can you tell me?"

As George tried to shift his mind into high gear, he realized he'd drunk more than he thought. He'd vaguely noticed that the level in his drink never went down thanks to the attentive staff, but hadn't thought much of it. Despite his buzz, he remembered how strongly Pia felt about the kidnapping episode and how adverse she was to talking about it, even to him. He knew he had to be careful to stay in her good graces.

"I don't know much," George said, stumbling over his words.

"Oh, come on!" Berman said with a touch of irritation. "I can understand Pia's reticence but not yours. Was it traumatic for you as well?"

"It was, but mostly because Pia was in physical danger."

"I'm sure Mr. Berman doesn't want to hear about any of that," Pia said, speaking up for the first time.

"No, I do. I'd like to hear about the whole episode. Actually, I'm most interested in the use of polonium-210 to kill the doctors. I'd heard about that case in London like everyone else. Did they ever figure out where the stuff came from? My understanding is that polonium-210 is hard to come by."

"It's very difficult," George said, thinking that it was a safe subject as far as Pia's sensitivities were concerned. "It is involved with triggering nuclear weapons."

"Well, I don't know why you two are so secretive about it. It was big news out here for several days. My understanding is that you, Pia, were given full credit for uncovering the role that polonium-210 played."

"It was the only solution that fit all the symptoms."

"You're not giving yourself enough credit. I read that the deductive reasoning was brilliant in the minds of several analysts. You see, Dr. Wilson, that's the quality of scientists we have here at Nano."

Berman was talking as if he were recruiting Pia, which confused George, since he knew Nano already had her loyalty. Before anyone could respond, Whitney Jones announced that dinner was ready.

The dinner was predictably excellent. Berman didn't mention the Rothman affair. Instead he took great pride in pointing out that all the food was locally sourced. He was especially loquacious about the elk tenderloin, which was the centerpiece of the dinner. Despite George's general discomfort of being in such a foreign, elegant environment, he thought Berman was entitled to brag about the meat, which was slightly gamy, but not intensely so, and superbly tender.

Without giving it a lot of thought, George proceeded to knock back several glasses of red wine he knew was far superior to the one he had brought. By the end of the meal, the buzz that he'd felt earlier had intensified. When Berman and Pia got up to return to the deck to look at the abundant stars through his impressive electronically controlled telescope, George concentrated his attention on Whitney, who remained behind as the epitome of the charming, endlessly indulgent hostess.

"So what's the story here?" George asked, leaning in to talk to Whitney conspiratorially. He had become inebriated enough to lose all appropriate restraint. He still had one burning question, and he had the mistaken notion that Whitney was taken with him.

"The story?" said Whitney, lowering her voice, playing along, suppressing a smile. "What do you mean?"

"Listen, I know I've had too much to drink and God knows I'd never normally ask a question like this." George took another swig of wine.

"Like what, Dr. Wilson?"

"Is Berman sleeping with Pia?"

Whitney laughed softly. "You're asking the wrong person. I wouldn't know either way. And isn't that a question you should be asking Pia?"

"Yes, yes, of course. But . . . well, she wouldn't necessarily tell me."

"And why's that?"

"She's very willful, which is an understatement, if you know what I mean. She hates anyone probing into her life. But I'm interested, and it's not just jealousy. I've never known her to have a lasting intimate relationship with anyone."

"What about you?"

"Yes," George said, sinking back in his chair, "that's a very good question." George was slurring his words. "I'm afraid it includes me. I tried for four years to break through her shell."

"I'm sorry," Whitney said. "That must be difficult. I applaud your persistence."

"It's not been easy."

"Let's go outside," said Whitney suddenly. "It's such a beautiful evening." She stood up and walked out to join Berman and Pia.

For a few minutes George stayed where he was, now convinced

that in all likelihood, Berman was probably sleeping with both Pia
and Whitney Jones. He then berated himself for saying what he had
to Whitney. Even without alcohol, George knew that social adept-
ness was not one of his strong points. Asking Whitney the question
he had was exactly the kind of weak behavior Pia had tried to shake
out of him, if not explicitly, then by example. George helped himself to some more wine and then headed outside to join the others.
He was now plainly dizzy and had to move slower than normal, running his hand along the furniture to maintain his balance.

Outside, Berman was still showing off his telescope and had
turned off the lights in the living room to help the viewing. Joining
in, George found he was impressed again, in spite of himself. He
had never seen the rings of Saturn, which were clearly visible. After
viewing several more celestial objects, including a distant, sprial-
shaped galaxy, George went and stood next to Pia. The alcohol had
not only loosened his tongue but made him more demonstrative and
even possessive.

"This has been lovely, really, but maybe we should head home,"
George said out of the blue. He daringly slipped his arm around Pia's
waist. He was surprised when she didn't make an effort to elude his
grasp as she usually did. If Berman noticed, he didn't give it away.
Whitney on the other hand gave him a discreet thumbs-up.

"The evening is still young," Berman said, hearing George's
comment.

"It is getting late," agreed Pia. As far as she was concerned, they
had already been there too long. "And I have a lot to do, as you
know, Mr. Berman."

"Zachary. My name is Zachary, or Zach."

"Okay. Zachary. Thank you for a lovely dinner. And, Miss Jones,
thank you, too."

"Of course. Our pleasure."

George stayed rooted to his spot next to Pia until she pulled away
and headed for the door with Whitney. Berman waited for George,

who was taking his time navigating the step up from the deck into the house and crossing the darkened living room.

"Will we be seeing you again?" Berman asked.

"You never know," George said flippantly.

At the door, George gave Whitney a kiss on the cheek, and she said she was pleased to have met him. George shook hands with Berman and took Pia's arm as they descended the stone stairs, pretending he was helping her. When they got to the car, both he and Pia looked back up at the house. Berman and Jones were standing at the door, waving.

"That was an odd evening and an odd couple," said George. He climbed into the car and fell into the seat, leaning back against the headrest. He exhaled noisily as if he were exhausted.

"Are you drunk?" said Pia.

"Oh, absolutely. That was the only way I was going to get through the evening."

"You were very . . ."

". . . drunk, is what I was. Am. C'mon, Pia, we're sitting in the car again. Let's get out of here."

11.

At first George kept quiet in the car. He felt very full, of food and wine, and the motion of the car was doing unpleasant things to his stomach. He put his left arm around Pia's shoulders, and while she hadn't drawn closer, she didn't pull his arm away, either. The evening had definitely been taxing, and George was tired and reeling. He felt Berman had skillfully choreographed the event, keeping Pia to himself while allowing Whitney Jones to apply her considerable array of charms on him. He was again irritated at himself for what he'd said to Whitney. Guiltily he looked over at Pia, but she was concentrating on navigating the dark, twisting road. As usual, she looked beautiful. He wondered if Whitney was going to tell Berman what he had said. If she did and Berman told Pia, there was going to be hell to pay.

"What were you talking about with Berman?" George asked.

"When?"

"Most of the evening. It was obvious that he was dominating your attention."

"Work stuff, mostly, except when he was trying to get me to talk about Rothman and my being kidnapped."

"He tried to pull me into that."

"I know. I heard and I have to commend you for not allowing it to happen. Thanks."

"You're welcome."

"He did pay me some compliments about my immunology work vis-à-vis the microbivores."

"That's not surprising. It's deserved, too." George shook his head, trying to clear the cobwebs.

"He also told me that he wanted me to get back to work on the flagellum issue I told you about, which is really what I was hired to do."

"Do you have any ideas for that?"

"I do. In fact, while I was talking to him, I gave it some more thought. I had the idea of programming the microbivores that are sent to deal with flagellated bacteria to roll their targets into a ball. You know what I mean?"

"Can't say that I do." George put his palm against his forehead. Its coolness felt good. He was beginning to get a headache.

"I've explained to you how the microbivores have specific binding sites for the bacteria they're sent to deal with. My idea is to program the microbivores to roll the bacterium over and over a few times before bringing it into the digestion chamber. That way the flagellum would be wrapped around it and would get digested at the same time as the bacteria's body. I think it is a masterful idea. My only worry is how much code it is going to take. What do you think?"

"Sounds good to me," George said, but he was having trouble concentrating. What he really wanted to ask Pia was whether she'd had an affair with Berman, like Whitney suggested, but he didn't dare.

"Berman seemed to think it was a good idea, but he's not a scientist. His job is to get the funding, which he seems very capable of doing. I really don't know how he does it. He hinted that he has found almost unlimited funding. It's extraordinary."

"You seemed to be getting on well with him."

Pia glanced over at George, whose comment implied he was jealous.

"And you seemed to be getting on well with Ms. Jones. She's very beautiful, isn't she."

"I guess so."

"'I guess so.' George, she's stunning! And you had her all to yourself."

"I think Berman wanted her to sound me out," said George, half to himself.

"What about?"

"About you and me. It would be unseemly for Berman to ask me directly. He strikes me as a guy who's concerned about appearances, so he had his assistant ask me some questions."

"It didn't look like you minded being interrogated by her."

"You're right, I didn't." A thought passed through George's mind. Was Pia even a tiny bit jealous?

"Did she ask you?"

"Not in so many words."

"I hope you didn't say very much, particularly anything personal."

"Oh, no," George lied. He was trying to remember what he did say, but it wasn't easy. Whatever it was, he wished he hadn't.

"He did apologize for that incident that I mentioned to you."

"That's nice. What did he say, exactly?"

"He said he was sorry. He said he'd been under a lot of pressure concluding the funding deal and had had way too much to drink. He said he wanted our relationship to start anew, since he appreciates my contribution to Nano."

"Did you believe him?"

"So-so," Pia said. "Not enough to see him socially without you around. But then he went on to say something I found really interesting, something I'd suspected."

"Oh?" George questioned. He sat up straighter and struggled to clear his mind.

"He admitted that there's a very specific personal reason he's interested in medical nanotechnology in general, and microbivores in particular, and what's driving him to raise the kind of money he has. He thinks that microbivores can possibly control or prevent or cure Alzheimer's. His mother is struggling with the disease in a nearby assisted-living facility."

"Very noble of him."

Pia's eyes left the road for a moment and darted over at George. "Are you being sarcastic?"

"I don't know," he admitted. "I had too much to drink."

"At least it was good wine," Pia said.

A few minutes later Pia pulled into her apartment complex's parking area. She hopped out of the car and headed in, leaving George in her wake. The cool evening air was refreshing for George, so he made it last. Once back inside, he drank three full glasses of water and took a couple of ibuprofen tablets to preempt the headache that was sure to get worse.

When he walked back into the living room, Pia's door was already closed. George could see the light was still on in her room. He sighed and started to undress, another uncomfortable night stretching out before him.

The door to Pia's bedroom opened, and she stood in the doorway looking at George. "Thank you for being here so that I could see Berman's house. I enjoyed it."

"My pleasure." George tried to make eye contact, but she looked away.

"Do you really have to leave tomorrow?"

"I do. I was only able to wrangle two days."

After a pregnant pause, Pia's eyes zeroed in and locked onto George's for a fleeting moment.

"Why don't you come in. I don't think it's fair to make you sleep on the couch again." A second later she disappeared. George fumbled with his clothes half-on, half-off, trying to get to the doorway. He didn't want her to change her mind. Now he truly wished he hadn't drunk as much as he had.

12.

It had not been the best morning for Pia. First she had to get up earlier than usual to take George down to the bus station to catch a bus to Denver Airport. She hated saying good-bye in general, especially with the potential for a scene since George had ended up wanting to drag it out, sitting in her car. She'd come to appreciate his visit, especially as it had allowed her to see Berman's house and make sure he knew she had a boyfriend. But the previous night after they had gotten back from the dinner party and she had warmed up to him and wanted to have sex, he'd proved to be incapable with all the alcohol he had foolishly drunk. So she was glad he was leaving, but then couldn't get him to get out of the car. She had been eager to get to work, looking forward to asking some of the programmers at Nano about the feasibility of her mechanical solution to the flagellum problem. When George finally did climb out of the VW, Pia had made sure to leave quickly, lest he return to ask her to promise yet again to be better about answering his communications and pressure her into making a commitment to come out to L.A.

As if saying good-bye to George wasn't enough, Pia's morning at work had been a disappointment. First she found out that none of the programmers associated with the microbivores project was available, at least until the following day and maybe not even for the rest of the week. Next, Mariel had the same chip on her shoulder that had epitomized her behavior on Monday. Pia had to work closely with her, and that was difficult when Mariel was in one of her passive-aggressive moods.

But the worst event of the morning was the sudden appearance of Berman in an uncharacteristically jovial and expansive mood. To Pia's chagrin it seemed that the previous evening's festivities had not dampened his interests in pursuing a social relationship. Pia had hoped to convey the proper message by showing up with a boyfriend, but it was apparently not to be. If anything, Berman had seemed emboldened, even in Mariel's presence, making Pia wonder exactly what George had said to Whitney Jones during their conversations.

Berman had invited Pia to a festive dinner for the visiting Chinese delegation and maybe even a movie over the following weekend. On both accounts, Pia had begged off, saying she was going to be busy entertaining her houseguest, which, as it turned out, was not the right thing to say. Berman had responded with: "Didn't he take an early flight to L.A. this morning?"

Pia had tried to cover her tracks as best she could. Berman had actually helped by finding enough humor in the situation to laugh. "You'll have to come up with something better than that. And factor this into your thinking: I promise no repeat of my boorish behavior before my China trip. Scout's honor." He'd held up his three middle fingers in the form of a scout salute as convincing proof of his sincerity. "You don't have to respond immediately," he had added. "Think it over. I'd just like to show some appreciation for your contribution here at Nano. No strings attached."

Pia had sheepishly agreed to think about the invitations but felt foolish not to have guessed that George couldn't be trusted not to blab when he had too much to drink.

When noon had rolled around and Pia was able to clear her lab bench, she was relieved to leave and go out for a run. This was part of the new Pia, the Pia who had begun to embrace exercise and out-door pursuits, as advocated by the company's healthy-lifestyle pol-icy. If employees exercised and didn't smoke there was a significantly lower premium on health insurance.

As often as Pia was able, and weather permitting, she would change into her company running gear, most of it emblazoned with the Nano logo, and head out for an hour or so in the middle of the day. As a creature of habit, she always took the same unpaved public road up the mountain and away from the Nano complex.

Running helped Pia center herself. On this particular day she maintained a steady metronomic pace and focused on the physi-cal acts of running and breathing. Her work, and the distinct and different social problems that Berman and George presented her, were forced to the back of her mind. Breathing in the crisp moun-tain air, she pushed herself to greater effort, reveling in the sen-sations coming from her quadriceps, hamstrings, and calves. The sun was out and felt strong against her face in the 5,000-foot-plus elevation.

The run was going particularly well, and Pia checked the running app on her iPhone, which was strapped to her upper right arm. The GPS was on, and the app marked her progress on the route, keeping logs of times and distances. As she passed a distinctive weathered pine tree, she saw that she was making great time. The activity calmed her. It was as if she didn't have a care in the world.

Then, ahead of her in the road, she saw a male figure lying face-down, legs straight and arms stuck out to the side, as if he had been crucified and tipped off the cross and onto the ground. He didn't seem to be moving, and Pia's pulse, which had been holding steady at a moderate rate, suddenly picked up speed. Her intuition told her the man was in trouble, and her first thought was whether she was up to lending a hand. She'd been through medical school, but as far as emergency medicine was concerned, her training only made her aware of what she didn't know. How to actually be a doctor was

learned in residency training, which Pia had yet to do. She knew all
too well that there was a reason a trainee could not get a license to
practice medicine until after some level of graduate medical educa-
tion had been achieved.

Controlling her anxieties as best she could, Pia ran up and knelt
beside the stricken individual, who was dressed in the same running
gear she was. He was Asian. Quickly determining the man was
seemingly not breathing and had no apparent pulse at the wrist, Pia
maneuvered him over onto his back. She shook him forcibly, trying
to rouse him. Leaning over him, she put her ear close to his mouth.
Now she was certain. The man was not breathing! His mouth was
partially open, and along his lips she saw a bit of foam, making her
wonder if he'd had a seizure.

Wasting no time, as she knew time was critical, she again felt for
a pulse and found none. With the flat of her hand she pounded the
man's chest several times. She had remembered that maneuver from
a lecture. What she couldn't remember was why it was done, but she
did it anyway. She then reached for her phone to dial 911 in hopes
of summoning help. Thanks to the GPS device in her phone, she
could give very precise details of where she was located, which
she did rapidly after telling the operator she'd come upon an unresponsive man who wasn't breathing and had no pulse. Her final
comment was that she had no idea how long the man had been lying
next to the road.

After being reassured that an EMT vehicle was being dispatched,
Pia started administering CPR. Her first priority was thirty chest
compressions, using the heels of her intertwined hands. At least she
could remember the outlines of the procedure. While she was doing
it, she made certain that she was getting at least two inches of chest
compression. It was not difficult. The man was lanky, perhaps in his
forties, and seemed in good shape and hence was supple. The ratio-
nale she knew was to propel blood through the one-way valves of his

heart and out into his system to keep the man's brain alive until his heart could be restarted with a defibrillator.

After thirty compressions, Pia stopped. Quickly she pinched the man's nose closed, fought successfully against her reluctance to seal her mouth over the victim's, and forced her breath into the man. She saw that his chest rose appropriately. After two good breaths she returned to the chest compressions. Following thirty more, she broke off again to repeat the breathing. Before doing so, she quickly tried for a pulse at the man's wrist. Unsuccessful at feeling a pulse, she pushed up the man's sweatshirt sleeve on his right arm to check for a pulse in his ante cubicle fossa—his elbow. What she saw surprised her: the man was tattooed on his forearm with a series of numbers, reminding Pia of concentration camp victims of the Nazis. She tabled the thought and moved on quickly.

To her surprise, at the elbow she thought she felt a pulse. Encouraged, she then felt for the man's carotid artery. Here there was a definite pulse! It was rapid and faint but definite, a good sign, provided the circulation was adequate to get oxygen to the brain. With her hand on his neck she noticed something else: the man's skin seemed hot, but there was no perspiration on his forehead. The thought went through her mind that he might have been suffering from heat stroke despite the cool outdoor temperature.

Pia was confused by the conflicting range of symptoms. In addition to his problematic cardiac status, she saw what looked like urticaria, or hives, on his forearm. It was also apparent that he had vomited, because there was some vomitus on the ground next to him. And there was that foaming at the mouth she'd noticed initially. Pia worried that despite the thready pulse, the man might be about to die of shock, possibly septic shock, with his elevated temperature.

Pia again leaned over to recommence the breathing part of the CPR and suddenly felt resistance when she tried to blow into the man's lungs. To her astonishment, the man spontaneously started breathing. He even coughed. Pia checked the pulse at the wrist. It was stronger. Then the man quickly woke up.

As if waking from a slumber, he gazed up at Pia with obvious surprise and gripped her by the arm, shaking her as if shocked she was there, and wanted to make sure she was real. He spoke quickly and excitedly in what Pia took to be Chinese. The man then pulled on Pia's arm in an attempt to sit up, but only managed halfway before falling back. Pia was transfixed, as if she were confronting a ghost. It had been such a sharp recovery: one minute the man was dead, as far as she was able to determine; the next he was very much alive. His eyes were darting around. He seemed terrified.

"It's all right," Pia said, trying to calm him. She checked her watch, wondering just how long the man had been without breathing and heart action. She also worried when the EMTs would arrive, hoping they were close by.

The runner again tried to get up. When he again faltered, he spoke quickly—what was he trying to say? The two of them had no language in common, but Pia could tell by the man's face that his terror was mounting, not lessening.

"It's okay," Pia repeated. "It's okay. An ambulance is coming. Just try to lie still." She knew it was common for people who'd just suffered a medical crisis to be anxious, but this was different. The man was trying to get up and leave. Who was he afraid would find him?

Pia's fear was that the man would lapse back into cardiopulmonary arrest, as nothing had been done to alleviate what had caused his heart and breathing to stop in the first place. Yet the man seemed to become more alert as the few minutes passed. When the man heard the wail of the approaching ambulance's sirens he looked even more scared, and started shaking his head. "No, no," he said to Pia. They were his first English words. "Please." He sat up, and this time didn't fall back.

"It's okay," Pia repeated calmly while keeping her hand on the man's shoulder. "It's okay. It's okay. You'll be safe."

The ambulance and a Boulder Police car came to a screeching halt, and two EMTs and a police officer hurried to the downed runner's side. It was clear they were surprised to see the victim sitting up with his eyes darting about.

"I'm a doctor," Pia announced hastily. "Maybe not a practicing doctor, but a doctor, nonetheless. I was running and I found him collapsed on the road, not breathing, and he had no pulse. I did CPR and got a thready pulse. Then he suddenly woke up. I thought he'd be in shock, but he suddenly seems pretty normal."

The runner was clearly more agitated with the arrival of the policeman and the EMTs. He was talking loudly, gesticulating madly, and struggling to get to his feet. Pia kept her hand on his shoulder to keep him in a sitting position.

"Hey, sir, take it easy. What's your problem?" said one of the EMTs.

"He doesn't seem to speak much English, if any," said Pia. "He's very agitated."

"I can see that," said the EMT. "We can't take him to the hospital if he doesn't want to go. I mean, he looks normal."

"He has to go. He wasn't breathing for I don't know how long. We have to check his brain function and try to figure out why his heart stopped. I'm telling you, when I first got here the man was dead as far as I could tell."

"Bill's right," said the police officer, indicating the EMT. "If he refuses treatment . . ."

"I think he works at the same company as I do, Nano. You've heard of Nano, no doubt."

"Obviously," the policeman said.

"He's wearing the same jogging clothes as I am, as you can see. We're all given this equipment as employees of Nano."

The EMT named Bill stepped forward with a blood-pressure cuff, but the runner yelled at him and tried to pull away from Pia's grasp.

"We're trying to help," Pia said to the man. "We have to take you to the hospital."

Pia had been kneeling by the man's side and now stood up. With Pia's restraining hand gone, the runner tried to stand, but his knees gave way. Some of the fight went out of him.

"I'll come with you," said Pia to the man, indicating herself and pointing to the ambulance and making driving motions. She pointed to the Nano logo on her sweatshirt and then to the one on his. It was the best she could do. The man nodded, as if comprehending. The EMTs then tried to get him onto the collapsed gurney, but the man refused. Instead they helped him first to his feet, something he insisted on, and then into the back of the ambulance. Inside the ambulance they secured him to the gurney. At that point he was no longer resisting, but Pia could see that the fear remained in his eyes. When one of the EMTs jumped out to get in the driver's seat, Pia climbed in the back.

As the ambulance started and headed back down the mountain, Pia could see that the patient, although calmer than earlier, was still agitated. She wondered what he was so afraid of. She also wondered, if he worked at Nano, which wasn't a given, what department he worked for. He didn't look much like a scientist, but what did she know? Since he apparently could only speak a couple of words of English, he seemed like a stranger in a strange land. To try to calm him, she grasped his hand. He seemed grateful. He squeezed hers in return.

13.

As the ambulance bumped its way down toward Boulder proper, Pia continued to try to communicate with the runner. While Pia distracted the man, the EMT riding with them in the back of the ambulance used the opportunity to take a blood-pressure reading, pulse, and body temperature.

"Do you work at Nano?" she asked the patient. She pointed to the logo on the man's sweatshirt. "I work at Nano," she continued, placing her hand flat on her chest. Unfortunately the charade got no verbal response whatsoever.

"Holy smokes," the EMT said, looking down, raising his eyebrows in surprise at the gauge on the ear thermometer. "His temperature is almost a hundred five." As if he didn't believe the thermometer, he put his hand on the man's forehead. "It must be right. He's hotter than hell!"

"What about his blood pressure and pulse?" Pia asked. From feeling his skin earlier, she had assumed the man's temperature was elevated.

"They are entirely normal," the EMT technician said.

"What about heat stroke?" Pia said. "Maybe we should try to cool him down."

The EMT communicated the vital signs to the driver, who in turn contacted the ER physicians. The EMT in the back got an ice pack and offered it to the runner. The man looked at it questioningly. The EMT put it on his own head as a demonstration, then handed it over. The runner held it to his head and seemed to appreciate it.

"I don't get it," Pia said to the EMT. "He must work at Nano like I do, but his English is nonexistent. "By the way, my name is Pia."

"Mine is David. Bill is driving. Nice to meet you."

"How long before we reach the hospital?"

"Ten minutes or so," said David, and he confirmed it with Bill.

Pia undid the Velcro and took her phone from her arm. She made a call. As it went through she had to brace herself against the wall because of the lurching and swaying of the ambulance. The siren was not being used since there was no traffic and the patient appeared to be remarkably stable.

"Mariel. It's Pia. I'm calling from my cell phone. I was on my run, and I came across a man dressed in Nano running gear collapsed on the road."

"A man? Who is he? Is he conscious? Where is he now?" Mariel sounded surprisingly anxious.

"I don't know his name. He's conscious, but he doesn't speak any English. He has no identification with him. We're in an ambulance on the way to the hospital."

There was silence on the other end of the phone. Pia checked the screen to see if they were still connected. It seemed they were, since there was a good signal.

"Mariel, are you still there?"

"Pia, listen to me, this is very important. Where are you going?"

"Hold on, Mariel. David, where are we going?"

"Boulder Memorial in Aurora," said David.

"Boulder Mem—"

"Right, I heard. Boulder Memorial. What's the man's status right now? Is he conscious?"

"He's conscious but confused and paranoid. The problem is, as I said, he doesn't speak a word of English."

"Okay! Here's the plan: I'll meet you at the hospital. I'll try to be right behind you. Listen. Pia, don't let the ER staff touch this man. They're not qualified. I repeat, no one is to try to examine him, do you understand?"

"I heard you, Mariel, but, no, I don't understand. When I came upon him he'd been in cardiac arrest for God knows how long. He wasn't breathing with no pulse. He's breathing now, but they're going to have to examine him. It would be malpractice not to do so. What exactly do you want me to say?"

Mariel didn't answer Pia's question, so Pia again pulled her phone away from her ear and looked at the screen. The connection had been broken. Not sure why the call had been terminated, Pia tried to call back, but it went directly to voice mail. Mariel had apparently ended the call abruptly.

Pia strapped her phone back on her arm. Did Mariel really say that the man shouldn't be examined? Pia looked at the runner, who was still acting fearful. While Pia had been on the phone with Mariel, David had tried to run an EKG, but the man had pulled off the EKG leads. The man wouldn't even let David take off his sweatshirt or start an intravenous line. On the positive side, at least he wasn't trying to get off the gurney or loosen the buckle across his abdomen.

David sat back down on the chair next to the man. For the moment he was content to complete the ride to the ER without trying to do anything else, as the man wasn't in any obvious medical distress, other than his extreme anxiety. The ice pack must have felt good to him because at least that was still on his head.

The man's agitation increased when the ambulance arrived at the hospital and backed up to the unloading bay. He began babbling to himself and looked around continually, as if he were a caged wild animal. The man barely allowed himself to be wheeled into the ER, where he was sequestered in a room separated from the main emergency area because his high fever suggested he might be infectious. But at that point the man had had enough, and he started to undo the buckle restraining him. When he was prevented from doing this, he let loose a rapid flow of angry Chinese. He wouldn't let any of the nurses near him. It wasn't until Pia stepped up to him from the periphery, where she had been standing, that the man calmed down a degree.

One of the nurses took pity on a shivering Pia and gave her a white coat to cover up her jogging outfit. The ER was air-conditioned to a temperature well below seventy degrees. The nurse also told Pia that a request for a Mandarin interpreter had been placed, but unfortunately the only one available was off duty and wouldn't be arriving for perhaps an hour.

Pia was standing next to the man's bed, keeping him relatively calm, when the head ER doctor on the shift entered. One of the nurses told Pia that he had been called in because of his standing order that he be notified whenever anything out of the ordinary occurred. In this case it was the communication problem. He had been briefed by the EMTs even before they made it to the hospital.

Pia did a double take. From her medical school experience back at Columbia in New York, she was accustomed to seeing harried ER doctors looking like something the cat dragged in. In her experience they were always beset with dark circles under their eyes, always dressed in soiled scrubs that looked as if they had been slept in, always sporting one or two days' growth of a beard if they were male, and always with hair in a state suggesting they had just arrived in an open convertible if they were female. In the few minutes she'd been at the busy Boulder Memorial ER, Pia had already seen several doctors scurrying around who met this description.

This man was the absolute opposite. He was in his thirties, tall and trim and well proportioned, looking like the athlete she was later to learn he was. His grooming was impeccable, and he was tanned from outdoor mountain sports. Under his whiter-than-white doctor's coat, he wore a clean, starched white shirt with a handsome silk tie done in a perfectly symmetrical knot. He wore cuff links that could be seen peeking out from his jacket's sleeves. His stylish glasses gave him an intellectual air. His voice was calm and assured and projected confidence. He was in charge, and Pia was impressed. There weren't many men whom Pia found attractive, but he was one of them.

"What do we have here? A bit of a conundrum, I hear. A patient who seemed to be dead and now can't wait to get out of our ER." His eyes scanned the ER chart, which was essentially blank. He turned to Pia. "I'm Dr. Paul Caldwell. You found him, I understand."

"Yes, my name is Pia."

"And you're a physician, I've been told."

"Sorta," Pia said, not wanting to misrepresent herself. "I graduated from Columbia Medical School, but I put off my residency to do research."

"Okay," said Paul. "Tell me about the patient."

"I found him while out jogging. Apparently he was running as well when he collapsed. When I came upon him, he wasn't breathing, and I couldn't feel a pulse. Not knowing how long he had been in that state, I did CPR. The only things I noticed were that his skin was very warm to the touch, and it looked like he had some urticaria on his forearms. After a few minutes of CPR he came to, and it was an extraordinarily rapid recovery. One minute he was unconscious and the next he was wide awake. He has been agitated ever since."

"So there's no history whatsoever?"

"None. He doesn't speak English, and my Mandarin, which is what I think he is speaking, is nonexistent."

Paul smiled. He found Pia intriguing, especially because she was one of the most exotically beautiful women he had ever seen. He tried to guess her genealogy but couldn't. His best guess was a North African and French mixture.

"Columbia University. Interesting. I'm an East Coast transplant myself. I went to Harvard but came out here to the University of Colorado for my residency. I even did a rotation here at Boulder Memorial. So what do you think is going on here with our patient, Miss . . . Ms. . . . Mrs. . . . ?"

"Pia Grazdani," Pia said, not willing to rise to the obvious bait. "Beats me what's wrong with him, but I'm telling you, as far as I was able to see, he was in full cardiopulmonary arrest when I found him. I thought about heat stroke because he felt so hot, with no perspiration. There was also a question of a seizure. I also thought of septic shock. But none of those goes along with the other thing I noticed: he had hives on his forearms, so maybe it was an allergic reaction of some sort."

"Well, the best part is he seems to be doing quite well," Paul said. "Let's just run some tests on this fellow if we can."

Paul then tried to talk to the man, but he stayed silent, glaring at Paul as if to dare him to come closer. Paul took an ear thermometer out of his pocket and found a cover for the probe. The only positive finding on the nascent chart was the elevated temperature.

"I just want to . . . wow, easy there, friend!" As Paul had lent over the man to take his temperature, the man angrily swatted Caldwell's hand away.

"Let me try," said Pia. She took the thermometer from Paul, showed it to the man, and put it in her own ear. She then let the man look at the display. After switching out the probe cover, all the time smiling at the man, she took his temperature. She was surprised. Just like her own temperature, the man's had fallen to normal: 98.7 degrees.

"That's incredible," Pia said. His temperature had been 105. Such a precipitous drop called into question the veracity of the initial reading.

"Can you do a quick basic neurological exam?" Paul asked. He was as surprised as Pia about the apparent sudden dramatic fall in the victim's core body temperature.

"I can try," Pia said, not too sure of herself. She took the flashlight he offered and shone it in each of the runner's eyes. The pupils constricted equally. She proceeded with a neurological exam, and although it was difficult to perform many of the basic tests because of the lack of communication, it seemed to Pia that his general brain function was normal. She was able to get the man to touch her finger with his finger and then touch his nose while Pia moved her finger into various locations. That tested cerebellar function. Whether he was oriented to time, place, and person was just a guess, but he seemed to be.

"I'm impressed with your technique," Paul said with a smile. He was enjoying Pia's company as well as her help with the difficult patient. He was surprised she was doing as well as she was without any residency experience. "I think you have demonstrated that there doesn't seem to be any apparent neurological deficit. What about trying to get an EKG?"

With the runner far calmer than he had been since he'd awakened, Pia was able to attach the leads, and the patient left them in place. Paul turned on the machine, and it kicked out an entirely normal EKG.

"This is amazing," Paul admitted. He studied the printout more closely. "Are you sure he was in total cardiac arrest when you came upon him? I don't see any abnormalities."

Pia shrugged. "I was reasonably sure he had no pulse, and he wasn't breathing. So I'd have to say yes."

"And you say you saw some hives on his arms?"

"I did." She pointed to the man's forearms.

"I don't see any now," Paul remarked, and Pia agreed. Whatever it was, it was now gone.

Paul motioned for the runner to take off his sweatshirt, but the man vociferously refused, shaking his head in the process.

"Okay," Paul said. He wasn't going to force the issue, at least not yet. He wanted, at a minimum, to listen to the man's chest, but he decided to wait until the man was more amenable. "We need to take some blood," said Paul. "Maybe I should do that."

Pia glanced at him. The patient had not let Paul do anything. Why did he think he could draw blood, a far more invasive activity than taking a temperature or attaching EKG leads? "Maybe I should try."

"But you're not insured," Paul said.

Pia looked at him questioningly. Paul's comment seemed like such a non sequitur.

Paul laughed at Pia's expression of confusion. "I'm just teasing. Obviously the guy's not going to let me near him. For sure you'll have to do it."

Pia smiled. It seemed that Paul had a sense of humor, too. "I'll give it a try, but I'm not very experienced. Although he does seem to trust me."

"So I've noticed." Paul handed Pia a needle used to take blood samples along with a vacuum tube. He held two more tubes in his hand. He wanted to do a whole battery of tests.

Pia made a point of showing the needle to the man and made a motion as if taking blood from herself. The man watched her but didn't respond. Pia went ahead with the process of pushing up the man's left sleeve. In plain sight were a number of other relatively recent puncture wounds over various veins. Pia looked over at Paul standing on the opposite side of the patient. "Do you see these?" she questioned, trying not to be too obvious about what she was referring to. The thought went through her mind that the man was probably a drug addict.

"I do indeed," Paul said. He didn't elaborate.

Pia applied the tourniquet and went ahead with the venipuncture. The man flinched but otherwise didn't complain, as if he were accustomed to the process.

After filling the first vacuum tube, Pia pulled it out and pocketed it so she could take the next two from Paul. She was pleased with herself as the process was going smoothly. Of course it helped that the man was thin, with good veins that stood out like fat cigars.

"Good job," Paul said as Pia slipped off the tourniquet and then withdrew the needle. She handed off the filled tubes and the blood-drawing paraphernalia to one of the male nurses standing by. They had remained in the room in case they were needed. It had quickly gotten around the ER that the patient might be a physical challenge.

Taking out his stethoscope, Paul was about to go back to trying to listen to the patient's chest. He motioned to the man that he was going to pull up the man's sweatshirt, but before the man could respond, the sounds of doors crashing open and raised voices could be heard just beyond their curtained-off area.

"What the . . . ?" Paul questioned. He pulled the stethoscope from his ears and reached out to pull back the curtain, but it was flung back sharply. The runner yelled in fear and grabbed Pia's arm as two uniformed men stormed in and positioned themselves on either side of the bed. Pia could see that the men were carrying side arms. She recognized the uniforms. They were Nano security people.

"This him?" one of them called out to someone who had yet to arrive.

"Yes, it is," a familiar voice said.

Pia turned and saw Mariel Spallek come through the parted curtain. Behind her appeared two Chinese men in suits and dark glasses. One of them said something to the runner in Mandarin and the man cowered.

"Who's in charge here?" Mariel demanded. She didn't even bother to acknowledge Pia.

"I am," said Paul. "My name is Dr. Caldwell. What the hell is going on? You can't come in here like this. This man is a patient." Paul reached out and pressed a red call button on the wall. A wall speaker crackled to life. "Nurse, we need security in here on the double!" Paul barked.

"Dr. Caldwell," said Mariel, speaking authoritatively. "We've come here to take charge of this patient. Without even examining him, I can assure you he is fine. With whatever minor setback he had, he will be looked after properly. As you can see, he is very keen to leave."

The runner had immediately heaved his legs over the side of the bed and was talking to the Chinese suit who'd addressed him, but in a way that suggested he was acknowledging a superior. The patient was still visibly agitated, but at the same time he seemed relieved to see people he apparently knew.

"Mariel," said Pia. "What's going on? This man works at Nano? Be that as it may, I don't think he should leave here. He needs to be observed at the very least. We believe he had a cardiac arrest, Mariel, why are Nano security people here? And why are they armed?"

Mariel studiously ignored Pia. The Chinese man who hadn't been talking to the runner reached out and snatched the two tubes of blood from the nurse's hand before the nurse knew what was happening. The nurse stepped forward with the intent to grab them back, but Paul restrained him.

"Dr. Caldwell," Mariel continued, "please have the man's discharge papers prepared. He has already told his colleague he would like to leave. Mr. Wang, confirm again that the patient wants to leave the hospital, please!"

The Chinese man Mariel had addressed spoke with the runner, and the runner nodded his head in reply and seemed to acquiesce verbally at the same time.

"Wait a second!" Paul said, not about to be so easily duped. "How do I know that's what this gentleman asked? He could have asked the patient anything. Let me get someone from hospital administration down here."

Paul exited from the room out into the hall but was immediately confronted by two more sizable, uniformed Nano security men. They blocked his way, arms crossed, determined expressions on their faces.

"Step aside!" Paul ordered, but the men held their ground. "Hey!" Paul shouted down the hall toward the ER desk. "Where the hell is our security? Get someone down here from administration stat!"

Pia again tried to speak to Mariel, but Mariel continued to ignore her. Instead Mariel snapped her fingers for the patient to get to his feet. When he did so, he faltered, requiring the two Chinese men in suits to step forward to help support him.

"Mariel!" Pia yelled. "This is outrageous. What the hell is going on?"

Mariel treated Pia to one of her signature disdainful expressions. "What is going on is we're signing him out of the hospital and over to our jurisdiction and our responsibility. I told you on the phone we were going to take care of this situation." The last sentence was hissed quietly, through clenched teeth.

"I know what you told me," said Pia with disbelief. "But I'm telling you he needs to be monitored and completely examined."

"The patient can be better monitored at the Nano infirmary, which is better equipped to handle this kind of emergency, and he will be looked after by Nano's physicians, who are intimately aware of the totality of the man's health status. I thank you for helping the man, but I told you not to let them treat him, and they took his blood."

Now Pia was openmouthed. Not the least of the surprises was the suggestion that Nano had a fully staffed infirmary. Dr. Caldwell was still protesting out in the hall, saying that the man should be kept in the hospital, that his patient was being essentially kidnapped, that he and the staff were being held hostage in their own hospital.

Pia watched as the strange group prepared to leave. The two Chinese men were supporting the patient, followed by the two security guards and then Mariel. Before the patient left the room he treated Pia to a weak smile and a wave as if to say thank you.

"Come on!" Mariel ordered Pia before exiting. "You can ride in the vehicle with me."

Dutifully, Pia followed. Out in the hallway the group joined the other two security guards, who then let Paul run down the hall toward the ER desk. With two security guards in front and two bringing up the rear, the group headed for the main ER exit.

When Paul reached the ER desk his timing was opportune. Arriving at that very second was a gaggle of suited hospital administration functionaries that included the hospital president, Carl Noakes. Along with this group were several uniformed hospital security people. Adding to the confusion were several uniformed Boulder policemen who also arrived at the same time, including the officer who'd gone out with the EMTs to get the stricken runner.

"Ah, Dr. Caldwell," said Mr. Noakes, slightly out of breath. "Perhaps you can explain what is going on here."

Paul groaned inwardly—Mr. Noakes, the hospital president, was a figurehead as far as Caldwell was concerned, and not the man you wanted to see in a situation like this. He was a bottom-line bureaucrat.

"We have a problem here where a non-English-speaking patient who presumably had had a cardiac arrest is being signed out against my orders."

At that critical point the two disparate groups met head-on. Noakes held up his hand for everyone to stop. Then he cleared his throat. "I think we have a misunderstanding here. What is the patient's name, Dr. Caldwell?"

"We don't have his name," said Paul.

"Yao Hong-Xiau," the runner shouted out, and a Chinese suit yelled at him.

"We should clear this area and move into one of the unoccupied exam rooms," Noakes suggested. He gestured with his hand after being shown where to go by the ER charge nurse. Everyone complied. Many of the ER patients waiting to be seen watched with utter fascination. It looked to them like some sort of a movie involving international intrigue was being filmed with police and armed security people eyeing each other.

"There is no misunderstanding," Mariel said calmly once everyone had regrouped in relative privacy. "This man is a representative of the Chinese government and a guest of the United States government, and he has expressed his wish to come back to our facility forthwith. These two gentlemen with me are Chinese nationals with diplomatic status who are visiting Nano." Mariel pointed out the two men in suits, and they both nodded in acknowledgment.

"How about we wait for our translator who will be here very soon?" Paul suggested.

Mariel regarded Paul with a supercilious expression. "We're not waiting. We would like to get this man into our infirmary."

As if to underline her point, the patient apparently asked to sit down, and the two men supporting him pulled over a chair from a desk.

"What about hospital charges for the visit?" questioned Noakes.

Paul groaned inwardly. It was typical of Noakes to be consumed by economics at a time like this. ER charges were certainly secondary to the ethics of prematurely removing a potentially vulnerable patient from an ER under armed guard.

"I'm glad you reminded me," said Mariel, forcing a smile. "I am fully authorized to take care of any charges."

She pulled a stack of bills out of a bag she was carrying, and Pia could see they were hundred-dollar bills. Mariel made sure Noakes could see, too, and reeled off a stack. There had to be several thousand dollars in her outstretched hand, and more where they came from.

"This should take care of it," she said.

"This is very unorthodox, we don't usually accept cash without an invoice . . ." Noakes said, eyeing the money.

"For your inconvenience," said Mariel, and separated a few more bills from her stash and added them to her offer. When Noakes seemed paralyzed, she reached out and forcibly placed the money in his hand. "That should more than cover it, And we are truly sorry for any inconvenience."

"Mr. Noakes . . ." began Paul, unhappy with the proffered resolution, but Noakes had stepped aside and the runner's group quickly made their way out of the room and then out of the ER.

Pia followed, hoping to talk to Mariel. She had a hundred questions, so she trotted alongside Mariel, who was striding quickly toward the second of two black vans idling in the parking lot. The uniformed drivers with dark glasses had the vans conveniently positioned to make a fast exit. The patient was helped into the lead vehicle with the Chinese suits.

"Mariel, what's going on?"

"Pia." Mariel stopped and fixed her with a cold stare. "There's a lot more to Nano than just our little area. The world is full of people who'd love to get their hands on what we're doing throughout the company. Nanotechnology is one of the most important fields of research, which we are leading, but we're vulnerable. We have to protect ourselves."

"With men with guns? And what does that have to do with this man? He was out for a jog, for God's sake. He collapsed. And you come with armed guards? And then you say he's a representative from the Chinese government? And Nano has an infirmary? And . . ."

"Pia, I thank you for calling me. But now you have to trust me, and stop asking questions! We have to leave. Are you coming? We need to get this man back to the facility a-sap."

Pia was still dressed in the borrowed lab coat, and, more important, she realized she'd set down her phone somewhere in the ER. "My phone . . ." she said, looking over her shoulder, momentarily torn about what she should do.

"We can't wait for you. If you want to stay, you'll have to make your own way back. But come back immediately, Pia, we have a lot of work to do."

Pia nodded and turned to walk back to the ER. Mariel spoke up once more. "And, Pia," she called out. Pia faced Mariel and squinted against the low sun behind her.

"Just forget about all this, okay?"

Without waiting for an answer, Mariel hauled herself up into the front seat of the black van and slammed the door behind her. Pia stood there and watched the two trucks drive away.

14.

Pia walked back to the ER, her head full of questions. Most of them centered on Mariel Spallek. Mariel wasn't an overly friendly person, which was something that Pia usually appreciated, as she thought it was more honest. She was authoritarian, to be sure, but was knowledgeable and a good supervisor, both constructive and demanding. She could also be passive-aggressive, which she'd been that morning, but Pia didn't care, she wasn't looking for a social interaction. Pia had gotten to the point of knowing what to expect from Mariel, at least up until having called her for help in regard to the downed Chinese runner.

But Pia could never have imagined that Mariel would show up with four armed guards and proceed to sign out a patient without a diagnosis or even a hint of an explanation for the man's apparent cardiac arrest!

Pia reentered the ER in somewhat of a daze. She saw the place was getting back to normal. There were still a few clusters of people standing around, talking about what had happened. The cop who had shown up with the ambulance to pick up the runner was still there, but he was deep in conversation with several of the hospital security people. Pia couldn't help but wonder where he'd been when the Nano contingent had first shown up and stormed into the ER. A few of the administrator types were still there, but not the hospital president. Apparently, with the acceptance of Mariel's money, he felt the situation had been resolved; the patient had been seen and the bill paid.

On a side table in the room where the runner had been taken, Pia found her cell phone. She figured she'd take a cab back to Nano—in her cell phone case she kept a twenty-dollar bill for emergencies.

As she retreated toward the ER's front desk where she intended to inquire about getting a taxi, Pia recognized she was more shaken up than she initially had admitted to herself. The sight of guns disturbed her. It was a common enough occurrence to see armed guards with weapons, even assault rifles these days, especially at an airport, but the memory of seeing Will McKinley getting shot in the head at point-blank range was still fresh, and she herself was kidnapped by men with guns. She'd seen firsthand what a bullet could do to flesh and bone.

As Pia approached the desk, she heard her name being called. It was Paul Caldwell.

"You're still here. I thought you had abandoned us with the rest of the Nano contingent."

"My phone," said Pia, showing it to Paul. "I left it behind."

"Are you okay? That was a weird experience."

"Sure, I'm fine. But it was weird, as you say."

"Hey, how about we get a coffee in the hospital coffee shop," Paul suggested. "Now that things are back to the usual emergency room stuff, the team here can handle it. I want to hear more about this Nano place. It must be very exciting if things like this are going on every day."

"Hardly," Pia said seriously. "At least not in the section I work in. It's a research facility, and nothing exciting has happened since I've been there for almost two years." As Pia spoke she realized that a lot of things could be going on at Nano that she would have no idea of, given the size of the facility and the staff.

"I'm teasing," Paul laughed. "But I'm not teasing about the coffee idea. What do you say? I'd like to hear how you happened to come out here to Boulder rather than start your residency."

A red flag went up in Pia's brain. Although she was ravenously hungry, having missed a meal following her attenuated run, she couldn't but help wonder about Paul's motives. He was a man, a good-looking man, but she had had quite enough of men since she'd been a young girl in foster care. Perhaps more important than her need for food, she was really curious about the Chinese runner's situation. She wanted to find out what Paul might be thinking as to his diagnosis. And she wasn't excited about getting back to Nano quite so quickly and having to face Mariel. With such thoughts in mind, she decided to ignore the red flag, at least for the time being.

"What do you say?" Paul repeated. He could tell that Pia was miles away.

"Okay, sure," Pia said. "Would they have something to eat as well as coffee?"

"Absolutely," Paul stated. "But for food I'd recommend the cafeteria. A much bigger selection." He motioned for Pia to follow, and together they went to the hospital cafeteria, still bustling with its lunchtime crowd.

Paul guided a tray past the food selections, and Pia absentmindedly placed a prewrapped egg salad sandwich and a bottle of water on it. She was not a finicky eater. She tried to pay, but Paul would have none of it, saying her money wasn't good at his hospital. They took a table in the back of the room.

"So where do we start?" he said, taking a sip of his coffee. It was the only thing he had selected.

"What do you mean?" Pia asked, unwrapping her sandwich and opening the water bottle.

"I mean, that was pretty intense, right. You obviously know that woman who showed up. And what exactly is this Nano place? I don't know anything about it."

So Pia told Paul Caldwell about her work and about Nano. Paul had cycled on that same mountain route that she used for jogging, but he had no idea what went on inside the sprawling complex. As Pia talked, he began to think she didn't, either.

"Your specialty is salmonella?"

"I did a lot of work on salmonella," Pia said. "It's what got me the invite to come out here to try to solve a problem that salmonella and other flagellated bacteria cause with a new way to fight sepsis through nanotechnology." Pia stopped herself, remembering what Mariel had told her about secrecy. But Paul was an ER doctor—what interest could he have in nanotechnology, other than a professional curiosity?

"Go on," said Paul. As he listened to Pia, Paul reconfirmed that she was undeniably gorgeous, with exotic features and lovely skin. He knew she had an athletic runner's body, having caught a glimpse of her in her spandex when she'd first come into the ER and before she'd been given the white coat she was still wearing. And she was a medical researcher, operating on some technological frontier he knew almost nothing about. He was enthralled with her. But he sensed she was aloof and not completely comfortable talking with him. He wondered why. There were lots of things he wanted to talk to her about, but he restrained his usually ebullient and talkative side and concentrated on the medicine. He didn't have to pretend. That, too, fascinated him.

"Tell me," Paul said when there was a pause in the conversation. "Have you been taking advantage of the great Colorado outdoors? That's what lured me here."

"I have," Pia said. "Mostly running, but I have been biking a bit, too."

"No skiing?"

"Some. I at least tried it. It's more of a commitment than I'm willing to make. How about you?"

"Skiing, mountain biking, running, even mountain climbing. I can't get enough. It's a major reason I'm in emergency medicine. When I'm off, I'm really off, and I'm out there doing something. Maybe we can hook up sometime and go for a run or something. I have to say, I like you."

"That's nice," Pia said noncommittally. She wondered if coming to the cafeteria had been a good idea, remembering the red flag issue.

Pia's reaction to his innocent offer to get together was hardly encouraging, so Paul quickly turned the conversation to their recent shared experience.

"So this runner you came in with. You said when you found him he was unresponsive. How long would you say it was that he wasn't breathing?"

"I have no way of knowing," said Pia. "All I know is that he wasn't breathing when I examined him. And I couldn't feel a heartbeat, not until I had done CPR."

"And yet the neuro seemed fine, and the EKG was absolutely normal," said Paul. "Very curious, to say the least."

"He recovered as if he had been sleeping. I know no Chinese at all, but it didn't sound as though he were slurring his words when he woke up. And he had full motor function. Immediately he tried to get up."

"If you had to guess how long he'd not been breathing, what would you say?"

"I saw him on the ground from quite a distance, and noticed he hadn't moved. I mean, it had to be fifteen, twenty minutes at least. I know that sounds impossible."

"It would be very interesting to get some follow-up. Since he's somehow associated with Nano, do you think you could ask about him? Do you think he works there?"

"I haven't the slightest idea," Pia said. "He didn't strike me as a scientist, for some reason. But my boss said he was a representative of the Chinese government, whatever that meant."

"That woman is your boss?"

"I'm afraid so," Pia admitted. "Actually my direct boss. I have to work with her every day."

"My sympathies," Paul said.

"Actually, she's not that bad. Professionally, she's very good at what she does. She's trained as a molecular biologist and oversees most of Nano's bio-research. She's very helpful with my research."

"I'm glad she's not my boss," Paul said, making an exaggerated expression of disgust. "She's so bitchy. And that hairdo . . ."

Pia couldn't help but reflect on Paul's choice of an adjective to describe Mariel. Accurate as it was, it seemed somehow out of place.

"If you can find out anything about him, I'd appreciate hearing," Paul said.

Pia finished her sandwich, and Paul could see she was lost in thought again.

"Let me drive you back to work," said Paul. "It's the least I could do, after all your help."

"Oh, no," said Pia, "I'll get a cab. Really!"

"No, I insist. I'm part of a large group of ER docs contracted to run the Memorial's ER. I called one of my colleagues to come in early. I'm off at three anyway, but I was going to go up to see the president, Noakes, and tell him what a spineless buffoon I think he is. The way he handled that situation was inappropriate, to say the very least."

"That doesn't sound like a good idea," said Pia.

"No, it isn't, so you'd be doing me a favor by saving me from my foolish self."

Paul slid a business card across the table to Pia. "I want to stay in touch in case you find out anything about the Chinese runner. And I'll let you know if there is any fallout here at the hospital. Do you have a card? I suppose you don't, given that you were out for a jog. Give me your cell number, and I'll put it straight in my phone."

Pia stood up and took the card. "It's okay, Paul, I know where to reach you."

Paul winced inwardly. He knew Pia thought he was being pushy, and he was, a little, but not for the reasons she probably thought. He liked Pia's detached calm, and he sensed they shared a lot of the same interests, which he couldn't say for a lot of people. And she was so damned gorgeous. At least Pia had taken the card.

"So are you going to save me from making a fool of myself, getting myself fired, even? My car's right outside the ER entrance. One of the perks is my own parking slot."

Pia eyed Paul. She debated. One of the realities was that she didn't know if twenty dollars would be enough for a cab all the way to Nano, and even though Paul was socially aggressive, there was something about his nature that suggested it wasn't the boringly typical male sexual come-on. "Okay," Pia said suddenly. "To save you from yourself, I'll accept a ride." She smiled. "But let me tell you a little secret. I'm black belt in tae kwon do." Now she laughed.

"You're joking?"

"I'm not joking at all. I learned it at school, starting when I was fourteen." What she didn't say was that the school was essentially a reform school, and she had used martial arts to protect herself.

A broad smile spread across Paul's face. To him, she was getting more and more interesting. "Fabulous!" he said, and meant it.

They walked in silence to the car park and found his Subaru with combination ski and bike racks. A dark blue Trek Madone bike was locked into the rack. In the back of the station wagon were loops of climbing robe. As Paul unlocked the car he looked over the top at Pia.

"Pia, you aren't going to need tae kwon do when you're with me."

"I know," Pia said. "That's why I told you about it. If I thought I'd need it, I wouldn't have said anything."

They both climbed into the car, which was as clean and ordered as Paul's person. Paul turned the ignition and looked across at Pia. "The reason I asked for your cell number is that I'd like to call you, and not just about this runner guy. Perhaps we could go for a drink and talk about medicine, or whatever floats your boat."

"That's a possibility," said Pia. She wasn't used to people being so disarmingly frank. Pia also felt safe with Paul. She could usually tell that a man thought she was attractive because he would check her out and leer. Here was a man who just said he liked her. It made a nice change.

They drove out of the hospital parking lot, and Pia directed him to Nano. When they got to the gate, Pia showed the security guard her ID and said that Paul was just dropping her off. Paul pulled up to the front of the main building. He was clearly impressed.

"This place is huge. And that landscaping is to die for. The whole effect is intimidating, I have to say."

"It is," said Pia, who was seeing Nano from a new perspective after the strange episode with the Chinese runner. She didn't like the feeling. She got out of the car, and Paul did, too.

"So stay in touch," he said, leaning on the car's roof. "No pressure, remember."

"I have your card," said Pia. She remembered she was wearing a Boulder Memorial lab coat, and slipped it off. Folding it over, she held it out to Paul. "This is yours," she added.

"Not mine personally. I'd say it belongs to Mr. Noakes, in which case, you can keep it. Seriously, keep it as a souvenir of your visit to Memorial."

"I have plenty of lab coats. I really don't need it. It's going to go to waste."

Pia continued to hold out the coat, but Paul refused to take it. Instead he just smiled and raised his arms as if in surrender.

Pia relented and unfolded the coat to put it back on. As she did so, something fell out and landed on the tarmac of the parking lot.

It was the first blood collecting vacuum tube used on the runner. Pia had forgotten she had jammed it in her pocket. The tube bounced on its rubber stopper. Responding by reflex, Pia reached down and snatched up the tube before it could bounce again and break. She held it up, and both Paul and Pia could see that the tube was intact.

Paul walked around and Pia offered him the tube.

"Hey, clever you! I never knew you kept back a blood sample."

"I didn't. I mean, I didn't do it deliberately. I stuck it in my pocket to keep it out of the way when I was drawing the second and third samples."

"Great to have this, since they confiscated the other two. I'll keep it, if you don't mind. It will be interesting to see if it's normal, which is what I suspect, since he was acting so normal himself."

"Please," said Pia. She thought about checking out the blood herself, but she knew there was a chance it could get confiscated on her way into Nano. She thought it would be in safe hands with Paul.

"Just don't use it all up," she said. "I might want to look at it, too."

"I won't," he said.

"You want my mobile number?" she said.

"Absolutely," Paul said. He got out his own phone to add it directly into his contacts.

Pia told Paul her cell phone number. She had yet to change from a New York plan. Paul took it down and put the sample of blood in his own lab coat. He gave Pia a salute of sorts and a friendly smile before climbing back into his car to drive out of the parking lot.

When Paul stopped at the security gate to be let out onto the state road, he glanced in his rearview mirror. He could still see Pia standing where he'd left her. Once the security gate had been raised, Paul accelerated toward Boulder.

A few minutes later he found himself whistling. He was happy despite the run-in with Noakes over the Chinese runner. Paul was not currently in a serious relationship, thanks to a recent breakup, and he thought that meeting Pia was just what the doctor ordered to take his mind off negative thoughts. He was definitely looking forward to getting to know her. She was the most interesting and intelligent woman he'd met in a long time. He was also looking forward to seeing what the Chinese runner's blood chemistries might show, if anything.

15.

After watching Paul's Subaru until it disappeared from sight, Pia
stood in the parking lot for a few moments, taking in the expanse of
the Nano, LLC, buildings and grounds. The sensation of unease
she'd felt when she and Paul had driven into the complex a few minutes earlier had only increased, and Pia's analytical mind clicked into
gear. What did she know about Nano now that she hadn't known less
than two hours previously? She knew that there was a Chinese man
somewhere in one of the many buildings who had a strange medical
condition, and that Nano security was very protective of him. She
also knew that Nano had its own medical staff and operated its own
medical infirmary on-site. And she knew that there was a lot she
didn't know about her immediate boss, Mariel Spallek.

For Pia, Mariel's role in the removal of the Chinese runner from
the hospital was the most perplexing aspect of the whole affair. It
was obvious that Mariel was familiar with the runner, or at least familiar with what might possibly cause his collapse and apparent cardiac arrest. Mariel had been extremely confident that Nano's medics
could treat the man when Paul, as a board-certified emergency medicine specialist, had little idea what was ailing him. What this told

Pia was that Spallek was clearly a higher-level Nano operative than Pia had previously thought, and she wondered what this implied for her. How would the fact that it was Pia who happened upon the man affect her status at the company?

This last concern was fleeting for Pia. What was more insistent and urgent for her was her instinctive drive to find out what was going on. Unlike most people, Pia was the kind of person who, sensing danger, would seek its source rather than run away from it. Early in life she'd learned that no one was going to suddenly appear and rescue her. She had to go for the jugular when threatened or cornered.

Pia had to smile at the timing. She knew George would immediately do everything he could to persuade Pia not to investigate the Chinese runner, but George was gone. There was no one who would try to dissuade her from getting to the bottom of this weird episode. Besides, she felt a moral and ethical obligation to know what kind of an organization she was involved with and hence supporting.

Pia passed through the elaborate security system, paying more attention than usual to the process, and headed up to her lab. She looked for evidence that Mariel Spallek had been in the room recently and found nothing. That morning, before she set off for her run, Pia had started to set up yet another batch of roundworm experiments, utilizing the new design with polyethylene glycol molecules incorporated into the microbivore shell. Everyone, including Berman, had been very keen for Pia to keep pressing forward with this work in hopes of preventing any immune response, especially before moving on to animal subjects and eventually human volunteers. Pia had filled out all the required requisition forms as dictated by the overzealous bean counters in accounting.

As was her custom whenever she returned to the lab, Pia checked the status of all her ongoing experiments, but she found herself unable to concentrate. Her mind kept reverting back to the Chinese runner. She figured that he had been brought to the Nano infirmary

that Mariel had mentioned, which Pia had been hitherto totally
unaware of. That thought begged the question of where such an
infirmary might be located, and if she could find out. If she could,
then perhaps she could go to the infirmary and talk to the medical
staff, to at least satisfy her medical curiosity and quiet her mind,
which was racing with all manner of outlandish scenarios.

But where to start?

Pia took the elevator down to the first floor and walked back to
the main security area, through which she had entered the building
just minutes before. She approached one of the guards who was
marginally more personable than any of the other four or five usually manning the day shift. He was standing alone in front of a pane
of floor-to-ceiling glass, watching as a UPS driver unloaded a number of parcels.

"Excuse me, Mr. Milloy," she said, reading the man's name
tag, which was pinned to his uniform. "Could you direct me to the
infirmary?"

"I'm sorry, miss," said Milloy, "I'm not sure what you mean.
What's an infirmary?"

"An infirmary, a small hospital facility. I was told that Nano
has one."

"Not as far as I'm aware, miss. But let me ask. Excuse me a
second."

Milloy walked over to the pair of guards stationed by the front
door and with a particularly serious demeanor, which was the normal style of all the Nano security people, spoke with the taller of
the two. Pia had never seen that particular man do anything other
than stand front and center, eyes forward, like a soldier on guard
duty. Even now, as Milloy spoke with him, the man continued to
look straight ahead, not acknowledging his interlocutor at all. Finally, the man nodded, almost imperceptibly, and said something to
Milloy. Milloy came back to Pia.

"I confirmed it, miss. Nano has no hospital. There's a nurse employed by the company who has an office near the cafeteria, but I expect you know that. She probably gave you a flu shot last fall."

"Right, I'm not talking about the nurse. Thanks." Pia started to leave, then turned back.

"Mr. Milloy, do you always work this building?"

"Why do you ask?" said Milloy. He hadn't sounded terribly pleased to field Pia's first question, and now he was sounding decidedly irritated. He'd tried to talk to Pia on several occasions before, but had felt she had deliberately snubbed him.

"There are a lot of buildings on the grounds," Pia said. "I have no idea what goes on in them. I thought that if you occasionally worked in other buildings you might know which building might have the best chance of having the infirmary."

"Sorry," Milloy said with little sincerity.

Pia went back through the iris scanner, took the elevator back to the fourth floor, and followed the corridor back to her lab. She stopped at the door but didn't enter. Instead, as she had never done before, she kept going. She knew there was a bridge extending from the building housing her lab to the adjacent building on the fourth floor, the same floor as her lab. She had no idea how to get to the bridge, but out of curiosity, she thought she'd try to find it. After about a hundred feet or so, there were some twists and turns until the corridor ended at a set of double doors protected by another iris scanner. Pia looked around. She couldn't see any obvious cameras, but assumed there would be some built into the fabric of the ceiling, as there were outside of her own laboratory, so there was a reasonable chance she was being observed. If asked by security what she was doing, she decided she'd be truthful, saying she was a curious employee wondering what was behind the doors at the end of the hall where her lab was located.

Pia put her eye to the iris scanner and pressed the scan button. It was of the same design as other machines she was familiar with from the entrance to the building and her own lab. But this one gave an unfamiliar result: a harsh buzz and a momentary red blinking light. Pia tried again and the machine turned her down once more. Pia tried the door. It was locked, as she expected. She shrugged and turned back. So much for trying to check out the bridge.

Before reaching the door to her lab, she had an idea. She took out her iPhone, went to the settings, and made sure location services was on. Then she tried to map where she was in relation to other buildings. But there was no result despite there being a strong Wi-Fi signal. Being more specific, she went to the Maps app and put in Nano's address. All she got was a blank. When she used double-tap to back out, she could see that the totality of Nano's footprint was a blank. Apparently Nano had gotten into the Googlesphere and removed the information.

Pia was getting nowhere. She knew of no other entrance to Nano that was accessible from the main road besides the one she and apparently everyone else used. But there were other side roads in the area. Perhaps she could go outside and try to walk the perimeter of the facility to see what she could find. Pia was determined not to be thwarted, but tromping around in the woods at that moment was not a high priority.

Returning back to her own lab, she again looked to see if Mariel had been around. If she had, there was no sign of her. With some ambivalence, Pia wondered when the hell she was going to see the woman. Mariel had been less than pleasant that morning and had mostly ignored her at the hospital, but Pia had some questions despite what Mariel had said in the hospital parking lot. Whether Mariel would answer them or not, Pia had no idea, but she was going to ask them just the same.

Pia went to the lab bench area she used as her personal space, since she did not have a separate office. She had had yet another idea. The Chinese runner had yelled out his name and suddenly it popped into her head. Pia used one of the lab's phones to call the main operator and asked to be connected to Yao Hong-Xiau.

"Could you spell that?" the operator asked.

Pia could only guess at an Anglicized spelling of the name, but after she made a stab of it, the operator said there was no record of anyone with "Yao" or "Hong" in their name. Still connected with the operator and with a piece of paper and a pen in hand, Pia wrote out the name. She gave the operator several different possible spellings, certain only of the first couple of letters. When the operator still could find nothing, Pia persisted by asking if there was a number for any Chinese group or office. When she got another no, she switched tactics and asked to be connected with the Nano infirmary.

"Infirmary?" the operator questioned. "What's an infirmary?"

Pia defined the term as she had with the guard downstairs, sensing irritably that it must be an East Coast term that hadn't made its way across the Mississippi River.

"There's no infirmary at Nano," the operator declared with certainty.

"How about hospital or medical facility?" Pia suggested. She was feeling discouraged but kept trying.

"Sorry! There's nothing like that. How about the nurse's office? I have a number for that."

Pia hung up the phone. It was frustrating. She tried to think of what else to do, but nothing immediately came to mind. Instead her eyes wandered over to the LCD display of the readouts coming from all the biocompatibility experiments she currently had running. One of the many figures on the screen was blinking, suggesting there had been a change in a parameter being monitored.

Pia walked over to the experiment in question. Almost immediately she could tell that the suggested change was mere artifact, indicating that a slight recalibration was called for. It took Pia only a few moments to accomplish the recalibration, and the blinking disappeared.

The heavy click of the door to the main corridor opening was the next thing to catch her attention. A moment later Mariel Spallek appeared in the open doorway, clutching a folder to her chest. Her face reflected her usual disdainful imperiousness.

"A sight for sore eyes," Pia murmured to herself. Yet for the first time since she had been at Nano, she was glad to see her immediate boss.

16.

"Pia, I'm glad you are here," Mariel began. She strode directly over to Pia, crowding her space with the help of her four inches of extra height.

"Mariel."

Pia stood her ground, gazing up into Mariel's arctic blue eyes.

"I got your paperwork from accounting," Mariel said. "I'm pleased you are pushing ahead with this work. The more corroboration we can get of immune compatibility of the microbivores, the better off we will be. I've already green-lighted everything you have asked for."

Pia found herself nodding as Mariel kept speaking and waited her turn.

"And Mr. Berman and I are pleased that you are attending to the flagella problem. That needs to be solved. Is there any way I can help in that regard?"

Finally Mariel stopped talking.

"You can get the microbivores programmers to give me some time."

"Consider it done," Mariel said agreeably. "I'll be handing this paperwork to the purchasing department, and I'll make sure it's processed at once. But I do want you to sign the requisition form, which you haven't done. Anything else?" Mariel handed Pia the form.

"So we're really not going to talk about it?" said Pia, taking the paper.

"Talk about what?"

"Come on, Mariel, the runner, the hospital, the armed guards! I bring a man into an ER, and the next thing I know, you show up with the U.S. Cavalry and forcibly remove him, which doesn't make a lot of sense. He needed a diagnosis and needed to be monitored, at least in the short term. He'd had an apparent cardiac arrest, a life-threatening condition if ever there was one. A mysterious life-threatening condition that you seemed extremely confident you could take care of here."

Mariel looked at Pia. A patina of irritation penetrated her haughtiness.

"Furthermore," Pia added, "I wasn't even aware that Nano had the kind of medical facilities that could deal with that kind of thing. I called the operator to be connected to the infirmary to find out if the man is doing okay, but she said there is no infirmary."

Mariel said nothing for a couple of seconds, the expression on her face not changing at all.

"The man wasn't forcibly removed," Mariel said finally.

"I'm sorry?" Pia said, rolling her eyes. Mariel was clearly avoiding the issue of who this man was, and Nano's role in his treatment. Whether he was taken against his will was significant, of course, but the fact that Mariel had arrived there at all with her goon squad was a more pressing concern.

"You said we forcibly removed a man from the Boulder Memorial ER department, and I'm telling you that the man consented to have treatment at our facilities. If you believe you saw anything to the contrary, then you're mistaken."

"Okay, I'll believe it if you say so. But tell me this: how is he doing in Nano's medical facility? Wherever that may be."

"I'm sure he is being well taken care of."

"You're sure, but you don't know? You haven't checked on him?"

"My expertise is in the bio labs, the same as you. This is where you need to concentrate your mind. We have important work to do here. The microbivore project is the most important one here. Everything else is designed to support it. I assure you the man is being well looked after, by a team of highly skilled staff."

"But Nano is a research lab," said Pia. "My understanding is that in the rest of this facility they are working on paint additives and the like. And we here in the bio labs are presently using worms. We're not even using animals yet. Why does Nano need a staff of medics? And why are you involved with them?"

"Miss Grazdani. As I indicated to you at the hospital, it would be best if you forgot all about what you saw. Or what you thought you saw. Ultimately it is none of your business. It is time you got back to work."

Although Mariel Spallek had no way to know, such admonitions were likely to have the opposite effect on Pia from the one intended. Pia felt strongly that it was for her to decide what was best for her to know, not a functionary like Mariel. In Pia's mind there had been enough international tribunals to proclaim that individuals in organizations bore an ethical responsibility about what such organizations did, and, ultimately, ignorance was not a defense.

"What is the role of the Chinese government at Nano?" Pia demanded.

Mariel had redirected her attention to the forms she held in her hands, but at Pia's question, she jerked her head upright and bore her eyes into Pia's.

"I said to forget it. I mean it. Sign the damn requisition forms!"

Pia shrugged and turned to sign the paperwork for Mariel. Judging by the force of Mariel's reaction, Pia was confident she'd touched a nerve, and, having done so, found that her curiosity was stimulated, not blunted.

17.

For the rest of the day, Pia found it almost impossible to concentrate on her work. Mariel's evasiveness under her questioning had certainly made Pia more interested in what she'd witnessed. And Mariel's reaction to Pia's mention of the Chinese government definitely seemed significant. China frequently competed with the United States in commercial interests, including the medical arena. From her time growing artificial human organs with Dr. Rothman in New York, she knew that the best work being done outside the United States was in China. And in China there wasn't always the same level of respect for the binding nature of patents in general, and medical patents in particular, as there usually was in the United States.

For an hour, Pia played devil's advocate, taking the opposite point of view and trying to bolster the case that Mariel wasn't dissembling or hiding anything significant and that the runner's ailment could easily be explained away. The man certainly didn't want to be treated by Paul Caldwell, that had been clear, and he seemed to want to go with the Chinese men and the guards who came to pick him up, even if they did come armed to a civilian hospital ER. And by the time he was discharged, the man appeared against all the odds to be in decent health. He was weak, to be sure, but otherwise reasonably okay. Pia remembered he had the presence of mind to acknowledge her help.

And what about those guards? Pia thought. If they were employed by Nano, they represented a much higher level of paramilitary security than she'd seen before. Their uniforms were different from the regular security personnel Pia encountered downstairs in her building and at the vehicular entrance to Nano's grounds. And who were the two Chinese men in business suits? Were they part of the Chinese contingent currently visiting Nano? The more Pia pondered the situation, the more questions she had.

But what puzzled Pia the most were the runner and his medical issues. As Pia thought back over the episode, she was convinced that he had been in full cardiopulmonary arrest when she had came upon him on the road and had probably been in that state for a considerable length of time. But by the time he left the ER two hours later, mostly under his own power, he didn't seem impaired in any way. He certainly was a medical curiosity, if not a total anomaly. She also recalled seeing the numbers tattooed on his right forearm as well as the puncture marks on his left arm when she went to take his blood. The blood!

Pia reached into her pants pocket and found Paul Caldwell's card. She dialed his number on her cell phone, but Caldwell didn't answer. She cursed and declined to leave a message. She wandered into the kitchen but realized there was no food in the house, as if that were ever not the case. Then the phone rang.

"Pia, it's Paul. Sorry, I put the phone down and couldn't find it for a second. I do it all the time."

"Thanks for calling back," said Pia.

"Sure. Did you find anything out at work? "

"No, I found nothing. I couldn't find out anything about a medical facility, or the Chinese man, or anything. What I'm calling about is to ask if you ran any tests on the blood."

"Yes, I sent a sample out to the lab late in the day. We won't hear anything till tomorrow at this point. I've been thinking about the runner, and I wonder if we were totally off base right from the beginning. Can he have been truly as ill as he appeared when you came upon him? Because the symptoms and signs, as meager as they were, don't add up to anything I'm familiar with. And he walked out of the ER under his own steam with only a little help, which would seem impossible if he'd been in cardiac arrest for God knows how long."

"I know, it doesn't add up," Pia agreed. "I've been thinking about the whole affair since you dropped me off. But I'm about as sure as I can be that he had no pulse and wasn't breathing when I came upon him."

"So what are you going to do? Let it drop? It was pretty clear that woman who showed up was in charge of the situation. If she's your boss, it puts you in a difficult position, I'd imagine. Then again, I guess we should wait and see what the blood tests show, right?"

The symptoms and signs didn't add up. Caldwell was entirely correct, Pia thought, the clinical history didn't make sense at all. But she was sure he was wrong in thinking they were totally off base from the start. She was 99.9 percent certain the runner had been clinically dead when she happened upon him. And now, miraculously, he had all but totally recovered and seemed to have suffered no ill effects.

Pia corrected herself. She couldn't be 100 percent certain the runner had not suffered any ill effects since she could not talk to the guy to find out, or find anyone at Nano who would tell her. Maybe he wasn't doing so well now. But if he was, then there had to be some medical Lazarus program running within the four walls of Nano that enabled a man to survive a massive, normally lethal medical crisis apparently unharmed.

"Pia, we'll have to wait and see, right? Pia, are you still there?"

The fact that she was on the phone with Paul Caldwell had slipped from Pia's mind entirely. She ended the call without saying another word and sat on the arm of her rented couch. It was suddenly obvious to her what she had to do to find out what was going on at Nano. There was one person who undoubtedly knew everything. That was Zachary Berman.

Although she had been avoiding it, she was going to have to get closer to Zach Berman. With security at Nano as tight as it was, as evidenced by iris scanners and armed guards, his house was possibly the weak link. She assumed he had a home office, even if she hadn't seen one when she'd visited with George. A few minutes in his home office could probably answer all her questions. The question was, how to arrange it? Pia felt her pulse quicken as her mind shifted into high gear. There was a way to do it, but it involved considerable risk.

18.

Ensconced in his private Nano office, Zach Berman nursed a mild hangover as he waded through online editions of *The New York Times*, *The Washington Post*, and select German and British papers. Nano paid for subscriptions to a number of Chinese publications, and Berman entrusted that part of the morning ritual to Whitney Jones, whom he didn't expect to see until considerably later in the day. Outside it was still dark.

Berman had spent the previous evening entertaining his Chinese guests, who had been pleased with their early-morning tour of Nano's facilities and had worked the rest of the day in the restricted areas, watching their compatriots being tested and put through some basic, and safe, exercise routines for the dignitaries' benefit. For the celebratory dinner, he again used his imposing home as the venue. He found it impressed Chinese visitors far more than the fanciest restaurant in either Boulder or Denver. It was also easier to arrange for a bevy of escorts at the house than at any restaurant.

By now, Berman was familiar with the long rounds of toasts that always accompanied such an occasion. Although he usually drank wine or beer while eating, with Chinese visitors he drank whiskey, which was their preference, hence the hangover, thanks to the number of toasts. Yet the meal had been a great success.

After dinner, Berman had made his formal PowerPoint presentation, detailing how nanotechnology was poised to become a global medical phenomenon, and how, through mutual respect and cooperation, Nano, LLC, and the People's Republic of China would be able to capitalize on the unlimited potential they would soon unleash together. Everyone in the room had heard the spiel before in some previous iteration, but Berman's bravura claim on this occasion had turned the last toast of the evening into the loudest and most emotional, requiring Berman to toss back an entire shot glass of scotch. Within minutes, as he reclaimed his seat, he had already felt the dull throb of an oncoming headache. A half hour beyond that, citing the need to get at least a few hours' sleep, Berman had excused himself as his guests began playing poker in his living room with the escorts.

As Berman had gotten up to take his leave, the leader of the delegation, Shen Han Li, took him aside. He thanked his host for his generous hospitality and said that everything he had seen that day convinced him that his colleagues had been correct in their previous assessment of Nano's progress. He reminded Berman that his superiors were still anxious to see concrete evidence of the efficacy of the particular nanorobots they were interested in. Such a demonstration would go a long way toward securing Berman his capital needs for the foreseeable future. Berman thanked Li for his candor and the generosity of what the deal could be. After the many hours of the meal and the innumerable, mutually congratulatory toasts, this was what Berman needed to hear.

It had been a successful evening indeed.

But now in the cold light of morning, Berman again felt the pressure of time and the need to assure himself that the athletes' performances would be enough to ensure the full investment from the

Chinese. There had been three recent setbacks, and even if all of the incidents had been contained, he couldn't afford any more potential disasters. If the Chinese found out, it could unravel the whole deal. He was going to have to talk with Stevens that morning to be absolutely sure.

While glancing through the London *Times*, Berman became aware of what sounded like a knock on the outer door of his office suite. Berman thought his woozy head was playing a trick on him, but then he heard it again. It was too early for any of his regular secretaries, and Whitney Jones had told him she was going home to power down for a few hours. Even compulsive Mariel never came in before seven or seven-thirty. With mounting curiosity, he flicked on the screen that showed the feed from the security camera outside his office, and what he saw surprised him.

"Well, well," Berman said aloud, and he happily buzzed his visitor in. "Through here," he called out. Berman was shocked but pleased. Pia Grazdani was coming into his office! He stood, mildly flustered. The surprise made him feel like a smitten teenager. Nervously he smoothed back his hair and made sure his shirt was properly tucked into his slacks while his mind conjured up a mental image of George with his arm around Pia. It was a fleeting image from the other evening as the two were leaving his home, which at the time had bothered him. But not for long. Whitney had told Berman that George had been drunk and talkative, and had actually asked if Pia and Berman were sleeping together. Berman and Whitney had gotten a laugh out of it. Whitney had further said that George had admitted that his relationship with Pia was not intimate. Berman had found the information encouraging, especially now that Pia was coming into his office at the crack of dawn.

"Good morning, Mr. Berman," said Pia brightly, appearing in the open door into his inner office. "I hope it's not too early to come and see you."

"It's never too early for a pleasant surprise such as this. To what do I owe the pleasure?" To Berman she never had looked quite so good. He found her unbelievably alluring. "Come in! Please. Sit down!" He pointed toward a leather couch, while clearing away some papers that littered its cushions.

"I wanted to thank you for having George and me over to dinner the other night. We enjoyed ourselves immensely, particularly me. I'm afraid George ended up drinking more than he should have. Anyway, thank you."

"And you wanted to come and thank me at six-fifteen in the morning? Not that I don't appreciate the gesture." Berman was amused—he couldn't imagine this was the reason Pia wanted to talk with him.

"I know you come in early, and I thought it might be easier . . ."

". . . if Whitney and or Mariel wasn't around?" Berman's imagination began running away with itself.

"Well, since you mention it, yes," Pia said, smiling. She felt transparent but forged ahead.

"Miss Spallek can be a little . . ." Berman let Pia finish his sentence.

". . . possessive?"

"That's a good description. But don't let it bother you. Please, sit down!" Berman again gestured to a couch positioned in front of floor-to-ceiling windows that looked out onto a Japanese rock garden. He patted one of the cushions with an open palm as if Pia needed further direction.

Pia ventured into the room, checking out the memorabilia, including what was labeled as the horns of several different types of African gazelle. The place oozed of a stereotypical, old-school masculinity that she thought had died with Hemingway. Pia sat down where Berman had indicated. She was inwardly surprised and relieved at the apparent ease with which she seemed to string Berman along. She was pleased that men like Berman were so predictable.

Pia wondered whether she could simply drop the pretense and

just go ahead and ask about the Chinese government runner. Just as quickly, she thought better of it. Her intuition was telling her that Berman would most likely not tell her anything. In her mind's eye she remembered the number tattooed on the runner's forearm. There was something unnerving about it when she had seen it, and it jarred her again now that she recalled it.

"Mariel might be possessive," added Berman, "but she has a good heart and she's loyal. What I'm trying to say is that she is a terrific lieutenant."

"Lieutenant? That's a curious choice of words," said Pia.

"Can I offer you an espresso?" Berman questioned while pointing toward a modern machine built into the mahogany paneling.

"That would be nice," Pia said. Before she'd arrived, she felt nervous about what she was doing, remembering uncomfortably how Berman had tried to force his way into her apartment. Yet now she felt confident and in control. She'd dealt with guys more intimidating than Berman. The Albanians who had kidnapped her, for instance. Much more intimidating guys.

"I always think of her as having a somewhat military air. She is very well organized."

"She's a good boss."

"Absolutely. She keeps me abreast of everything you're doing in the lab." Berman handed Pia a cup of espresso, then made one for himself.

Pia was sure Mariel had briefed Berman about Pia's role with the Chinese runner and was curious why he wasn't mentioning it.

"She's very impressed with you," he went on. "As I mentioned the other night, we're very appreciative of the great strides you and she have been making on the microbivore biocompatibility issue."

"I hope we're making good progress. It's really fascinating work, and I very much want to make a contribution to the science. That's what my goal is."

With his coffee in hand Berman sat in an upholstered swivel club chair situated on the opposite side of a coffee table from Pia. For a second, he regarded her with a slight smile on his face.

"So, speaking of the possessive type, how's your friend, Dr. Wilson? Did he get back to L.A. okay?"

Pia smiled a little herself.

"I assume so, I haven't heard. It's good to have the apartment back to myself. I'm not equipped for company."

"That's understandable," Berman said.

"Does Miss Jones live with you in your house?"

"Hardly," Berman said.

"I'd like to see it again. It was so overwhelming; I think I missed a lot of detail."

Berman tossed back the rest of his espresso. This was all going so much better than he could have imagined.

"You'll have to come back for dinner again."

"Sure," said Pia. "I'd be happy to come to dinner."

Berman eyed Pia. She truly was one of the most exotically attractive women he'd seen in a long time, and here she was, seemingly offering herself on a platter. He tried to calm himself. It was more than he could have hoped for. "Okay," he said. "So when are you free?"

"I'm free tonight, I believe. If that's not too presumptuous."

"That's not presumptuous at all. So tonight it is. Does eight o'clock suit you?"

"It suits me fine," said Pia, who smiled. "But there is one thing I would like to make clear."

"And what might that be?"

"You promised no repeat of what you called your boorish behavior that happened before you went on your trip to China. I want to hold you to that promise."

Berman raised his hands palms out. "On my mother's honor." His lips curled into a slight smile.

"Okay," Pia said simply. "See you at eight!" She stood up and left

Berman's office, feeling his eyes burning into her back. "Let him enjoy his fantasies," she whispered to herself. Once outside in the cool morning air she further murmured: "Mission accomplished."

For his part, Berman rocked back in his plush rocking swivel chair and thanked the gods for such an unexpectedly promising start to his day. Even his hangover had miraculously disappeared.

19.

After looking at the security logs as she did every day, Mariel Spallek had to concede that since Pia had started work before six o'clock that morning, she was certainly entitled to take an extra forty-five minutes at lunchtime to go for a run. Pia had also told her that jogging restored her when she felt tired, and that she did much of her best thinking when she was pounding the pavement on the mountain road above Nano. It helped that Mariel was in a good mood. She had purloined another lab on the floor below for Pia's use as well as more testing equipment so that Pia could run twice as many tests on the various levels of the polyethylene glycol incorporated into the nanobot surfaces that they were experimenting with. Once Pia had gotten all these apparatuses set up, Mariel told Pia she could go for her jog, but added that she would prefer that Pia not come across any more Nano employees in extremis. That comment had brought a laugh from both women.

It was Pia's custom to run up and away from Nano to get to a higher elevation, but this time she turned right out of the gate and back down the road toward town. After a few hundred yards, she turned on a smaller secondary road that she had never been on before. After another hundred yards or so, she stopped and made her way up the embankment at the edge of the road and into the forest that surrounded Nano. Pia's plan was to try to determine if there was a second entrance into the facility, which she now strongly suspected, or anything new she could see from the outside. There were plenty of back roads in the area, and she could have tried driving around to see what she could find, but doing it on foot seemed like a better idea. Her plan was to circumambulate the complex along the perimeter fence, even though Nano occupied a considerable area. She was hoping for some success, since she'd gleaned precisely nothing of consequence since she'd left the emergency room the previous day.

Pia plunged into the woods. It had been a dry spring so far, and a fine dust hung in the air as small branches and twigs snapped underfoot. The undergrowth thickened as Pia made her way deeper into the trees, and she fended off branches with her forearms and got some scratches for her trouble. After just five minutes she felt she could have been in the middle of nowhere. Ahead, the trees were taller and fuller and she had a hard time seeing down into the valley-like depression where Nano was situated. As Pia strained for a look ahead, she walked straight into a dark-green, thin-mesh chicken-wire fence, scraping her nose in the process.

"Dammit!" Pia put her hand to her face but there was no blood. Now that she focused on what was right in front of her, she could see the nearly invisible fence. A narrow trench had been dug and it extended to the left and right, as far as she could see, so that the fence went into the ground. Brown metal stanchions were set into the ground at fifteen- to twenty-foot intervals, and the ten-foot-high fence was strung between them. Pia shook it—it was taut and strong, possibly coated with a dark green material that might have been a nanotechnology product. She heard a sound, and straight ahead on the opposite side of the fence she saw a young deer standing stock-still, staring right at her.

"No need to be afraid," Pia said. "Neither one of us is getting through this fence."

So Nano had a second, outer perimeter barrier significantly beyond the imposing concertina wire–topped chain-link fence closer in. Pia had no reason to believe this new barrier didn't run all the way around the facility except, obviously, at the main gate. It was yet another example of how seriously Nano took security. It also changed Pia's estimate for how long it would take her to walk around the complex.

Pia's iPhone sounded and she gasped. Running into the unexpected fence had made her jittery, and she didn't expect a phone call while in the woods. She released the unit from the strap around her arm and recognized Paul Caldwell's number on the screen. Pia's hopes were raised—perhaps he'd found out something useful from tests on the runner's blood.

"Pia?"

"Paul, yes, what can you tell me?"

"Pia, I can hardly hear you, it's a bad connection. Listen . . ."

Pia could hear nothing. She turned and headed back toward the road where she had entered the woods. She could hear Paul's voice trailing in and out when the line beeped a couple of times, and the call was lost. Reaching the road, Pia waited for Paul to redial—she wanted to avoid the exasperating situation when both parties try to call the other when a connection is lost. She hoped Paul wasn't waiting for her.

Her phone rang again.

"Paul?"

"Pia, is that you?"

"Yes Paul, it's me, what's up? What did you find out?"

"Okay, I can hear you. Listen. There was a problem with the blood."

"Problem? What do you mean? What did they find?"

"They didn't find anything, Pia. The blood never got tested. It never made it to the lab."

"What do you mean? When we talked last night you said you'd just sent it. You expected some sort of results today."

"I said I sent it, yes, but I was just saying what usually happened. Except it didn't happen in this case."

"So what the hell did happen?" Pia was mad, and even though she felt self-conscious yelling into her phone, standing by the side of a road, yell she did. She could hear Paul apologize on the other end, but that was no help. Except for her seeming success with Berman in scheduling another visit to his lair, nothing else was working out. And now there was a problem with the blood. It didn't seem fair.

"I put the blood in the usual pouch and left it in the secure box outside for the courier. He picked it up and dropped it off at the lab. He's our regular delivery guy and I trust him, but I also checked, and there is a record of his signature at the other end. That proves the blood was received, but after that, no one has any record of it. It didn't make it to the lab."

"How can that happen?" said Pia. "Paul, you should have walked it down to the lab yourself."

"Come on, Pia, give me a break. This has never happened before. Sure, a sample gets mislabeled once in a while, but no blood sample has ever disappeared into thin air like that. Believe me, I've got them turning the place upside down over there. That lab does half its business with us, and I said we'd take our blood somewhere else if they don't find it. I doubt Noakes would have it in him to do that, but I've made the threat on his behalf."

"What was the label on the vial?"

"There was a standard bar code from the hospital. I wrote my name on another label, and 'runner' on it, as shorthand. There's a lot of blood going over there with my name on it. I was trying to be careful, in case the bar code came off. Pia, I'm sorry this happened but it's not the end of the world—"

"Right," Pia said abruptly, and ended the call. It may not be the end of the world for Dr. Caldwell, but it left Pia in a mess of frustration. She was back to square one—she had nothing. And she felt a certain amount of anxiety. The fence seemed like a sinister presence to her, an unnecessary second protective curtain around the border of Nano, shielding it from the outside world. The main fence that flanked the parking lot was taller than this one and was impressive enough on its own. She supposed this outer boundary could be breached more easily, but she had no doubt there were sensors that would indicate any intruder. Or was it the case that Nano was more concerned with stopping people from getting out rather than preventing them from getting in? She had no answer.

Before she could think too much along those lines, cutting through the still mountain air, Pia heard the high-pitched whine of an engine. An approaching motorbike, she thought, and she ducked back down into the fringe of the woods, where she wasn't visible from the road. Before she could see any motorized transportation she saw first one, then a second cyclist dressed in black gear with Nano logos and wearing solid black bike helmets and dark, wrap-around sunglasses. They were breathing evenly and climbing the hill at an impressive speed, their shoes clipped into the pedals, their rhythmically swaying bodies centered over the handlebars. As the first one passed, he glanced back over his left shoulder toward his colleague, and Pia caught a glimpse of enough of his face to tell his background. He was Asian, possibly Chinese.

Close behind the cyclists was a man in biking leathers on a dirt bike wearing a full-face helmet, maintaining the same speed as the larger road bikes. Further back, a white van followed at the same pace, but keeping more distance than the motorbike. Pia could see nothing through the vehicle's blacked-out windows. A couple of

minutes after the group had passed and no one else appeared, Pia
followed, running, half expecting to see the group heading back in
the direction from which they had come.

Rounding a hairpin turn at the top of the rise, Pia had a view into
the distance. Ahead was a long, steep uphill grade. Up near the summit she could just make out the cyclists who had not slowed. Even
from that great distance she could tell they were moving remarkably
fast despite the gradient. Who were they and why were they wearing Nano logos? While Pia watched, they disappeared over the crest
of the distant hill, followed by the motorcycle and then the van.

For a moment Pia stood where she was, staring at the spot where
the group had disappeared, straight up into the Rocky Mountains.
She shook her head in disbelief. It was all too much of a coincidence.
As there had been a runner, there were cyclists apparently operating
out of Nano in some way, and they were important enough to be
trailed and shepherded by a motorbike and a white van.

The interruption had stopped Pia from fully assimilating what
Paul Caldwell had told her. Blood from the Chinese runner that had
been accidentally saved had been sent to a lab and then lost. Such a
loss had never happened before, and there was no good explanation
for the sample's disappearance. The lab was being turned inside out
in a desperate attempt to locate the missing sample, or so she had
been told by a contrite Paul. *Good grief*, she thought dejectedly.

Pia was sure the lab workers were wasting their time. She had no
doubt that someone from Nano had taken the blood sample before
it could be tested. Nano knew that blood had been taken from the
runner but they may have assumed it was all intercepted in the ER.
This later action meant they were very thorough and had a long
reach. They must have stationed someone at the hospital or, more
likely, at the lab, to intercept anything coming in from the ER at
that particular hospital. Such an action wouldn't be difficult to pull
off for an outfit with Nano's resources.

All the same, she cursed her foolishness in trusting Paul Caldwell with the blood. He could just as well have attached a giant sign to the blood saying, STEAL ME! He'd not only written his name, but indicated the sample was from the runner.

Then Pia's more rational self kicked in. Despite the odd encounter in the ER, Pia had given Caldwell no reason to act in a clandestine or secretive manner with the blood. Sure, Nano had snatched the other samples away, but it was too much to expect an ER doctor to anticipate something that had never happened before: the loss, for whatever reason, of a blood sample after it had reached the lab. The message that Pia got from the unfortunate episode was that the stakes were raised and that she would have to be more careful in the future. With the enormous amounts of money involved with nanotechnology, she was up against a formidable foe carefully clothed in secrecy.

Pia turned around and started jogging back the way she'd come. She'd take her run and skip the idea of circling Nano on foot. After all, what difference would it make if there was a second or even third entrance to the complex? Such a discovery wasn't going to tell her anything except add to the sense of secrecy. What was becoming progressively clear to her was that her only and most promising resource of learning any secrets about what Nano was doing was Zachary Berman. There were no iris scanners at his house, or at least she hadn't seen any, and no razor-wire barriers. But thinking about going back into his house unaccompanied by George sent an involuntary shiver down Pia's spine. Intuitively she knew that if Berman was anything, he was a dangerous snake in the grass.

20.

Before she went home and changed and showered for her dinner date, Pia had one stop to make after leaving Nano for the day. She knew Dr. Caldwell was on duty because she had called the hospital. When the receptionist heard the caller was a doctor, she offered to page Dr. Caldwell. Pia declined and hopped in her car and drove straight over. Her task at hand couldn't have been done on the phone. She needed a favor that required person-to-person contact.

Pia walked into the ER, and as luck would have it, Paul Caldwell was standing in the second bay she looked into, having been called in to check a first-year resident's care of a young boy who'd taken a serious blow to the head from falling off his bike. Pia watched as Caldwell finished assuring the anxious mom that the kid would be fine. When he was finished and had turned the case back to the first-year resident, he turned and came out of the cubicle, on his way to the main desk. He saw Pia, smiled an uncertain smile, and raised his eyebrows.

"I didn't expect to see you here," he said. He'd hoped to see Pia again, but not so soon, especially after her reaction to the lost blood sample and precipitous end to their phone conversation. He was quite sure she had hung up on him.

"I'm sorry I gave you a hard time about the blood," she said, lowering her voice. They were standing in the middle of the busy ER. "I realize it wasn't your fault."

"You realize I didn't lose the sample on purpose. Well, I'm glad you're giving me the benefit of the doubt. That's very generous of you."

Paul continued on to the ER desk, where he dropped off his paperwork on the head-trauma case. Pia followed close behind. She noticed he was dressed impeccably, just as he'd been the day before when she had first met him.

"Do you have a moment to talk?" Pia asked.

"I think so," Paul said. He leaned over the ER desk and asked the head nurse if there was any other case waiting for him. Paul's role was mainly supervisory unless the ER was overwhelmed. In that situation he saw cases cold. The nurse gave him a thumbs-up sign, meaning for the moment he wasn't needed.

"Come on!" Paul said to Pia. He led her down the hall into a doctors' lounge. Inside the windowless room were several club chairs, a couch, and a single desk. The desk was occupied by a resident physician dressed in rumpled scrub clothes, looking much more like the ER doctors Pia was accustomed to seeing from her medical school experience. The doctor was doing paperwork and didn't look up when Paul and Pia entered.

"I think Nano had something to do with the blood disappearing," Pia said quickly and quietly once they had seated themselves. "In fact, I'm sure of it."

"What makes you think so?" Paul studied Pia's face. Her comment sounded paranoid to him. He also noticed something else. She wasn't maintaining eye contact.

"It's really just a hunch." Pia looked over at the doctor at the desk. He was paying them no heed. "The place has a lot of secrets, I'm coming to find. The security is extraordinary. I'd not given it much thought until now, but it seems excessive, even considering the need to protect nanotechnology patents. I mean, there are iris scanners. It's like the Pentagon or the CIA, for shit's sake. And on top of that, it's not just runners who have some sort of association with Nano. This afternoon, while I was out supposedly to jog but really to reconnoiter the Nano complex, I saw a couple of cyclists with Nano logos who I think were also Chinese, being followed by other people I assume work at Nano: one on a motorbike and others in a white van with heavily tinted windows."

"Cyclists?"

"Yes, Lance Armstrong types: professional-looking with all the paraphernalia, including flashy racing bikes. And I discovered that Nano has two fences, the inner fence you saw with razor wire, for chrissake, and another fence a couple of hundred yards back in the woods that's camouflaged. I didn't even see it until I literally walked into it."

"You were out in the woods?"

"Yes. That's where I was when you called me. I was going to walk around the property to find out where the other entrances are. There has to be at least one more way into the place."

"Okay, but I don't see how that adds up to Nano stealing my blood sample."

"You said nothing like that had ever happened before. If there was a flaw in the lab's system, you'd expect it to have happened at least once before, wouldn't you? The amount of blood the hospital must send out for tests."

"It's true, they test a lot of blood," said Paul. "We have a lab in the hospital, but the bulk of it is outsourced. It is more economical."

Pia realized her logic was shaky at best. She was saying Nano must have taken the blood because they were secretive and a little sinister. But she stood by her instincts. Last year, George Wilson had tried to shoot down all of the outlandish-sounding conspiracy theories she came up with surrounding the deaths at Columbia, but in the end, she had gotten to the heart of the matter by instinct and deductive reasoning. She'd been very wide of the mark on the way to her conclusion, but she was basically right in the end. With Nano she was getting another gut feeling, and she was determined to follow through with it. There was definitely something strange transpiring, on, and she was going to find out what it was all about.

"Let me say this," Pia continued when she sensed Paul's dubiousness. "They certainly have the personnel to pull off something like stealing a blood sample from a clinical lab. You saw those guys yourself who came here with my boss. They looked like a private SWAT team. Come on! It's a company that makes paint additives, or so they want us to believe. Why all the security and strong-arm tactics?"

"I did think their barging in here was a bit over the top," Paul said, although he was reluctant to buy into Pia's idea completely. He liked his life to be stress-free and uncomplicated and this affair was becoming complicated. He liked to work, and have enough free time to enjoy nature, at least when he wasn't spending his spare time noodling with computer code, a hobby that was a holdover from college robotics courses. Paul loved the relative autonomy of being an ER physician, which was why suits like Noakes drove him crazy, and why the idea of a company like Nano stealing evidence, if that was what had happened, was so antithetical to his beliefs. But he didn't want to complicate his life.

"So how are you going to find out if they did it?" Paul asked after a pause.

"Paul, trust me, I have a nose for this stuff. They did it."

"All right, how are you going to prove it?"

"I'm going to do a little undercover work," Pia said. She waited for Paul to reprimand her, as George would undoubtedly have done, but he said nothing.

"Which is another reason I'm here." Pia paused.

"Go on."

Pia lowered her voice and leaned closer to Paul. "I need a scrip. I need a prescription, or better still, maybe you could just give me a few pills if they're available in the ER."

"What kind of pills are you talking about?" Paul questioned warily. Pia asking for drugs raised an immediate red flag. Obviously he didn't know her well, having met her for the first time the day before. He also noticed that she was still continuing to avoid looking at him, making him wonder if she had been like that yesterday. He couldn't remember.

"Sleep medication," Pia said. She was studying her hands. She felt awkward. "Not a lot. In fact, only a few pills or capsules or whatever. I hardly slept a wink last night. Thanks. I really appreciate you doing it."

Paul leaned back, "Hey, I haven't agreed to do it!"

"No, right, sorry, I'm jumping the gun. I need some Temazepam."

"That's a benzodiazepine, a controlled substance."

"I know, I know. I'm having terrible trouble sleeping. I can't sleep at all, in fact. I had some Ambien, it doesn't work at all. I mean, look at me."

Paul looked at Pia, and she seemed completely fine to him. In fact, she looked totally gorgeous. Like Pia, Paul relied a lot on his intuition to guide him. He was suspicious of Pia's claim that she wanted the narcotic to help her get to sleep. Something wasn't right, and she wouldn't look at him.

"Look, sorry," Pia said. She stood up. "I can ask someone else, it's not a big deal." She started toward the door.

"Pia, there's something I didn't tell you."

And Pia turned back. She noticed that the other person in the room was still ignoring them as if he wasn't even aware of their presence.

"I didn't send all the blood to the lab. I kept a few cc's here in the ER. They are in the fridge."

"You did?" Pia's face lit up. "Why didn't you tell me?"

"I would have told you earlier, but you hung up on me. And I did tell you I sent a sample of the blood over to the lab. I didn't send all of it because you said you might want to take a look at it. I sent enough for standard diagnostic tests and kept the rest."

"I wish you'd told me."

"I'm telling you now. You could have used a little time to chill out when we were talking earlier. I'm not going to come running after you like a lost puppy who got scolded. I've got my own stuff to worry about, you know."

"Okay, I get it," said Pia. "And you're right. Okay, great! You keep the blood. We don't know what we're looking for, so you should hold on to what you have till we have a better idea."

"Okay, I'll keep it, but let me ask you another, personal question."

"What's that?" Pia asked. She stiffened, not knowing what was coming.

"Why are you avoiding looking at me? It makes me nervous, like you're being secretive or you're not telling me the truth."

Pia forced herself to lock eyes with Paul at least for a few beats. It was hard for her as always. Then she came back to where she had been sitting and sat back down. Looking at her hands, she shook her head. "You're right, but you're wrong."

It was time for Paul to shake his head. "If I'm supposed to understand that comment, you're giving me far more credit than I deserve. What the hell are you saying?"

"You're right about me not telling the truth, but you're wrong about it being the reason I have difficulty looking you in the eye. This is probably more than you want to know, but I've been diagnosed with adult attachment disorder. Are you familiar with that?"

"I can't say that I am."

"Let's put it this way and keep it simple. You can look it up online if you want. Basically I have trouble with social relationships." Pia went on to give a quick explanation about her foster-care past. It

was unusual for her to be as open as she was, but she liked Paul intuitively. She felt there was a beginning of a bond and she was willing to be uncharacteristically open in return. When she was finished,
she forced herself to look at him again and try to hold it. She couldn't.

After a moment of silence Paul said, "Thank you for telling me
what you have. I feel honored. I felt yesterday I wanted to get to
know you more, and now it is an even stronger feeling. But what
about this comment you made that you weren't telling me the truth?
Do you have a drug problem, Pia?"

Pia couldn't help herself. She laughed, and it wasn't just a titter.
It was a belly laugh, making her again glance over at the resident
working away at the nearby desk. She was relieved to see he was still
totally ignoring them. Pia redirected her attention back to Paul.
"Oh, no," she said, trying to control herself, and lowering her voice
even more. "No, I don't have a drug problem. What I wasn't telling
you the truth about is why I need a couple of Temazepam tablets.
It's not for me to go to sleep. It is for a particular gentleman to go to
sleep. To be bluntly honest, I guess I need a kind of date-rape con-
coction but not for the usual reasons. I'm not going to rape anybody,
at least not literally."

Paul made an exaggerated expression of confusion. Now it was
his turn to lean forward. "Okay," he said. "I think you'd better tell
me exactly what you have in mind, because I haven't the slightest
idea." He and Pia's heads were almost touching. He could smell her
perfume. It was one of his favorites.

Sotto voce Pia told Paul of her idea of trying to discover the truth
behind Nano by putting herself potentially in harm's way at Zachary
Berman's extravagant home.

"You're not joking, are you?" Paul questioned.

"Not in the slightest. I think it is the only way. The irony is that
I'd be willing to bet that he's probably done something similar to
not a few women. Maybe not with Temazepam but at least with
alcohol."

"What made you think of Temazepam?"

Pia was encouraged. Paul had not dismissed the idea out of hand. "This afternoon I looked up date-rape drugs on the Internet. Apparently it's one that is used quite frequently, and it's readily available. Truthfully, I'm not choosy. You have a better idea?"

It was Paul's turn to chuckle. "It's not something I've had experience with except on a couple of rape cases that have come through the emergency room. We test for drugs like that if there is any indication to do so, meaning if the victim might have been given a Mickey Finn."

"What do you say, now that I have told you the truth? Will you give me a couple of tablets or what?"

"I can't, in good conscience as a doctor, give you medication, even two tablets, for you to commit what might be interpreted as a felony, provided you don't sexually abuse your victim."

"Fat chance," Pia said. She couldn't help smile. She liked Paul's sense of humor.

"But I tell you what. I'll give you a couple of Temazepam if you tell me they're for you to take yourself."

"Fair enough," Pia said.

"But they are not tablets. They're capsules. Is that okay?"

"That's even better," Pia said.

"And one other request. You have to tell me Berman's address. If I don't hear from you tomorrow by midmorning, I want to know where to send the police. I have to be honest: I'm not condoning this plan in the slightest."

"Fair enough," Pia repeated.

21.

So here I am again, thought Pia as she sat in her car in front of Zachary Berman's house. She was wearing the same black sheath dress she had worn on Monday, since it was the only cocktail dress she owned. But this time there was no George, and, she hoped, no Whitney Jones. Pia had gone over in her mind what she intended to do tonight, but she realized the whole thing was going to have to be played by ear. With all her heart, she'd rather not have to go through the unpleasant charade she was about to inflict upon herself, but she was unable to let go of her intense need to know more about Nano. And to do that, she knew she had to go through the boss, Zachary Berman. Being a realist at heart, Pia knew she was accepting a certain amount of risk.

Pia flipped down the VW's sun visor and reapplied her peach-shaded lipstick, which she knew set off her skin tone beautifully. Or so she had been told. She climbed out of the car and smoothed down her dress, aware that Berman was probably watching her. The security room he would be using, if he was watching her, was somewhere Pia wanted to locate as soon as possible.

As she walked up the steps and approached the front door, it swung open at just the right moment. As on the previous visit, Berman greeted her European-style with a kiss on each cheek. He was wearing a smart-casual getup similar to the one he had on her previous visit. The jacket was dark blue, and the mock turtleneck was a tan knit.

"You must have seen me coming," said Pia in reference to Berman's timing with the front door.

"I did," said Berman, showing her inside. Pia paused just inside the threshold.

"I didn't see a camera," she said.

"It's very discreet," said Berman. "See if you can figure out where it is."

Pia smiled. Berman had probably been the kid who loved to show off his train set. Like a lot of men, he had never grown out of the urge to point out his fancy toys.

"Okay," said Pia. She went back and looked around the frame of the door and above, where the timbers of the wood-framed house were visible in a kind of modern Tudor style. Berman was amused.

"You'll never find it." He then pointed out the camera. It was a tiny reflective glass bubble in the middle of the granite lintel. It was all but invisible.

Pia made an expression that suggested she was duly impressed. "Cool! Where's the monitoring room?"

"Please," Berman said as he motioned for Pia to precede him back into the house. Just beyond the foyer he opened what looked like a closet door. It was a small room with a bank of electronic gear and two large TV screens showing a succession of pictures of the exterior of the house, the gate, the swimming pool, the tennis court, and the rest of the property.

"What about the interior?" Pia asked. "Is that included in this system or is this just for the grounds?"

Without even answering, Berman reached up to one of the pieces of equipment and touched a screen. Immediately one of the TV monitors switched to a succession of interior shots, going from room to room.

"Does this record?" Pia asked.

"It does," Berman said proudly. "It records for forty-eight hours, then erases itself and starts again. It's a continuous feed."

"Let's turn it off," Pia said.

"Excuse me?"

"I want it off. I don't want to feel inhibited, knowing that a recorder is operating."

A slight smile appeared on Berman's face. He loved it. She had miraculously transformed herself into a woman of his dreams. He reached up to the same piece of equipment he'd touched to bring up the interior images and turned it off. The appropriate monitor went blank until he switched it back to the exterior images.

"Sometimes," Berman said with a wry smile, "it's fun reliving an evening's events, if you know what I mean." He raised his dark, bushy eyebrows provocatively, or so he thought.

Pia felt a flash of anger at the realization that her previous visit had probably been taped. She had enough experience of her uncle taking pornographic pictures of her when she was a kid to be disgusted by Berman's remark, but she had to keep her cool.

"There's no Miss Jones tonight?"

"There's no Miss Jones. And I let the cook and the housekeeper leave a short time ago. Our dinner is on low heat in the oven; the Champagne is on ice. We have the place to ourselves. Would you like to sit outside? It's a lovely night again. You could put a fur throw around your shoulders if you'd like."

"Sounds good," said Pia. *So the coast was clear,* she thought. But that worked both ways—there was nothing to stop Berman from trying to get what he wanted, either. At least initially it was to be a kind of Mexican standoff.

Pia took her seat outside while Berman went to the bar to fix their drinks. He returned with two Champagne flutes and proposed a toast.

"To Nano, and all who sail in her," he said, and laughed at his own little joke.

"To Nano," said Pia, "and its continued success."

"*Our* continued success. We're in this together. And we'll all share in the good times when everything we are working for comes to fruition. Mariel continues to tell me your experiments are going well."

"Yes, they are," said Pia, happy to be talking about work. She relayed that there had been no signs of any immunological reaction up until almost five o'clock that afternoon with the microbivores containing the polyethylene glycol molecules incorporated into their surfaces. "If this continues, we could be looking at starting mammalian experiments in the near future."

"Fabulous!" he said, standing. "Let me top you up." He indicated Pia's glass.

"I am driving, Mr. Berman, but don't let me inhibit you."

"Call me Zach, please! When we're out of the office, particularly here in my castle, I prefer you call me by my given name. And don't worry about driving. I'll have someone come up from the motor pool if necessary." He smiled that same unctuous smile that Pia found so nauseating. She stood up.

"Perhaps we should go ahead and eat. If the food's in the oven, we should not let it wait. I'd hate for it to dry up, whatever it is. The food was lovely on Monday night, and I've been looking forward to it all day."

"Do you cook in your apartment?"

"Never. I'm too busy with what Mariel and I are doing in the lab."

"Then it sounds like you don't like the food at the cafeteria?"

"It's fine. I just prefer yours."

"Well, that's good. I do, too. Come through to the dining room. I won't be a second." Berman walked toward the kitchen and kept talking, his voice echoing throughout the cavernous spaces of his house.

"I enjoy serving dinner to my guests," he shouted from the kitchen. "It reminds me of a time when I didn't have staff to help. They make me nervous sometimes, fussing around me. This is much more relaxed."

That's right, thought Pia, *you're just a regular guy at heart*.

"Anything I can do to help?" Pia shouted.

"Stay right there," Berman yelled back. He emerged from the kitchen with a tray. He gave Pia a bowl of steaming soup and offered freshly milled black pepper from an oversize grinder.

"Smells heavenly," said Pia.

"Vegetarian pea soup, with a lot of mint from my herb garden. And a dollop of crème fraîche. You can't beat it. *Bon appétit!*"

Pia had to admit the soup was lovely: fresh and delicate, high-lighted nicely by the fragrant pepper. She would have enjoyed it more if she weren't so nervous.

Berman had set down a fresh glass of Champagne and a glass of white wine that he claimed was a simple French white Burgundy but which Pia was sure was a pricey wine. As she sipped it, she reminded herself to be careful with the alcohol. As Berman drank his Champagne in a couple of chugs and started in on his wine, Pia took a few small sips of hers. She had to be particularly careful with the Champagne as it had a tendency to go to her head. Her obligation was to stay sharp.

As they continued with their meal, Pia had to admit that Berman was good company. He was solicitous, making sure her food was properly seasoned and that her glass of sparkling ice water was refilled. She finished a glass of the white wine, and took some of the extremely robust red Berman produced to complement the delicious buffalo steaks he served with local vegetables and some herbed orzo.

"The meat was so tender," Pia said as Berman cleared away her plate.

"It's good for you, too. Great protein, not so much fat. So let's take some dessert in the den."

Pia didn't think she had seen the den on Monday, and indeed it was a new room for her, off the living room, with yet another fireplace at the center of the back wall. There was a huge TV on the wall at right angles to the fireplace, and a deep burgundy-colored leather couch in front. There was no other furniture in the room at all. Like his office at Nano, the décor and furnishings oozed stereotypical masculinity. There was a bank of photos of Berman on a countertop that ran along the wall behind the couch. They were mostly location sporting photos with Berman holding guns, fishing poles, and mountain climbing gear. Pia sat on the couch and Berman fiddled with his iPhone, changing the lighting, bringing on some jazz music, and closing the drapes all in the space of a few seconds.

"That's very high tech . . . or something," said Pia. She imagined she was supposed to be impressed.

"I'm sorry," said Berman. "Is it too corny? I didn't conduct that little performance just for your benefit. I actually do it when it's me here by myself. I like the convenience of this custom app on my phone. I got some of the programmers at Nano to rig this up for me. It took me a while to learn how to use it, but now I can turn on faucets in the garage with this." He held up the phone in triumph.

No wonder I can't get any time with the microbivores programmers, Pia thought, but didn't say.

"So what can I get you?" Berman asked, playing the considerate host. "After-dinner cordial, some dessert wine? I do have some homemade ice cream in the freezer. I'm assuming you're not interested in a cigar. But I don't want to be sexist. If I were here by myself, which I'm infinitely grateful I'm not, I would indulge in a cigar."

"Are you by yourself very often?" Pia asked.

"Sometimes. Why do you ask?"

"I don't know. You have these attractive women working for you. Whitney, Mariel . . ."

Berman sat down next to Pia.

"Maybe they are attractive . . ." He reached out and ran his forefinger along Pia's jawline as she turned to face him. Her initial response was to knock his hand away, but she controlled herself. She knew she had to maintain the pretense or the evening would be a flop. At the same time, she hated to be in the position she was. It reminded her of being attacked in the residence mansion of the superintendent of the Hudson Valley Academy. She struggled to keep as much eye contact as she could.

"Whitney and Mariel are definitely attractive," Berman continued, totally unaware of Pia's thoughts. "But they are not you." He now reached around Pia's shoulder and put pressure on her to draw her toward him. Pia acquiesced to a degree, then pulled back gently. She fought with herself to stay in control and not lash out at this man, who at the moment represented everything she found repulsive about the opposite sex.

"Let's slow down," she said softly. "Let me get you another drink." Her goal was to get him to drink as much as possible as soon as possible.

Berman sat back and looked at Pia. "You're making me work very hard, Pia."

"I think we need to get to know each other better."

"I thought when you came to see me in my office at the crack of dawn today that you were ready to take things to the next step."

Pia stood and leaned over Berman, one hand on either side of his legs. Her face came close to his. She fought against the urge to give his neck a sharp karate chop that probably would have made him as limp as wet spaghetti.

"Maybe I am ready, but my Italian mother told me that the man had to show he respected me before I should let him do anything."

Pia was amazed at herself coming up with a line like that. In reality she could not remember one single thing her mother had said, as she'd had died a violent death when Pia was just a toddler.

Pia knew she was driving Berman crazy. He was shifting in his seat as if he were going to explode. Pia stayed where she was, and shimmied her hips a little and smiled. She couldn't believe herself. "So what can I fix you?" she questioned. "I remember from Sunday night that you like scotch, right? I've always admired men who drank scotch. It's such a masculine drink."

"Yes, I do like my whiskey."

Berman could hardly speak. He actually licked his lips.

Pia smiled again. The method acting she had done during her undergraduate days at NYU was coming in handy.

"So which way's the bar?" She stood and took a step for the door.

"There's one right over there," said Berman. "I keep whiskey in here, so it's close at hand."

Pia swore under her breath. She had left what she needed in her clutch purse on the dining-room table. She assumed she'd be able to fix a drink in the wet bar in the living room, from which Berman was getting the wine and Champagne. She looked over and saw a built-in cabinet she hadn't noticed. She walked over and pulled on what she thought was a large drawer. Instead the whole front of the piece swung aside to reveal cut-glass decanters and whiskey glasses.

"Which one?" asked Pia.

"The lighter of the two. A Laphroaig single malt."

"Ice!" Pia said, triumphantly. "I need ice."

"Pia, I really can't allow you to sully a lovely single-malt whiskey with ice. It's really not the way you drink it."

"I'm sorry, but if I am going to try it, I need ice. Where do I go?"

Berman stood. "You should let me get it, please." He'd regained a modicum of composure. He took a glass and poured himself a dollop. Pia reached under his elbow to encourage him to add a bit more. She smiled. He smiled back.

"I need to use your bathroom," said Pia. "So I can get the ice on the way back."

"You know where the bathroom is, you used it the other night. It's off the foyer. The wet bar is in the living room, and I should—"

"Now, you sit down and don't move!" said Pia with trumped-up authority. "I'll be right back."

Pia hurried out of the den, picked up her clutch purse, and headed for the foyer. Her pulse was racing. In the bathroom for a couple of seconds, she located the two thirty-milligram capsules of Temazepam. Then she flushed the toilet and washed her hands. Back at the wet bar in the living room, she filled a wineglass with ice from the icemaker, tucked her purse under her arm, and headed back to the den.

Berman was sitting on the couch, nursing his scotch. On the cocktail table in front of him was a second tumbler half-filled with neat whiskey, normally enough alcohol to knock her out cold. Pia realized that her plan was in danger of backfiring badly at the crucial moment. She could not get drunk herself. How much had Berman had to drink? A couple of glasses of Champagne, a couple of glasses each of white and red wine. Some, but not enough for a man the size of Berman and with a tolerance gained from being a heavy drinker. And herself? So far, she had had most of a flute of Champagne and less than half a glass of wine. She could take more than that, but with whiskey, that would be pushing it. She had no real experience with hard liquor.

Pia poured the whole cup of ice into the whiskey and mopped up the overflow with a napkin.

"Sorry, spilled a little. Well, good health."

"Santé!" said Berman, taking a sip of his whiskey and relishing it.

Pia took a sip, and the booze made her cough.

"Steady on," said Berman. "Are you enjoying it, or would you like something else?"

"I like the taste. I developed a liking for this stuff a while ago. But

when I was at middle school it was more often Crown Royal I drank."
She was warming to the role she was playing. Looking over her
shoulder, she gazed at all the photos. "I get the impression you're an
active guy."

"I think that's a fair description."

"Is that one of you on the top of a mountain?" Pia asked, pointing
to one photo in particular.

"It is," Berman said proudly. "It was taken on the summit of one
of the lesser peaks in the Himalayas."

"I'm impressed," Pia said. "Would you mind showing it to me?"

"Not at all!" Berman got up and walked around the couch. As he
did so, Pia reached her tumbler down under the cocktail table and
managed to pour out most of the liquid while holding in the ice with
her fingers. When Berman came back with the photo she dutifully
pretended to admire it. In actuality she thought rich man's mountain climbing was one of the more ridiculous endeavors.

Berman came back around the couch.

Pia laughed as she put her tumbler down onto the cocktail table.
"Now, that was a treat." She pretended to belch and laughed a bit
more. "Come on, with your drink. You're losing."

"I wasn't aware it was a race."

Pretending to be getting high, Pia said, "Can you change the
music? Come on, let's have a proper party." She snatched Berman's
glass and handed him his iPhone. The glass was still about half-full.

"What do you want to listen to?" Berman asked.

"How about something a bit more contemporary," Pia suggested
as she stepped over to the open liquor cabinet and filled Berman's
glass to just below the brim. She looked back at Berman, who was
busy with his custom app, apparently scrolling through music selections. Pia dropped both of the Temazepam capsules into the amber
fluid and tried to get them to sink.

"How's this?" said Berman. What sounded to Pia like the Beatles
came on.

"No, too old," said Pia. She used her finger to stir the whiskey, but there was no effect. The red-and-blue capsules floated around like miniature buoys. "Shit," Pia quietly hissed. She put the glass down and fished out the troublesome capsules.

"This?" Berman called out.

The new music was unfamiliar to Pia. "I don't recognize it. What is it?"

"It's an old band I used to like in the eighties. Is that fun enough for you?"

"The eighties? Do you have anything from the last ten years? Something I might have heard of?"

Pia struggled with the capsules, finally managing to break them in half. When she did so, she poured the white powder into the drink.

"Oh, for God's sake," she shouted out.

"What is it?" yelled Berman over the music.

"I spilled some more of your whiskey, I'm sorry." Pia found a long glass stirrer in the cabinet and started frantically trying to get the powder, which was now floating on the surface, to dissolve. She cursed herself for not having tried a dry run.

"How about something else," she suggested. Finally the powder seemed to start to dissolve.

"Okay, but you're not being much help." Berman found a radio station playing some kind of electronic music, slow and languid.

"There," said Pia, "I like that."

"Really? Sounds god-awful to me," said Berman.

Pia looked into the bottom of Berman's glass. There was a small piece of blue capsular material. She tried to get it with her finger, but it agonizingly kept moving away from her fingertip. Instead, she poured most of the spiked drink into a second tumbler, leaving the pill debris where it was. She then carried the glass over to the cocktail table and rescued hers. Making sure Berman could not see what she was doing, she filled hers with bottled water and some whiskey for color. With her heart racing, she returned to the cocktail table and put her glass down.

"Come on!" she said in a lively tone, reaching out to Berman. "Dance with me!"

Pia moved her body to the rhythm of the hypnotic music, swaying, holding an arm over her head, apparently lost in the moment. Berman sat back and drank his whiskey. What a woman!

"I'd prefer to watch you," said Berman. As he watched, he drank. Pia snatched glances at Berman, afraid that the medication might have a bitter taste that would alert Berman to its presence. She knew one capsule was the recommended dose for someone with anxiety or insomnia, but she wasn't sure how much of the two capsules actually got into the drink.

Pia had absolutely no experience of dancing, let alone exotic dancing, but she could move in sync with the music, which thankfully retained the same tempo from one song to the next, if *song* was the right word. She took the whiskey bottle and refilled Berman's glass. He had already drunk about a quarter of it. Apparently the taste wasn't bad.

"Hey, no fair," he said, and it looked to Pia as if he were having trouble focusing on her. Pia grabbed her own glass and made a point to knock back most of it. This was enough for Berman to slip into a binge mode himself, taking healthy gulps of whiskey as Pia went back to her provocative dancing.

As Berman kept up his drinking, Pia was encouraged to be progressively more creative. After a number of songs and several more additions to Berman's glass, she began to wonder what was keeping the guy awake. She wondered if maybe Berman popped benzodiazepines every night and had a tolerance for the drugs. But then, while she was refilling his drink, Berman's eyes seemed to disappear up inside his head, and his glass slipped from his grasp. Pia lunged forward and caught the glass before it rolled off his lap. His head sank back, and he began snoring gently.

"Thank God," said Pia. She took the iPhone and found the control that switched off the radio. Suddenly the house was plunged into absolute silence. Quickly she ran back to the kitchen with Berman's tumbler and the other two glasses and rinsed them all out in the unlikely scenario that a Mickey Finn was suspected the following day. She even made certain the pesky blue capsule material was properly disposed of before she put the glasses back in the den and poured a little whiskey into two of them.

"Okay," she said to no one in particular when all was ready, "let's see what we can find."

22.

Pia reckoned she had four or five hours to search Berman's home. The fact that her host was drunk and drugged up didn't stop Pia from going back and checking on him twice in the hours since he'd finally succumbed. Pia had arranged Berman in a kind of a recovery position on his large couch with his head a little over the side in case he became nauseous. She was confident that to the world, he appeared to be sleeping like a baby. Pia spent ten minutes in the kitchen, drinking several glasses of water until she felt slightly more human herself. She wanted all her faculties.

Pia had no notion of what she was looking for in Berman's house. She walked through the whole place, making a mental note of the location and function of each room. The property was on three levels, with guest rooms, a workout room, a wine cellar, and access to the garage downstairs. She had seen the whole of the first floor, but nothing of the second. The two main rooms up there could be reached by a main staircase from the living room, and by a back stair from the kitchen.

Berman's giant master bedroom, with two huge baths, occupied most of the space. But there was another room as well, and it was the one Pia was most interested in. It was clearly a home office.

Wearing a pair of latex examination gloves she'd picked up in the
ER when Paul Caldwell was off getting her Temazepam capsules,
Pia sat at Berman's desk in his chair and looked around. The table
was glass and on it sat a large Mac, the latest model with retina display. To the right was a six-inch-high stack of papers; to the left, a
flat-panel charger for Berman's iPhone and Android. To the side,
below the table, was a cherrywood filing cabinet that was locked. Pia
swiveled around and took in the room. Unlike the rest of the house,
there was a smooth finish to the walls, wood paneling that lent the
room a more businesslike air than the rest of the timbered home.

There were a couple of low cabinets against one wall and Pia tried
the door handles on both. Each was locked. Bookcases lined the
other wall, filled with what Pia saw as a standard guy's collection of
business books, sports biographies, and thrillers, with a few coffee
table books on the Rockies thrown in. She pulled a few of the books
back but the wall behind was solid. There was no drawer in the glass
desk, and Pia ran her hand along the flat surfaces in the room, looking for keys. Nothing.

All Pia had ready access to was the pile of papers on the desk.

Pia read through the pile meticulously. Most of the papers turned
out to be printed-out copies of intra-company emails. Many were
anotated in pencil in Berman's hand. The majority were status reports of tests and experiments going on throughout Nano, and Pia
recognized a few of them as her own. Her unfamiliarity with some
aspects of other applications of nanotechnology hindered her ability
to decode some of the more technical language. Scattered among
the emails were copies of requisition forms that Berman had signed,
including hers for the additional biocompatibility experiments.

One paper was a form for a new office chair for someone named
Al Clift that Berman had turned down. He drew vigorous circles
around the price—$359—and wrote "request denied" next to it. All
Berman could be accused of from the evidence in this pile of paperwork was being a micromanager, and a cheap one at that.

Pia slumped down in the seat and stared at the Mac. It was powered down and she thought if she turned it on, Berman most likely would know someone had been in his office, and she'd be the prime suspect. She was frustrated and extremely tired. It was now a quarter of four. She decided to take one more tour around the house, come back to the office and look at the papers again, and then leave before Berman woke up.

The lower level yielded nothing. She could see into the wine vault but couldn't open the door, which had a separate lock. Through the window she saw row after row of bottles but no safe or cabinet or any other out-of-place piece of furniture. The climate-control system hummed along, keeping the room at a steady temperature and humidity. Pia hesitated to go into the garage in case Berman considered it part of the outside and her visit would be recorded. She had a moment of panic when she wondered if Berman had been lying about cameras inside the house being off, but it was much too late to be concerned about that.

She carefully checked the door into the garage. It didn't seem to be wired. When she opened the door, she kept herself out of view until she could be sure there were no switches on any of the door-jambs. It seemed that the outer doors of the garage were the ones wired to the alarm system. It made sense, considering what was in the garage.

There were three vehicles: a Ford F-150 with a snowplow attachment, a Range Rover, and an Aston Martin. There was also a sailboat on a trailer. The room had two freezers, which on inspection were largely filled with venison and elk meat. One wall was covered with power tools and gardening equipment mounted on hooks. This was a meticulous and well-prepared man, Pia thought.

As she followed that line of reasoning, Pia realized it was unlikely Berman would store sensitive material in plain sight in his home. Why risk having documents lying around at home, no matter how good the security system, when he could leave everything at work?

Nano had fences, armed guards, iris scanners, multiple cameras, and who knew what else. Pia sighed. She'd give the paperwork one more look and then cut out.

Pia walked up to the main level of the house. As she passed the small room where Berman kept his TV monitors, a movement caught Pia's eye on one of the screens. She moved closer and was horrified to see something walking up the steps toward the front door that was barely ten feet from where she was standing. It was the tall and unmistakable figure of Whitney Jones.

Pia did an immediate one-eighty and hurried back toward Berman and the den. As she ran along on her tiptoes, she pulled off the surgical gloves and held them in her hand. In the den, Berman hadn't moved, and he was still snoring peacefully. Pia imagined Whitney was approaching the front door. Quickly she pulled the den door to without shutting it. By then she could hear the sound of heels on the hardwood floor, so she made her way over to the couch. She plopped herself down and curled up in the corner with Berman's feet in her lap. She hoped she looked as if she were asleep. Once again her heart was pounding in her chest.

Whitney had walked into the dining room but hadn't looked in the den. Pia peeked and saw from a display on the TV console that it was 4:42 A.M. Did she always show up that early? Maybe the garage had been wired, after all. Pia knew Whitney would have seen her car in the driveway. As the footfalls receded, she figured Whitney was going to check on the bedroom, the logical place. Pia reached under her short dress and stuffed the exam gloves into her panties. Her heart was thumping so loudly in her ears, she thought Whitney could probably hear it from upstairs.

After what seemed like a half hour, the footsteps returned, louder and faster this time. Whitney hadn't found Berman in his bed, perhaps she was now worried. After another circuit of the living area, the door to the den opened slowly, and the room was filled with light. Pia breathed more loudly. Now her head was pounding from anxiety, and she felt nauseous. Whitney must have surveyed the scene from the doorway because the door quickly closed and the den was plunged back into darkness.

Pia lay still, thanking her luck in seeing Whitney on the monitor and not having to run into her someplace else in the house, wondering if she had left any evidence of her nocturnal visitation. She figured Whitney was still in the house, and she didn't relish the idea of lying here in the dark, listening to Zach Berman snore. She needed to grab a couple of hours' real sleep in her bed. Pia swung her legs over the couch, fumbled for her purse in the dark, and stepped over to the door.

23.

Whitney Jones was sitting at Zachary Berman's dining-room table, expertly tapping a message on her iPad. She was good at it and often sent more than a hundred texts a day. She heard the door to the den open and close. Whitney was pleased someone was taking the initiative, as she wasn't sure how to handle the situation. She sensed that someone had appeared in the archway into the dining room and gathered it was Pia, as Berman surely would have announced himself. She further sensed that Pia had entered the room and walked over to her, but she didn't look up. Whitney was being deliberately passive-aggressive—she sensed her boss's infatuation with Pia and thought it could only lead to trouble.

"Oh, hi, Miss Jones," said Pia, genuinely embarrassed despite not having been discovered in flagrante delicto. Pia hoped she was doing as good an acting job as the one she had with Berman, albeit in a completely different role. But still, she felt if what she'd been caught doing was not illegal, it was at least naughty. She was glad it was only being found asleep on the couch first thing in the morning with her boss's boss, and not wandering around Berman's house, looking for incriminating evidence of what Nano was up to with the Chinese, as she actually had been doing.

"I thought I heard the door open," said Pia, waiting for Whitney to react in some way. "And of course I saw the light."

"One second," Whitney said, and went on typing rapidly with her thumbs. After a long minute, she looked up with arched eyebrows and addressed Pia. "I'm sorry if I woke you. I was looking for Mr. Berman. Obviously enough, I guess. He has a call to make this morning before certain people leave their offices."

From Pia's perspective, Whitney appeared to be completely unperturbed by Pia's presence. Either she was hiding her feelings and doing an acting job, too, or she really was as cool as they came. It also made Pia wonder what the relationship was between Whitney and Berman. Obviously she had a key to the house.

"It's still very early, isn't it?" said Pia, looking around as if to see a clock. "What time is it?" She decided to try to be as nonchalant as Whitney, as if this were no big deal. And it really wasn't, Pia thought, apart from the fact that Berman was drugged rather than asleep. Pia had no idea if he would suspect anything when he woke up, but the thought of it made her anxious to leave. At the same time, she wanted to stick around to see if Berman was okay, because if a doctor examined him, it might be hard to evade the difficult questions that would almost certainly arise.

"It's a quarter of five here," Whitney said, interrupting Pia's train of thought. "But it's not that time all over the world." Whitney looked back to her device as an answering text came in, and she went back to tapping on the keyboard.

Pia imagined that in China it was approaching five P.M., since it was on the opposite side of the world. Perhaps that's where Berman was calling. It certainly made sense.

"Yes, well, he's asleep in there," said Pia, suddenly feeling the need to say something. "We both had rather a lot to drink, I'm sorry to say." Pia didn't have to fake feeling tired and slightly hungover. She rarely drank alcohol of any kind.

Whitney finished typing and looked at Pia.

"Don't worry, Pia, you won't hear any judgment from me," she said. "One of the reasons Zachary likes me is my complete discretion. But the call has to be made. Excuse me!"

Then she walked off in the direction of the den. Despite herself and after a moment of indecision, Pia thought it would be inappropriate to leave at that point, so she followed. Whitney went over to Berman and tapped him on the shoulder, but he didn't wake up. She squatted down and shook him more forcibly while calling out his name. There was still no response. She stood back up, looking down at him. "He's sleeping like a baby. What on earth were you drinking? He looks like he's out cold."

"This," said Pia, holding up the almost-empty decanter of whiskey. The scent wafting up made her feel sick. She picked up the soiled glasses, including Berman's tumbler, which she'd washed right after Berman had passed out but had brought back to the den. She was glad she had, because it might look odd that there were no glasses with the whiskey. But only if she was acting guiltily, which Pia was now very afraid she was doing.

"You can leave those for the housekeeper," said Whitney with a wave of her hand.

"It's no trouble," said Pia, who wanted to clean the glass a second time, somewhat like Lady Macbeth washing her hands, in case any residue of the narcotic remained. Before Whitney could protest further, Pia exited the room and went to the kitchen, where she scrubbed the tumbler clean under the hottest water the faucet could provide.

Again, Pia didn't know whether to stick around to see if Berman woke up or to take her leave, but when she got back to the den, Berman was sitting up, drinking a glass of water. He looked as if he'd been in a bar fight. His eyes were reddened and his hair was sticking straight up in the back.

"How are you feeling?" said Pia. This was a moment of truth. "You went down pretty hard last night."

"I feel like I've been hit in the head with a hammer," said Berman.

He kept his head down, eyes away from the light. "How many whiskeys did I have?"

"Plenty, but you're okay?" said Pia. Meaning, you don't feel like you've been drugged, do you?

"Yes, I'm fine," he said. He looked at Pia and tried to smile. "I usually have a good head for that stuff. But don't worry about me, you should go home." Now it was his turn to feel embarrassed. Behaving like an inexperienced college kid had not been his plan. "Miss Jones tells me I have an important call to make in a few minutes, so I'd better get myself together. And thank you for coming. I had fun, what I remember of it."

"I had fun, too," said Pia. She felt vastly relieved, and she didn't know whether to go over to Berman and shake his hand or kiss him on the cheek. In the end, she did neither, and thought it was best if she just left before it got more awkward. She waved wanly, made sure she had everything she came with, and walked out of the house.

It was still dark outside, and Pia felt as if she might still be drunk as she uneasily descended the front steps down to the driveway level. Fearful of possibly falling, she hung on to the handrail for dear life. She was exhausted and even a little depressed after all the effort she'd expended for naught. On top of that was the realization that she had probably opened the floodgates as far as Berman was concerned. Up until this evening she'd made it a point to keep Berman and his ardor at arm's length. Now she had no idea what to expect.

Pia drove back to her apartment with extreme caution, maintaining five miles per hour below the speed limit. She parked her car very carefully and made her way into bed. She looked at the clock. It was five-thirty. Berman was on his call or he had finished it. But what the nature of his business was, Pia was no nearer to finding out than she'd been before showing up at Berman's house. Before she could think about it too much and feel too disappointed, she fell into a deep, dreamless sleep.

24.

Pia awoke with a start. She emerged quickly into consciousness—
damn, she thought right away, *what time is it?* Pia found her phone
and was horrified. Although she had expected to sleep for a couple
of hours at most, it was ten forty-five. She saw that she had emails
and texts from Mariel Spallek asking where she was, and to get in
touch with her immediately. And voice mails, too. Pia didn't need to
listen to them to know what Mariel wanted. Not wanting to delay
the inevitable, Pia called Mariel, who answered immediately.

"It's Pia, I'm really sorry, I'm sick. I'll try and come in after lunchtime, if that's okay."

"I guess it'll have to be," said Mariel. "What's wrong with you?"
Her question was posed in the same tone an irritated motorist would
use to ask a mechanic what was wrong with her car. There was
no hint of sympathy or concern. Mariel had been inconvenienced,
and she didn't like it. Pia wasn't particularly surprised by Mariel's
reaction—she, too, would have been frustrated by someone not
showing up for work, even though this was the first time Pia had ever
called in sick. Although some of Pia's morning timekeeping could be
somewhat erratic, such episodes had always been due to her working to the wee hours of the morning.

"Headache, dizziness, nausea. Basically, I feel like shit." Pia had chosen her rude syntax on purpose, hoping to cut off conversation.

"Sounds like the same thing Mr. Berman has," Mariel said, unable to resist the opportunity for a little dig, and suggesting to Pia that she had learned of Pia's second visit and felt jealous. "I'll see you at two o'clock if not before."

Pia was about to ask a question, but Mariel had hung up. Had Berman not made it into the office? she wondered. That seemed unlikely. Pia surmised that he had come in, and Mariel had seen him looking hung over. The few hours' sleep she had stolen had done Pia a world of good, and she felt almost back to normal.

To help with the process, Pia downed two ibuprofen tablets, drank two glasses of water, and took a shower. As the hot water further revived her, Pia went over her options. Again, she took the position contrary to her own and challenged her concerns as to what she had witnessed over the last few days and asked if there couldn't be a rational, innocent explanation for all of it. And again, presumably with humans involved, possibly as subjects of experimentation, she couldn't convince herself there was and that she should do nothing.

Pia decided she needed a sounding board. She first thought of George, but there was too much personally invested, on his side, for that to be an efficient use of her time. Two years previously in medical school, he had been helpful, even if it was his negative energy that Pia sometimes fed off. He'd pointed her in the right direction for the polonium discovery, although he had done so inadvertently. Today if she called, he'd want to talk about his recent visit and what it meant, and how they needed to make better contact, blah, blah, blah. That was the last thing Pia wanted to discuss. Pia truly liked George, even if he was hopelessly conservative. The problem was that she knew she could never be what he thought he needed. She also knew instinctively that he'd oppose her doing any kind of investigation of Nano and would be unable to understand her need to do so.

Then she thought of Paul Caldwell, and when she did, she remembered she'd promised to call him by midmorning, otherwise he promised he was going to alert the police. She quickly checked the time. It was beyond midmorning; in fact, it was after eleven. Frantically she called him.

"Pia, how are you?" he said with no preamble. He'd obviously seen her name on his phone's screen.

"Paul, thank God I got you! I almost forgot to call you. You said you'd call the police if I didn't. You haven't, have you?"

"No! And I would have tried you before I called them."

"Good," Pia said with relief. "Are you in the ER?"

"No, actually I've just left there. I filled in on the night shift for one of my partners with a sick kid. I'm on my way home, but I was going to call you when I got in. I hesitate to ask, but how did it go last night? Did you get a good night's sleep with the Temazepam?"

"I just woke up," Pia admitted. It sounded to Pia like Paul was teasing her, so she ignored his question. She also didn't fill in the part about going to bed at five A.M. "Listen, I was wondering if we could have a chat sometime today. In person; the sooner, the better."

"Aren't you going into work? It's after eleven." Paul set aside his worries about giving Pia the Temazepam, as apparently there were no repercussions, and now he was curious if she'd found out anything about Nano. But he was following her lead, and not asking any questions over the phone.

"I'm going in later," said Pia. "I'm a bit worse for wear. Alcohol and I are like oil and water."

"Well, let me tell you my plans. I'm going home and jump into some hiking gear and get out on a trail somewhere. Why don't you join me? We can chat then. I'd certainly like to hear more about your evening." Paul wanted to know if Pia really was okay.

"I suppose that's a possibility. I would like to talk with you. Tell me more about this hike. I'm not up to a real challenge."

"It will be nice, trust me, nothing too strenuous. I had a hard night in the ER. More than the usual couple of drunken college kids, I'm sorry to say. Like, we had a nasty car accident that I'd rather not think about. C'mon, Pia, come with me and get some fresh mountain air. I promise, you'll feel a lot better. It works for me every time."

In truth, the last thing Pia felt like doing was going on a hike, but if that was the price she had to pay to bend Paul's ear, so be it. She felt she needed someone else's counsel, even if only to hear herself talk. "Okay, Paul, I'll come. Just tell me where I have to be."

FORTY-FIVE MINUTES LATER Pia was standing at a trail head with Paul, dressed in her running gear and a light rain jacket. Paul had on a stylish hiking outfit and professional-looking boots, and he looked good, as if he could hike all day despite having been up all night. Pia felt underdressed, and also unready physically for hard exercise. But Paul assured her that he planned just a two-hour round-trip jaunt up through the pine trees on this popular circuit.

"This time of day it shouldn't be too crowded up here," Paul said, immediately setting a brisk marching pace that challenged Pia to keep up with him. Paul breathed in deeply and exhaled. They were walking on a bed of fragrant pine needles. "This is what I live in Colorado for. The air is fantastic, don't you think?"

"It's a little thin for my sea-level tastes," said Pia. "But it is clean and crisp." Usually she would agree with him more enthusiastically, but today she didn't want to waste time on pleasantries, so she launched right in, filling Paul in on what had happened the night before. The only omission she made was not confessing to using the Temazepam capsules she'd gotten from Paul on the unwitting Berman, saying instead simply that he got drunk and passed out. As she spoke, she acknowledged to herself that her suspicions about Nano depended on circumstantial evidence: the disappearance of the blood sample, Mariel showing up with armed guards at the ER, the level of Nano's security, the odd cyclists, and the Chinese runner's strange illness and miraculous recovery.

When she finished talking about Nano and the fact that she'd learned absolutely nothing at Berman's house, Pia went back two years and told Paul a bit about the episode surrounding the deaths of Rothman and Yamamoto at Columbia and some of her part in uncovering the truth about them, and how that effort had nearly cost her her life. She was much more scant with the details than she had been talking about her visit to Berman's house. By the time she finished, she was out of breath from talking so much while walking hard. The hiking was easy for Paul, and he was obviously thinking about what he was hearing as evidenced by a few pointed questions. After a couple of minutes' contemplation after she was finished, he spoke up.

"So let me be blunt, because that's the way I am, okay? There are two possibilities that I see. One, you have a well-tuned instinct for sensing trouble and a very good analytical mind that can think your way through evidence and see the way to a solution. And from what you've told me, you're brave enough to follow it up. Or foolish enough to try."

"If that all is one," said Pia. "What's two?"

"That you are a bit crazy," said Paul. "I mean, no offense. Are you offended?" Paul looked over at Pia, whose face was impassive. "I guess you're not offended. Good. Because actually I don't think you are crazy. Dogged is a better word. Also clairvoyant. From what you just described, you were the only one who thought anything was amiss for a long time following the deaths at Columbia, isn't that right?"

"Yes. No one believed me. I felt like a Cassandra. It seemed so obvious to me."

"Okay, well, I believe you. I'm not normally one for conspiracy theories, but there is definitely something strange about Nano, based on what I saw in the ER and what you have told me. So what are you going to do about it now that you have flamed out at your boss's mansion?"

"I'm glad you agree with me about Nano. It's reassuring, to say the least. The problem for me is that I have the same sense here that I had back in medical school. I can't help feeling what I feel, and I have an obligation to look into it if just to dispel it. I had a visitor here just this past weekend. His name is George Wilson . . ."

"Ah-ha!" Paul said with a mischievous smile. "I like this. A love interest?"

"Hardly," Pia said with a wave of her hand. "At least not from my side."

"Oh, no!" Paul complained. With an exaggerated gesture he let his face and shoulders fall. "You're so gorgeous; you must have hundreds of boyfriends."

"Sorry," Pia said. She couldn't help smile. "As I suggested yesterday, I'm not much of a social animal. Sorry to disappoint. George and I have been friends for the whole time we were in medical school, and he did help me with the Rothman investigation, breaking into a few places where we were not supposed to go. Anyway, that's another issue.

"The point I wanted to make was that when he was here over the weekend, he asked me an interesting question that set me thinking. After I told him how enormously nanotechnology was going to affect the medical field and the huge amounts of money being spent in research and development, he asked who was overseeing it all, making sure that corners weren't being cut on issues like safety. At first his question just irritated me because I was already irritated he'd shown up uninvited."

"That's a no-no," Paul interjected.

"But later I realized he was right. There is no oversight of nanotechnology research. No one is checking what might be the health risks of some nano products or violations of ethical standards, like premature human experimentation."

"Ah, so that is what you think might be going on?"

"Truthfully, I don't know, but, yes, that is a worry. And here I am in the thick of it, so to speak. I want to be sure I'm not abetting something unethical or even possibly illegal. I need some evidence of what is going on at Nano. I can't call the authorities like the FDA or a newspaper, because I don't have anything to show them, and it is not at all unreasonable for a nanotechnology company to be secretive.

"It's the same as when I was in medical school. It's down to me. I'm going to have to get inside the other buildings at Nano where I'm officially not supposed to go to find out what is going on. I tried to look around a little the other day, even the building connected to the one I work in by a bridge. Frankly, it is my first choice to look in, because it seems to have the most security, but I got nowhere. An iris scanner blocked my entrance to the bridge."

"Isn't snooping around Nano going to be dangerous? You saw those guards who came to my ER."

Pia shrugged. "Maybe yes, maybe no. I don't really know. But I am a Nano employee. If I end up being found in some area where I'm not supposed to be, I can just say I got lost, or I'm running an errand for Mr. Berman, now that I know him socially. The only other thing I can think of is to try to get him to invite me to participate in other aspects of Nano's research efforts. The trouble is, I don't know what it is, exactly, and I can't tip my hand. My immediate boss, Mariel, has told me on several occasions how important secrecy is considered, even with the work I am doing. You see, I could be fired at any time. I'm helping them, but I am certainly not indispensable."

"How do you know you're not already working on the secret stuff?"

"What do you mean?" said Pia.

"I just mean you may not know all of the uses the projects you're working on are put to. I mean, do you?"

"And I thought *I* had a cynical side," said Pia, with a sarcastic chuckle. She hadn't thought of that possibility. The microbivores seemed to have a benign purpose, but with the technology she was helping develop to counter the biocompatibility issues, she couldn't be so sure. Pia was silent for a few minutes.

"I'm sorry," said Paul. "I didn't mean to upset you."

"You didn't upset me. I'm fine."

"Okay. Good." Paul came to a halt and gestured around them. "This is the turnaround. Let's enjoy the view for a few minutes and head back." They had emerged from the trees and reached a rocky ledge, which offered a striking view of distant mountains.

After another few minutes of silence, Paul spoke again. He wasn't out of breath in the slightest. "So how do you want me to help you? I have a sense that this is where your monologue is leading. So just talk it through or is there something more concrete? I won't do anything illegal, mind. And I'm not breaking in anywhere like you just told me George did with you."

"I got it," said Pia. "There is something you can help me with."

"Okay, shoot."

"When we first met, you told me you liked to play around with computer code, yes?"

"I may have said that, yes." Paul sounded wary.

"Don't worry, I'm not asking you to hack into anything. But I need to get past the iris scanners at Nano. When I tried to cross the bridge from my building to the neighboring building, an iris scanner wouldn't allow me access. Is there some way I can dupe such a scanner without smashing it with a hammer? It has to be something that might look like the scanner made an honest mistake if I got caught."

"Are these scanners manned?"

"What you mean?"

"I mean is there a security person standing there watching you when you stand in front of it?"

"Some but not all," Pia said. "On the first floor of my building there are certainly security people, but they have never paid any attention when I go through the scanner. And when I tried but failed to get past a scanner blocking the door to the bridge from my building to the next, there was no security person."

"I think I can help you, in that case," said Paul. It sounded as if it might be illegal, but only if he was the one to break in somewhere he didn't have a right to have access to. It also sounded like a fun challenge, the type he used to love when he was in high school. "My understanding is that an iris scanner uses mathematical pattern-recognition techniques that take advantage of the fact that people's irises are as different from one another as fingerprints. I'll tell you what, I'll look into it for you."

"Thanks, Paul, that's great."

"Listen, I don't want to pour cold water on this, but it sounds dangerous. Do you think it's a good idea?"

Pia rolled her eyes. Paul was channeling George.

"I'm going to try whether you'll help me or not."

"I figured you'd say something like that. I'll see what I can find out."

25.

Mariel Spallek made a point of checking her watch when Pia walked into the lab at 2:15. "You're late," she said. "I thought you said you'd be here by two P.M." She turned her attention back to the ledger book spread out on her desk.

"You said two P.M., not me. You're lucky I'm here at all, the way I feel. I'm certainly allowed a sick day." Pia had reached the end of her rope with Mariel. She wasn't used to taking the kind of aggressive manhandling and nitpicking that Mariel was subjecting her to without pushing back.

"I never take a sick day, and I don't expect my staff to take any, either," said Mariel without looking up. "Some days I feel better than others, but I come to work anyway, short of hospitalization. I expect the same from others."

Pia conjured up a number of pithy retorts but thought better of saying any. She hoped she'd have an opportunity to tell Mariel what she thought of her at some juncture in the future.

For the next two-plus hours, Pia kept her head down and worked hard. Mariel had commandeered some more staff to help in the new space she'd gotten previously on the floor below. Pia got them up to speed, and they began to set up more biocompatibility experiments.

The more experiments that could be run, the better the conclusions would be statistically.

What now began to bother Pia was that Mariel would not give up her tendency to micromanage, meaning everything had to be run by her, even the most mundane details. For Pia, part of the excitement of doing research was challenging herself first to get to a solution, and second to get corroborating data. She felt constrained by Mariel's overbearing supervision of everything she did and every step she took. When she had a break, she again sought out Mariel, who was still engrossed in the same ledger book, no doubt compulsively going over details.

"Listen, Mariel, I know the work is going well, and you've got staff running tests that I don't even know about in other Nano buildings. Are any of these other tests related to what I am doing, and if they are, wouldn't it make sense to have some of the techs report directly to me? That way I can analyze what they are doing myself."

"That's my job, Pia. Your job is to be creative about the specific problems that we assign to you. What other people are doing is not your business."

"Yes, okay, but who are they? Why can't I at least talk to them? I'm slaving away here, and I have no idea what anyone else is doing. To me that is frustrating and seems like a recipe for redundancy."

"Nano is a large, high-security company that is very compartmentalized because of security needs. There is a need-to-know policy with all our staff and all our research. You don't need to know what other people are doing, nor do they need to know what you are up to. Ultimately it's more efficient that way and certainly more secure. You'll be informed if there is any redundancy. You concentrate on what you're paid to do. If you knew Mr. Berman better, you would understand the way his mind works. He's the father and supporter of Nano's organization. I am his eyes and ears."

And a jealous bitch, Pia thought but didn't say. Instead she said:

"You suggested on the phone he was not feeling up to par. Did he come in today?"

"He came in, yes. Of course. He's a dedicated man, in contrast to yourself. Why do you ask?"

"I'm just interested, Mariel. Why are you giving me such a hard time about everything?"

Mariel stopped reading her ledger and looked up at Pia. She affected a flinty smile.

"I'm sorry if you think I'm giving you a hard time, but I'm really not. We're all under a lot of pressure. That pressure comes from the top, and I have to act accordingly. My pressure is coming directly from Zachary Berman, and I assure you he's giving me a much harder time than you think I'm giving you." Mariel kept her smile fixed on her face, then looked back at her ledger. Pia marveled at how someone could smile with such great insincerity.

Pia had to do something, get her mind grounded—Mariel Spallek was becoming unbearable and making it difficult to concentrate. Pia had checked on all the experiments that she had running and saw everything was in order. There still were no signs of any immunological response in the lot. The polyethylene glycol in the microbivores' skin was doing wonders at all concentrations, even what she would have thought were minuscule amounts.

"I'm going to take a breath of air," said Pia. Before Mariel could respond Pia added, "Don't worry, I'll be right back. One way or the other, you'll get your full day's work out of me."

Needing a few moments away from Mariel, who'd made a point of shadowing Pia for the whole time that she had been there, Pia descended in the elevator and marched outside. Needing to talk to someone, she called Paul Caldwell. Before the call went through, she remembered he said he was going to sleep when he got home. She disconnected.

Impulsively, she called George despite the can of worms such a

call might unleash. Luckily she got his voice mail, which wasn't surprising, given that no doubt he'd be hard at work somewhere in
his L.A. hospital. Mostly out of desperation, she called the internist
who was responsible for Will McKinley's treatment in New York to
see if she had any new information for her, but she didn't pick up her
phone, either. For Pia it was a complete strikeout. Still, the break
had been therapeutic. Fortified, she headed back into the building
and anticipated another couple of frosty hours with Mariel Spallek.

When she got back to the lab, Pia stopped in her tracks. She saw
that Zachary Berman was there, talking with Mariel. Unfortunately
he looked up and saw her, which meant that Pia couldn't act on her
first instinct, which was to turn tail and disappear. The idea of having to put up with Berman and Mariel at the same time was more
than she wished to bear.

"Ah, Pia, there you are. How are you feeling? Mariel tells me
you're under the weather."

"I'm fighting something off, maybe a cold or flu, but I'm here. And
you? She told me you were feeling ill yourself." Pia girded herself.
She had no idea what to expect, although Berman's voice seemed
calm and not accusatory. She couldn't help but worry that he might
somehow suspect she'd slipped him a Mickey Finn.

Berman smiled. He'd progressively recovered from that morning,
when Mariel Spallek caught him with his head down on his desk in
the office taking a catnap after a string of calls to China.

"I'm doing quite well, but thank you for asking." Berman turned
and with raised eyebrows looked at Mariel. Mariel took the hint,
although she was clearly displeased, and she walked away. She busied herself at the far end of the room, well out of earshot.

"You got home safely?" Berman asked, keeping his voice low.

"I did. I made it a point to drive below the speed limit the
whole way."

"Good choice. At the time I'm not sure I would have had the

good sense to do likewise. Luckily I didn't have to go anyplace for several hours, and then I was driven."

"I hope your call, or calls, went well."

Berman looked at Pia questioningly.

Pia averted her gaze. "Miss Jones told me you had a call to make."

"Right!" Berman said. His eyes roamed about the lab. "So how's it going here?"

"It is going well. We've increased the number of biocompatibility experiments by a factor of ten, which will surely give us highly significant results, especially if they all continue to show no immunological reaction at all. Mariel has gotten me more lab space and some tech help. We're getting it done."

"That's music to my ears. From my perspective, the microbivores project is the most important one under way here at Nano."

"What other projects is Nano currently involved with?" Pia asked. She suddenly decided to throw caution to the wind and go for broke.

Berman smiled at her the way a father might smile at a young girl asking too many questions. "I'm sorry, but for security reasons, I can't tell you that. I hope you understand."

"Mariel said essentially the same thing. But isn't there a chance that there could be overlap of my work with others? We could all mutually benefit if each of us knew what the other was doing."

"Mariel and Allan Stevens make sure that any appropriate cross-pollination, if you will, is taken advantage of. Believe me, your work has definitely influenced some other work that is going on concurrently. I can assure you of that."

"What aspect of my work? The biocompatibility issue?"

"I'm not going to be specific," Berman said. His voice hardened. His smile disappeared. His patience was nearing its limit, but he checked himself. "Let's go back to more pleasant subject matters."

"You asked me how it was going, and I'm being frank. I'm sorry if I overstepped any line."

"No, I'm glad you feel comfortable talking to me directly. I know how Mariel can be. It's a virtue of hers to be so diligent. Except when it isn't. But enough of that. What I really wanted to come over here for is to apologize for my adolescent behavior last night. The last time I passed out was freshman year at Yale. It is not my usual modus operandi. I'm sorry."

"There's no need for an apology. I drank more than I usually do, too. I fell asleep as well."

"Is it out of line to ask if you had fun last night?"

Berman was still smiling, so Pia thought she could relax. "Yes, I did have fun. Thank you for having me over." She glanced around for Mariel to make sure she had not approached. Pia wouldn't have put it past her, but she had left the room. "The only part I regretted was when Miss Jones found us crashed out in your den. That was a little embarrassing."

"Oh, I don't think you have anything to be embarrassed about. I've woken up in much more compromising situations than that one, believe me. I have to say that I enjoyed myself immensely before the scotch got the better of me. You are quite the dancer."

Pia felt her face flush. Of all the things he should remember. Thinking about it embarrassed her far more than Miss Jones's showing up. "It's amazing what alcohol can do to one's inhibitions," she said.

"You were delightful. The next time you come, I'll make sure I stay awake and be a more attentive host. How does that sound?"

"Sounds good," said Pia, thinking the opposite. "I'm up to my neck in here for the next few days, though."

"Alas, I'm traveling myself, so I won't be around for a while. It would be good if you could come with me, but you're much too important here."

"Oh, going anywhere fun?" Pia was horrified at the idea that Berman even considered the idea of taking her with him, and she had to make an effort to sound as casual as possible.

"Yes, actually, I'm going to Italy. But it will all be work, unfortunately, so don't be jealous. I must run. I'm very glad I saw you. Keep up the good work. Don't worry about Mariel, she does what I say. And we'll be sure to have dinner again when I return."

"I'll be here," said Pia as Berman walked away. "I'm not going anywhere."

26.

In the week since she had last seen Zach Berman, Pia worked harder than ever, pushing her new lab technicians and coming ever closer, she thought, to being able to declare that biocompatibility issues, at least with roundworms, had been solved by incorporating the poly-ethylene glycol into the microbivores' skin. Prior to using the compound, the roundworms had shown a 30 to 40 percent immunologic response. Although weak, it had been significant. Afterward there had been none, even with a low level of the oligosaccharide polymer. The results had been so good that Pia began thinking about what animal subjects she should try next. She also continued to develop the spiraling technology for the anti-salmonella robots. That concept continued to be promising, although she was still not able to arrange time with the programmers.

Much of her downtime was spent with Paul Caldwell. They'd been on a few more hikes, including an all-afternoon, challenging affair on Sunday that left Pia tired and sore the following day, but still exhilarated by the views from the high Rockies route Paul had taken her on.

Her friendship with Paul was growing by leaps and bounds. It was such a relief to Pia to be around a man who liked her for herself.

She was still reserved and knew she was aloof in other people's eyes—maybe even his, to a degree—but it was easier to try to be involved in a relationship that wasn't at all sexual. Paul insisted they drive into Denver on Tuesday night to go to a bar he knew. He claimed he wanted to show Pia off, so once more she got into her black dress.

Although reluctant to go at first, she ended up having a better time with Paul's friends than she'd imagined. They were a mixed group in terms of their professions but shared a creative side that Pia appreciated. She didn't feel creativity was her strongest suit, but she enjoyed it in others. Yet what she liked the best was that there had been no sexual pressure in the slightest, and hence no awakening of any atavistic fear in Pia's psyche, a problem that Pia recognized in herself from her recurrent nightmares.

Paul had done some research on iris scanners on the Internet and talked in general terms to a couple of his techie friends. On Wednesday evening, he told Pia he believed it was definitely possible to fool a scanner, particularly a first-generation scanner, which was the kind generally in use, with a high-resolution photograph of an eye, or even of a whole face, including both eyes. If the picture was good enough, he didn't think it mattered if the image was in two dimensions and not three, because the iris itself is flat. After a light supper of vegetarian lasagna that Paul had made, he and Pia tested a single-lens, high-resolution camera that could take close-ups as well as normal photos.

"Where did you get this camera from again?" asked Pia.

"It's from a friend from medical school. Okay, an ex-boyfriend." Paul looked over at Pia. It was the first time he had implicitly mentioned his sexual orientation. He felt Pia knew, and was as comfortable as he was in not considering it an issue. He noted that Pia hadn't batted an eyelid.

"We still see each other occasionally. They use these cameras in the lab at his clinic. I don't even know what for, but it is definitely high resolution and can even take pictures through a microscope. He told me once he got hold of this thing for some art project he was working on. And I'm borrowing it for a few days."

"It looks normal enough to me," said Pia.

And it did. It was a little boxier than a regular commercial camera, but Paul told Pia the operation was the same.

Paul wanted to do a test on Pia, so she sat on Paul's couch and he stood in front of her with a light behind him.

"Keep still, miss, this won't hurt a bit." Paul made a leering face and Pia opened her eyes wide.

"Does it matter which eye?" she asked.

"I don't think so. Anyway, that's why we're trying it out, to find out if it works. Okay, hold still."

Paul took a number of pictures of both of Pia's eyes in close-up and also of her face from as close as a foot and as far away as three feet. He told her that he was done.

"So where will you get these printed?" said Pia.

"On my printer here in my apartment. But it may not be necessary to print them, but rather just to leave them in digital form. What I'm thinking of doing is transferring the best image to your phone, and you can try that. Actually, we might even try using the camera in your iPhone. The resolution on the screen of a phone is really very good, particularly the iPhone."

"Will it be good enough to fool the scanner?"

"We'll see about that. Has a scanner at Nano ever not let you in?"

"Yes. As I told you, it was the scanner at the door to the bridge connecting the building I work in to the immediately neighboring building. It refused me passage."

"And no security person was standing there?"

"No. No one."

"Good."

"You understand the science behind this, don't you?"

"In general, I suppose from what you told me."

"To review, it is based on the fact that irises are unique, like fingerprints. Even identical twins have distinct irises. What the scanner does is use mathematical and statistical algorithms on certain visible characteristics, and digitalizes them, and then compares them with its library of stored scans. In a place like Nano, the results of a scan are then compared with its list of people who have access at the particular scanner. It is then yes, you have access, or no, you don't."

"I appreciate your taking the time to do this," Pia said.

"Hey, I'm enjoying myself. This is exactly the kind of computer stuff that I find interesting. I'm also kind of a movie buff, and it reminds me of that movie with Tom Cruise. What was it?"

Pia shrugged. She'd only seen a handful of movies in her life. Her life had enough drama. She never felt that she needed more.

"*Minority Report!*" said Paul, happy that he'd remembered. "Tom Cruise got his eyes switched out, which of course is going a bit overboard, which is what Hollywood's all about. . . . Anyway, we're not doing anything so drastic, thank goodness. But I think the system has a flaw that we can exploit, at least the system that is currently in use."

"This is fun for you, I can see," said Pia. "What did you do in high school, hack into ATMs?"

"What I did in high school is none of your business," said Paul, but with a smile on his face. "Seriously, what are you going to do if this works? Whose eye are you intending to photograph? The only actual people you told me about at Nano are Berman and that Spallek woman I met. He's the big boss and she's a horror show. How are you going to get those pictures?"

"Now you're asking too many questions," said Pia. She hadn't told Paul much about the development of her relationship with Berman, or what Berman had perceived as such. But she thought that Berman would be the most likely target, especially because of the nascent social connection she had with him. She knew she was playing with fire, but so be it. There seemed to be no other way if she was serious about finding out what Nano was up to. The other benefit of using Berman was that he undoubtedly had access to everything.

"This is all great fun for me, but to be truthful, I'm worried about you. My guess is that you will try to take a photo of Berman, which I also imagine you're clever enough to pull off. But if you use this to get access to secure areas, you'll be trespassing, and no one knows what the consequences of that might be."

"I appreciate your concern," Pia said. "And I recognize the risk. If I use this to get into areas where I'm not authorized to be and something happens, it's not your fault. It is mine and mine alone. But let me say this: I would have learned about these iris scanners and how to get by them if you hadn't helped. It just would have taken longer. I'm determined to get a look around Nano, particularly in the building next to where I work: the one connected to mine by the bridge."

For a minute Pia and Paul stared at each other. Pia held the contact as long as she could before turning away.

"Can you at least appreciate what I'm saying?" Paul questioned.

"Absolutely," Pia snapped. She looked back at Paul, her eyes blazing. "But don't carry it too far if you want to stay my friend. I've had too many people making decisions for me in my life. I don't need that anymore, and I don't want it."

"Fair enough," Paul said. "I just wanted to get it off my chest."

"Okay, it's off your chest. Shall we move on?"

"Right!" Paul said. He stood up and walked over to his desk. Using a connector, he attached the high-definition camera to his computer. "Let me have your iPhone. Let's see what we can do."

There was no conversation while Paul played around with the images of Pia's eyes and face. A sense of unease hung in the air until Pia broke the silence.

"There is something else I would like," Pia said. When Paul didn't respond immediately she continued: "What do you say about giving me a couple more of those Temazepam capsules."

Paul eyes left the computer screen and moved over to Pia. "You're getting as bossy as Mariel, if I may say so."

"Sorry," Pia said without sincerity. She didn't think of herself that way, just that she was her own person and hated to be bossed herself.

"I have to say no," Paul said. "You'll have to get someone else to fill your drug needs if you want to remain *my* friend. That's where I draw my line in the sand as well. I told you I wasn't going to do anything illegal, so I'm not going to abet the misuse of controlled substances, especially when I think it puts you at risk. Once, maybe, without giving the idea the thought that I should have, but not twice."

"Okay, okay," Pia said, holding up her hands as if Paul needed to be calmed down. "Your point's well taken. And I think you're right. I don't need any drugs. All I need is the camera and a bit of creativity."

"The camera you can borrow."

"And I might not even borrow that if I can't fool the scanner with my own image."

27.

Pia hustled across the Nano parking lot, clutching her cell phone. She knew the night guards were replaced at six. Her hope had been to get there earlier, but she was not a morning person, and had not gotten up immediately when the alarm had gone off. If this ruse with the iPhone and the iris scanner didn't work, she thought the tired and generally less attentive staff who were just about to go home would be less likely to notice anything was amiss. To some degree she also knew the men who manned the shift from all the times she had gone into or out of the lab in the wee hours of the morning for various experiments. In contrast to the day and evening shift, they were more conversational, apparently out of boredom.

On the screen of her phone, Pia had ready the image of her eyes at a zoom of just slightly less than normal. As she had expected, there were two guards on duty in the foyer of her building, half the daytime or evening complement. She even knew both of their names.

"Morning, Russ. Morning, Clive."

"Morning, Dr. Grazdani. Early start for you," said the older man, Russ.

"Yep. I've got lots of experiments running. Gotta go—have a good day, you guys."

Pia walked over toward the scanner positioned to guard the entrance to the bank of elevators. Russ and Clive ignored her as they concentrated on making their shift-change entries into the logbook. At home, in the bathroom mirror, she'd practiced what she was about to do. Although when she entered she had her phone pressed flat against her right ear, as if on a call, now she moved it to a horizontal position lateral to her eyes with the screen pointing forward. When she was in front of the machine and it indicated it was ready to take a reading, Pia leaned back slightly and moved the phone such that it was directly in front of her eyes.

She waited impatiently. Nothing happened.

She jiggled the camera up and down slightly, but still there was no familiar beep from the machine, as she had hoped. Quickly she glanced at the scanner over the top of the phone. Instead of the usual green light coming on, indicating a successful match, there was nothing. The scanner clearly wasn't happy. The ruse hadn't worked.

"Crap," she said, under her breath. Quickly she turned the iPhone around and looked at the screen. It had gone blank. She'd forgotten to extend the time of the auto-lock, and the phone had switched itself off.

"Everything all right, Dr. Grazdani?" called Russ from the desk in front of the lobby.

"Yes, thanks, Russ. I must have blinked at the wrong time. I'll just try it again." She smiled over to the men, who waved and went back to their preparations to leave.

The machine reset, and with the image back on the screen of her phone, Pia tried again. After a couple of seconds, in which time Pia thought her heart was going to stop, the usual beep sounded and the green-for-go light came on. A second later the door lock in the glass partition clicked open.

"It worked," she said, rather too loudly. In some respects she was surprised. It was a good example of technology chasing technology. The designers of the first-generation of iris scanners probably had never imagined the advances in resolution of smartphone touch screens.

"It usually does work," said Russ, his voice much closer than it had been the last time Pia had heard it.

Pia jumped and turned. The guard was standing no more than six feet away.

"I'm getting a call," said Pia, who turned back to her phone and went to adjust its display. At the same time she walked through the glass door and into Nano proper. After pushing the elevator button, she turned her head and saw that Russ had retreated back to the main entrance doors and was in conversation with the daytime security shift that had just come on. Pia resolved to be more careful next time.

Next time.

It was early in the morning, so up on the fourth floor Pia passed the door into her lab and retraced her route to the double doors that barred the way onto the bridge. There she tried the trick with her phone again. She had no reason to believe the phone would work when her own eye didn't, but she wanted to try. When the predictable happened and she couldn't get in, Pia walked back to her lab. What the hell did Nano have hidden on the other side of that bridge? In her bones, Pia felt it had to be something serious to justify all the security.

While she checked all the biocompatibility experiments she had running, she again went over all the options of whose eye she was going to capture in a high-resolution photo. She came to the same conclusion: it had to be Berman for a number of reasons. She'd considered Mariel and even Whitney, but she kept coming back to Berman. She reasoned that only with Berman could she be certain she would have total access, as there was a chance the others could have their access restricted for reasons that Pia could not anticipate. There was also the issue that the chances of her being able to take a bunch of photos of Berman without his becoming suspicious were higher than doing the same with the women.

Pia was under no illusions that getting the kind of photos she needed meant that she most likely would have to put herself at risk again by returning to his house. As much as she hated the idea of doing it, she'd have to repeat her charade, but this time without the benefit of the Temazepam. She would have to get herself reinvited, which certainly would inflame Berman's passions and expectations. For many reasons, it was obvious to Pia that the man was a libidinous brute and accustomed to getting his way.

There were so many problems with the plan, but one rendered all the others moot. For at least a week, Zach Berman hadn't been at Nano.

28.

A little more than two hours after Pia started her early day's work, it was after four o'clock in the afternoon more than five thousand miles away in Milan. Zach Berman sat at his computer in his room at the Four Seasons Hotel, going over progress reports emailed to him on the various projects that were running at his company, particularly the microbivores program, which was closest to his heart. He was pleased with what he read, and it made him eager to get back. But he couldn't go just yet. The Giro d'Italia, one of Europe's top cycle races outside of the Tour de France, was about to start. It was his reason for being in Italy, but Berman had no interest in anyone making that connection.

A week earlier, almost immediately after his conversation with Pia, Berman flew in his Gulfstream to Milan, where he had met up with yet more Chinese dignitaries. At least he wasn't meeting any new people: this delegation was made up of individuals he had encountered over the last two years in Boulder or in China, and Whitney Jones had coached him for hours on their names and personal interests and government jobs. Such information made it far easier to converse with these people and avoid the painful stretches of silence he'd endured in his early encounters with them. Raising capi-

tal wasn't his favorite job, particularly with the Chinese, because
their bureaucratic mind-set was contrary to his value system. In
fact, he freely admitted he hated dealing with them, save for the
rare few who had an entrepreneurial streak, however suppressed.
Yet on the world stage the big money was in China. That was the
long and short of it.

One man Berman now saw regularly and who was easier to deal
with than most of the others was Yan, who insisted on being called
Jimmy. Jimmy spoke excellent English and was apparently a man of
some status in the bewilderingly complex government hierarchy.
Jimmy was actually good company, Berman had been happy to find,
and it was really to meet him that Berman had come to Milan. Jimmy
was a cosmopolitan man who had studied for a time at Stanford, so
he was able to converse with Berman about American matters in
American English. He wore a Western-style suit and sported a better
haircut than the other officials Berman had met. How old he was,
Berman didn't know, although he suspected Jimmy was younger
than he, and in good physical shape, as compared with the other Chinese bureaucrats Berman had to spend time with.

Berman knew Jimmy was very smart. Politics was a particular
area of interest, and he quizzed Berman closely about recent American presidential elections. He seemed amused by the process. How
did Americans know if the people they supported would make good
leaders? he wondered. To Jimmy it all seemed absurdly random,
more of a popularity contest. Berman's response was that was the
way democracy worked. "The people pick the person they think will
make the best leader," Berman said. "The people?" Jimmy asked enig-
matically, and left it at that.

Berman knew the drill with the Chinese, and he was calm and
confident when he spoke to them as a group. He'd picked up a few
words of Mandarin, and it always amused his guests when he tried a
new phrase, even if he almost always mangled it.

After several days of acclimating in Milan, Berman, Jimmy, and

two more of the senior Chinese bureaucrats, together with a translator, had visited their investments as they were training. The cycle
team was doing sprints around the track in an indoor velodrome,
cycling impossibly fast and close together, it had seemed to Berman.
The last thing he wanted at that stage was a serious crash. The five
visitors had stood at the back of the arena, trying not to stand out
too much. The main coach from the team had expected them and
walked over when it was appropriate.

"Welcome to Milan. I am Victor Klaastens, team coach. Nice to
meet you all." The man had a heavy Dutch accent.

"Ah, Mr. Klaastens, I'm glad you're here," Berman had said.

"Where else would I be but with my team?"

"Indeed. So how is everything going? I'm sure our visitors would
like to hear from you."

The translator had struggled to keep up, and that was okay with
Berman. He'd wished he could have talked to the coach in private
before the meeting with the Chinese delegation, but it had not been
possible. Klaastens was stocky, in his mid-fifties, and definitely had
been around the block a few times, with a protuberant beer gut that
proclaimed as much. The team's bright blue, red, and green warm-
up suit looked decidedly out of place on him.

"Everything is good," Klaastens had responded. "Though I'm not
happy to have to talk through a translator. And there's no need to
translate that." He looked at the young woman who interrupted her
translation to bow her head hurriedly.

Berman had looked at Jimmy but gave no indication that he was
perturbed at what Klaastens had said. Berman wanted everything to
go smoothly. Jimmy had seemed to be taking it all in stride. The
English of the two other men was iffy.

"This is how sport is these days," the coach continued. "I'm a
Dutch coach on a cycling team from Azerbaijan who these Chinese
gentlemen show up to watch, and they have a well-off American
with them whose name I don't know. Ignore that, too, miss."

"'Well-off American.' I've been called many things. . . . I'm merely an observer," said Berman.

"I don't really care who you are. Maybe it's for the best I don't know. I'm happy with the situation," said Klaastens. "Even if I have to accept some riders at the last minute who I can't even converse with, since all they speak is Chinese. We're a poor cycle team from a poor country. Why Azerbaijan needs a cycling team, I don't know that, either, but Kazakhstan has one, and they wanted one, too. Which was very lucky for me, because I was out of a job. When I heard we would have our whole season taken care of, I was even more happy. Someone told me that the government got money from outside and they're very happy to take the credit for having a successful team. What it meant for me was no more chasing down cell phone providers in Belgium for ten thousand euros of sponsorship. That kind of thing is not fun for a man, particularly given my age and experience."

"So how are the new men doing?" Berman had asked to try to steer Klaastens's conversation into a more neutral arena.

"They are doing very well." The coach looked closely at Berman as he spoke. "Extremely well. Maybe a little too well."

"If they are performing beyond your expectations, I don't think that should be a problem. The reverse, in fact."

"The fact is, they are so good, they make our team leader nervous. I don't know how much you know about our sport, but when a team's leader is entering a race with anxiety, it is not good. The leader is a little past his best, I know, but he has a following in France, and our team wants to win a stage at the Tour in July. No one thought anything when I put these two guys in the pack because, to be frank, you and I could have got a place on the team. But these guys are fast, and strong. And no one knows who they are."

"They have been training in China. I heard about them by chance when I was in China on business. I ride myself, I have always been interested in team cycling, so I made some introductions. If these guys are good, then, well . . . good. This is the first time they are in international competition."

"It shows. They never talk to anyone and they have their own doctors."

"Chinese people are suspicious of Western medics. There is a lot of herbal medicine, all perfectly tested and legal, that they use. And these two guys have never been outside of China. Even being in Italy makes them nervous. I've been through this all before with the team president."

"I know you have," Klaastens had said. "But I know more about cycling than he does. What is that phrase in America? I've forgotten more about it than he knows. Is that right?"

"Very good."

"Okay. I'm asking for my own benefit. I need to be prepared if one of these guys wins a stage in this race."

"You think there is the chance of them winning?" *If either of these guys wins a stage, I'd be surprised*, Berman had thought. Both riders knew the consequences of performing too well too soon. The consequences not only for themselves, but also for their extended families in China. Having heard how fast the two men were, Berman had worried that they had seemed to have stretched their legs too much already, despite instructions to the contrary.

"Probably not. We see a lot of guys who look great in training but flame out and fail on the road. Perhaps they're like that."

"Perhaps."

"Okay. I am not worried, as I said. They passed the drug and blood doping tests we administered several times over, the same one that the race uses. And you tell me everything is fine. So it is fine. I hear there are more than seven hundred million cyclists in China. At least two of them have to be good, right? I found that number on the Internet, and I like it. If anyone from the media asks, which they will, that's what I'm going to say. Two from seven hundred million. That should quiet most skeptics."

The translator had talked for a good minute after Klaastens finished, and Zhu, one of the Chinese delegation, had responded with a few agitated words.

"Is everything okay?" Berman had asked the translator. But it was Jimmy who had replied. "He's just wondering if everything is okay. He says this man here is very serious."

"Yes, please assure him that everything is fine. Our friend here is very eminent in the world of cycling. He is just expressing some personal opinions. He likes to talk, as you can see. But everything is perfectly fine."

Berman then had steered Klaastens away from the group. "I don't want them to think you are not grateful for their support," Berman had said when they were just beyond earshot.

"I am grateful," Klaastens had insisted. "But they're not officially supporting us, you see? It's the anonymous part that is strange to me. You usually can't stop sponsors from putting logos on everything that moves. So I appreciate it from that angle, but really I don't know who these guys are any more than I know you."

"I assure you, when the time comes, they will come out in the open, and I will, too. These are all early steps. They don't want to be embarrassed if the men fail. Failure is very bad in their culture, particularly on the world stage. That's why there is all this intrigue. But your contact was correct. The funding for the team came from a third party and was funneled through the Azeri government. Ultimately the connection is through oil."

"Oil?"

"It is widely known that the Chinese are interested in cornering the market for raw materials in general."

Klaastens had shrugged and nodded. Having heard that information, he had become Berman's accomplice of sorts. Ultimately he didn't care about the details in that he valued his job more than he cared about the answers to any questions he had. Klaastens figured he had enough deniability should anything untoward happen. The two walked back to the Chinese men and Klaastens addressed the translator.

"Please assure the gentlemen that our team is very grateful for their support for the whole team, and we look forward to a long and fruitful partnership. We just want reassurance that their riders will continue to be team players. Although a lot of people don't know it, cycling is, in the final analysis, a team sport."

"Well put," Berman had said, who then had taken his leave before Klaastens put on a demonstration of the prowess and speed of the team, particularly the two new Chinese riders.

At the desk in the Four Seasons, Berman finished up his emails. He looked at his watch and wondered if he had time for one more dish of fried gnocchi. He found he loved the food in Milan, especially at the cheaper restaurants. His new favorite dish was beyond delicious, but healthwise they weren't such a good idea. Berman wouldn't dream of eating such a thing at home, which made them so much more alluring.

These had been a fun few days. He found that Milan had an exciting nightlife, which he had avidly taken in, with Jimmy as a surprisingly knowledgeable guide. He found certain venues in which there was a seemingly endless chain of attractive women from Eastern Europe, particularly the Czech Republic and Hungary. As a result, he was looking forward to a long sleep on the way home.

With Jimmy, he'd visited the team a few more times in training after that first visit. He reminded the doctors who worked with the riders that they should be sure to follow the protocols they had established. Security was paramount. Never carry anything yourself— use the couriers. And remember, the riders couldn't win. They should be consistently fast, but always ride in support of the team leader. It was likely, especially on this year's course, that they would be much stronger than the leader, but at all costs they had to hold back, even if they felt strong enough to sprint ahead. The idea was just to introduce their presence, no more at this stage.

There would be ample opportunity down the road for heroics. After all, as far as the Chinese were concerned, that was what this was all about.

29.

Zach Berman felt he was just about over his latest bout of jet lag. No matter how much sleep he got on a flight, no matter how diligent he was about taking his melatonin supplements, which he was convinced helped, and not sleeping during daylight on his return to Colorado, he was always knocked off center a little for a few days after flying home.

He had been back in Boulder by the time the first stage of the Giro d'Italia—a short time trial—was held on Saturday. The next day there was a longer stage, more than two hundred kilometers. Berman followed the team's progress on the Internet. He was pleased to see the Azerbaijani team's riders had performed decently without being embarrassingly bad or improbably good. Although Berman had no control over the team leader's performance, he was pleased to see he lay in thirtieth place overall; his Chinese riders finished each day in the middle of the peloton, the main group of supporting riders, which was just as it should be. Berman was looking forward to being back in Milan on the twenty-seventh for the end of the race, even if he had to travel there via China. But the long trip would be well worth it if the latest training results were replicated over the course of the next couple of weeks.

On Sunday Berman had forced himself to pay another painful visit to his mother at the Valley Springs Assisted Living home in Louisville. Each time he went, he thought he detected a tangible decline in his mother's capabilities. On this occasion, she was just a little more belligerent toward him, and just a little less capable of completing a coherent sentence. The inexorable decay was frightening, not for his mother, as he had given up any hope of stemming her disease, but for himself.

He felt his going there was like those juvenile-offender programs in which at-risk teens are sent to a hard adult jail in the hope that they'll be scared straight. Except Berman was trying to make sure he worked even harder to make sure his Nano team had the funds to make progress with the science. His ability to comprehend the technical aspects of the program had long ago been left behind by the advances his scientists were making, but he kept on top of it the best he could. What Berman could do was ensure he secured the money.

To that end, he closeted himself away for hours in the nerve center of Nano with his senior scientist, Allan Stevens, and his small inner circle, the molecular manufacturing guys, listening in as the team revised the scientific protocols over and over again. The margins they were working with seemed minute: in the nano universe, an infinitesimal number of molecules, too few or too many, could lead on the one hand to underperformance and on the other hand to overwhelming stress on the body and, potentially, catastrophic failure. That much had become clear. It was a tightrope walk.

The bulk of his time Berman spent with Whitney Jones, being debriefed about the intelligence she had gleaned from the latest group of Chinese dignitaries and their competitive nationalistic mind-set, and combing over the Nano strategy for the upcoming weeks. From what Whitney and Berman could divine, the huge injection of financing to take the microbivores project to the next level, namely the move to mammal and then human safety studies, was still on track, and once that had taken place, the sharing of the advances in nanotechnology would begin in earnest. But the performance criteria remained as challenges that Nano had to meet. For that reason, Berman spent more time with the premier athletes still in training, and through interpreters he tried to get a fix on their psyches. Were they going to be ready to assume the responsibility that was being placed on them? Could he trust they would act as instructed? Some of the expendables obviously hadn't, although ultimately they had contributed in unexpected but valuable ways.

Berman was consumed by his work. The preparations were meticulous in every detail, and Berman was on hand for each and every aspect of their development. He could leave nothing to chance. He undertook a monkish existence, rising even earlier, working even harder. For these few weeks, Berman needed his head to be as clear as it could be. He was a grown man; he could delay his inevitable gratification till the time he could truly appreciate it. So he made a pact with himself. No red meat; no alcohol; no cigars. And no Pia. She was simply too much of a distraction.

30.

Pia was too busy to be bored, but whenever she stopped work and tried to focus on the bigger picture, she felt restless. She was consumed with trying to get back to Zachary Berman's house to create a set of circumstances by which to get the photograph of his eyes that she hoped would give her access to the rest of the Nano buildings, but Berman was either away or not available, thanks to more visiting Chinese.

She tried visiting his office early before the day began, as she'd done the first time, but he was never there, so she'd given up after three·or four attempts. She had dared go to Berman's office only twice during normal business hours, and each time his secretary, a woman who worked nine to five and dealt mostly with Berman's correspondence, said he wasn't available. Pia didn't want to push her luck by appearing to be stalking the head of the company. There was as little sign of Whitney Jones as there was of Berman. Pia tried not to be paranoid, but she couldn't quite dispel the idea she was being intentionally ignored.

Uncharacteristically, she then had tried hard to befriend the two assistants she had been assigned, Pamela Ellis and Jason Rodriguez, looking for some institutional gossip about Berman and Whitney.

Pamela was impossible, Pia decided very quickly. She was a clone of Mariel Spallek, minus a few years. As clumsy as Pia's attempts to engage the young woman in conversation may have been, there was no reason Pia could think of for Pamela to rebuff them so categorically. On a few occasions, Pia was sure she could feel Pamela's eyes burning into the back of her head, and when she turned, she was sure Pamela had just looked down or away. The possibility that she was a spy installed in her office by Mariel Spallek struck Pia almost as soon as she met the woman, and Pia made sure their relationship was strictly cool and businesslike.

Jason Rodriguez was also slightly standoffish but, in comparison, much more friendly. He was, as he freely admitted, a science nerd. He was eager to learn about nanotechnology, so he was happy to pick Pia's brain as often as he could. He was smart and understood the potential for the science and was as ambitious as he was oversized. Jason admitted to being six feet six, but Pia wondered if he wasn't taller. For college, Jason told Pia he had a choice between sports and study—he couldn't imagine devoting as much time as he wanted to each, and he chose science. He happily talked about his undergraduate and postgraduate studies at the University of Michigan, but about what he had worked on at Nano before being assigned to Pia, he wouldn't say anything at all.

Pia had gone so far as to ask Jason if he wanted to go out for a drink one evening, but he declined, citing pressure of work. Jason had talked to Pia more than once about his girlfriend at Michigan, and in the past tense, so Pia was fairly sure he was neither taken nor gay. Her pride was slightly dented when he turned her down a second time, at which point Pia backed off, in case she was making herself too obvious. She knew there was an element of irrationality on her part, being accustomed too often to having to fend off unwanted advances from men.

Pia's main concern continued to be, What the hell had gotten into Zach Berman? Pia asked herself the question day after day. She was aware of the irony of the situation. Prior to the mysterious jogger episode, she had been fighting him off for months, but now that she was trying to make herself available to him, he had vanished. Or at least he was not around to ask about another dinner date. Pia was so anxious to try out the next phase of her plan that she'd agree to almost anything to get herself back inside Berman's home with him. But he wasn't giving her the chance.

Meanwhile, Nano was moving quickly with preparations for mammalian safety experiments, beginning with mice using Pia's microbivore design. But as her results with the roundworms got more and more encouraging, the pressure on Pia had let up. Mariel checked in on Pia less frequently, and was herself much less objectionable. Pia almost missed the haranguing. Wouldn't Mariel want her to ramp up the preparations, to push the science as far as she could take it, so that they could at least start the prolonged FDA approval process? And what about the microbivores computer software guys with whom Pia had yet to meet up? Continually Pia had been told that they might be available the following week but it kept getting put off.

Then Pia was told by Mariel that Pamela Ellis was being reassigned within the building. Mariel gave Pia an experiment to run involving a commercial product, a DNA array for a pregnancy testing kit that was, as far as Pia was concerned, the equivalent of busywork.

On Sunday, Pia sat on her couch, nursing her ongoing unease and frustration. Something Paul Caldwell had said stuck in her mind. How much did she know about what Nano was doing with her ideas? Perhaps Pamela Ellis was somewhere in the locked-up confines of the secret Nano, performing experiments Pia should be doing in her lab, maybe using mice with the oligosaccharide-shielded microbivores. Or other experiments they did not want her to see or even know about.

Pia's iPhone rattled on the tabletop in front of her and snapped her out of her daydream. The display identified the caller as Paul. Pia was pleased with the distraction.

"Hi, Paul, I was just thinking about you."

"That's nice, but listen, Pia!" His voice was low as if he didn't want to be heard by anyone around him. "This is serious. I think we've got another one."

"Another what?"

"An athlete from Nano, on his way into the ER. A cyclist this time. Where are you?"

"I'm at home, give me ten minutes and I can be there. What do you know about the cyclist?" Pia pulled on her sneakers and grabbed her car keys and a jacket and left home running as she talked into the phone jammed between her shoulder and her ear. She'd been sitting around waiting for something to happen, and now it seemed like it had.

"He's at the far end of the Carter Lake Loop," said Paul. "I know the ride. A member of the public was a couple hundred feet behind him and saw him go down and called nine-one-one. The ambulance relayed the details of the call to us so we can prepare the ER, and they said the rider is supposedly unresponsive. He's an Asian male, and he's wearing a cycling suit with a Nano logo."

"Oh, God, that's great! I mean, it's not great, but we can try to keep this guy in the hospital once we have him, right? And we can get some more blood."

"We can try, Pia."

"Does Nano know about him?"

"That I don't know."

"Okay, I'm in the car, how much time do I have?" Pia was pleased. Paul was keeping the small blood sample from the jogger that he had held back from the batch that had disappeared at the lab. At first Pia was going to bring it back to her lab to run some tests on it, but then had hesitated. The problem was that there was such a small amount, she couldn't waste any. She decided that before she did anything, she would need to have a better idea of what kind of tests she wanted to run. Besides, Mariel Spallek had been riding her too hard to risk any kind of extracurricular activity like that, but a larger sample of blood would give Pia an incentive to find a way to test it to see if it could explain what had happened to the victim.

"The ambulance is about halfway there, so my guess is he won't be back here for a while, depending on what they find at the scene. Come over and we can strategize. Noakes isn't here today, thank goodness, and I've called the police. So yes, let's try and hold on to this one."

Even though the ambulance hadn't yet reached the rider, Pia raced over to the hospital and excitedly found Paul in the center of the ER in front of the main desk.

"Do they have him?" Pia demanded. Her face was flushed. She was out of breath in her excitement.

"I don't know, Pia. You need to calm down. We hope the guy is okay, right?"

"Yes, yes, I'm sorry, Paul. I've just been going crazy at work thinking about that jogger. It is driving me insane not to have any answers, I'm not the patient type. I need answers."

"I know you do, Pia, you've told me enough times," said Paul. He smiled at Pia. He was calmness personified, making Pia's anxiety that much more pronounced. "I've talked to our in-house counsel, and she is on her way in. I seem to have lost Mr. Noakes's contact information, so he is not on his way. Oh, well. We have two Boulder police officers here, and I have told them that there might be a disturbance. I said that we're expecting a cardiac patient who's going to need attention but who might possibly be essentially kidnapped by a third party. Actually I didn't use the word *kidnapped*. I just said that other people might come and demand to take custody and have the patient discharged against our medical advice. I've also asked for our Mandarin translator to be called in, and she is on her way. That's about all we can do for the moment."

Paul was wearing a radio headset, which was linked into the communications between the EMTs and the ER. He pressed the TALK button and asked the ambulance driver his ETA to the scene of the accident. Pia couldn't unscramble the static-ridden half of the conversation that Paul was having. When he finished, he turned to her.

"They're there. It's David and Bill, the same guys who were with the runner, which is good. We'll find out if the man is presenting the same symptoms."

"What can they see?" Pia questioned nervously. "Tell them to get the patient into the ambulance right away."

"Give them a chance! They have to stabilize him, see what's going on. You know the drill. Excuse me a second, Pia, I really have to check on another patient."

Paul marched from the reception area of the ER over to a nearby bay where there was a lot of activity. Pia looked at her watch every thirty seconds and back at Paul. Pia was too far away to hear what was being said. After what seemed to Pia like a long fifteen minutes, Paul came back and smiled at her.

"Okay, let's check in. They should be on their way back." Paul called up the ambulance, and relayed what the EMT was telling him.

"Okay, you're still at the scene. Initially very similar signs, yes . . . Apparently unresponsive . . . You performed CPR . . ."

"Ask about the tattoos," Pia said.

"What, hold on a second. What's that, Pia?" Paul held his hand over the radio set so he could hear Pia's question.

"Ask them if he has tattoos on his right forearm."

"We can find that out when they get here, they apparently just revived the patient. A tattoo isn't going to be germane to the immediate situation. What's that?" Now Paul was straining to hear the EMT. He pulled the unit off his belt and looked at the controls. He had lost contact.

"I can't hear them, dammit. Dispatch! We lost contact with Dave and Bill. Dave? Dave? Can you hear me?"

"What's the matter?" asked Pia, although it was obvious that Paul couldn't hear the EMT.

Pia and Paul stood there, useless, for a couple of long minutes. Then Paul's radio crackled into life.

"What's happening?" demanded Paul.

"What is it?" said Pia. Paul held up his hand, palm forward, telling Pia to wait while he heard whatever the story was.

"Are you serious? . . . The patient's name was Yang. . . . And it was the same people who arrived, you're sure of that. . . . Okay, I understand. You stay there, of course, get the police on the radio. . . ."

Pia experienced a sinking feeling in her stomach as she listened to Paul's end of the conversation.

"Okay, wait there." Paul broke off the call.

"What the hell?"

"They never got the guy in the ambulance. The same crew as came in here swooped in with a white van this time and took the man away. It sounds like it was practically at gunpoint, and just like with our guy, he'd completely revived. In the blink of the eye he went from moribund to fully conscious, and they don't know how long his heart had been stopped and how long he'd not been breathing. . . ."

"Where is this loop place? Where did they pick him up?"

"I guess it's thirty, thirty-five miles north of here. Why?"

"Because from where they are to Nano is about the same distance as it is from here to Nano, but they have to go on twisty back roads, and we can go mostly by freeway. Let's go, we can head them off."

"Head them off? What are you talking about?"

"We have to stop them getting back into Nano if we can or, at the very least, see where they enter the Nano grounds to be sure that's where they have taken him."

"How are we going to do that?"

"We'll think of something. We know which road they have to take on the way in from Carter Lake Loop. Paul, are you coming or not? He's supposed to be your patient. You were worried they might kidnap him here. But they didn't wait this time, they took him before he even got in the ambulance. Let's go, Paul, we're wasting time!"

Pia set off at a run, and much against his better judgment, Paul followed.

31.

Paul had no time to argue with Pia's decision to take her car; she ran out to the ER parking lot and jumped in the VW, barely waiting long enough for Paul to hop in and get his door closed. As he struggled to fasten his seat belt, she was already on the way.

"Pia, let's think about this. What are we going to do, even if we see the right white van? And how will we know it is the right van? And you forgot your seat belt."

Pia cast Paul a dirty look as if to say "you are not my keeper," and accelerated out of the hospital lot. Aggressively she zigzagged through traffic on her way to the freeway, heading northwest.

"We're going to find them, then improvise. If nothing else, we'll follow them to Nano."

"And then what?"

"I don't know! What I do know is that we can't sit around and wait for the police to go see the EMTs. I'm sure Mariel had some excuse . . . whoa! Look out!"

Pia swerved to avoid a car that was trying to execute a perfectly legal lane change with blinkers flashing. The driver didn't see Pia coming up fast.

"Pia, we're going to get into an accident, if not arrested."

"No, we're not! There's the freeway ramp."

Pia drove onto the highway, where her speed was less conspicuous. She pushed on, driving over eighty, till she slowed and took an exit.

"What are you doing?" Paul gripped what he could to keep himself righted.

"This is the fastest way to Nano, plus it intersects the road to Carter Lake Loop, which is coming up right now." She rolled through a stop sign, then accelerated again. "This is actually the Carter Lake Loop road now. The Nano main entrance is coming up on the left in just a few minutes."

"How are we going to recognize the van other than the fact that it's white? A white van is not much of a description. Pia, this is crazy." Paul's knuckles were blanched holding on to the armrest.

"I'm going to drive right past Nano, and then we'll follow the road north heading for Carter Lake Loop. There can't be that many white vans around."

They drove for a few minutes in a tense silence. Pia was hunched forward, holding the steering wheel tightly in both hands. She was on a mission.

Paul allowed himself to look out the window and recognized where they were. He saw the logic in Pia's plan, but still wondered what they could do once they saw the van, provided they did see the van.

Pia drove quickly but attentively. She passed the turnoff to the Nano security gate on the left without slowing, and had to blare her horn to warn a black Suburban, which threatened to pull out in her way. She continued on, banking to her left, accelerating again.

"Okay, now what?" Paul questioned.

"We're just going to head out toward Carter Lake Loop. I estimate we probably have ten minutes or so on them. I think it is better to drive out and intercept them. I have a suspicion there's a separate entrance to Nano that I'd like to find. I don't think they'll use the main entrance."

"Why don't we just call the police and let them handle this?" said Paul. Pia's determination and rashness were making him nervous.

"The police have already been called, and they're up with the EMTs. Besides, I'm sure Mariel has some kind of watertight legal explanation for what's going on, just like when she stormed into the ER to get the runner. The local police are not going to help with the situation."

Pia continued the gradual left-hand turn following the road until it straightened out. They were now passing the Nano property on the left and a few of the Nano buildings could be seen poking up through the evergreens and aspens. To the right the road fell off into a gully containing a tree-lined mountain brook. She was traveling at more than fifty miles an hour.

Pia glanced over to Paul and was about to say something, but suddenly something caught her attention. Out of the corner of her left eye, Pia saw a shape in her side mirror bearing down on her car. Before she could even respond, she felt the shuddering impact as her VW was rammed hard across the rear on the left side. Try as she might, she couldn't keep the car straight as the giant shape pushed and pushed, grinding her car toward the edge of the road. Pia may have screamed, but the sound was drowned out by the rending of metal as the car hit the soft gravel at the side of the road, followed by a second of silence as it flew off and down the embankment toward the tree line. Then she felt a sickening thud, accompanied by the smashing of glass, as the car rolled once, then twice, and perhaps again, but Pia couldn't know how many times, because everything went black and was perfectly still and quiet.

32.

George Wilson looked down at Pia lying in the hospital bed and felt sick to his stomach. When he received word of what had happened some forty-eight hours after the event, thoughtfully sent along by Zach Berman through Whitney Jones, he dropped everything, made a plea to his chief of radiology about having to attend to another family emergency, this time relatively for real, and rushed straight to Boulder. Since he had arrived two days previously, he hadn't left the hospital once, and had only slept fitfully for forty-five minutes at a time slouched in a backbreaking hospital room chair.

George's mind kept sliding back to the time he and Pia had stood in a different hospital room, in New York, watching their fellow medical student Will McKinley fight for his life. McKinley was still worrisomely ill with a recalcitrant, antibiotic-resistant infection in his skull. Even though George had been told that Pia's injuries now weren't life threatening like they were initially, he couldn't help but think of Will and how close he and Pia had come to being in a permanent state of limbo, hanging between life and death. Head injuries could be like that.

Pia had been severely injured. She had fractured her left arm in two places, mid-humerus and radius, and four ribs. The ribs were apparently from the steering wheel. As the roof of the car had compressed when the vehicle rolled over, Pia received a serious blow to the head and a resultant concussion, and her neck was badly strained with bleeding into the para-spinal muscles, so she was wearing a neck brace. She had suffered some internal injuries as well, trauma that couldn't be seen but was more life threatening than the broken bones and cuts and bruises, a very familiar sight to George. The blunt force of the crash and probably the steering wheel had ruptured Pia's spleen, causing blood to pump into her abdominal cavity, and without the rapid response of an ambulance and EMTs from this same hospital, Pia could well have bled to death as she lay unconscious in the wreckage of her new automobile. Luckily they had accurately diagnosed the problem and had alerted the ER so that when she had arrived, she was taken almost directly to surgery to stem the bleeding. There was no doubt it had saved her life.

Pia was still currently in a drug-induced coma to allow the swelling of her brain to subside, and was being artificially respired to make sure she got full aeration of her lungs. To monitor this, she was given round-the-clock nursing care. George understood all this, but he was desperate for Pia to wake up so that he could hear her voice, but he knew he had to be patient, and he was learning that that was a virtue he had in short supply. There was nothing he could do, and he hated the feeling of powerlessness.

George heard the door to the room open and felt someone come in and stand next to him. At first he thought it was one of the nurses, but it wasn't.

"Any change?" asked Paul Caldwell.

"Hello, Paul. No, nothing new." George met Paul when he had first arrived. Paul, too, had been standing vigil in between runs back down to the ER. George's first reaction was anger and jealousy, but he soon realized that both emotions were uncalled for. When he heard that Paul had been in the vehicle involved in the accident with Pia, he had assumed Paul had been driving and was responsible for what had happened. And he had further assumed that he and Pia were an item, which seemed to make superficial sense, as George recognized Paul as a handsome and intelligent doctor. When George learned that he was wrong on both accounts, he felt foolish and was moved to admit his mistake and apologize. He also quickly came to be grateful for Paul's concern and the fact that Paul had been an effective ombudsman for the most difficult period of Pia's hospitalization, making sure the best surgeon available had come in to take the case.

"Listen, George, my offer that I made yesterday still stands. You should go over to my apartment and lie down for a couple of hours. And have a proper shower and change your clothes. Frankly, if you did that you'd be doing us all a favor."

George looked over at Paul, and he was smiling. George appreciated Paul's attempt to defuse the tension with a bit of humor, and as soon as Paul mentioned lying down, George suddenly felt an overwhelming fatigue come over him.

"You know, Paul, I may just do that. I don't think much is going to change here for the next few hours."

"No. The plan is to reduce the drugs over the next day or so and bring her out of this sleep. Everything seems to be nice and stable. My sense is that she knows you've been here, George, I'm sure of it. But I imagine you want to be in good shape when she fully wakes up."

"Yes, you're right. Maybe I will take a couple of hours."

"Good. I'll get a cab for you. I wrote the address down, and here's a key."

Paul handed over what George needed.

"Paul, how are you feeling? I'm sorry I never asked."

"Me, oh, I'm fine."

In truth, Paul's left hand was causing him a lot of discomfort, but he wasn't going to complain, given how lucky he had been to walk away from the accident with nothing worse than a mild concussion from his head hitting the roof of the car—like Pia, he, too, had been knocked unconscious for a time—a couple of broken fingers, and bruising on his chest and thighs.

Paul had spent enough nights in the ER dealing with the aftermath of car crashes to know that there was often a strange randomness to the severity of injuries drivers and passengers suffered. He had seen pictures of crashes that left cars an unrecognizable tangle of mangled metal, which was how Pia's VW looked, and killed three, yet a fourth person escaped with only a broken leg. In another instance, one he had thought about frequently since this accident with Pia, the driver had died while the man sitting next to him had been left without so much as a scratch. It was so random as to be astonishing. It also made him feel slightly guilty, considering how banged up Pia had been.

Paul remembered fastening his own seat belt, which certainly had been a good idea, and that Pia had not fastened hers. He even remembered trying to get her to do it, only to be rewarded with a dirty look. But he discovered later that Pia had been wearing her belt, and thank God, for without it, she would certainly have died. He couldn't remember her actually fastening it, and wondered when she would have thought to do it, as fixated she was on catching the van from Nano carrying the injured cyclist back to the ER. He was very thankful that she'd paused long enough to take the precaution that saved her life. There were other things about the accident that Paul had trouble remembering, which made him recognize that he apparently had a certain amount of post-traumatic amnesia.

"All right!" George said finally. "I'm out of here for a few hours. You'll check on her, won't you?"

"Absolutely," Paul said. He gave George a reassuring pat on the back. "Every time I have a free moment in the ER, I'll pop up here and make sure all is in order. You have a nap. You deserve it."

"Thanks," George said. He smiled weakly, gave Pia's leg a squeeze through the sheet, and left the room.

Paul watched George go, then, as he did every time he came into Pia's room, looked around at the ostentatiously large displays of flowers that Zach Berman had been sending over from Nano on a daily basis. Paul had taken it upon himself earlier that day to throw out the first huge bouquet, which had seen better days. Berman himself had yet to put in an appearance, and neither had any other company official, although Pia's new colleague tech, Jason Rodriguez, had been to see her. Paul noted that Pia's direct boss, Mariel Spallek, hadn't been in either, but he was not surprised, given what Pia had said about her.

What was really bothering Paul, however, was a feeling about Nano and the accident, made worse by the fact that no one from Nano's administration had shown up. Try as he might, Paul could not remember much just before the accident nor immediately after, which was why he thought he'd suffered traumatic amnesia. All he remembered was waking up in the ambulance with the siren screaming, and this lack of memory left him with a vague feeling of foreboding that kept nagging at him, making him question if it truly had been an accident, and if it hadn't, whether there was some complicity on the part of Nano.

This was Paul's second day back at work, but with these thoughts, he was finding it hard to focus on the ER. On top of that, he was worried about Pia, despite what he had said to George. He hoped to God that she would be the same person when she woke up. But even that had a slight downside, having come to understand her mild paranoia, her tenacity of purpose, and how prone she was to conspiracy theory. What was worrying him was the fear that when she woke up, she would resume her search for answers to all the questions she had about Nano, only with even more vigor, especially if she shared Paul's questions about what caused their car to go off the road.

Paul had initially told the police about his vague sense that the accident had not been an accident, meaning Pia's vehicle might have been forced off the road. But he recognized that this idea was not given a lot of credence, and he could understand why. Then a day after the accident, two officers had quizzed Paul more closely, especially on the reasons why Pia was driving so fast since it had been ascertained she'd been traveling at approximately fifty-five mph in a thirty-mile-an-hour zone. Paul had been honest and had explained that he and Pia were trying to intercept a van that had taken a patient before the individual could be loaded into an ambulance, a fact that the police had confirmed. Paul had also told them about the previous incident in the ER involving the Chinese runner and Mariel Spallek coming to collect him and sign him out against medical advice. Paul's natural reticence and caution kept him from mentioning any of Pia's suspicions about Nano, as he didn't know how much credence to give them himself.

When the two officers returned to the ER the following day to ask further questions, Paul was glad he had been circumspect the day before. The officers asked him repeatedly about the supposedly planned intervention with the van carrying the cyclist—why did they deem it necessary to dangerously race around Boulder, chasing a man who had turned down the offer of help from an ambulance from the Boulder Memorial Hospital? Why were they so concerned about this one patient? The police seemed less interested in the possibility that the VW had been rear-ended on the road than the fact that Pia had been speeding, particularly because, according to them, the VW showed no evidence of having been hit by another vehicle, as banged up it was. Paul knew Pia would be far less sanguine about accepting the line of questioning than he was, but he was being honest. The fact remained that he truly couldn't remember much at all about what had actually happened.

But in his own mind, Paul had asked himself over and over about the causes of the accident. Sure, Pia had been driving fast, but she was in control and was not being reckless, as far as he could recall. If another vehicle had been involved, where had it come from? Was the car racing Pia for some reason, or was it a third car that no one knew about? The idea that they had been pushed off the road had occurred to Paul almost immediately when he'd become oriented to time and place, but it seemed outlandish, like something that happened in a movie. It would mean that someone had tried to murder him and Pia, or at least Pia, and he would have been collateral damage. He had shared Pia's suspicions, mostly unvoiced, that Nano might be experimenting on human subjects somewhere in the facility, but this line of reasoning about the accident struck Paul as being close to paranoia. Of course, he guessed that Pia would almost certainly feel differently when she came to, especially if, by some slim chance, she remembered more than he.

Paul looked down at Pia's face. Despite the turmoil of his thoughts, Pia appeared to be in a deep but contented sleep. The contrast made Paul realize he was exhausted. He would have liked nothing better than to lie down next to her and catch a few minutes' rest himself.

33.

Despite the noise in the room, Zach Berman was practically asleep on his feet. Two Chinese trainers were shouting instructions to a pair of riders crouched over racing bikes on stands that converted them to stationary mode. The riders were wired up to banks of instruments, and as they pedaled furiously they yelled back to the trainers, begging to be allowed to stop, or so Berman assumed, going by the little Mandarin he'd been able to pick up. The air in the lab was so thick and close that the riders were perspiring profusely and adding to Berman's sleepiness.

He had spent hours in the room as the scientists and trainers tried again to replicate the conditions under which the rider might go into arrest, as the runner and now two cyclists had done in the open. Indeed, the same cyclist who'd had the mishap previously was one of the test subjects, but try as the scientists might, adjusting dosages, degree of hydration, various stressors, and varying riding conditions, both men were riding as hard, and complaining as loudly, as ever after almost ten hours of work, with absolutely no change in their relatively slow heart rates and their normal cardiac rhythms and shallow breathing.

These had been a frantic few days for Zach Berman. Despite

strict orders for all the subjects not to go out on their own, no matter how confident they felt, here he was, presented with yet another problem. The cyclist's crisis had come just weeks after the jogger's similar public collapse, over which Berman believed he had finally prevailed and ridden out the storm of questioning that had emanated from China. Having another similar episode would be inconvenient timing, to say the very least. Berman's backers believed the technology was close to being perfected, and any technical glitch like this seemed to throw the whole project into doubt. Berman knew he couldn't help much with the science, but he had to be in the room to witness the work, as being away from it, speculating on what was going wrong, proved unbearable for him. His only consolation was that it was better that it should happen now rather than when it really counted.

The other problem driving Berman nuts was that he couldn't stop thinking about Pia. The emergency contingency plans put into place by Berman's head of security had worked smoothly. As soon as the rider had gone down, the team assembled their van and got ready to retrieve him, and they were aware, through their contact at Boulder Memorial, that the ambulance was getting there ahead of the Nano team. But the pickup from the ambulance went well and the situation appeared to be under control when the chief of security heard a report that the head of the Boulder Memorial ER and "some young woman" seemed to have set off in pursuit.

When the head of security quickly called Berman and said he could "deal with it," Berman had reluctantly acquiesced. Berman paid people handsomely to take care of problems like this. The security chief had told him not to worry; there was no chance of the incident being deemed anything other than an accident; he could deal with that end of the matter, too, if it came to it.

Later, Berman had heard that Pia was involved in a car accident on that same road, and he quickly deduced that she was in the vehicle with the doctor racing after the cyclist. Berman knew it was

Pia who had found the runner who had gone down, and she had asked Mariel Spallek a lot of questions about it, but he convinced himself then that he had nothing to worry about. This time, he wasn't so sure. Still, he found that he was very glad Pia was alive, because he felt the unfinished business he had with the woman trumped any minor threat she might pose.

More than anything else, Berman wanted to redeem his masculinity with her. At his house, when she had essentially invited herself to dinner, her seductiveness had driven him wild. The fact that he had passed out like some immature teenager was a monumental blow to his ego and self-image. When she was better and out of the hospital he wanted to make up for the lost opportunity, especially replaying in his mind her exotic and erotic dance. As far as her curious streak was concerned, he was confident he could deal with that himself, but in his own way. After all, he had dealt with Whitney and Mariel without a problem after he'd gotten tired of their personal favors.

Berman rubbed his eyes and drank cold coffee from a cup that had been filled about three hours previously. The thought occurred to him that perhaps these apparent cardiac arrests were just anomalies, one-off events that couldn't be explained and would even out statistically. If that was the case, Berman thought he would be consumed by anxiety waiting for the next one. Berman resolved to have the trainers threaten the subjects more convincingly to make sure they never went out alone, and to have the scofflaws punished more seriously, so that if such medical disasters did reoccur, no one would find out about them to draw attention to Nano.

Berman was snapped out of his troubled musings by Whitney Jones, who suddenly shook him hard by the shoulder. She'd slipped into the lab unseen and unheard by Berman.

"Mr. Berman, are you okay? You look like you're fading."

"No, Whitney, I'm fine. Where did you come from? What are you doing still up?"

"I should be up if you are. And I'm glad I was. I was waiting for you in your office and took a call that came in on your direct line. I said to the caller that I'd find you. You have to come back to take the call. He'll be calling back."

"What now? Another problem?"

"Yes, I'm afraid it must be. It was Klaastens, the trainer from the cycling team. He said it's very urgent and involved one of the Chinese cyclists."

"Shit!" Berman mumbled. "I hope to hell it isn't another cardiac arrest. Did he say what it was?"

"No, he didn't, and I didn't press him. He was insistent about talking directly with you. He said he'd tried your home number, but there was no answer."

"How the hell did he get the direct-line office number?" Berman had a private phone in his office that was restricted to a very few trusted cohorts and certain high-ranking Chinese dignitaries, but Victor Klaastens was not part of either group. "I'd given him the home number but not the private office number."

"I don't know, you can ask him that yourself." Whitney started to guide Berman out of the room. "He's calling back in fifteen minutes from now, so you have to move it."

Berman could hardly put one foot in front of the other, but he knew he had to go back to his office if he wanted to speak with Klaastens. The direct line bypassed the Nano switchboard, so he couldn't take it in the aerobics lab. On top of that, all cell phone and data transmissions were blocked in this part of Nano, thanks to one of Nano's own products, a wall paint that blocked radio frequencies.

As soon as Berman dragged himself into his office, the direct-line phone rang. Berman let it ring three times to allow himself to take a deep breath before he picked up.

"Yes?" he said.

"Mr. Berman, it's Victor Klaastens—"

"How did you get this number?" Berman's irritation at what he considered a security problem had woken him up. He wanted to be absolutely certain that the direct line was never bugged.

"Mr. Berman, please, I may not have your resources, but I'm not a stupid man. You should listen to what I want to tell you, because it's more important than a restricted phone number. And don't worry, no one can trace this phone or where I'm calling from."

"Okay, so tell me."

"It's one of your riders, Han. He's injured."

"Injured? How? His heart . . . ?" Berman stopped himself from saying more.

"His heart? That's curious you should say that. No, not his heart, it's his Achilles tendon. A complete rupture, I'm afraid."

"That's odd," Berman said. He was relieved it hadn't been a cardiac problem, which is what he fully expected. An Achilles tendon rupture was an injury that could happen to any athlete who was pushing the limits, and therefore less worrisome vis-à-vis the Chinese. At the same time, it was a problem, and problems were not something he wanted happening now. Was this another anomalous injury? Did cyclists ever have this kind of injury—wasn't it more associated with contact sports? Even if it wasn't a direct result of the program, what was China going to say about this? Shit.

"Mr. Berman?" Klaastens said, unsure if Berman was still on the line.

"A complete rupture, you say."

"Yes, he was doing some aerobic work on the stationary bike this morning, warming up, when it went. He wasn't even pushing himself particularly hard. One minute everything was fine, the next minute he said it felt like someone kicked him very hard in the back of the leg. I'm sorry, I know this is not what you want to hear."

"And Han, what's happening to him?"

"He was taken to the hospital, of course, but he won't be there very long. I spoke briefly with one of the doctors. He said that they will wait for the swelling to go down, and then an operation can be done if it is desired, but it can wait a while. It can be treated conservatively as well; it just takes longer to heal."

"Okay, don't do anything. I'm coming to Milan for the last stage, on the twenty-seventh, can he wait that long?"

"I am the trainer, not the doctor, I don't know. It's a shame, he was performing well, very comfortable. I think he shows more promise than Bo. Next season, he can be back, and stronger."

"Next season," said Berman, as much to himself as Klaastens. He knew if the next phase of his master plan wasn't successful, there would be no next season.

"So I will see you in Milan on the twenty-seventh, Mr. Berman." Klaastens waited for a reply, but Zach Berman had already ended the call.

34.

She knows she's asleep, but she feels awake at the same time. She feels as though she is looking at the world from the bottom of a swimming pool, and she can breathe, but she can't move. Sounds are oddly muffled. Some familiar faces come to her, as if people are swimming down to meet with her as she lies down here, looking up. She knows they're familiar, and they're friendly, so she is content to see them.

Someone else has come to see her. She needs to get away, but she's held back, as if the fluid in which she is suspended is more viscous than water. Looking down at her arms she can see she's constrained by straps, like seat belts, and suddenly she's moving forward quickly, then tumbling down, falling and falling through the bottom of the world. Somehow, she knows that if only she could open her eyes, she'd be okay. But it's so hard to do, so hard. . . .

"Pia?"

Pia sensed she was in the hospital, and felt more conscious of her surroundings than she had in a long time. There was discomfort, even pain. She tried to move but she couldn't, at least not her arms. She knew time had passed, but where had she been? Someone was with her in her room. She was aware that people had been coming to see her, and had been comforted by their familiar voices. George. George had been one of them. And her new friend Paul. Pia's head throbbed, and she knew she was drugged, and there was a dull ache in several parts of her body. But still, she should be able to recognize this new visitor. Then she realized she had yet to open her eyes, so she did.

"Pia? Are you awake? They said you were more awake now than you have been."

She did feel more awake, the man was right. But who was he? She studied his face.

"Pia. Maybe I should leave you to sleep."

Suddenly, Pia knew who it was.

"Pia, it's me, Zach. I wanted to see you before I left. I have to go on a trip, but I will be back." Berman studied Pia's face and glanced down at the curves of her body beneath the white bedsheet. She was as alluring as he had remembered, maybe even more so despite the sterile hospital environment. He wanted her. He wanted to own her, to tame her, to control her. She had teased him mercilessly, and it had worked: he was beguiled, enthralled, even bewitched, and he loved it. Screw Whitney and Mariel and their petty jealousies. Berman was going to make it happen. The fact that Pia had survived was an omen he was committed to exploit.

Pia was going to try to speak, but before she could form words, she became dimly aware that another person had entered her room. This time she recognized the voice at once.

"Excuse me, may I ask who you are?" said Paul Caldwell, firmly. "This patient has restricted visiting status."

"I know," said Berman, facing Paul and taking measure of the man. He recognized who he was from his name badge and having seen the name in the police report of the accident. "Dr. Caldwell, I am Zachary Berman, president and CEO of Nano. Dr. Grazdani is a highly valued employee, and I wanted to be sure to pay a visit before

I have to leave the country on a business trip. My assistant spoke directly with the hospital president, who cleared my quick visit to check on her status. I was assured it was not a problem."

"Visitors except immediate family are inappropriate, no matter what Mr. Noakes might have said. Did you clear your visit with Gloria Jason, head of nursing? That would have been more appropriate."

"I believe it was only cleared with Dr. Noakes."

"It's Mr. Noakes. He is not a doctor and frankly not involved in patient care."

"Well, I apologize for the intrusion. I will be leaving right away. May I just inquire how she is doing? Obviously I care." Berman affected what he thought was a concerned expression.

"You could have found that out with a phone call," Paul said curtly. "But to answer your question, she's coming along." Paul was purposely taciturn. He had taken an instant dislike to Berman. From what Pia had said and from his own questions as to Nano's possible complicity in the accident as well as his immediate observations, Paul thought he recognized Zachary Berman for what he was: a power-intoxicated male predator, and Paul had met a few in real life.

"May I also inquire how you are?" asked Berman, maintaining his concerned expression. "I understand you were in the same accident as my employee."

"Yes, I was," said Paul. He wasn't surprised Berman would know that he had been. It had been in the papers and even on the evening news. "In comparison to Dr. Grazdani, I am fine." Paul held up the forefinger and middle finger on his left hand palm toward himself. The fingers were bound together with white adhesive tape. "This is the extent of my injuries."

Berman looked at the fingers. Was the doctor giving him the middle finger, knowing the digits were attached? Berman allowed himself to smile. In spite of the situation, he liked the guy. He had an attitude that Berman could appreciate. "I'm glad there were no other consequences," added Berman.

"Other than this," said Paul indicating Pia with a nod of his head.

"Perhaps her driving skills are not what they should be, or maybe she was just in the wrong place at the wrong time. When she's better, we're looking forward to having her back at Nano, where she belongs."

"We'll see," said Paul. This man was truly reprehensible, he thought.

"If there's anything I can do, please let me know," said Berman, looking back at Pia. He smiled to himself, knowing what he'd like to do.

"There is one thing," said Paul. "You can stop sending the flower arrangements. It's a bit much. Too funereal. And particularly the lilies are stinking up the place."

Berman smiled again. This guy was a trip, but he held his tongue. Instead he just nodded and left.

Paul looked back at Pia, who surprised him by staring at him with heavy-lidded eyes.

"Well, hello, stranger. What a nice surprise. How do you feel?"

"Paul! Where am I?" Her voice was hoarse. She tried to cough but it was feeble.

"You're in the Memorial. You've been here a week."

"A week?" Pia managed with consternation. "What happened?"

"There was an accident. A car accident."

"I'm starting to remember. We were looking for the white van."

"We were," Paul agreed. "But I don't think you should be worrying about it now. There will be time. How do you feel in general?"

"I hurt. I feel groggy and like I've been run over by a garbage truck."

"I can imagine. I'm sorry. Listen, we kept you in a drug-induced coma for a few days because we were a little worried about you. Among other things, you had a bad concussion. But you're going to be fine. You'll feel progressively less groggy as the drugs wear off."

"My head hurts."

"I'm not surprised. You probably hurt elsewhere, too. We'll have a self-administered narcotic piggybacked into your intravenous line as soon as I let your hospitalist know you are awake. But don't worry about it now, just rest." He stepped up alongside the bed and lifted the call button attached by a safety pin to Pia's pillow. He showed it to her. "If you need pain medication before the do-it-yourself is in place, just push the button."

"Why are my arms tied up?" Pia had tried to raise her arms but couldn't.

"They are just wrist restraints," Paul said as he undid Velcro straps. "We didn't want you pulling out your IV."

"Tell me! Was that Zachary Berman who was just here?"

"It was."

"What was he doing here?"

"Beats me!"

"Was George here while I've been out of it or was I dreaming? I seem to remember his voice."

"You're right. He is here in Boulder. At the moment I made him go get something to eat. He's going to be very pleased you are awake."

"Why on earth did Berman come here? That makes me feel . . . I'm not sure how it makes me feel. But it's not good." Pia's speech was getting clearer, and Paul could tell from its timbre that she was getting agitated.

"Try to stay calm! Don't worry about anything for now. If you'd like, I'll tell the powers that be that you don't want any visitors except George and me. You should just concentrate on feeling better. Berman will not be allowed back in, trust me!"

"Thank you, Paul. I appreciate it."

35.

Zach Berman knew his rider wasn't in contention to win the rather short final stage that was the finish of this year's Giro d'Italia, let alone the race itself, but he felt extremely nervous nonetheless. A huge crowd had gathered in Milan's main square, which was dominated by the massive yet somewhat delicate cathedral. Berman had marveled at the structure on a visit with Jimmy Yan earlier that day, not least because it had taken six hundred years to complete. The fourteenth-century stonemasons and artists would probably have loved to know that their work was going to be part of a team effort that would go on for literally hundreds of years, all for the glorification of their God. Berman felt his task of marrying nanotechnology to medicine was as monumental as the cathedral, but unlike the builders of the cathedral, he had so little time to finish his own work.

Berman looked at his watch. The riders had left the Piazza Castello fifteen minutes before, and if they rode at forty to fifty kilometers per hour, they would come into sight in ten minutes or so. From his aluminum bleacher seat next to Berman in the temporary grandstand, Jimmy Yan stood and tapped his watch. Berman nodded and stood up. Yan was prepared, as Berman knew was his habit.

"They are close," said Jimmy, watching events through a small pair of opera glasses. The throngs of people were waving flags of all the nations represented in the race, but they were all outnumbered by Italian flags. The loud cheering of the boisterous crowd was punctuated by klaxons and car horns, and even some fireworks, which made the din deafening.

Jimmy stood on his tiptoes, looking at the lead group. This last short stage was mostly a formality. A dominant Spanish rider was going to win the Giro overall, as long as he didn't fall down, but three Italians were vying for second, and it was these riders who were causing the crowd's excitement. From the spectators' point of view it was a great way to finish the nearly monthlong race. Now everyone in the grandstand was on his feet, and Berman couldn't see through the phalanx of raised arms. Then he caught a glimpse of the peloton as they made their circuit of the piazza—did he see the blue, red, and green of his team? He couldn't be sure.

"There!" Jimmy grabbed his arm and pointed, and Berman definitely saw the team's colors, all the riders in a group in the middle of the pack as the massed ranks of riders crossed the line.

"I saw Bo," Jimmy said. "I'm sure of it."

Thank God, thought Berman. His rider had to finish the race, and this was only the first hurdle of many to come in the next few months. Not that finishing a race was a great obstacle in itself, but the officials in China had made it clear, there were to be no more problems or failures: certainly no injuries during public events; no more riders going down on the back roads of Boulder; and no more visits to emergency rooms in American ambulances. Berman wished he had the power to control each situation to such an extent.

"We should go down and see the team," said Berman, who felt that their finishing the race without any disasters was a cause for modest celebration.

"As you wish," said Jimmy. "I will go and see Liang once more before we leave."

Liang was the rider selected to take the place of Han, who had been flown back to the United States to have his Achilles operated on out of sight of potentially curious European surgeons. Han's injury had baffled Nano's scientific team. They knew of such injuries to juiced-up baseball players who had added too much muscle and overtaxed their tendons, sometimes shearing them clean off the bone. But Han hadn't been putting on bulk to hit home runs, he was leaner and built for speed and endurance. If anything, his muscles had become smaller in girth, just much more efficient and able to avoid lactic acid buildup entirely.

Doctors in both Shanghai and Boulder had spent days poring over MRIs of Han's legs taken well before his injury when he was being considered to be a subject, but found no minute tear that might have caused the rupture, or any other structural weakness. Eventually the Chinese and American scientists agreed that his injury was an unhappy fluke. "Shit happens" was how the phlegmatic, down-home Victor Klaastens had put it, and Berman finally had to agree that it applied in this case, just as it did in the rest of life.

Jimmy had gotten Liang holed up in an apartment somewhere in Milan. Berman didn't know where it was, he only knew that Liang had flown back to Milan in the same Chinese plane that had taken Han to Colorado, and that he was being attended to by a Chinese doctor who had spent the past two years at Nano. The Chinese were leaving nothing to chance, or leaving nothing to the Americans, which might be the same thing as far as they were concerned.

"How is Liang?" asked Berman as Jimmy got his things together.

"Liang is well. He feels strong and wants to start racing. Despite his situation, it turns out he enjoys this."

Berman preferred not to think too much about the "situation" of the people brought in from China to be trained at Nano.

"He knows if he succeeds, he can win freedom for himself and for his family."

Berman smiled at Jimmy.

"Of course. That is a great incentive for him."

"Fear of failing is a better incentive, don't you think," said Jimmy, making a statement rather than asking a question, and Berman didn't have an answer for him before the two split up. Berman watched Jimmy head off before he himself hustled toward the crowd grouped around the riders. He wanted to have a few words with Victor Klaastens.

36.

Before the accident, and for most of her adult life, Pia always had a
hard time getting out of bed in the morning. She would read too late
at night, and her sleep would frequently be interrupted by nightmares, so invariably when her alarm went off, she wasn't rested and
the temptation to grab another hour was often too much to resist.
But in the weeks since she had been released from the hospital,
she'd woken up at six o'clock, seven days a week, ready and eager to
start her rehab work.

For Pia, being out of action was torture. Other than her slight
problem in getting out of bed in the morning, she hated inactivity, as it never failed to awaken her latent sense of vulnerability. Vacations were a pointless waste of time, as far as she was concerned.
They allowed too much time to think. Pia needed to have a purpose
in her life, a reason to get out of her warm and cozy bed and something to keep her going though the day. And now, following the car
crash, she had two.

One was that she wanted to get back to work. After being eman-
cipated from foster care, Pia always had work. First it was getting
her high school equivalency and her chores at the convent. Then it
was college, and finally medical school and her brush with death.

After Pia's sojourn away from civilization, it was Nano that dominated her life for eighteen months, and even after she started to have questions about Nano and what might be going on there, she remained totally absorbed by keeping her work separate from concerns of what other people there might be up to. She was absolutely sure that what she had been doing was honorable and ethical and might even serve to help her friend Will. So she wanted to get back to work. She wanted to find out what had happened with the compatibility experiments with mice: if the results had been the same as with the roundworms—that is, if her idea of incorporating the polyethylene glycol into the microbivores' diamondoid outer shell had continued to solve the immunological problems.

On top of that was the flagellum issue. Had the programmers looked at her idea of writing code that would cause microbivores to tumble a flagellated bacteria over and over on itself, thereby rolling up the flagellum before the bacteria were drawn into the digestion chamber?

Pia was excited to answer these questions. But there was a problem, a major problem. When she was still in the hospital after the accident, Mariel had called Pia and told her that she would not be permitted to return to Nano even for a visit until she had been completely and totally cleared by her general surgeon, the hospital physical therapy team, and her orthopedic surgeon. It had not been a discussion. In her usual harsh manner, Mariel had told her not to show up or call until she was completely over the sequelae of the accident with letters from her physicians to that effect.

Even though Pia was used to being on her own and liked it, her forced separation from Nano bothered her more than she had expected, making her realize she was not quite the introvert she thought she was. She had come to count on the minor interactions she had with other people in the course of a regular day, a circumstance that without Nano had to be fulfilled by visits to her physical therapist. Unfortunately that didn't do the trick. In her small, ten-unit apartment building, she knew no one by name and only a couple of the other residents by sight.

Her only visitors were Paul, whom she saw regularly, and the physical therapist who came to Pia's home until she was well enough to drive over to the gym to work out on her own. Paul had been a godsend to Pia in many ways. He had even arranged to borrow his parents' second car for Pia to use. The VW was destroyed, and Pia wasn't in a position where she could ask Nano for a replacement.

The second major motivation in Pia's restricted life to get her out of bed in the morning was Berman. Whenever she was lying there, reluctant to get up, as she was that morning, she thought of him. When her broken arm ached, as it did at that moment, or her ribs hurt, or her splenectomy incision burned, she pictured Berman. Pia wanted answers from him, answers to her original questions about Nano and, more pressing to her, answers about the car accident.

Paul confirmed to Pia that in her feverish near-waking state, she had seen Zach Berman in her hospital room. It was awkward, Paul admitted, but Berman had tried to give off the air of a concerned boss coming to visit a colleague. Paul hadn't bought it. He actually told her what he had really thought, namely that Berman was a predator and that she should stay the hell away from him.

"You mean a sexual predator?" Pia had asked.

"Of course a sexual predator."

"What made you think that, not that I don't believe you?" In her mind's eye Pia could see Berman trying to force his way into her apartment.

"His attitude and his person," Paul said with a shake of his head. "It's too bad, because he's a nice-looking guy."

As Paul Caldwell suspected, Pia was totally convinced that their accident had not in fact been accidental, even though she had total traumatic amnesia about the event. What swayed her was that she knew herself: there was no way under the sun that she would simply drive off the road. In her mind, the only explanation was that the VW had been run off the road, and Pia wondered how the authorities could even suggest otherwise.

Paul told Pia that he had been interviewed, and the incident was officially described as an accident, caused in part by Pia's excessive speed. He said the police had come to this conclusion even though he had told them, despite his own memory problems, that he vaguely recalled the involvement of another vehicle behind them just before the accident. When Pia had heard this, she insisted on talking to the officers who had interviewed Paul. But in spite of her protestations, they said there was nothing to investigate, a recommendation that was accepted all the way down the official line. They said that their examination of the mangled car revealed no suggestion that another vehicle had been involved. There were plenty of scrapes and dents but no other paint and no damage that couldn't be explained by the multiple rollovers the car had experienced.

Still, Pia continued to believe there was a cover-up. When Pia persisted in this vein, Paul questioned that if it was true that they had been forced off the road and if it had been done by Nano, how did Nano know to come after them? They had left the hospital only minutes before. Pia didn't have an answer to this question except to suggest that there could have been a tracking device on the car, or a spy at the hospital. With that, Paul told her she'd been watching too many movies.

George had come to visit again three weeks after she was released from the hospital, but it was very hard for him to get away from L.A., and he couldn't stay for more than a single night. Pia had mercilessly run all her theories past George, who listened with half an ear, worried sick she was going to get herself in trouble, and he certainly agreed with Paul that she should steer clear of Berman, even though it had been Berman who had called George about the accident. George even went so far as to tell Pia that she was becoming paranoid and letting conspiracy theories dominate her life. He reminded her that it wasn't the first time she had allowed such thoughts to get herself in trouble.

"That might be so," Pia had agreed. "But back in New York I was ultimately right."

"But being right in New York, and only partially right, I might add, doesn't make you right here in Colorado. If you want my advice, I think you should just let it all go. I think you should relocate and start over because I think your prospects at Nano aren't so good after everything you have told me."

At that point in the conversation, Pia waited for George to tell her to come and stay with him in L.A. once she was fully recuperated, but he didn't. She gave him credit for biting his tongue, but she knew the invitation was coming sooner or later. But moving to L.A. was not in Pia's game plan, even if she ultimately had to give up on Nano.

More than anything, Pia was just plain frustrated. She hated the inactivity and her feeling of impotence. She couldn't do anything when she was so feeble. So this day, as many others, after she'd given her situation some thought, she hopped straight out of bed and did a set of stretches that made her aching body feel more limber and ready for exercise. She had stopped all painkillers, other than over-the-counter anti-inflammatories as needed, and she was tackling her injuries head-on. Pia was delighted that the hard cast she had endured on her arm was coming off later in the week, to be replaced by a gauntlet version although still with the sling. Her ribs were still taped, and the hair on the very top of her head was still short from having been shaved to get the ten or so stitches needed to close a laceration.

As she showered, Pia went through a series of homemade memory tests and aced them all to prove to herself that her memory was getting better and not worse since the accident. The neurologist she'd seen had warned her that symptoms like memory loss could appear months after the accident, and warned her of depression that could follow. Pia had replied that she was too mad to be depressed, and demurred when the doctor asked what exactly she meant.

It looked like it was going to be a nice summer day today, and Pia set herself new, and higher, workout goals. Best of all, she was due to meet Paul for dinner that evening at a casual Italian place in Boulder, and Pia looked forward to working up a good appetite.

37.

The air felt great to Zach Berman at 5,000 feet above sea level in the Jura Mountains of France. After years in Colorado, he felt very comfortable at this altitude. Weather-wise it was a beautiful, promising day, with a warm, bright sun and a faraway blue sky, and Berman's body tingled with anticipation. This was the day when the years of hard work and sacrifice would pay off. He was confident but not over-confident, because he still had a nagging, anxious feeling that something could go wrong, as had happened over the last few months.

But that was in the past. Since that disturbing morning when he'd gotten the call that the rider Han had ruptured his Achilles tendon, Berman had enjoyed nothing but good news. Bo and Liang, the new tandem in the Azeri race team, had meshed well with the team. Through the coach, Victor Klaastens, Berman had circulated a couple of stories in the cycling trade press about these two young Chinese riders who were showing such great promise in training. By the arrangement of the government, a Chinese newspaper had interviewed the two men, and a transcript in English appeared on the Internet and had been followed up by a few Western sports outlets. The success of Chinese cycling wasn't going to come as a complete surprise to those in the know.

And the success was coming. Berman's scientists believed they had cracked the problem that had caused the athletes' cardiac failures, associating it with a kind of oxygen toxicity that in turn created a hypermetabolic state, a problem that turned out to be amenable to subtle changes in dosage, actually lowering the loading dose. Ever since those changes had been incorporated into the protocol, no one had encountered any problems whatsoever. What's more, performance levels had gone up further, adding to Berman's sense of comfort that what had been planned for this stage of the Tour de France was about to be realized.

Liang was the stronger of the two cyclists, physically and mentally, and it was decided that he should enjoy the honor. The team was positioned so that Liang's triumph would be a surprise but not a complete shock. He showed himself to be a good climber, and in two earlier medium-difficulty mountain stages, he had picked up points, leading the pack up major climbs, earning a good standing in the "King of the Mountains" race, a prestigious competition within the larger Tour itself.

At each stage, Berman and Jimmy Yan had spent a little time with the team. A few days earlier, they set up a base in western Switzerland from where they could drive into France and catch up with their riders. Berman had never spent so much time with one person, and he doubted that even the most devoted married couples ate every meal together like they did, not to mention nearly all their other waking moments. Berman liked Jimmy, but he knew the man wasn't being paid to be his friend. But now, as the two men stood amid a crowd at the top of the brutal eighteen-kilometer climb to the summit of the Col du Grand Colombier, Berman felt he could confide in Jimmy.

"I'm very nervous, Jimmy, I don't mind admitting it. There's so much at stake."

"I am also nervous."

"Really?" said Berman. It was unlike Jimmy to admit to such a weakness.

"Sure. I know what you have on the line. And I know how serious my superiors are about seeing proof that your methods will work. They have a lot at stake as well. But you are a sincere man, so I am hoping you succeed, and when you succeed, China succeeds. It is, as you Americans say, a win-win situation."

"Sincere?"

"You believe what you say, and it is hard to argue with that confidence. But a lot of what you promise is outside your control, so your sincerity may not always help you, as it raises expectations."

Berman was unsure how to respond. Should he be less sincere? Or make fewer promises? Jimmy helped him out by speaking again.

"You're sure you really want to be here, not at the finish?"

The stage finished in the small town of Bellegarde-sur-Valserine, more than forty kilometers past the mountain, with another, less vigorous climb between the riders and the end.

"No, this is the spot I want to be at. If Liang is leading here, I know he's strong enough to win the stage. This is what this race means to me, the rider struggling to the top of the mountain, on his own, fighting his pain and fatigue as much as he is taking on the other riders."

"I know you like the sport," said Jimmy.

"It's a metaphor for me," said Berman. "I'm a competitive guy." A moment later a cheer went up from the crowd as the people pressed forward.

"They are coming," said Jimmy.

The police were now fighting to contain the crowd so that they could keep the road open. In the next instant a police car summited the peak with siren blaring, then another car, then a car from the Azeri team and a motorbike with a cameraman facing backward, training his camera practically in the rider's face. Berman strained to see through the flags—he saw the rider being patted on the back and heard the cheering for the leader. It was Liang, he was leading the stage! Berman had been following the race online, so he knew what was happening, but he needed to see it for himself. It was sweet victory.

Liang looked strong, his face set in rugged determination, breathing evenly. He was standing on his pedals, straining for every last ounce of effort, then sitting as he rode a short flat before the descent began. He reached down and took a water bottle, zipped up his shirt, which he'd opened for ventilation on the climb, stuffed his mouth with some food, drank, and then was out of sight, followed by more team cars and motorbikes fighting through the crowd that had closed up behind Liang.

A loudspeaker was booming news of the other riders in French, but Berman couldn't make out any of the information. He looked at Jimmy, who gestured with his head for the two of them to leave. Berman followed him and looked down below as the road snaked away. He could see Liang and the caravan following behind him, rounding a bend far below. Jimmy was looking at his watch, then at his cell phone.

"He has a four-minute lead," Jimmy said. "The rest of the race is spread out, and there is no organized pursuit. Liang will win the stage."

Although he had seen his rider crown the mountain in triumph, Berman now was second-guessing his decision to avoid the finish of the stage. He realized that he and Jimmy would be stuck on top of the mountain for hours. But he knew that in less than an hour, Liang would win a stage of the Tour de France, and Berman would be halfway toward his goal: unlimited funding for microbivores. An image of his mother came into his head and he shook it away. Not now. He breathed in a deep draft of mountain air and allowed himself a short, self-satisfied smile.

38.

Pia stood in the familiar Nano parking lot, composing herself. She was hoping that the trouble she had just encountered getting through the guard station wasn't a harbinger of her general reception and was merely the result of a misunderstanding. She had been held up at the security gate because she was driving Paul's parents' old Toyota, not the VW that she was logged into the system with. Even though the guard had seemed to recognize her, he was not willing to let her pass. What had bothered him more than the make of the car was that Pia's ID no longer worked when he tried to swipe it into the system through his computer. She explained that she had been off work for a considerable period, and she probably had to renew her ID. The guard agreed that she should go straight to the security station and then finally let her through.

Now, as she stood next to her car, Pia wondered if her nerve was failing. She could never recall such a thing, but the Nano buildings suddenly looked huge and foreboding. The sky was low and dark, which didn't help, and she felt unwelcome. The origin of that feeling was not difficult to discern, because she had received only one piece of correspondence from Nano other than the less-than-friendly call from Mariel while she was still in the hospital. The letter confirmed what Mariel had said, that Pia would have to submit to a physical before she could restart work, but gave no timetable. Pia knew her hospital bills and physical therapy charges had been taken care of by Nano's insurance plan, but she had no record of the transactions. In the meantime, Mariel Spallek didn't return any calls or emails, and recently when Pia called, she received an automatic reply that the voice mailbox was full.

Pia couldn't help but wonder if she was still a bona fide employee of Nano or if she was in a kind of limbo, such as administrative leave. She had been getting her regular pay statements through the mail, so she was still being paid, but these were coming through the bank, not from Nano directly. She had in her possession letters from both of her surgeons and the physical therapy department documenting her considerable progress. She wasn't totally finished with her rehab, but she believed she was certainly able to work. She felt she had very little alternative to showing up in person to find out what the story was.

The threatening rain began slowly with just a few drops, then it increased. As she stood in the drizzle, trying to summon her resolve, Pia saw a familiar figure recede away from her toward the building entrance. He had pulled in after her but had parked in a reserved section.

"Jason! Hold up a second."

Jason Rodriguez turned, saw Pia, gave an embarrassed wave, and kept walking. Pia ran after him and planted herself in front of the much taller man.

"Jason, what's going on? Can't you stop and say hi?"

"Late, I'm late, Pia, so I can't stop, really."

The man's eyes darted left and right, avoiding Pia's gaze.

"Paul told me you came to see me in the hospital, when I was asleep. That was kind of you. I wish you'd have come back when I was awake."

Jason looked down momentarily and caught Pia's eye. She could see a pained expression on his face.

"What's the matter, Jason? You seem very uncomfortable talking to me."

"Mariel . . ." said Jason quietly, before his voice trailed off.

"Mariel? Mariel what, Jason? Mariel told you not to talk to me? What did Mariel say about me?"

"Okay, listen." Jason's attention was now fully trained on Pia to the point that she herself had to look away. "Mariel knew I had gone to see you in the hospital, and she wasn't happy about it. She said you were bad news, and that I needed to keep away from you if I wanted to continue working at Nano. I tried to say that I thought you were a bit aloof but an excellent scientist. Her reply was that there were a lot things I didn't know."

"Like what? What was she implying?"

"I don't know exactly."

"And you just believed her."

"I'm sorry, Pia, this job is my big break. I've been trying to get a job like this for years. You know how it is out there."

Pia stared at Jason for as long as she could before looking off. She couldn't believe it. It was as if she were some kind of pariah. She felt like trying to goad Jason into talking to her and tell her what he really thought since he was certainly holding back. But she didn't have the energy.

"Good luck, Pia," Jason said after an uncomfortable moment. "I hope things work out, I really do." He turned up the collar of his jacket and hurried on toward the building.

Pia needed an outlet for her anger, so she took out her phone and, despite the light rain, dialed Mariel Spallek's number. It was probably best the woman didn't answer because Pia wasn't sure what she would have said. On this occasion Mariel's voice mail did pick up, but Pia didn't bother to leave a message. Instead she shut and locked the car door and walked quickly toward the Nano entrance.

Normally, she would walk though the doors and directly to the iris scanner by the glass doors leading into the facility, but after what had happened at the security gate, she headed to the security office as she had been advised. Guests and delivery people were instructed by notices to visit the reception desk to the left of the main door. There were a handful of people waiting there. Other Nano employees were arriving in small groups. It was a busy time of day. Security guards were attentive, making sure people went through the scanner and glass partition one at a time. Pia recognized most of them.

In the security office things were calmer, and she went directly to the counter. After the conversation with Jason, she thought there was a good chance that she was going to have trouble. Pia did not recognize the woman staffing the counter. Her name tag read HARRIET PIERSON. An imposing woman of color, she wore a military-style uniform like all the other security staff. Pia had her ID in her hand, which Harriet took without comment. She was obviously expecting Pia. She tried to swipe it into the computer, but as had happened at the gate, it apparently didn't work, because she then disappeared into the back room.

Pia waited. To pass the time she looked back into the main foyer of the building. People were arriving in greater numbers, so a short line was starting to form in front of the iris scanner.

Harriet returned to the counter and handed Pia her ID. "Okay, Dr. Grazdani," she said, "I guess you haven't been here for a number of weeks."

Pia nodded and raised her left arm, which was still in a sling with a forearm cast. She knew she looked slightly bedraggled with the sling, cast, and baseball cap to conceal her uneven hair. She was wearing jeans and a plaid flannel shirt.

"Anyway," Harriet continued. "I've updated your ID. You shouldn't have any more trouble with it at the gate."

Pia thanked the woman. She left the security office and headed out toward the short line waiting to go through the iris scanner. She was more sanguine now about getting up to her lab since the visit to the security office had been so easy. As she waited, she recognized the guard standing off to the side, monitoring the people as they passed through the checkpoint. It was Milloy, the particularly officious guard she'd had a mild run-in with before.

When it was her turn, Pia stepped up to the scanner and faced it. She waited but there was no expected beep. Instead it flashed red for fail.

Pia was trying for the third time when Milloy approached her.

"Miss, please step aside. May I see your ID?"

"Of course," Pia said, not bothering to conceal her frustration. At least she was confident the ID was going to work.

"One second, miss." Milloy took the ID with him to a nearby computer station. To Pia's chagrin, he spent a good three minutes two-finger tapping at the computer and reading the screen. He looked over at Pia, who rolled her eyes and shifted her weight in her frustration at the delay. Finally he walked back to her.

"I'm sorry, miss, your general clearance has been suspended pending medical reinstatement."

"Well, can you let me in so I can go to HR and try to get my clearance restored?"

"Can't do that."

"What do you suggest?"

Milloy pointed. "I suggest you go into security and see what they can do."

"I was just in there getting my ID updated."

"You'll have to go back."

"Look, Mr. Milloy, this is outrageous. I'm an employee here, I had an accident."

"So I see. But I have no authority to let you in."

"Call Zachary Berman, he'll tell you."

"Zachary Berman, the CEO of Nano." Milloy laughed. "And what would I say to him? Sorry, lady, I can't help you."

"He knows me," said Pia indignantly. But she knew she wasn't going to win this argument. She had one last attempt in her.

"Okay, call Whitney Jones, his assistant."

"I know who she is. I happen to know she's away on business with the boss man. Why don't you give her a call in a couple of days, and I'm sure she can help you. Now I have to go."

Pia could tell Milloy was enjoying himself at her expense. Normally, Pia would have stood there and argued with Milloy, but she found she didn't have the strength. As she walked back to her car, Pia's anger increased. She got in and drove fast out of the Nano lot. When she came to the state road, she made an impulsive decision. Instead of turning right back to town, she turned left and headed directly to Zach Berman's house. Perhaps he was away, as Milloy had said, but maybe he wasn't. Even if he wasn't there, Pia needed to blow off some steam. At the moment her anger and frustration were directed at the CEO. He was, ultimately, responsible.

The gate. Pia had forgotten about the gate at the bottom of Berman's drive until she was almost upon it. She pulled directly up to it and leaned on her horn. The raucous sound startled the birds in the immediate environs, and Pia saw them flee up into the higher branches of the surrounding evergreens.

After several blasts, Pia eased up and the din ceased. Her ears were ringing. Then she noticed the buzzer and pressed it repeatedly. A minute passed, then another, with no response. She then got out of the car and faced what she thought was the remote camera, defiantly putting her free hand on her hip.

"Hey, Mr. Berman, I can't get into my lab. It's not fair. I helped you fix those microbivores. I should not be treated like this. If you're not there, maybe you'll see this tape. We have unfinished business. You know it, and I know it."

Then Pia felt foolish, shouting at a stone gatepost with what she thought was a camera mounted on top. She looked up one more time, flipped a finger, and then got back in her car to drive home.

39.

Pia sat on Paul's couch, drinking her third glass of wine of the evening. Nothing about Pia's story of her difficulties getting into Nano had changed since Wednesday, but she had recounted it again over dinner, and it appeared to Paul as if she were about to do so again.

"Okay, Pia, I don't wish to be rude, but I know what happened. Nano has revoked your access to your lab until you have a medical release, and you're pissed. Understandably. I get it, they're ungrateful bastards with all the work and help that you have given them. But I don't see what you can do about it other than hire a lawyer to get you that meeting with human resources."

"I don't need a lawyer!" said Pia, for the tenth time.

"An employment lawyer. I'm not talking about a personal-injury lawyer or anything like that. Nano hasn't terminated you, but you can't get into work, even though they are still paying you. Funny, a lot of people would love such a situation."

"It's not the money," Pia complained.

"I know. Come on! Calm down! I'm talking about an employment lawyer who will get this resolved, and if he can't get you into the lab, then he will get you a settlement. Then you can move on with your life. You can't go on like this."

"Like what?"

"Like this, Pia, going over and over the same things like you're picking at a scab. Not every mystery gets resolved. Go to the newspapers with your story. See what they can do. Perhaps the Chinese runner and this more recent Chinese cyclist will remain a mystery. Right now, only you and I even know it's a mystery, and I must admit, I've lost most of my interest in it."

"If I go to the newspapers, even if they pick up on it, I'm sure Nano has contingency plans. It's not going anywhere unless I find out what they're doing and can be specific with the press."

"But your hands are tied. If you can't even get into the place, there's no way you can figure out what they are doing. It's as simple as that. Frankly, right now, I don't even want to think about it anymore."

"So I'm on my own. Is that what you're telling me?"

"Of course not. I didn't say that. I will help you get a good lawyer. I know lawyers. In fact I know the scariest lawyer in Boulder who happens to be involved in labor law. He'd be perfect. As soon as he calls, they'll roll over and give you whatever you want."

"I want access to my lab."

"A lawyer is not going to be able to get you access if Nano doesn't want you to have access. Be reasonable. Let's talk about something else."

"Will a lawyer be able to make them tell me why they tried to kill us?"

Paul let out a sigh. "No, Pia, that's not going to happen. Nor do we know for sure that they had anything whatsoever to do with the accident. I just have this imprecise recollection of a vehicle behind us just before we went off the road. But I'm not sure about that. You're not going to get anywhere trying to reopen that can of worms. Because there are no worms!"

"I'll never accept the idea that I just ran off the road. It's absurd."

"You are entitled to your idea, but I'm telling you that you can't keep on with this monomania. It's like *Moby-Dick*."

"What?"

"Never mind. Do you still want to come down to Denver with me? We both could use a diversion. Come on, Pia, what do you say?"

"I'm good," said Pia. "I'm not in the mood."

"You sure?"

Pia nodded. She wasn't in the mood for socializing and small talk at all. And she'd had enough wine for the night.

"Hey, Paul," she said. She sounded brighter. "Do you still have that camera you borrowed from your friend? The one we fooled around with that time?"

"Yeah, it's still here. Why?"

"Can I borrow it?"

Paul hesitated. He tried to look Pia in the eye, but she quickly looked away. "Why do you want to borrow it?"

"I don't have a real camera, and I feel like going hiking tomorrow while you're in the ER. I think my ribs can take it. I want to take some pictures of the wildflowers that are blooming in the foothills."

"Pia . . . ?"

"C'mon, Paul, don't be so suspicious. I'd use my phone's camera, but I have in mind to make large blowups for all those bare walls in my apartment you're always complaining about. So I need the high definition."

"Exactly what's brewing in that mind of yours?"

"Nothing," Pia said casually. "I just feel like being creative, seeing as I have all this free time. What do you say? Or do I have to go out and buy one?"

"Okay. I'll get it," Paul said. She could be so damn willful.

"And can I have that cord that connects it to the Mac, too?" Pia called after him. "You're an angel."

"I know," said Paul. "And probably a fool," he said under his breath.

40.

Zach Berman clicked off the Web site he had been looking at on his computer. The Tour de France had finished that day, won by the Spanish rider who finished the last stage among the leading procession of riders enjoying the final ride down the Champs-Élysées. But Liang Dalian had taken his place on the dais during the awards, wearing the red polka-dotted jersey of the King of the Mountains, the rider with the best record on the hills over the whole race. He was lauded as the first Chinese to win a stage at the Tour, and the first to win one of the prestigious in-race competitions. Liang was featured for a minute or so on the cable TV coverage of the race ("Was China about to invade the sport?"), but there was far more about his triumph online.

Berman saw an interview with Liang, conducted through the same translator he had met numerous times with the team. Liang was well coached in his responses. He was delighted and amazed at his own achievement. He humbly thanked his teammates and the sponsors and his trainers. He explained that coming to Europe to race was difficult for him and his teammate Bo because neither of them had been outside of China before. He concluded by saying that he hoped this was the first victory of many for his fellow countrymen—and he said perhaps he could win the whole Tour next year, who knows?

Alas, that wasn't going to happen, Berman thought. Berman guessed that there was some teenage peasant riding his bike for fun in a far-off province who would get that honor, and he would be raised in China and trained in China and be a professional who could be a star in the new China if he wanted to. But the risks with persevering with Liang were too high lest his true biography came to light, and Berman knew that something would happen to him in the next few months that would wreck his dream.

Berman located another Web site he felt he needed to check on. The opening ceremony of the World Athletics Championships in London was now less than a week away, and he would be in town, waiting for the competition with the same anticipation he felt for the Tour, only doubled or tripled in intensity. It was coming down to this watershed event. Berman's whole future rested on just one race. But the trainers told him repeatedly not to worry. They said the same things Liang's personal trainer told him one morning somewhere in France during the Tour. Berman had nothing to worry about—the rider was performing extremely well, even though he was utilizing only about 85 percent of his physical capacity. The trainer said Liang could win the whole race if necessary, and with ease. In London, they said the same. The problem wasn't going to be winning, it was winning by too much.

Berman took heart from all the comforting words, but still he was unable to relax. So for the umpteenth time, he visited the Web page for the Chinese athletics team. It was the biggest team of any coming to London, and it was stacked with medal prospects. He found the marathon team, and there was the familiar face of Yao Hong-Xiau, a late entrant who had missed the trials in March but who had put up a stunning time in a private race in June. Berman knew strings had been pulled to get Yao in the race, but his name was still there. Yao would be running in London.

Berman's concentration was gradually interrupted by a strange sound. It was a distant noise that had seemingly taken some time to penetrate the thick walls of his post-and-beam and stone house with its triple-glassed windows. Looking away from the computer screen so that he could concentrate, he strained to listen. The sound was just beyond his hearing threshold, but it was definitely there.

"It's a goddamn car horn!" Berman said out loud. "Where the hell is that coming from: the East Coast?" He scraped back his chair. Leaving the den, he passed through the foyer and entered the monitoring room.

"Well, well, what do we have here?" One of the monitors had halted its sweeps to stop at the view of the driveway gate. The system was programmed to zero in on any significant movement beyond the swaying of tree branches in the wind. There in full view was Pia Grazdani, looking directly up into the camera, eyebrows raised expectantly. She was sitting in the driver's seat of a sedan with the driver's-side window down. Berman could see that she was leaning on the car horn.

"Looks like manna from heaven," Berman said, answering his own question. His heart beat a little faster and a sense of excitement quickened in the reptilian centers of his brain. Pia had come to see him, and it seemed her timing was immaculate. He was in the mood to celebrate, and he couldn't think of anyone he'd rather celebrate with than Pia Grazdani. He was going to make up for having passed out on the occasion of her previous visit.

PIA KEPT THE car horn pressed. She had planned on doing it for five minutes, and it was now approaching that point. Coming to Berman's house had been a sudden, impulsive decision born out of desperation and frustration. She had tried the same trick four days earlier without success, after failing in her attempt to get into her lab, but she thought things might be different tonight. She had no idea whether he was in Boulder or not, as he hadn't returned any of her calls, texts, or emails, just like Mariel, but Paul had said that he thought he was in town, thanks to a tip from a friend who worked in general aviation at the airport. The report was that at least the Nano jet had returned. Whether Berman had been on it was anybody's guess.

When she had first arrived at the gate at the base of his driveway, she'd been encouraged seeing lights in the distant house, even though that was no guarantee he was there, and even if there, that he'd be willing to see her. Nonetheless, she was going to be persistent, as Berman was her last shot. She knew it was unrealistic to hope to solve both her problems—her lack of access to her lab and her need for answers about what was going on behind the scenes at Nano. And Pia was realistic enough to understand that continuing her employment at Nano might well be an untenable proposition. But her desire to find out more still burned, and Berman was her only hope.

Pia had debated a long time about what to wear for this occasion, in case she actually got to see the missing CEO. Her black dress seemed inappropriate for an impromptu visit, even though it might be what Berman wanted to see. She thought it better to look casual, as if she were just dropping by. In the end, from her hardly extensive wardrobe, she picked a pair of skinny jeans and an embroidered, tailored black shirt that she thought flattered her athletic figure. Her hair looked reasonable pulled back in a ponytail that masked the six-week-old shaved spot. More bothersome were the gauntlet cast for her distal radial fracture and the sling for the break in her humerus, but there was nothing to be done about them until the following Wednesday, when they were scheduled to come off.

Suddenly the massive wrought-iron gate shuddered, and then with a screech of metal on metal it began to swing open. Pia let up on the horn, allowing the nightscape to return in a rush to its previous silence. Pia's ears were ringing from the harsh clamor. For a second she hesitated. Not fully recuperated from her accident, she knew she wasn't in fighting form and therefore felt more vulnerable. But her determination trumped any reservations. She put the car in gear, passed through the gate, and motored up the long serpentine drive.

Pia parked in the cobblestone turnaround at the base of the stairs leading up to the house, as she had done on both her previous visits. She put the camera strap over her shoulder and let the camera rest in the small of her back. She started up the stairs. As she topped the last step, the door opened, and Berman stood at the threshold. He was dressed surprisingly similar to her in jeans and a dark cowboy-style shirt with snaps instead of buttons. His feet were bare. His lips were pressed together in a self-satisfied smile.

"Well, well. Hello, stranger."

"Hi." Pia winced but gave Berman a coy wave with her free hand. She realized she was very nervous.

"You're waving, that's nice. It's a different gesture from the one you gave me a few days ago."

"What?" said Pia before she remembered that on her previous, unsuccessful visit she had flipped off the camera.

"Oh, yes. Sorry. I was frustrated. I was gesturing at the world in general rather than you in particular."

"You were frustrated that I wasn't here?"

"Well, yes," said Pia. Berman was making it all about him, as usual, and Pia played along.

"There was a lot I wanted to talk to you about, and no one at Nano was returning my calls or emails, including you."

"Whitney and Mariel thought it best," said Berman. "But now you are here. Do you want to come in? As you said, we have unfinished business together." He laughed before stepping aside to give Pia room. Pia sensed he winked at her, but it was out of the corner of her eye as he moved to the side. Was he that brazen?

"Yes, I would like to come in," Pia said. "Thank you." It was all she could do to keep from rolling her eyes at the possible wink, knowing he had a completely different take on what she meant by unfinished business. Did his BS actually work on women? "I know it's late but I was up in the foothills taking photos of wildflowers." She hefted the camera and stepped past him. "I was driving by and I just thought I'd see if your lights were on. Hope you don't mind. I wanted to ask you why I can't get into my lab."

"Mind? I'm thrilled." Berman closed the door behind Pia before he strode into the depths of his home.

Pia followed into the living room. She noticed that the door to the den was closed when she passed. Otherwise the place looked as it did the last time she'd been there. As it was with her own apartment and despite all the home's accoutrements, in general it had a decidedly impersonal atmosphere except for the den.

"First, let me get you a drink," said Berman, smiling. "I should be a good host."

"Maybe a single glass of wine, thank you. I don't want a repeat of what happened last time I was here."

"Yes, you're right. But I will have a proper drink just the same. I have a lot to celebrate, but believe me, there's not going to be a repeat."

"What are you celebrating?" said Pia, but Berman had retreated into the kitchen to fix the drinks. Pia breathed deeply in and out. She needed to keep her nerve. Berman returned with a glass of what looked liked neat scotch and a glass of white wine. Tucked under his arm was the white wine bottle wrapped in a cloth napkin.

"This okay? It's a Pinot Grigio. I rather like it, although I don't drink a lot of wine, except with meals. Will it do?"

Pia nodded and took the glass. She intended to drink very little, so it didn't matter what it was.

Berman directed Pia to one of the living room's oversized couches. He took a neighboring matching club chair.

Pia shifted the camera around so that it was by her side. The strap was still over her shoulder. She wondered how she was going to get around to taking pictures of the man.

"So you say you can't get into your lab. Well, I understood you were asked to wait for a medical evaluation."

"Mariel called me while I was still in the hospital and told me not to come back to Nano until I was fully recuperated, which I believe, for all intents and purposes, I am even if I still have a cast and a sling. By the way, I heard you came to visit me in the hospital, and Jason Rodriguez came one time as well. Thank you. But you didn't return, and nor did Jason."

"I've been doing a lot of business travel lately. Funding issues are coming to a head, and I've been away far more than I've been here. I checked that you were doing well. If there had been any complications, I would have been there."

"As far as my medical bills are concerned, they have all been paid, or so I've been told, and I have to assume that is Nano's doing. This past Wednesday I tried to go back to my lab just to check things out, but I couldn't get in. My clearance had been 'revoked,' according to security. It was after that incident that I came looking for you here. I was a good employee. I *am* a good employee, and I think I deserve better treatment."

"I'm sure you do, Pia," said Berman. His face was noncommittal.

"You're sure I deserve better treatment, or you're sure I think I do? Which is it, because there's a big difference."

"Okay, Pia." Berman leaned forward in his leather chair. "Of course you deserve better, but Nano demands the highest standards of discretion from its employees, as we made clear on many occasions. Security is our biggest concern here at Nano, as it is in all nanotechnology companies. Competition is fierce, as you know. Billions of dollars are at stake. We are averse to publicity, particularly negative publicity, on all accounts."

"When was I not discreet?"

"When you went with that ER doctor after the van from Nano

containing the cyclist. To do what, I have no idea, but it is obvious you had in mind to intercept it."

"Ah, so you did know where we were going." Pia's tone had risen. Berman seemed to be admitting something important. Had she been under surveillance?

"I didn't say that we knew. But you admit you were chasing after Nano employees going about Nano business that had nothing to do with you or the Boulder Memorial Hospital. We pieced together what happened after the accident. The radio conversations with the EMTs in the ambulance, the phone call to you from Dr. Caldwell from the Memorial's ER . . ."

"How did you know the ER doctor and I were trying to intercept the van with the cyclist?"

". . . the story you and your doctor friend are trying to concoct about Nano's involvement in causing your accident. Good grief, woman!"

Pia stopped trying to talk above Berman.

"You haven't exactly been discreet, have you?" he said.

"You're admitting to a lot of things here . . ." said Pia. Berman was being transparent, and Pia found it hard to know how to respond. She expected more lies and evasions.

"I'm admitting to nothing. Someone overheard Dr. Caldwell call you from the ER. Your statement to the Boulder police about the accident is in the public record as well as his. You later accosted a Nano employee in the parking lot who had been warned not to talk with you . . ."

"I talked to Jason Rodriguez. He was my colleague. And I thought he was my friend, but obviously I was mistaken."

"Pia, I am the best friend you have right now, believe me. Mariel Spallek wanted to—"

"Wanted to what?"

"Pia, please calm down. And sit down." Pia had gotten up from the couch and was pacing around the room, furious with Berman's calm and calculated indictments. The camera was dangling from its strap over her shoulder, forgotten.

"Listen. Look at it from my point of view, from Nano's point of view. All of this behavior I have just outlined, which started, by the way, because of your unfortunate discovery of a Nano jogger who had been in momentary distress."

"Momentary distress! The man was in cardiac arrest when I came upon him."

"Impossible. The man is perfectly fine, I'm happy to report, and back to full participation in his duties here at Nano. You were mistaken about his condition, I assure you. And you were specifically asked to forget about the incident. Obviously you didn't take that advice. I'm sorry, Pia. Yes, you have been a good worker and have definitely contributed to Nano's primary project as well as everything else that is being done to support it. But you haven't been cooperative, especially with your outrageous suggestions that Nano had something to do with your unfortunate accident while recklessly speeding. And now, on top of all that, I have you on security tape, showing up at my home uninvited, making lewd gestures."

"Oh, come on. That was purely out of frustration. Childish, maybe, but certainly understandable."

"I'm not convinced everyone would find your behavior understandable. That doesn't sound like much of a defense to me."

Pia sat down, deflated, and bit her lip. What now? "So you told people not to call me back?"

"Mariel insisted that I terminate your employment, although she's not really in a position to insist, but I preferred to leave a door open. I was going to request the medical letter that had been asked for, stating you had totally recovered, and then talk to you myself. But you've jumped the gun, and here we are."

"And what were you going to talk to me about?"

"I thought we could have an adult conversation, man to woman."

Berman winked and smiled again, reminding Pia what kind of an individual she was dealing with. She looked off, tempted to flee, but remained seated. He had said man to woman, not CEO to employee, which said it all.

"I had in mind a conversation like we are having now," Berman continued after taking a sip of his drink. "What I am hoping is that you will see fit to change from a kind of dangerous maverick and security risk into a team player. Personally I'd like to keep you aboard."

"What's going on at Nano?" Pia blurted. "Who are these runners and cyclists who are falling down in the road and appear to be dead? Why can't I get past those double doors on the fourth floor? That's the adult conversation I want to have."

"Oh, Pia. Nothing's happening at Nano that isn't happening at the top nanotechnology research facilities all around the world. It would be naive to think otherwise. We're all pushing the envelope. What's different is that we have a small jump on the competition because of our lead in molecular manufacturing. We've been able to move from theory to reality with nanorobots. But we have to be discreet, as I said, because the competition could catch up to us in a heartbeat. We have tried to patent our breakthroughs with molecular manufacturing, but it is difficult. It is based on the way ribosomes of living cells function, which the good Lord has ingeniously devised. As it is in the public realm, we can't totally protect it, although we have certainly tried."

"I'm sorry, but I need to know more. I need to be sure these people are not being abused."

"Oh, Pia!" Berman repeated, as if talking to a child. "No one is being abused, trust me. Everything is totally voluntary. We rely on employing talented people who are content to work in their area and not concern themselves with . . . other matters. We call it compartmentalization. There are only a very few who know everything. As I said, I want to keep you around, but if you feel you need to know what's going on behind every door in the whole place, I don't think it's going to work. We'll come to an agreement on a settlement of your contract, a very generous settlement. Of course there will be some restrictions on your being able to work for another nanotechnology company for a reasonable period of time. You don't know everything going on at Nano, but you know enough about our most important project. Leaving Nano will give you a chance to finish your medical training somewhere else."

Berman took a healthy draft of his scotch, finishing the glass. It was his first of the day, so he wasn't concerned. He played his hand pretty much the same way with Whitney way back when, and now it was time for what he had said to sink into Pia's brain.

He stood and walked to the den, only to quickly emerge, stirring a fresh drink. He looked at Pia, and within, his ardor was unrestrained. Berman knew he shouldn't be talking to Pia at all. Mariel was right—Pia was very intelligent, very nosy, very persistent, and very dangerous. Berman knew he couldn't trust Pia, but he couldn't abide the idea of losing her, whether by firing her or by some more drastic arrangement that would scare her off completely. He wanted to have her, to possess her until he tired of her. He was a man used to succeeding in all areas of his life, and vain enough to think he could have what he wanted. And he wanted Pia with all his damaged soul. He thought he was making progress, but she hadn't budged. She was still sitting on his couch, looking sexier than ever, despite the cast and the sling. He wanted to see her dance again and then have wild sex. His imagination led him off to that wonderful place.

On her part, Pia was pretty sure she had Berman figured out. He was rich and sophisticated, as if that made a difference, and he controlled a large and apparently thriving company that had some curious relationship with the Chinese, probably for capital in exchange for proprietary secrets. Nano had its share of secrets, and she knew China was sitting on an ungodly amount of foreign exchange. He obviously thought he was special and entitled, and could engage in these games with her as he probably had with many women. He had all but admitted there was something going on at Nano that she shouldn't know about. No, he *had* admitted it, but there he was, smiling smugly, lounging in his chair as if he were the king of the world. And behind that facade was just another horny guy hoping to get lucky.

In her relatively short life, Pia had had experience with plenty of men like him. Men obsessed with their own power who wanted to possess her in some way, even when they knew they shouldn't, either because they were in a position of trust and responsibility over her, or were her boss, as in this case, or, in the worst instance of all, related to her. Pia saw Berman as just another predator who wanted to misuse his power and have his way. Although she knew she was playing a dangerous game, she was intent to turn the tables to get what she wanted without succumbing to him.

41.

"How about a little more of the Pinot Grigio," Pia said, extending her empty glass in Berman's direction. They'd left the question of her future hanging. When Berman had disappeared into the den, Pia got rid of her glass of wine in the same manner she had with the scotch the last time she'd been to Berman's house: under the furniture. She wanted to play the tipsy role and thought it would be more convincing.

"Absolutely," Berman said, pleased with the request. Perhaps Pia was relenting. He got up with the bottle and filled her glass. As he finished topping it off, he smiled and Pia smiled back. After making it look as if she had taken a sizable drink of wine, Pia set her glass down on the cocktail napkin. She then hefted the camera and took off the lens cap. She stood up and pretended to have trouble with her balance.

Berman watched her antics with a slight smile but then his brows knit as she brought the single-lens reflex camera up to her face, peering through the viewfinder and aiming directly at him.

"Wait a second!" Berman said, reaching out with his hand and extending it toward the camera. "What are you doing?"

"I've been taking pictures all afternoon," Pia explained with a giggle. "I wanted to take a few more. I want to take some of you."

"Why?" Berman questioned. The fact of the matter was that he had a reflex aversion to being photographed. He'd been burned before by overzealous paparazzi. Cameras made him leery.

"You're a handsome man," Pia said.

"I don't like cameras."

"Oh, come on! Relax!" Pia lifted the camera back in position for her to see through the view finder. Berman's hand stayed in the middle of her field of vision. She lowered the camera. "Hey, it's digital. If you don't like it, it can be erased."

"Maybe later," Berman said. "Maybe we can take some photos of each other."

"Just a couple?"

"No! Sit down. Let's talk about your settlement."

Pia settled back into the couch, placing the camera next to her. The charade was going to have to be extended.

"Okay," Berman said, visibly relaxing. "Here's what I propose." He went on to outline the terms of a settlement for Pia, and it was very generous indeed. As he kept talking, Pia became confused.

"Wait, are you offering me a job?"

"Yes, it's a personal services contract, not with Nano but with me directly. Rather like the one Miss Jones signed when she started working for me. And she is, as you know, a very valued and well-compensated employee."

"You mentioned confidentiality agreements."

"Yes, of course. They're an integral part of the negotiation. You need to sign a confidentiality agreement that covers the nature of this conversation."

"You mean before we negotiate the details of the job."

"Yes, it's standard for top-level employees who work directly with me. And extremely watertight. I have one here for you to sign, as well as a contract."

"You have one ready for me?" Pia had noticed that when Berman had emerged from the den with his refreshed drink, he had been carrying several sheets of paper.

"Not exactly. As I said, it's standard. It's what I had drawn up for Whitney."

"Wait, you're going much too fast. What would I be doing for you?"

"Well, that would remain to be arranged. With certain employees, I prefer to secure their services under contract and then find the niche that they fit into. I know you will be a valued member of my staff, because of your scientific expertise and your other . . . talents."

"And what might those be?"

"I said that the lab might not be the best place for you to work, but I want to keep you around. I'd like to have you here and with me on some of my travels. You're very intelligent and perceptive and persuasive, and frankly I'd much rather have you working for me than against me. You'd be a great asset. Also I am very attracted to you, Pia. I think that is rather obvious, especially after that regrettable episode on your doorstep."

"So you want to get me under contract. How romantic."

"Come on, Pia, you came here voluntarily after nine o'clock at night. What was your idea for this evening? What did you think we were going to talk about? Or do? We're healthy adults."

Berman was speaking softly, leaning forward so that he was very close to Pia, who was sitting catty-corner on the couch.

Throwing caution to the wind, Pia stood and went to sit on the arm of Berman's chair and draped an arm over his shoulder. She put her mouth close to his ear and whispered.

"Just tell me you had nothing to do with my accident."

Berman tilted his head up and said softly, "I swear."

"You're a liar," Pia said abruptly, and gave Berman a sharp jab in the kidney with the arm she had had over his shoulder. She stood up and ran around the other side of the glass coffee table as Berman came after her.

"Come here you, little bitch," he roared. He was smiling broadly, enjoying the chase.

"What are you going to do, beat me up?"

"You hit me . . ."

Pia skipped around the furniture until she stood near the lobby. She held up her arm.

"That's nothing. Look at me. My arm is broken in two places, and I had broken ribs and had a head injury. And I lost my spleen."

"I had nothing to do with it," Berman said, raising his hands in mock surrender. He was laughing and, at the same time, pleading almost.

Pia knew she'd judged him correctly. He was most likely a physical coward who probably enjoyed inflicting pain. Berman reminded her of her despised uncle.

"Do you enjoy thinking about women being hurt?'

"No, Pia, believe me. Maybe I like to play a game or two, but it's always consensual and in good fun. Come on, Pia, you're torturing me."

"I know."

"Is it the money? I can offer you more money."

"Okay, offer me more money."

"I'll double the money."

"So write it down."

Berman scurried back to the desk and scratched on the contract with a pen. To Pia, he was weak, desperate, and pathetic. If he couldn't control an issue, he wanted to buy his way to a solution. Pia's confidence grew with her realization that she'd seized control of the situation.

"Let me see the number."

Berman handed her the contract.

"That's more like it. Now come here."

He walked toward her, and she pushed him back down into the club chair.

"Where do you keep your toys?"

"My toys?"

"You know what I mean. A man like you in this big house."

"In the bedroom. In the cupboard on the right next to the bed."

"Stay here."

Pia killed the lights in the living room and went up to Berman's bedroom. She found the cupboard and, indeed, as she suspected, it was full of sex toys, masks, and a coil of nylon rope and a lot of things she didn't recognize. She worked quickly before she lost her nerve. She found a blindfold and some handcuffs and took the rope, not exactly sure what she was going to do. Then she struggled out of her jeans and shirt, leaving on her panties and bra. She gathered up the sex paraphernalia along with her clothes and returned downstairs.

Berman's eyes opened wide when he saw her near nakedness and the booty from the cupboard in her free arm. "Don't you move!" Pia ordered as she dumped everything onto the couch except the rope.

"I haven't. What are you going to do to me?" Berman was good at role playing. He was transfixed by her activity and body, watching her every move.

"You'll see," she said. She stepped behind him, told him to lean forward, and to put his hands behind his back. He complied, trying to catch sight of her over his shoulder. With some difficulty with her cast, Pia managed to tie his hands, but not too well. She wanted him to be able to free himself but only after some effort. She then returned to face him and pushed him back into the chair. "I said you'll see. But I was lying." Pia slipped the blindfold over Berman's head. She then popped all the snaps on the front of Berman's shirt, exposing his chest and his admirably flat abdomen. "Is this what you like?"

She ran her hand down the contours in front of him stopping at his belt. She gave his belt a tug.

Berman groaned and shifted in his seat.

"What I'm trying to do here," Pia explained, "is give you a good premonition of what it is going to be like when I fully recover. I told you I have broken bones, so unfortunately we'll have to wait for the real thing, won't we."

"What are you talking about? I don't want to wait!"

Pia got the camera and, standing directly in front of Berman, made sure it was in focus. She then reached out, pulled off the blindfold, and snapped a rapid series of photos of his face with his eyes thrown completely open in surprise.

"What the hell!" he shouted.

"Perfect," Pia said. "These will go well with my wildflowers."

"I told you I don't like having my picture taken," he said.

"You said you didn't like cameras," Pia corrected him. Quickly she replaced the blindfold before Berman knew what was happening. He shook his head violently in an attempt to get rid of it.

"Hey. Take this thing off!"

"Sorry," Pia said. She took another picture of Berman with the blindfold in place, and then quickly retrieved her clothes and the camera lens cover.

"What are you doing now?" Berman demanded as he struggled to free his hands.

"You have to wait for next time. I want to be fully healthy. And in case you are interested, I wanted to have a few photos in my possession just so you don't hold all the cards, Mr. Berman. I assure you that they are for my use only."

Berman struggled to his feet and then buried his head in the chair in an attempt to dislodge the blindfold.

Pia grabbed the contract from the table and ran to the front door, carrying her clothes. She didn't want to be there when Berman got himself free. Nor did she bother to put on her clothes when she got down to her car, not wanting to take the time. She didn't know if Berman could remotely keep the gate closed at the base of his drive-way, but she assumed so and didn't want to take the chance of being caught on his grounds. When the gate opened as she approached it, she felt a great sense of relief. As she drove away on the county road, she suspected there would be some consequences to what she'd done, but at least she had the photos.

42.

The first thing Pia did when she got home was take a quick shower to get Berman's scent off of her. Then she uploaded the pictures from the camera onto her computer and found that the shot of Berman could not have been any better. With the shock of the blindfold coming off and the flash of the camera, his eyes were fully open. Pia could see white sclera all 360 degrees around the iris. And the focus was so sharp it practically looked three dimensional. It was a better picture than the one of her own eyes, and that had worked well.

As she had done with her own photo, Pia enlarged the eyes to life size, then transferred the image to her iPhone. She worked fast, maintaining the intensity that had a hold on her since she ran out of Berman's house. She'd never bothered to dress even when she pulled up to her apartment in her complex. No one was around at the time, as it was almost midnight, and she just ran in, carrying the camera and her clothes.

She hadn't stopped moving since. Now she prepared to go to Nano immediately. She found her lab coat where it had been hanging for over six weeks and her ID, then tied her hair back in a ponytail before returning to her car. On the way to Nano, she ran down a checklist in her head. She knew she needed a lot of luck if it all was to work, and the closer she got, the more nervous she became. The confidence she'd felt back at her apartment melted away. The only thing in her favor was her familiarity with the graveyard-shift security staff from having interacted with them so often, probably more than anyone else on the scientific staff, coming in as often as she did on off hours. She was betting on the fact that they hadn't seen her in over a month wouldn't arouse any suspicions. In the past there had often been equivalent intervals. Still, the closer she got the more nervous she became. There were lots of reasons why what she was about to attempt might not work.

By the time Pia pulled up to the gate, she was shaking. She bit her lip as she handed over her ID to the guard. To Pia's delight, the man merely glanced at it before handing it back. He touched the peak of his hat in a kind of salute before saying "Evening, madam" and raising the gate.

Getting through the gate as easy as she did buoyed Pia's spirits, even though what was ahead was going to be more of a test. At the same time she was reasonably certain she would recognize at least one of the security people, and he would recognize her. She had frequently chatted with the guards when she was leaving and they often teased her about being so committed. She hoped that familiarity would mean they wouldn't watch her too closely.

Pia parked and walked as confidently as she could to the entrance. Two guards were on duty. One, Russ, she recognized, but the other was a much younger man she didn't know. She guessed he was new.

"Hello, Dr. Grazdani, long time no see," said Russ. "Sorry to hear about your accident."

"Yes, hi, Russ. I'm back." Pia groaned inwardly.

Russ had been on duty when Pia had gained entry using the picture of her own eyes. Pia looked over at the reception desk, and was relieved to see that no one was sitting by the computer. Pia worried that a guard stationed there might see that the system was admitting Zachary Berman, CEO, and not this woman no one had seen for more than a month. But if she couldn't get in, it didn't matter who was sitting where. Pia switched her attention to Russ, but he was back talking to his youthful colleague and paying her no mind.

Pia whipped out the cell phone and without looking back placed the image of Berman's eyes in front of her own. There was a reassuring beep. A green light flashed. It worked the first time. Pia swung open the glass door and was about to march through.

"Dr. Grazdani."

It was Russ.

"Yes," said Pia, knowing there was nowhere to run to.

"Welcome back."

"Thank you, Russ," said Pia. "It's nice to be back."

Pia scuttled away, slapped the elevator call button impatiently, and boarded the moment the doors opened. The whole time she was worried she'd hear her name being called out a second time. She breathed a sigh of relief when the doors closed and the elevator began its smooth ascent. Once she arrived on the fourth floor, she wasted no time walking down to her lab. Again she used the phone trick and again the scanner cooperated. A moment later she was in her lab.

Although she was tempted to wander around to look at the experiments under way and get a sense of what was going on with the mammalian experiments, she felt she didn't have the time. Berman might well be madder than hell, as well as sexually frustrated, and possibly might react by making her persona non grata. She doubted it, knowing what she did about the man, but she couldn't be sure and wanted to get in as much searching around Nano as she could in case it was the last time she would be able to get in the facility.

Knowing that there were security cameras all over Nano, Pia understood she couldn't just wander around in her lab coat and jeans, looking out of place. Many employees wore scrubs, as in a teaching hospital, and she wanted at least that much anonymity. Pia found a set in Mariel's office that were a bit too large but she put them on anyway, topping off her disguise with a surgical mask and a hood.

A FEW MILES AWAY, on a bedside table in an upscale apartment, a cell phone trilled. A text was delivered. A couple of minutes later, the phone sounded again, and this time a hand reached out from under the bedclothes and picked up the phone to check it. Whitney Jones was irritated at having forgotten to mute the phone when she'd turned out the light. The fact that it had rung wasn't unusual. Her phone number was linked to numerous systems across the whole company that alerted her to certain people's movements, but the only person who really mattered was Berman, and if he wanted to reach her, he could use the house phone, which he did on a regular basis. Sometimes it was for the most trivial of reasons, including that he couldn't sleep.

Whitney looked at the screen. There were two texts: The first informed her that Zachary Berman had entered Nano at 2:05 A.M., then, at 2:08, he had gone into one of the labs on the fourth floor. Whitney sighed. There was nothing unusual about Berman showing up at Nano at any hour of the day or night, but she wondered sleepily why he wanted to visit that particular lab. She shrugged and put the phone back on her night table. Quickly, she fell back asleep before she was able to speculate any further.

FULLY ATTIRED IN SCRUBS, Pia headed for the door to the hallway. The lab was much as she had left it, with the same banks of equipment she had spent hours and days and months poring over. She wondered for a second who worked there now, but quickly discarded the thought. She had no time to reminisce; there was work to be done. What she did notice were banks of mice cages.

Leaving the relative safety of her familiar lab, Pia stepped out into the corridor. Her plan was to head down to the doors leading to the bridge that she had tried to go through unsuccessfully on several previous occasions. They were the doors from which Mariel always emerged whenever she had been off doing whatever it was she did elsewhere in the complex.

As Pia approached the doors she began to wonder what she might find. There were other buildings in the Nano complex, but the one to which she was headed seemed to hold the most promise. It was close to the building that housed most of the biotech labs, and it was physically connected. If there was an infirmary on the grounds, it most likely was there.

Pia tried to walk at a normal pace. She didn't want to appear in a hurry, nor did she want to look as if she didn't know where she was going. As she approached the door, she cupped the iPhone in her hand in an attempt to make it less obvious and made sure the photo of Berman's eyes was on the screen. Pia brought the phone up along the right side of her head. To the left, on the ceiling, was what looked like a security camera: a small, inverted, dark brown plastic bowl. Stepping up to the scanner, Pia moved the phone in front of her eyes. As soon as she heard the telltale beep, she quickly lowered the phone and slipped it into the pocket of her scrub pants. The light flashed green. The door clicked. She was through.

Once again, Pia's heart was pounding, now with a mixture of fear and anticipation. But on the other side of the storied doors the corridor looked exactly the same as it did on the near side: brightly lit with white walls and white composite floor. To Pia it didn't even look like she was on a bridge connecting the two buildings. But after walking fifty feet or so, she guessed she had passed into the new building, and that knowledge lent the sterile corridor a sinister feel. There were a few blank doors but no signs or numbers. Above were occasional inverted plasic half spheres, probably cameras. She passed a bank of elevators on her left with oversized doors.

Suddenly, she saw someone walking along the corridor toward her, a man, judging by his size, but with his face concealed behind a surgical mask like hers. He was carrying a modern-looking white valise that blended with the environment. Pia's heart skipped a beat as he glanced in her direction as they closed on each other. At about ten feet of her, he nodded slightly before looking forward in the direction he was headed. Pia nodded back and kept walking. They passed without a word like two ships in the night.

Pia let out a breath. Holding it in had been instinct. Of course there were to be people around, she reasoned, as well as other people possibly following her on TV monitors. She had to expect as much. She had to stay calm and continue walking. But where was she going? She passed several doors with iris scanners. Which ones should she enter? She assumed she was on the fourth floor as the bridge came from the fourth floor of the biotech building. But she couldn't be sure. In theory, the idea of exploring the building seemed straightforward. In reality it was anything but.

The corridor took a left-hand turn and soon reached an intersection. Lines painted on the floor pointed in opposite directions: green to the left, and red the right. Which one to take? In either direction, the way ahead looked the same: more corridor. *Green for go*, thought Pia, but then changed her mind and went the other way, turning right. After what seemed a hundred feet, there was another left-hand turn, and then in front of Pia, past an unmanned guard station, was a set of heavy, large double doors with an iris scanner set in the wall to the side. Whatever passed through these doors had to be big.

Pia still didn't know what she was looking for, but her intuition told her she had stumbled onto something. For the fourth time that night, she flashed her iPhone over the scanner and waited for the green light. When it came on, she opened one of the doors and walked in. When she saw what the room contained, Pia's eyes bulged and she swallowed hard. "Oh, my God," she said in a stunned whisper.

WHEN WHITNEY JONES'S PHONE woke her for the second time, she saw it was Berman again, moving around the Nano complex. Good grief! Now he was in the main room inside the inner sanctum, so only the hardwired devices like the iris scanners would be able to communicate with the outside world. If she could, she would have called Berman to find out if everything was hunky-dory and ask what was making him wander all over creation. She decided to send a text that would be waiting for him when he got back outside the infirmary building.

"What's up?" she typed. "Everything ok? Don't forget London calls at 8 am ur time."

Putting her phone back down, Whitney cursed before rolling over. She worried that she might have trouble going back to sleep.

43.

Pia stood in front of a large, almost ten-foot-high glass tank full of liquid. At her eye level, suspended upright in the liquid, was the body of a man, or, more accurately, two-thirds of the body of a man. He looked Chinese or Asian. The man's brain was entirely exposed, and over his mouth was a tight-fitting mask, like a piece of scuba equipment. His eyes were open, staring blankly ahead. Pia could see that the chest had been opened and a portion of the wall cut away to expose the inflating and deflating lung. One of the man's legs and one arm had been removed entirely, the stumps sealed tightly with a white material. On the remaining leg and arm, various muscles had been exposed, with electrodes inserted into particular muscle bundles.

The man was stationary, and to her horror, Pia could see what was holding him in place. He was anchored or impaled on a vertical pole that pierced his body in a cephalic-caudal axis, and also by various tubes that emanated from his body and disappeared into a number of sealed boxes on the floor. More lines ran from these boxes to the wall, where banks of signal lights were arranged in displays with a series of stopcocks. Pia looked at the lines more closely and could see that in one the red liquid was moving—it was bright red, oxygenated blood.

This half-man was alive, or mostly alive. And he was stuck on a spike like a butterfly collector's specimen.

Pia staggered back until she leaned against the wall. She looked around the warm, humid room and saw it was cavernous, with a high black ceiling with exposed piping and duct work. The light coming from above was dim and seemed to be ultraviolet with a decidedly blue cast. Most of the light in the room came from the tank, which was brightly lit from above like a kind of huge aquarium. Pia noticed that there were more of these tanks, maybe as many as ten, but couldn't see from where she was standing if they were all occupied. Most of them were.

There were people in the room, possibly lab workers or custodians, gowned with their faces covered with surgical masks. They stood about forty feet away, clustered around one of the aquarium-like tanks and were involved in a discussion. Pia couldn't hear their voices amid the deep-throated hum and bubbling of powerful pumps that dominated the environment. There were three, no, four individuals: it was hard for Pia to tell. One looked over and spotted Pia. Pia made it a point to walk over to a nearby countertop, where there was a clipboard. She picked it up and pretended to study it.

"Oh my God, oh my God, oh my God . . ." Pia said to herself under her breath. What the hell was going on here? In her mind Berman's comment only hours before kept replaying: "No one is being abused, trust me. Everything is totally voluntary." *Yeah, sure,* thought Pia. "These half-dissected people volunteered to be human physiological experiments." Pia's mind went back to the poor dogs they had used in the lab in medical school. That was sickening enough, but this?

"Volunteers?" Pia whispered. "My ass!"

A tank with a woman inside was lined up facing the first one, so that the two victims could look at each other Pia thought morbidly.

This female was submerged in liquid like the man in the first tank, and had obviously been partially dissected as well. Pia could also see a portion of her lungs expanding with each respiration. Pia shuddered. What she was seeing was far worse than her worst nightmare. These people were being kept in a semi-living state, artificially respired and monitored. But why?

The blood.

Pia looked at the tubes in each tank and saw blood leaving and entering both bodies. These individuals were being kept alive and their blood was being processed and analyzed. She looked more closely at the woman, and on her forearm, she saw tattooed numbers, much like the ones she had seen on the Chinese runner. She kicked herself for not following up on that lead at the time. For a moment she tried to imagine what the numbers meant, but instead her mind kept returning to the blood. If it was subject to so much attention in this room, Pia reasoned she should look at it herself. She now had a sneaking suspicion about what was going on, but she needed to prove it.

While pretending to look at the clipboard, Pia studied the room and the other workers. She could see they were wearing more protective clothing than she: full-barrier protection with gowns and booties as well as masks and hoods. Pia made sure she stood with a tank between her and the techs so that they couldn't see she was wearing street shoes and no gown over her scrubs. The lines carrying blood to and from the bodies pierced the huge containers and had ports, so Pia knew that if she found a syringe, she could draw a sample.

Halfway across the room Pia saw an equipment unit with all sorts of material, including beakers and other glassware, as well as tubing and, she presumed, syringes. But to reach them, she would have to walk toward the other workers. There was no chance they wouldn't see she wasn't properly attired and that she was out of place there. In short there was no chance, in her mind, that she wasn't going to be found out no matter what she did.

AFTER PIA HAD left his house. Zach Berman had barely moved. He didn't even untie himself immediately. He felt angry, humiliated, excited, unnerved, but mainly frustrated all at the same time. His anger came mostly from Pia's leaving and from her brazen willfulness in taking those photos after he had specifically warned her not to. Yet he wasn't truly worried that she had done it, after all, what could she possibly do with them? Pia seemed to think she had some ridiculous idea that having the photos would somehow work to her advantage. What was she going to do? Post a picture on a social media page? All it showed was him with his shirt off and a blindfold over his eyes. Big deal! It might be mildly embarrassing for a time, but most important it wouldn't have any effect on the Chinese dignitaries he was dealing with. They all had mistresses, and they all played around. In that regard they were more like the French.

What Berman was mostly thinking was what a woman she was! What a tease! She had taken him to the edge of something, and he wanted to go back, desperately, and be thrown over. His phone pinged, telling him he had a text, but what could be so important at that time of night? Berman had a sudden thought. Maybe she'd somehow gotten his private mobile number, and it was Pia texting him, continuing the evening's entertainment.

Quickly Berman extracted his hands from the slippery nylon rope, and pulled out his phone. Damn, it was from Whitney, reminding him of the calls he had to make that morning. How did she know he was still up? The woman needed to get a life, for God's sake. Berman tossed the phone onto the couch so recently occupied by Pia's delightful form. In his fantasy, she was coming back, and he slouched back in his chair and dreamed again about what he was going to do to her the next time he had an opportunity. She'd eluded him twice, first of his own accord and now of hers, but it wasn't going to happen again. A tease was fun, but there was a limit.

ABRUPTLY, TWO OF the lab technicians left the room, walking out through a second entrance on their side that Pia hadn't noticed before. The other two were preoccupied, apparently attending to a problem at the side of the aquarium structure, where they had been grouped. Quickly Pia took advantage of the situation and strode over to where the medical equipment was kept. She saw all manner of laboratory and medical paraphernalia, but where were the syringes? She opened a few drawers and found them. She grabbed three and went back to the first tank, nearest to the double doors through which she had entered the room.

A quick perusal of the port and Pia figured out where to attach the syringes. She plugged one into the line, toggled the stopcock, and drew a full syringe of blood, capped it, and quickly took two more. Hazarding a glance into the depths of the room, she noticed that a third tech had left. The remaining individual was still engrossed in whatever he or she was doing, so Pia pulled out her iPhone from her pocket, opened the camera app, switched off the flash, and quickly took a picture without raising the phone above the level of her hip.

Then Pia walked out of the room without looking back. Had she been seen? There must be cameras in there, she thought, but perhaps she didn't look suspicious. Still, if anyone compared the entry logs with her appearance, she didn't look much like Zachary Berman. She was afraid she didn't have a lot of time. As Pia walked, she tried to process exactly what she had just seen. They were living, human laboratory experiments, somehow being kept alive, their circulatory systems being run through banks of testing equipment. Pia stopped for a second and thought she was going to throw up. What Nano was doing was such a travesty of ethics that it was unspeakable. But she didn't have time to let herself become emotional. She gathered herself quickly. She had work to do.

As she retraced her steps back to her lab, Pia couldn't help but think of the Chinese runner she had helped take to the ER. Was that him back in that chamber of horror? If not him, it was someone like him, a tattooed person maintained in a fish tank for physiological experimentation. Berman had said there were things going on at Nano that were taking place at facilities like it all over the world. Did he mean that? What she had just seen? Again, she felt a momentary wave of nausea sweep over her, making her shudder.

When she reached the lab, Pia thought about calling the police right away, but she was still ruled by her significant distrust of authority. She was trespassing, and it would be easy for Nano security to prove she had faked her way in using fabricated ID. The authorities would get nowhere near that lab tonight, and Nano probably had some major contingency plan for emergencies. Maybe they could dismantle the whole setup or exchange the human bodies for some other animals if necessary. The more information Pia had, the better.

Pia needed to look at the blood. Her work at Nano had involved microbivores, but she knew Nano could easily have been making other nanorobots with the same nanomolecular manufacturing techniques the company had perfected. Having seen the bodies in the tanks, Pia wondered what else Nano might be making. Perhaps these were nightmarish versions of tests that normally would have been conducted on lab animals, but in their race to bring to market, maybe they were just skipping animal testing for reasons of expediency and going directly to humans.

Back in her lab, Pia subjected some of the blood to a gentle, selective centrifugation, utilizing a special kind of apheresis to separate the blood solids from the plasma and then the solids themselves. Pia knew the nanorobots could be converted to neutral buoyancy by ultrasound waves, which she had used on the sample prior to putting it in the centrifuge.

With the gentle centrifugation under way, Pia turned on the scan-

ning electron microscope to allow it to boot up. With that accomplished, and the remaining blood hidden in one of the many
refrigerators in the lab, Pia peeled off her scrub clothes. She had another thought. She had to test the Chinese jogger's blood that Paul
still had squirreled away. It made her task that much more hazard-
ous in that it would require leaving Nano and returning, but Pia knew
she had to do it. Whatever she might find in the blood of the dissected individual in the tank, she needed to know if it was in the jogger, too.

Leaving the lights on in the lab, Pia went back to the elevators
and descended to the lower level. As calmly as possible, she exited
through the glass partition and walked back across the lobby toward
the main exit. Russ was still on duty, reading a newspaper at the
empty reception desk.

"You done for the night, miss?"

"No, Russ. I'm coming right back."

44.

Like millions of other Americans. Paul Caldwell didn't have a landline in his apartment, relying solely on his cell phone for communication. When he was off, he was really off, so he never had night call like most other physicians. For Paul that meant that when he climbed into bed, the cell phone was switched off.

Pia had learned all this about Paul early on in their friendship. She knew that when he was off duty and away from the hospital, if she really wanted to get hold of him, she had to go to his apartment. If it happened to be after hours, she knew it meant getting him out of bed.

That information had been theoretical until now. Leaving Nano, Pia didn't bother trying to call Paul. Instead she drove directly to his apartment. Leaving her car running, she ran up to the front door of his building and leaned heavily on his intercom buzzer for a good minute before he answered.

"Who is it?" Paul asked, sleepily.

"Paul, it's Pia. I have to talk to you."

"Pia? Is that you? It's three-thirty in the morning, can't this wait?"

"No, it can't wait. If it could, I wouldn't be here."

"What's happening? Are you all right?"

"Paul, just let me in!"

Paul buzzed Pia in, and she ran up the three flight of stairs to his door.

"You have company?" she asked. She wanted to be sure.

"No. Only me." Paul held open the door dressed only in his boxers, his eyes half closed, and his hair askew. "What is it that can't wait?" He closed the door and stood in his foyer, looking pathetic.

"Where's the sample of blood? The blood from the Chinese runner."

"What? Why do you need that now?"

"Because I do. Where is it, Paul? I'm in a hurry."

"I can see that. The blood's at the hospital in the freezer of the refrigerator in the doctors' lounge. At least that's where I put it. Can't you sit down and tell me what's going on?"

"No, I can't, really. I don't have the time. I need to look at that blood. Look at it closely. You have to trust me, Paul. I know what I'm doing. If you get dressed, you can follow me in your car. We'll go to the hospital, and you'll get the sample and give it to me. Then you can be back here in your bed in thirty minutes or so. This can't wait for morning. By morning I might not be able to get back into my lab at Nano."

"I didn't think you could get in your lab now. What's changed?"

"I don't have time to explain. I've got to get back there right now. I've burned a couple of bridges, maybe all of them, but I have an idea of what's going on at Nano, what they didn't want me to know. Let's put it this way: it's worse than I ever suspected. Come on, Paul. A couple of hours from now I'll come back here and explain it all to you, provided I'm right."

Paul started to protest, but Pia was already gone, leaving his door ajar. He knew he could go back to bed, but he knew Pia would come right back and get him up again. He pulled on a pair of jeans and a

T-shirt, stepped into a pair of loafers and walked outside. Pia was sitting impatiently in her car with the engine running. Paul stepped up to the car, and Pia lowered the window.

"There's really no time for talking, Paul. If you get me the blood, I can be back here within the hour, and we'll have everything we need."

"Need for what?"

Pia's window rose, and Paul had no option. He got in his car and followed Pia to Boulder Memorial. All was quiet at the hospital, and they drove all the way up to the ER loading dock. Paul escorted Pia through the quiet ER to the staff lounge. It was the first time she had seen the ER without any patients waiting.

Without speaking, because one of the ER physicians was sleeping on the couch, Paul opened the fridge where the staff kept their packed lunches and reached into the back of the freezer compartment to retrieve a brown paper bag.

"You kept it in here?"

Paul shrugged. "No one ever cleans out the freezer. You had me paranoid about this after the other sample was lost, so I thought of here. Hiding in plain sight, sort of."

"But the blood's frozen. I need to look at it under a microscope."

"Yes, Pia, it's been in the freezer. I didn't know how long I was supposed to be keeping it. And I never imagined you'd need it at five minutes' notice in the middle of the night. "

"Okay, okay. You go home, and I'll be right over as soon as I can, okay?"

They quickly went back outside. Pia climbed back into her car, which she'd left running, but Paul kept her door from closing. "Do I have to worry about you? Where exactly are you going?"

"No, you don't have to worry. I'd love to tell you everything, but it would take too long to explain. I'll be back as soon as I can to your apartment to fill you in. Turn on your phone, and I'll call you, or I'll just ring your buzzer again. Whatever! Now let my door close!"

Pia's door slammed shut, and she backed up quickly and headed for the exit. Paul watched her go. She was a trip, that was for sure. *Headstrong* was not quite a forceful enough word for him to describe her. She could be exasperating, yet that was part of her charm. Paul found himself worrying about Pia, despite her protestations. He knew he wasn't going to fall back asleep until she showed up.

WHITNEY JONES OFTEN had trouble getting back to sleep once she'd been awoken. But when her cell phone had finally stopped informing her of Zachary Berman's movements, she'd fallen into a deep slumber. She'd heard the ping as Berman left the inner lab and, quickly, another as he apparently moved around the Nano complex. By the time the phone sounded again, when Pia exited the Nano bio-lab building, Jones was asleep.

But her rest was short-lived.

Now, as she woke again, she was irritated. Whitney snapped on the light to see what was going on this time. She wished she could just switch off the damn phone, but being apprised of her boss's movements was part of her job. Whitney got a glass of water from the kitchen faucet and sat at her counter. She saw that Zachary Berman had gone back into the Nano complex, just after four o'clock in the morning. But she knew he had just left—where had he been? What the hell was he doing?

Whitney scrolled back to her texts to see what her boss had said in reply to her query about what he was up to. But there was no text from Berman. She was momentarily confused, but then she realized that what she had assumed to be a text from Berman was the security system at Nano telling her that he had reentered the lab he had been in before. Why was he doing that? It didn't make sense.

Whitney saw that she'd missed another text as Berman left Nano. Whitney thrummed her fingers on the marble countertop. Berman hadn't responded to her text. That wasn't unprecedented, but it was unusual, given that he was so active at that time of night. She figured he must have seen his phone and just ignored her message. She could have taken that as an affront, but she had learned to know better.

The phone pinged as she held it in her hand. Now she was being told he was going back into that same lab in the common area at Nano for a second time. Why was he going in and out of that particular lab?

Whitney thought about the lab for a second, and then she remembered who had worked in it. Her mind raced with the possibilities that this realization presented her.

"Shit," she said quietly, and finally called Berman on his main house phone.

PIA LOOKED THROUGH the eyepieces of a high-power microscope to view the centrifuged blood from the submerged man. She backed up the objective and the field came into view. Just as she suspected, she saw a plethora of spheroid forms that looked for all intents and purposes like microbivores. Yet she doubted they were, because under the light microscope there was a cobalt bluish cast to the structures and the microbivores looked black. So far she felt her suspicions were vindicated. The blood from the submerged, dissected man contained billions of nanorobots of some sort.

Pia then moved over to the console of the scanning electron microscope. She had prepared a sample of the same blood and placed it into the specimen chamber and activated the vacuum pumps. There was now a complete vacuum, so she turned on the electron source. Sometime later she had an image on the monitor screen. She knew she was looking at nanorobots, and she knew they were definitely not microbivores. Microbivores were spheroid; the ones she was looking at were spherical. What kind of nanorobots they were, she had no idea. To get a better view, she upped the magnification to the order of 300,000 and waited for the scanning to take place. When it was finished, she brought it into focus.

Now she could see the nanorobots with much better clarity. She could not appreciate the blue cast that she had seen under the light microscope since the electron microscope image was only in black-and-white. What she could now see is that the nanorobots' surface, from the equator to about halfway up to the poles, was covered with what looked like nanoelectrical rotors. What they did, she had no idea.

Switching to the blood sample she had gotten from Paul, which was now thawed, Pia went through the same sequence. With the light microscope, she searched for any nanorobots. At first all she saw were blood cells, mostly red, but also some white. She searched for more than ten minutes and was about to give up when she found one of the bluish spheres. The Chinese runner had the nanorobots in his blood, just not as high a concentration, but their presence gave Pia the idea of what they might be.

When she had first arrived at Nano, and had done her due diligence in relations to nanorobots, she'd learned that Robert Freitas, the man who had originally designed the microbivores, had also designed a respirocyte, a nanorobot capable of carrying oxygen and carbon dioxide a thousand times more efficiently than a natural red blood cell. If Pia was forced to guess at that point what she was looking at, she would have said a respirocyte. The implications were obvious: Nano was using nanorobot artifical red blood cells prematurely in human subjects with disastrous results. The why she didn't even try to comprehend.

Knowing that she had accomplished all she could under the circumstances, Pia collected her samples and the extra blood and put it all into the brown paper bag she'd used to bring back the jogger's blood.

Pia powered down the equipment in the lab and checked her watch. It was now approaching five o'clock in the morning. She had wasted no time and was pleased she had not been interrupted. She wouldn't need to come back because she felt she had everything she needed to expose Nano and, in the process, Zachary Berman with her evidence of the vile, inhuman experiments that were going on. She had her proof: two blood samples from separate sources, one involving live and one mostly dead human subjects and hopefully one photo, which she had yet to look at.

Despite the reassuring quiet of the deserted lab, Pia knew she had taken a great risk leaving and then coming back to Nano, but she felt she had had to confirm the presence of the nanorobots in both blood samples.

Paul's involvement was the key. Without Paul, Pia's claims might possibly be written off as the desperate actions of a disgruntled employee who'd recently been terminated, or even a thwarted lover of the company boss, especially if she were to just disappear. Although she alone had seen the bodies in the tanks and was possibly easy to discredit, Paul Caldwell certainly could not be. He had been with Pia when the first blood sample was drawn, and he was a medical professional with an excellent reputation and credentials who could vouch that the blood had indeed come from the Chinese jogger. She had found out much more than she had expected that evening, and now that she had, she needed to act at once.

Pia texted Paul that she was on her way but didn't expect an answer, assuming he'd most likely gone back to sleep. Her plan was to return to his apartment regardless of whether he responded to her text. She'd just wake him up as she'd done earlier. Hurrying out of the lab, she descended to the reception area. As keyed up as she was, she had to force herself to walk at a normal pace. In the lobby it was the quietest time of the graveyard shift, and Russ must have been on a break, because only the younger, unfamiliar security guard was on duty. He merely nodded as Pia left. She only had to negotiate the parking lot, and she was home free.

The old Toyota started fine. At this point Pia was worried about every possible negative contingency. Without a problem she drove out of the lot and through the gate. There had been a moment of concern when the guard seemed to take longer than usual to raise the barrier, but he finally did, and Pia was able to pull out into the deserted county road. This was to be another careful ride, taken at just the speed limit, and she made sure that her seat belt was fastened. As excited as she was, she wanted no mistakes or lapses of appropriate judgment.

But then, despite her attention to detail and quite inexplicably, a police cruiser appeared in her rearview mirror. To her horror it came right up behind her, tailgating her. A moment later its emergency lights started flashing and the siren sounded once.

"Pull over, please!" said the metallic voice. Reluctantly she complied, wondering what on earth she could have done. She came to a stop, engine running.

What the hell? thought Pia. Perhaps she had a broken taillight, but she didn't think so. No one emerged from the cruiser. The question flashed through her mind if she should call 911, but she didn't. Then, two large SUVs pulled in behind the police car. Alarmed, Pia took her foot off the brake, but before she could move, another SUV sped up from the opposite direction, crossed from the other side of the road and stopped right in front of her, blocking her with its high beams directly in her face. Quickly, two men alighted from this SUV, one at either door. A third man apparently coming from behind rapped on her window, and then pulled open her door. He leaned down.

"Hello, Pia," said Zachary Berman. "Nice to see you again so soon. We need to talk." Berman held the door open for Pia, who saw no alternative to getting out of her car.

"I've already called the police," Pia said out of desperation. "You're just making it worse for yourself."

"As you can see, Pia, the police are already here. And they don't seem to be rushing to your aid. Ah, Miss Jones has arrived."

Whitney Jones walked up to where Pia was standing, and Pia felt slightly more at ease with the presence of another woman at the scene. Pia felt nothing violent was likely to happen with Whitney there.

"I'm sorry about this, Pia, I really am," said Jones, and before Pia could respond, Jones jabbed her through the sleeve of her shirt in the arm with a syringe and depressed the plunger.

One of the Nano security guards caught Pia before she fell unconscious to the ground.

45.

Thinking back over the course of their three-month friendship, Paul
Caldwell made a mental list of the number of times Pia had said
something along the lines of "I'll be right back," and then had not
followed through with her promise. Paul knew Pia could be unreli-
able. Often when they were on the phone, she'd say, "I'll call you
right back," and half the time, she didn't. A couple of times, Paul
had invited her to a drink with friends, and she said she was on her
way but then had changed her mind. It wasn't anything that irked
Paul about Pia particularly, it was just one element of her unique
and otherwise charming personality that he had learned to accept in
the face of her other, better qualities.

Paul had come to understand that the sensitivity to other people's
feelings that one might expect from a friend was not a strong point
for Pia due to her adult attachment disorder, which she'd admitted
to early on in their relationship. After she had confided in him, Paul
had made it a point to read about the condition, and the information
had made it easier to adjust to her quirks, such as her impulsiveness,
seeming lack of empathy, and resistance to trust. But Pia had never
been so insistent as when she raced out of the ER a few hours be-

fore, saying she'd be right over to his apartment. She'd even sent a
text saying she was on her way. Which was why Paul was worried
when she hadn't shown.

Paul had let Pia leave the ER without making any real effort to
stop her, which he now regretted. But on a number of occasions,
Pia had said she was going to do something when she clearly was
thinking of doing another, like seeing Berman or going into Nano,
as he was sure had happened in this case. Paul respected Pia's right
as an adult to take responsibility for her own actions, and he knew
she was going to follow through on a particular course of action
whether he approved or not. But still, the thought nagged at him,
what if?

Beyond that, the basic issue was that some five hours after she
had left, where was Pia? There was no answer when he tried her cell
phone.

If, as Paul surmised, Pia had left after picking up the blood sample, she may have run into trouble. There were three alternatives
Paul decided were plausible. The first was that perhaps Pia hadn't
gone into Nano at all—she had taken the sample somewhere else to
examine it and either hadn't had time to tell Paul where that was,
or for some reason decided not to. The problem with that idea was
that there weren't a lot of places where microscopes were available
at all, let alone at that time of day. The second alternative was that
Pia had gone about her business at Nano without incident and opted
not to return to Paul's apartment to wake him up for a second time,
and had gone home instead, turning off her own phone. Third and
most improbable was that she was still at Nano. First, Paul explored
the option that was easiest to check. Since he was not due at the ER
until late, he went out and got in his car and headed west.

When he reached Pia's apartment, he noticed that his parents'
Corolla wasn't in the parking lot. This wasn't conclusive proof that
Pia wasn't home, but it pointed in that direction. Undeterred, Paul

knocked on Pia's door a number of times, then retrieved the spare key from the top of the door frame. Paul had chided Pia for selecting such an obvious hiding place, but she reasoned that she owned nothing worth stealing, and it wasn't like there was any other convenient spot to hide a key. Besides, she told Paul that she always brought the key inside when she was home.

"Pia? Are you here?" As he called out her name, Paul half expected to hear a quiet fusillade of insults asking him what the hell he thought he was doing, but there was no sound. Pia wasn't in her bed, which didn't look as if it had been slept in, although with Pia, it was a little hard to tell. Housekeeping wasn't Pia's strong suit, and sometimes when she came home from Nano in the early-morning hours, she didn't bother to take off her clothes and just lay on top of the covers or on the couch.

The lack of possessions in Pia's apartment and the fact she kept little food there meant it would be hard to tell whether or not she'd been there recently. There never were any dishes in the sink; there never was a book open on a nightstand, because there was rarely any food, and no nightstand, and few books. A glance through Pia's clothing was of little use to Paul—there were garments he recognized, of course, but nothing he saw that was missing. Paul sat on the arm of Pia's couch and checked his phone again to see if he had missed a message from her. He hadn't.

What were his options? In his mind, Paul ran through the conversation he would have with the police if he called them. Yes, I last saw her maybe six hours ago. No, she's not technically missing. Why am I worried? Because I think she may have been caught at her place of employment, where she's currently not welcome. In fact she could have been considered a trespasser, meaning they might have called the police themselves. In that case, is there a Pia Grazdani possibly being held in custody?

Paul was not optimistic about such a call. If Pia had been arrested, and she had been allowed her famous phone call, the person she would call was him. As far as Paul knew, there was no family, and George was hundreds of miles away in California. Paul reasoned that he was there in Boulder and would know the circumstances. But there had been no call, from Pia or from anyone else.

All Paul could do was go home and wait.

46.

Whitney Jones wasn't helping Zach Berman's mood. With the muffled drone of the jet engines in the background, he went over the events of the last fifteen hours in his mind. Whitney was sitting in a seat across from him and openly glared at him from time to time. Berman felt duped by Pia, and made to look ridiculous. He was angry enough about it without having to be reminded by the look on his subordinate's face of how the whole Nano enterprise had been endangered because of his infatuation with one woman. "You idiot," said the look on Whitney's face.

But the more he thought about it, the more Berman was confident that his carefully laid plans and the countless hours of work and sacrifice over the years had been endangered, but not compromised. He went over every detail in his mind, looking for a loose end that remained, or a possibility that hadn't occurred to him that jeopardized everything. He had yet to find one.

Pia's penetration of what was called Nano's inner sanctum had initiated a hurried but detailed operation to rid Nano of all evidence of the vivisected bodies and to substitute dogs in the aquarium baths. It was something that had been planned for the near future anyway, since the physiological experiments that the bodies had been used for were already successfully completed. Berman also knew he was assisted by the fact that Pia was a remarkably private, secretive person, a lone wolf who had few long-term friends, save for George Wilson, who was way off in L.A. and, according to what Whitney had been able to find out, was kept at arm's length by Pia.

Berman had learned what he knew about Pia from the several times he'd had her followed by a local private investigator. From those reports he knew that the only possible problem was the ER doctor, Paul Caldwell. The head of Nano security agreed and considered Caldwell a potential difficulty, but as long as Pia had kept him in the dark, or neglected to tell him absolutely everything, which was assumed to be the case, then Caldwell was less of a threat alive than he was dead. One disappearance, that of Pia, would be relatively easy to explain considering her personality; but if a second person connected to the first went missing, too, then it became a pattern.

Berman was confident that Pia hadn't stored or transmitted the information she might have gleaned from the blood samples, that much seemed clear. There were a couple of photomicrographs in the scanning electron microscope, but no evidence that they had been transferred, uploaded, or copied. There was nothing in her laptop or on her iPhone other than the single, hurried picture of one of the tanks. She had sent one text to Caldwell and no emails. The photo was hardly a problem, because it wasn't possible to discern what was in the tank. Pia had told Caldwell she'd be right over but hadn't shown up. Again, it might present a minor issue, but he'd know she was gone soon enough.

As for hard evidence, Berman's security people had retrieved the blood Pia had collected from within Nano and the small sample from the Chinese jogger, and a viewing of the security recordings showed how much blood Pia had taken in the first place so that the amounts could be compared. Later, a discreet search of Boulder Me-

morial found no more hidden vials of blood anywhere in the ER—
the security tapes there had quickly been scrutinized as well.

Berman was not happy about the security failures that had afforded Pia access to Nano and his own regrettable and embarrassing
role in making them happen. It had taken Whitney Jones awhile, but
she had figured out how Pia had circumvented the iris scanners, assisted in her detective work by her knowledge that the system indicated that it was Zachary Berman himself who was moving around
inside the complex and not Pia Grazdani. Whitney was also the one
who found the images of Berman's eyes on Pia's iPhone. Whitney
was also the one who had shown the photos of Berman's eyes to the
embarrassed head of security. Jones told him to find new software
that would eliminate the future possibility of a two-dimensional
image that could fool the scanners.

Whitney had also left instructions that a security guard was to go
to Nano and swipe Pia's iPhone through the system twice more:
once in and once out, and he was to wait at least an hour from the
time that the Gulfstream was in the air before he did it. Whitney
thought that Pia had left behind the technology to dupe the system;
so why not use it to their advantage? The same guard was then to go
to Pia's apartment, leave a couple of items, and take some clothes
and destroy them back at Nano. One of the female employees was
driving the car Pia had been using east at that very moment, to be
abandoned somewhere remote with Pia's phone inside. Whitney was
securing alibis for Berman and herself, and leaving evidence that
suggested Pia had been home after being at Nano and had then
taken off, heading east to an unknown destination.

More than any of these matters, what Berman thought about
most in the hours of the flight to Europe was himself. He had been
fooled by this woman, and made to look laughably callow, but as she
lay unconscious in the back of the SUV on the way to the airport,
when he should have been furious, he found that he didn't desire
her any less. If anything, he wanted her more than ever. And he had

made a snap decision not to leave her fate up to the head of security
or even Whitney. He was still in control, and he wasn't done with
Pia Grazdani. Even before they had intercepted Pia leaving Nano,
Berman had phoned Jimmy Yan in China, where he was spending a
few days with his family before the semi-controlled chaos of the
athletics championships. Or at least that's where he said he was and
what he was doing.

Jimmy was calmness personified on the phone, and it reassured
Berman. In response to a specific question about privacy, Jimmy confirmed that he was speaking on a safe link as Berman himself was,
and that Berman could tell him exactly what had happened. When
Berman had finished with the saga about Pia, Jimmy was quiet for a
minute, and then told Berman what he had to do. Berman promised
Jimmy that he would personally deal with Pia, and that he was able
to leave immediately as requested.

Systems had been set in place for weeks in the event of the successful conclusion of the experimental phase of the relationship between Nano and Jimmy's higher-ups in the Chinese government.
Once the expected result in London was achieved, the first of the
new rounds of secure money transfers would take place, and China
would begin to receive access to the first of the equally secure Web
sites that contained thousands of pages of technical specifications
for some of Nano's proprietary secrets, mostly in the arena of molecular manufacturing, and even a number of its products. Jimmy
said that in two days he would pick up Berman at the airport and
take him to the house he described to him, and then ended the call.

Jimmy Yan's refusal to be rattled was comforting to Berman, but
he knew his friend would have some explaining to do if he chose to
mention these incidents to any of his superiors. Jimmy had alluded
to the politicking that took place inside the Chinese government
and had admitted that some individuals and factions disliked any
arrangement with foreigners in the West, especially Americans.
China could reach these technological goals on its own, it was ar-

gued. Yes, agreed Jimmy, of course China was capable of making such advances, but how long would it take? The opportunity was here, and they should seize it now with all the foreign reserves, particularly dollars, they were sitting on. And on top of that, they could get something else that they wanted almost as much: international athletic recognition to help make up for the loss of self-respect from having been subjected to centuries of abject colonialism by Western powers.

Berman turned his head away from the window and caught Whitney giving him the evil eye once again.

"Okay, okay! I screwed up," said Berman. "What do you want me to say?"

"I didn't say anything."

"You didn't have to, your face was doing the talking for you. I know what you are thinking: stupid Berman had to get involved with this woman. He couldn't keep away from her like some besotted teenager. Okay, I'm a guy with a weakness for beautiful women. I don't want to have to remind you of how you have personally benefited from my . . . interests."

"Zachary, I promise, I didn't say anything."

"So you said," said Berman. "Perhaps I need to talk it out for my own benefit. I'm confident Pia didn't tell anyone about anything she found, except possibly the ER doctor. She didn't have time. And if she had told the doctor, he would have rushed off to tell the police, which we know he hasn't done. Right now, he's sitting home in his apartment, and the only calls he's made have been to Pia's mobile phone. We know that for a fact. I predict he will go to work at three o'clock when he's expected and only start taking action if he hasn't heard from Pia when he gets off work, whatever ungodly time that might be."

"You're confident of that?"

"I am. You can't raise an alarm because a grown woman hasn't called you for a few hours. Can you imagine how flooded the switchboards would be? Even if it's a whole day, the police aren't going to do anything. And by then, we'll be in Jimmy's safe house."

"I think you're right," said Whitney. "I know we'll be fine." She was placated to some extent, but there was one huge mistake Berman had made, to her mind. If they were speaking frankly, she would bring it up.

"The only real problem is the woman." She nodded her head toward the back of the cabin. "What exactly do you have in mind?"

"So you have a problem with me bringing her like this?"

"Of course I have a problem. She's the weak link in all of this. She's caused this brouhaha, and she's still with us. She can ruin everything. If it had been up to me, she should have been left in the hands of the head of security. Ultimately he's the one to blame for all this by not keeping her out of Nano."

"Of course you know what would have happened to her if we had left her in his hands. You don't find that a problem?"

Whitney was quiet for a moment. She knew what would have happened, but she didn't want to think about it, like she had never wanted to think about the people in the Nano aquariums. She had been brought into Berman's vision, and her future was tied to his, she knew that. If he went down, she went down with him. But she did have her limits.

"Actually, no, I don't. I don't think about it. But the fact that she is here with us, that's a problem."

Whitney turned around and looked over her shoulder. Berman followed her line of sight, and there, as he was well aware, was Pia, unconscious and slumped back across two wide seats, her mouth open, her chest rising and falling in quiet, rhythmical breathing. She was handcuffed to the table in front of her, restrained like one of the many Chinese athletic prisoners who had traveled west on this plane.

"You bought her with us. She could ruin everything we've worked for. What are you going to do with her?"

"Well, that's what I've been thinking about," said Berman, and he smiled. "Her fate will depend on her willingness to become a team player. Maybe she could be your assistant."

"My assistant?" Whitney howled. "No, no, no! You're not going to saddle me with that willful bitch. I don't want to babysit your latest plaything, especially knowing you, you'll tire of her. She'll be hanging around my neck, and I don't have the time or the energy. Keeping you on track is enough of a job for me."

"Oh, come on! Whitney. Your job's gotten bigger and you need an assistant. She's intelligent and tenacious: a hard worker. You could use her."

"I don't know," Whitney said. She knew how much she owed Berman, and it was hard for her not to do his bidding. The trouble was she was reasonably certain the Pia business was going to end badly, and she didn't want to get to know the woman and then have to be involved with getting rid of her, really getting rid of her.

47.

Berman's body clock was shot. At two hours' notice, he had flown twelve hours from Boulder to Milan, then refueled, turned around, and flown back west, although the journey from Italy to Stansted Airport in the U.K., London's third airport, was much shorter.

Berman was very glad to have Jimmy Yan as his partner at this stage of his dealings with the Chinese government, as Jimmy was able to solve with ease and equanimity problems that might otherwise be intractable. Berman had established his own contacts airside at the Milan Linate airport with a general aviation enterprise, so coming and going discreetly had been no problem.

But now he had a piece of troublesome cargo he needed to get into the U.K., a country known to be more rigorous with import rules and regulations than the Italians. "No problem," said Jimmy, "I'll make your flight an official Chinese government one. No one will look at it. As for the cargo, a diplomatic pouch can be any size; just make sure the package is immobilized, and you can transport it in a large duffel bag. As for somewhere to stay, forget your West End hotel. What were you thinking anyway? The traffic in London is epically bad. The Chinese government has a house in the country

used for diplomats and diplomatic purposes that is much more convenient. And much safer."

Jimmy and his people had picked up Berman and his party and
driven them west from Stansted around London's orbital road, the
M25. Berman noticed signs for quaint-sounding towns such as Pot-
ters Bar, Frogmore, and Chorleywood, which was where they got off
the M25. They quickly decamped in a place he was told was called
Chenies—pronounced "Cheney's," as if it belonged to the former
USA vice president—in the county of Buckinghamshire.

Jimmy had been very quiet on the ride in the large, black limou-
sine, only to tell Berman that he and his countrymen generally traveled by Mercedes station wagons and vans in the U.K. because SUVs
stood out so much. With gas at $10 a gallon, only those with money
to burn, almost literally, drove an SUV. He said that the Chinese
delegation preferred to be more discreet.

Now Berman was sitting in the kitchen of a large, old stone house
in this tiny village, looking out over a well-tended lawn and picture-
perfect English garden surrounded by a sunk fence. He had noticed
the massive iron gates, the numerous cameras and guards that represented the visual security. Although Jimmy had said something
about diplomats, Berman thought that he was probably in a government safe house, perhaps belonging to the Guoanbu, the Ministry of
State Security, China's version of the CIA. Berman knew better
than to ask which host he should send a thank-you gift to.

"How is the tea?" asked Jimmy, who had made Berman a brew in
a mug adorned with the logo of the BBC.

"The tea is excellent, thank you."

"I have gained respect for the English way of making tea," said
Jimmy. "I take it strong, with milk and sugar. And the water must
be hot, but past boiling. No tepid cups of water with a tea bag on
the side, like in your country. That's an abomination."

"The tea is very restorative," said Berman, who felt that he needed more than a cup of tea to get back to a semblance of normality. "Where did you take her?"

"One good thing about English houses is that the old ones, like this one, have generous cellars. We have converted the one here so we can accommodate the occasional guest, particularly those who are, as we say, detained."

"How convenient," said Berman lightly.

Jimmy smashed his hand down on the table, and Berman's hand jumped, sending hot tea over his knuckles. Berman had never seen Jimmy lose his temper. It shocked him.

"This is not a time to be flippant. I am taking risks for you doing this. Big risks. There is no place more treacherous than a house full of spies, which is what this is in actuality. So we took her down there and only a couple of people know it. How would I explain this woman to my superiors? How would I explain how your mind is controlled by your libido like a teenager?"

"But you said I should bring her. It was your idea." Berman was momentarily taken aback.

"My desire would be for her not to exist at all, but she does. I realized that she could not be made to disappear adequately in Colorado, not with the resources that are available and with the bothersome independence of your police. Most of them, anyway. This problem must be contained. We are so close to fruition. I don't want our collaboration to be jeopardized." Jimmy looked pointedly at Berman. "So I will take care of things myself."

"Look, Jimmy, I have unfinished business—"

"You are a foolish man. There are millions of women available."

"Not like her," said Berman, and he could see Jimmy relax slightly.

"Look, I know that powerful men have such weaknesses," said Jimmy with a sigh of resignation. "I have a couple myself, as do all my superiors. We know how to handle this kind of situation. So we will handle this rationally. The precautions you have made are good ones.

There is nothing to connect this woman with this property, which is the important thing at this time. And you will keep her quiet."

"Whitney Jones is making sure of that. The woman is out cold and will continue to be sedated in the near future. All I want is a chance to convince her to join the team."

Berman looked at his watch. By his reckoning, it was eleven P.M. in Colorado, and Paul Caldwell would be due to come off his shift. *How long before he raised the alarm?* Berman wondered.

48.

Paul Caldwell had stayed at work at the hospital for more than an hour after his shift was due to end. He was exhausted, and gripped with anxiety about Pia, but there were hospital cases he couldn't abandon, even under these circumstances. It had been twenty-two hours since Pia had left his sight without getting in touch with him, and by the time Paul drove back to Pia's apartment, he was convinced something had happened to her.

Once more, he rang her bell, even banged on the door in frustration, and called her name. As he waited, a door down the hall opened a sliver and an elderly woman's voice called out.

"Do you mind, young man? It's very late."

"Excuse me, I apologize. May I have a word?" Paul walked toward the voice, and heard the chain going on the door. "I'm a doctor."

"I can see that," said the woman. She had mostly closed the door, exposing only a three-inch vertical slice of her face and one eye. "It's the coat. It's the only reason I haven't shut the door. What do you want with that young woman? I think I have seen you before. Is she your girlfriend?"

"She's a friend. I'm worried about her. I haven't seen her in a couple of days."

"I have seen you here before. You're only the third man I've seen visit her. Another one tried to visit her, but she wouldn't let him. I was about to call the police. She doesn't know I've seen people, but I have. I mean, I don't see everybody, but I see a lot."

"Look, madam, may I come in?"

"You may not. I saw her last night around this time. I don't sleep too well at night, and I hear things like with you coming here now. She came home just about this time, and she was carrying her clothes."

"Excuse me?" Paul said. He wasn't sure he'd heard correctly. "She was carrying her clothes. You mean she was naked?" That seemed hard to believe.

"No, she wasn't naked. For some reason she had on her under-garments and was holding her clothes. And a camera, I think. I saw her, but she didn't see me. I don't know if I should be telling you this or not."

"I'm glad you are. Did you see her again last night?"

"Yup. Wasn't too much after she'd come home that she went back out again. This time she had her clothes on and was in a hurry. I mean, I don't understand you young people, surely I don't."

"Did you see her after that?"

"No, I didn't."

"You didn't see her at all today or hear anything?"

"No, I didn't, but I sleep more in the day than during the night. I don't know why."

"Have you seen anyone else?"

"Yes. I saw you this morning. And a man who looked like a police officer was leaving the building earlier, but I don't know which apartment he was in. It's not like I stand here all day spying on people, you know."

"I'm sure you don't, madam."

"Well, if you're a friend, the key's on top of the door. But you know that already." And the door closed, indicating the conversation was over.

Paul checked the angle from the woman's door to Pia's and figured that she could see Pia's door only if she had her own door open
slightly, as she just had. It was likely she could miss someone coming
or going unless she spent the whole day peering out through the
crack in the door. If she heard a noise—and her hearing seemed reasonable—and she went to the peephole, she wouldn't be able to see
anything.

Which meant that Pia still might be inside.

Paul went back to Pia's door. Taking the key down, he opened up.
"Be here, Pia. Be here," he said quietly. But she wasn't.

She had been here, though. There were signs of life about the
place. A half-empty half-gallon carton of milk stood on the kitchen
counter next to a copy of the Monday's *Denver Post*. Paul went into
Pia's bedroom, and her chest of drawers was open and apparently
some of her clothes gone. He checked in the bathroom and there
was no toothbrush, although he couldn't swear there had been one
there earlier.

Paul digested the information he had gleaned. Pia had been here,
but why hadn't she been in touch? Was it so imperative that she
leave that she would do so without so much as a text? Paul thought
it unlikely. No, it wasn't unlikely, it was impossible. He looked at the
copy of the newspaper and the carton of milk. Did Pia drink milk?
He had never seen more than a pint of milk in the fridge, and there
was no new box of cereal to account for using so much. And a newspaper. To Paul's recollection, he had never seen Pia read a local
newspaper. And why buy one only to leave it behind, obviously un-
read? Paul tried to think like Pia would, first about the worst-case
scenario to explain a series of events. Someone had been here and
tried to make it look as if Pia had been here. Whoever was behind
this was trying to establish a timeline, and what better way to do
it than with a newspaper?

Continuing to think along those lines, Paul went over to Pia's
Mac and tapped on a key. The screen came to life, and showed an

open MapQuest Web page, with driving directions to a nanotechnology research laboratory in New Jersey. *That's a little too convenient*, thought Paul. But then again, in the absence of Pia herself to say otherwise, how else would anyone explain what he had found in the apartment?

Paul suddenly felt very uneasy, and he left Pia's apartment as quietly as he was able to, carefully replacing the spare key. He looked down the hall, but the old lady's door was closed. The thought went through his mind that if Pia was really gone and there was an investigation, would he be a suspect?

He sat in his car in the parking lot pondering his options. In the morning he would call the police, but he was pretty sure they wouldn't do anything. Before that, there was one call he could make and be sure of a quick response. He looked in his phone's contact list and found the number for George Wilson.

49.

It was a beautiful English midsummer's day. Zach Berman felt some-what better after his three-hour sleep, but he wanted to feel fresh air on his face. The interior of the vicarage was a warren of stale air, with corridors and passageways linking wings of the building. Most of the rooms, like his bedroom, were tiny, and all the ceilings were low. Running along the walls and framing doorways were massive wooden beams, some of which had been salvaged from British war-ships in the eighteenth century, according to Jimmy Yan.

The garden was lovely, with English summer flowers and a mani-cured lawn as flat as a green on a golf course. A game of croquet had been set up. In one of the distant, expansive lawns was a flock of sheep, which made the place resemble a nineteenth-century paint-ing. It was all terribly bucolic. It was as if the Chinese were playing the lord of the manor.

Berman walked around the house a couple of times and thought about what he might say to Pia and how to couch his argument. He knew it was going to be an uphill struggle, headstrong as she was and as self-righteous as he expected her to be. He could already hear her purported outrage. If the prize wasn't as important for him, he wouldn't bother to make the effort. From his perspective it was absolutely critical that she acted volitionally. Berman had never on principle paid for sex nor had he ever, in his mind, forced himself on a woman. His enjoyment depended as much on his partners' as on his own. What Berman wanted more than the physical rush was the boost to his self-esteem.

After his second circuit of the house, he stood in front, looking down on the village. He could see the village green in the center, with modest, storybook houses dotted around. They looked as if they had been molded from the landscape, as if they had grown rather than been built by human hands. In the middle distance a car was navigating a one-lane village road and kept disappearing behind the hedgerows. Beyond them, rows of golden wheat swayed in pocket-sized fields.

Berman was joined by Jimmy Yan.

"It's very pretty," said Jimmy, looking out at the scene.

"It is. And peaceful."

"Quite so. No one bothers us here; no one asks any questions; everything is quiet. We are careful to keep our traffic to a minimum."

The two men stood in silence for a moment. Jimmy turned slightly and indicated another large building to the west of where they were standing, almost obscured by a dense copse of trees.

"That is the manor house, built in 1460; a rather chaotic time in British history. We own that as well, but it has not been decided whether to renovate it. It will require a lot of money. It is ironic that we Chinese are here now buying such real estate after all the mischief we endured during the colonialism era. But it is a lovely building, and quite old. Of course, Chinese civilization is the most ancient of all, and I don't think much was happening in the culture of your country in 1460."

Actually, there was a lot going on in the North American continent before Columbus discovered the new world, thought Berman, but he didn't have the energy or inclination to engage in an academic debate with Jimmy Yan.

"So have you decided what to do with the girl?" Yan continued.

"I'm going over that in my head right now."

"Well, you should be prepared, because I've been informed that she is waking up. You need to go and see her. As I mentioned, we like things to be quiet around here. Not that anyone will hear what is happening, but we dislike disturbances of any kind. I hope you understand."

Berman nodded, and Jimmy Yan returned to the house. Berman listened to the songbirds another minute, then followed him inside.

She was standing in a room, but the light was so blinding she couldn't make out any details. When she tried to turn away from the light, she realized she couldn't move. She was rooted to the spot, her arms and legs glued to her side, and she couldn't even close her eyes to offer some protection against the light. Then the lights went off, and she was in complete darkness. All she could hear was her own breathing, until she heard voices and people moving around in the room. What were they doing? She couldn't speak; she couldn't see; she couldn't move.

The lights came back on, but not so bright, and she could see a body lying submerged in a glass tank of liquid. The person was dead, surely, as half of him was missing. From the waist down, there was nothing. She couldn't look away, so when the half figure turned in the water and stared at her, there was nothing she could do but scream silently. Then she felt a punch on her arm, and she was falling, falling straight down into a black nothingness.

Very gradually Pia could make out her surroundings more clearly, but what she was aware of most of all was a restraint on her right arm. She was lying on a bare mattress, shackled with a length of chain connected to a ring on the wall in a large, damp, musty room.

It was hot as Hades, and Pia's head pounded in time with her racing heartbeat. Where the hell was she? What had happened to her?

Pia picked up snatches of a dream.

She remembered being inside Nano and seeing the dreadful tanks with half-dissected people inside. Paul. She had seen Paul and made him go somewhere with her, but she couldn't remember where. Then it was as if she were looking through a powerful microscope, but she didn't know what she was looking at. Paul came to mind again; Paul was going to help her, but he couldn't because she never made it back to him. Zachary Berman had stopped her, and now she was here, wherever here was. She felt fear grip her throat, and she started to shiver despite the heat. *I've got to get ahold of myself,* she thought, taking a deep breath and letting it out slowly. The shaking stopped.

Pia looked around. The room was perhaps twenty feet long, ten feet wide, and as high as twelve feet, lined with red brick on all four walls. On the wall opposite the bed was what looked like a planked oak door with no details. There was a sheen of condensation on every surface. Next to the platform-style bed was a toilet with no seat. Next to that was a sink with a single faucet. In the corner of one wall, where it met the ceiling, was a tiny window, but the light in the room came from big fluorescent lamps that hung incongruously from above. There was no clue as to where she was, and Pia had no memory of being taken anywhere. But she thought time had passed. There was daylight outside, but what day was it from which she remembered those events? Monday, perhaps.

Pia closed her eyes and tried to concentrate on something other than her throbbing head. Sunday. Yes, that was the day she went to see Berman at his house. With that, the memories came back in a rush: Berman, the camera, what she saw at Nano, Paul Caldwell, the blood sample from the ER lounge, Nano again, seeing the spherical nanorobots and being stopped by the police on the way back to Paul's. Now she knew what had happened. She had been kidnapped by Zachary Berman. She knew she had to think hard about those events to recall all the details, but she was unable to concentrate.

In addition to her headache, Pia was stiff all over, especially where her injuries from the car wreck were still healing. Her broken left humerus in particular felt as if it had been broken all over again. The sling was still in place, as was the gauntlet cast for her left radial fracture. That felt fine. With some effort she got herself up into a sitting position on the side of the bed. She could see that there was enough chain for her to reach the toilet and the sink but that was about all. Sitting up made her left arm feel better.

When she was able to think a bit more clearly, Pia tried to figure out if anyone could possibly have seen her being kidnapped. Paul Caldwell must be expecting her back, but unless someone saw her getting taken, she would have simply disappeared. But she had been stopped by Boulder cops! They looked like Boulder cops, in what appeared to be a Boulder police cruiser, which was why she had pulled over to the side of the road, so unless Berman had bought them off, they would know. Pia considered the possibility, then sank back on the mattress. The cops had been in on it, she realized. The cops had stayed in their cruiser while Berman took her. If they were real cops.

She had been in a terrible predicament before, but Pia felt more desperate this time. Not only did she have no idea where she was being held, but she hadn't seen or heard a soul since she had started coming around. She thought about yelling out but didn't think her headache would tolerate it. Best to wait. Was she someplace within Nano? She had no idea.

So it was almost with relief that a few minutes later Pia heard dead bolts being drawn on the heavy wooden door opposite where she was lying. A figure ducked his head to pass through the low doorway, and Pia knew before he looked up that it was Zach Berman.

50.

Paul paced around his apartment, waiting for George Wilson to show up so he could tell him his news. After listening to Paul talk for two minutes on the phone in the middle of the night, George had told Paul to stop. He had heard enough, and he was coming out to Boulder on the next flight he could get. George had refused Paul's offer to pick him up from the airport, saying Paul should stay home in case Pia showed up. To Paul, George sounded much calmer than he himself felt. Impossible though it seemed, George had experience of a situation with Pia that was not dissimilar to what was currently going on.

The buzzer to the outer door rang and no sooner had Paul buzzed George in than he was in the apartment.

"Any word?" George asked the moment he came into Paul's living room.

"I got a text. An hour ago."

"From Pia?"

"Look." Paul handed George his phone. The text identified Pia as the source and read, "Heading home. Don't worry. Will call soon."

"Did you reply?" asked George.

"Of course. I called and texted back and got a reply: 'Don't worry.'"

"What do you think?" asked George.

"It's not Pia. That's what I think. Someone's got her phone."

Paul told George what he'd found on the screen on Pia's computer.

"I don't think Pia thinks of the northeast as home, do you?"

"No," said George. "I don't."

For a moment the two men looked at each other. The only way they were acquainted was through the prism of Pia, and their short interaction after Pia's accident when George had sacked out for some hours in Paul's apartment. The current circumstance wasn't the most opportune moment to expand their friendship, as both were nervous, on edge, and tired.

"Thanks for calling me," George said, and he meant it.

"I didn't know what else to do," admitted Paul. "You're our white knight."

George wondered about that comment but didn't respond to it. Instead he said, "And you kept trying her cell?"

"No luck, just voice mail. If it was Pia, she'd pick up the phone." Paul looked at George. He was a mess and had obviously pulled on the nearest clothes he could find, sweatpants and a sweatshirt over a cotton T-shirt. Paul would not have been caught dead in such an outfit, especially since George was wearing dress shoes with white socks. George noticed Paul looking at his feet.

"I know. I got the wrong shoes. My sneakers were wet after I went for a run in the rain. But after you called and after I cleared the trip with my chief resident, I flew out the door to catch the next flight to Denver, which was leaving in an hour. I came with nothing, but I did make the flight. I'll need to pick up some stuff. But we have to put our heads together first. So tell me everything again, but fill in the details."

The men took seats after Paul gave George a Coke. George had asked for one, saying he needed a quick caffeine hit. Then Paul went through the whole story, beginning at the end, the time thirty hours before, when Pia had texted Paul that she was coming right back to his apartment. George nodded every now and then, as if to say, "Got it." Then Paul was finished.

"So you don't know what she found at Nano?"

"No, but I think it was something extraordinary as she was so fired up she didn't want to take the time to explain. She told me she'd tell me everything when she came back and that she would be coming back as soon as she could, apparently after doing something with the blood samples. I believed her. Unfortunately. And she sent me a text that she was on her way. I'm sure that was her."

"Do you have even the slightest notion of what she might have found?"

"Only a very vague idea. She suspected Nano might have been pushing the envelope with human experimentation of some kind."

"You mean with the nanorobots she was working with?"

"I don't know any details. All we know is that there were some athletes involved somehow, one of which Pia had come upon while running and a second one. You remember all this, don't you?"

"Yeah, of course. So what else happened the night she disappeared that you know of?"

Paul told George about the iris scanner situation, about the camera, and about Pia testing the idea with photos of her own eyes, and then apparently going off to Berman's to get appropriate photos of the CEO.

"Damn," said George with emphasis. "That's so Pia. She puts herself in jeopardy back at that asshole's house just to get photos so she could sneak around Nano?"

"I tried to talk her out of it. It was the second time she'd gone up to Berman's house by herself. The first time she had gone in to search his house." Paul did not include the part about his giving her two capsules of Temazepam. In retrospect he was embarrassed about it. "On this second visit, my guess is that she was successful getting the photo she needed. Using it, I think, she got into a secret part of Nano and found something, as I said, extraordinary." Paul then went on to tell George the story of the blood sample he'd been holding, and how she had shown up in the middle of the night to get it, wanting to look at it under a microscope.

"I wonder what she found?" George asked, looking off into the middle distance, trying to imagine. He looked back at Paul. "This is all very worrisome, to say the very least."

"I couldn't agree with you more. The security guys that showed up in my ER looked like a SWAT team. And on top of that was the accident."

"Right!" George agreed, feeling anger well up inside of him. "Pia was convinced the car accident was no accident, and still you let her go back to Nano that night? And you also let her go and see Berman on her own, twice, with these crazy plans? What kind of a friend are you?"

George had promised himself that he wasn't going to yell at Paul and suggest her disappearance was his fault if it turned out that Pia had gone rogue again. He knew better than anyone that Pia was fearless and single-minded. In the days that he'd spent in Colorado when Pia was injured after the car accident, he came to like and respect Paul, and he knew he was a good friend to Pia. But now that he was here, George couldn't help himself.

"If you weren't prepared to go with her, why didn't you at least call me?"

"It wasn't a case of my being prepared, George. She didn't tell me anything. It was the middle of the night, for God's sake. I had lectured her in the past about being responsible but she's a grown woman. I had to trust that she knew what she was doing."

"Yeah? And look where it got her!"

"I know that, George! Do you think I haven't been thinking about all this the last thirty hours? 'You should have stopped her.' 'You should have called the police.' 'You should have called George.' I've thought all these things a hundred times. But at four o'clock in the morning, when she had woken me from a sound sleep, I wasn't thinking as I might have had it been four o'clock in the afternoon. She always had a good reason to go it alone."

"She always does, that's the point."

"Look, George, we can have this conversation later. Right now we need to concentrate on what we are going to do to find Pia. Agreed?"

George dropped his bluster and nodded. "You're right," he said. "And you're not the only one beating yourself up. I should have been here myself when she told me a little of what she was planning to do, that's the bottom line. So let's go through it again, and see what we can't figure out. We need to have all our ducks in a row when we go to the police, which I'm afraid we are going to have to do, even though we don't have much to tell them. We have a woman who just didn't show up when she said she was going to show up. I don't think the police are going to do too much. I mean, there's no sign of foul play or anything like that."

"That's part of the reason I haven't called them yet," agreed Paul.

"The obvious thing to do is check Berman's house. Come on."

"If he's there with her, he's hardly going to let us in," said Paul.

"We have to try, Paul. Can I borrow your car? If you don't want to come, that is."

"I'll come with you, of course."

As they drove Paul's Subaru to Berman's house, Paul raised a question, a scenario he thought was possible, given what he knew of Pia.

"Let me ask you this, George. You've known her longer, but we both know how willful Pia can be, and, I have to say, insensitive to other people's feelings. What do you think of the idea that whatever it was she discovered Sunday night, she just said, 'Screw it, I'm not having any more to do with Nano,' and actually did take off somewhere?"

George thought for a minute before responding. It was true Pia had a mind of her own, which was a major understatement, just as it was true that she often showed little regard for other people's sensitivities, his in particular. But would she just take off? George couldn't imagine it.

"No," he said eventually. "I don't think that's possible. She's what you have described, but a whole lot more, chief of which is tenacious. She's the most tenacious person I've ever met. If she found something, she wouldn't give up. She'd pursue it until hell froze over. Trust me on that."

Paul nodded in agreement.

When they reached Berman's gate, George got out and rang the buzzer, but there was no answer.

"He has state-of-the-art security, I assume," said Paul. He stayed in the car.

"We're being recorded right now. The camera's up there." George pointed it out to Paul.

"So what do we do now? I can't see the Toyota parked up there," said Paul.

"Berman would have moved it if she's still there," said George. "Maybe I can shimmy over the gate . . . Wait, someone's coming." Driving slowly down the long driveway was a white truck. The heavy iron gates swung open and the truck slowed to a stop. The men could see that the driver was not Zachary Berman.

"Let's ask this guy," said George. "See what he knows."

The driver of the truck sounded his horn—Paul's Subaru was blocking the way. The driver stuck his head out of the truck window. He was a blond-haired man with a deep tan. "C'mon, guys, can you move your car?"

"Is the boss man around?" said George.

"Mr. Berman? I'm his tree guy. I didn't see him, but I don't usually see him anyway. Look, I want to go to my next job and you know I can't let you in. Have you buzzed up to the house?"

"Come on, George," said Paul. "Get in! We're in the man's way."

"Just a second," said George. He wandered over to the truck and stuck his head in through the passenger-side window.

"Sorry, we don't mean to get in your way, and we'll move in a second, we're just wondering if Mr. Berman's around. It's important to us. We're old friends. I've come all the way from L.A. I just wanted to say hello." George was at his most amiable—in his ultra-casual outfit he looked quite benign, and the gardener just wanted to be on his way.

"I don't think he's here. One of the guys who looks after the flower beds says he went on one of his trips."

"Abroad?" said George.

"I don't know where he goes. I just know that when he's here, everyone's on their best behavior, and right now, there's a couple of the gardeners sitting out back drinking coffee and taking their time. I commented on that, and they said Berman's away somewhere. But where, you'll have to ask someone else. The gardener guys should be coming down within the hour."

"Thanks," said George. "We'll come back."

"If I see anyone when I come back tomorrow, who shall I say stopped by?"

"Just a friend," said George, and waved a casual good-bye.

George got back in the car, where Paul was waiting.

"What was that about?" said Paul as he backed out of the way to let the arborist pass.

"Berman's apparently gone on a trip, or so the guy heard from one of the gardeners. But he doesn't know if it's foreign or domestic or anything. But Berman's apparently not around, at least not around here. How about we stop by Nano, see what we can find there?"

"I guess it makes sense," said Paul, and they drove off toward Boulder.

"I don't think we are going to find anything out at Nano. They are extremely security conscious."

"We have to cover the bases," said George. He sounded more

decisive than Paul remembered. "Perhaps they don't know what car she was driving. Anyway, if we strike out at Nano, we'll go by her apartment again."

"Security would have noted what car she arrived in . . ."

"Okay," said George, raising his voice. "I know. But we have to look."

They rode the rest of the way in silence. Neither man thought it would be easy to get past the first security gate on the road into Nano, and both were right.

"We're here for a job interview," said George, talking past Paul, trying a line he had thought up on the way over on the first line of security at a gatepost by the main entrance to Nano.

"There are no interviews scheduled for today," said the guard, an efficient-looking older man. "They always let me know to be prepared for people who need temporary ID, and there's none today."

"It's unofficial. An informational interview with Whitney Jones, in Mr. Berman's office."

"I know for a fact that Whitney Jones is not here today. Can I see your driver's license, sir."

"What do you need that for?"

"Everyone who comes in here has to show ID. And you, too, sir," the guard said to Paul.

Paul and George looked at each other. If they showed their ID, Nano would know they had been here. If they didn't, they'd be turned away immediately. George shrugged and dug his license out of his wallet. Paul followed suit. The guard retreated into his small cabin and picked up a phone. A line of cars had formed behind Paul and a couple of impatient drivers were honking at him.

"Look, George, we should take this to the police," said Paul.

"It might not hurt to let Berman know we're around."

Paul said nothing. The guard put down the phone.

"Pull in over there," he said, indicating a cut-out to the right of the guard post. He handed over the driver's licenses. As soon as Paul parked, a black SUV drove up and a man in a suit got out of the passenger side.

"Can I help you fellas?" He was younger than the gatepost guard, fitter, more athletic, and much more intimidating, despite his smile and casual syntax.

"We're here for an interview," said Paul.

"There's no interviews today, Dr. Caldwell." The man knew exactly who Paul was. "Better check your calendar, I think you got the wrong day. You can drive out through the same gate." He indicated the same guard post, where the exit barrier was now raised. The security man had one more thing to say.

"Have an excellent day, gentlemen."

51.

"Hello, Pia."

Berman stood in the doorway of Pia's underground cell and looked at her lying on a dirty, bare mattress staring at the ceiling. He could see that she was chained to a ring secured to the brick wall. She looked very small and defenseless, and with her broken arm he knew how vulnerable she was. But this was the woman who had taunted and humiliated him and put what was to be his crowning life's achievement in jeopardy, and he felt that by rights he should be very angry with her. He certainly had been angry in Boulder the other night. He wasn't used to being toyed with and dominated, in any sense of the word. It wouldn't be unjustified for him to exact some revenge on this woman, perhaps even the ultimate revenge.

"Aren't you going to say anything?" Berman asked.

As his anger burned, Berman realized he wanted a reaction from Pia, any reaction. Again he was flustered by the mixture of frustration and desire that he was experiencing. He had never felt anything like it, or so he told himself. Despite all the evidence that he could see before him of a defenseless woman, he was as nervous as if he were the prisoner. In a strange, irrational way he almost believed that Pia could have the upper hand over him if she so chose. He knew such an idea was ridiculous, but that was how he felt. Berman moved into the room, and the Chinese guard pulled the door shut behind him and locked it. It was better now that the guard wasn't watching him, but still Berman was uncomfortable.

"Pia, I'm sorry it has come to this, but you must understand you left us with no choice. You came to my house and tricked me. And it wasn't the first time. I started to think I was more than just drunk that first time you came, and eventually I figured out what you had done, but I decided to give you the benefit of the doubt. I was hoping that on Sunday your motivation was more sincere, but I now realize it was all a charade so you could photograph my eyes for you to trespass onto Nano property."

Berman paused, but there was no visible reaction from Pia.

"You used the photographs to gain access to a restricted area and you stole a sample of blood from a sensitive physiological preparation. You had also obtained a blood sample from a previous occasion that Nano had taken the time and effort to obtain a court order to confiscate. We also know you used Nano equipment unauthorized to examine these samples. These are very serious matters."

"Mengele," said Pia, very quietly.

"I'm sorry, Pia, I didn't catch that."

"Do you know who Josef Mengele was?"

"Of course, he was a Nazi doctor in the concentration camps—"

"That's who you are. A modern-day Mengele."

"Pia, that is ridiculous, but I can understand that what you saw requires some explaining on my part. It is not what it seems."

"Some explaining! You bastard." Pia sat up and gave Berman a look of pure hatred and anger. Berman stepped back, even though he knew Pia was restrained. For him she had an intense power that was deeply unsettling.

"Where the hell am I? You have me chained to a wall in this me-dieval dungeon like something out of Robin Hood. You really are a pathetic, impotent little man."

Berman's face reddened. "I don't think you are in a position to make that kind of judgment. You've never given me a chance to show you who I am, personally or professionally. I am on the verge of leading the greatest scientific medical breakthrough of the last fifty years. Maybe a hundred. And here is the issue in a nutshell. I want you to join me as I suggested back in my home. I want you to join us. I'm making you an offer of a lifetime."

Pia laughed a mirthless laugh. She shook her head. "Sure you want me to join you? That's why you have me chained to the wall in a dungeon."

"You wouldn't listen to me the other night at my house. You never listen. It's always about your agenda. If restraining you is what it takes to get you to hear me out, then so be it. And I needed to make sure you wouldn't spoil everything at the last minute. Right now I just want to talk to you."

"Do I have a choice?"

"Unfortunately, no. But I ask you to think about what I am saying as a scientist, a researcher, a doctor who is interested in helping save millions upon millions of people, not someone who is immature and controlled by sentimentality and knee-jerk delusions of ethics."

"I suppose my ethics are 'reflex,' as you suggest, especially if I think there's something wrong with carving people up and keeping them half-alive in tanks."

"You are a good scientist, potentially a great one. Mariel Spallek said as much, and I trust her judgment, especially in light of your polyethylene glycol suggestion for the microbivores. But she also said that you can't help interfering in areas that shouldn't be of your concern."

"Isn't that what a good scientist should do? Be concerned? Isn't that what Robert Oppenheimer implied when he looked back on his career as the father of the atomic bomb?"

"That's what a philosopher does. A scientist should be looking to push the boundaries of science, which is what we are doing at Nano,

and what you have been helping with. Pia, you know what nanotech-
nnology is going to mean to the world, you probably know it nearly as
well as I. It is a revolution, a coming avalanche of techniques and
products, and we need to be in the vanguard, leading the world, and
not back in the pack with the Europeans and all the other myopic
nations who can't see the big picture."

"And that's where you come in, I imagine. Keeping the big picture in focus."

"Yes, that's what I do. I shoot for the moon, taking theory to
reality."

"So tell me more about the big picture, Zachary. Please fill me in."

Berman paused and looked at Pia. She was as defiant and sarcastic
as ever—really pissed, hissing like a cornered alley cat with no back-
down in her whatsoever. He'd come this far with her, literally and
metaphorically. He saw no reason to conceal anything from her at
this point. This game was going to end either with her compliance
or with something far more unpleasant, so he really had nothing to
lose. Most important, she was at least talking.

"Big picture, it's about money. Of course it is, isn't everything?
We can operate in the United States with relatively little supervision
from the authorities, but any significant amount of funding always
comes with strings attached. The government talks about compliance. We have to make sure we are in line with this regulation and
that statute to keep every wild-ass constituency fat and happy. The
red tape is unbelievable. And since the financial meltdown in '08,
private funding from within the U.S. is always complicated, if not
impossible. You sit down with financiers and talk to them for weeks,
and they get over their qualms and accept all your guarantees and
promises and warranties, and then the money they come up with is
chicken feed compared to what we need. You know, in the order of
ten million or twenty million. And they think they're big shots.

"But China is different. They know how to get things done, and
the bigger, the better. They are looking into the future, not bogged

down in the present, let alone the past. I may not know exactly what branch of the government I am dealing with, but their representatives sit down and they say, 'We want this technology. What do you need to make it happen and share it with us?' And I say, 'Oh, about a half billion to really get it started.' And they say, 'Okay.'"

"Half a billion dollars?"

"They are not intimidated by such an R-and-D budget, knowing that nanotechnology is already a seventy-billion-dollar-a-year phenomenon. They're smart enough to know they're getting a bargain, considering Nano's leap forward with molecular manufacturing. It is incredible how quickly they can make up their minds, knowing they are investing in the future. From the very first meeting I had with them, they wanted to be part of Nano's future. The only problem was that they wanted some proof that nanorobots would work as well as I said they would, so they made their investment in microbivores and future molecular manufacturing dependent on my showing them definitive proof. Someone high up the food chain apparently not satisfied in China's performance in the Beijing Olympics says, 'This guy has to prove this stuff works. If he takes a good athlete and makes him a world-class athlete, that will prove to us that he knows what he's doing.'"

"What stuff?" said Pia. "You said, 'prove this stuff works.' What 'stuff' are you talking about?"

"It's what I presume you saw in those two blood samples."

"The blue nanorobots."

"Yes. Do you know what they are?"

"My guess is that they're respirocytes."

"I'm impressed."

"It had to be something that contributed to the athletes' endurance. Superefficient oxygen carriers. I read about them when I first arrived at Nano at the same time I read up on microbivores. I suppose it would explain some of the medical anomalies seen with the runner."

"The respirocytes supply oxygen to the athlete's bloodstream far more effectively than regular red blood cells. A thousand times better, to be exact. They are so effective that the subject's heart doesn't even have to be beating for adequate oxygen to be available for several hours in a patient's brain. Which is why the subjects who had cardiac arrest showed no neurological side effects after being heart-dead for up to an hour or two. As we later learned, the initial cardiac arrest problem was caused by the respirocytes simply because they worked too well. They triggered what we found to be a hyperoxic, hypermetabolic state resulting in a kind of heatstroke with cardiac arrest. The first test subjects simply got too large of a dose, even though it was only five cubic centimeters of the nanorobot suspension. We had no idea at how efficient the respirocytes would prove to be. It is a great harbinger for the success of the microbivores."

"And the Chinese wanted proof that these nanorobot respirocytes, designed and manufactured by Nano, could make an athlete super-effective?"

"Essentially yes. We trained a cyclist, and he won a stage at the Tour de France. But the higher-ups were more specific. The goal was for a Chinese national to win an international race at a major championship. As chance would have it, the jogger you came across will be running in the marathon at the World Athletics Championships, which start on Friday."

"In London."

"In London."

"So is that where we are?" asked Pia. "In London?"

Berman's facial expression gave nothing away.

"But you're cheating and your runner will be found out."

"I don't think so. None of the doping tests will detect something as inert as a diamondoid surfaced nanorobot. Even if the authorities decided to do blood counts, with the low concentrations we use, it would be rare indeed for one to be seen. My feeling is that the Chinese runner will win, hopefully not by too large a margin, and I know he has been advised as such. And once this guy wins his race, Nano is out of sports. No doubt someone will figure out eventually what respirocytes do for athletes, and eventually there will be tests, but the Chinese and I will have moved on. I don't care, and the faction in the government that decided upon these tests will have their proof. And what's more, they'll have the glory that comes with athletic achievement on the world stage.

"The Chinese government doesn't just want to dominate economically, they want sporting success as well as proof their system of government is superior to the rest of the world's. In that regard they're as bad as the Soviets and the East Germans in the Cold War era, when they would do anything to beat the U.S.A. to a gold medal. I'm sure it also has something to do with the Chinese government wanting to erase the three hundred or so years of humiliation the country suffered under colonialism."

Sports meant nothing to Pia, but she could understand the significance of what Berman was talking about. It sounded so trite. She clearly understood the flaw. It was a classic attempt on Berman's part to justify means by supposedly honorable ends. All the time he talked, she couldn't get the image of the bodies in the tanks out of her head. Berman was willing to sacrifice people, to experiment on humans to reach his goals.

"So you're doing all this for the Chinese in order to get their money."

"Investment. To get their investment, so that it can be applied to the microbivores project, yes."

"And to what end? I mean, is this to speed up the process, investigating microbivores? How much time do you estimate this kind of investment will save? Two years? Five years?"

"How about ten years," said Berman. "Without the Chinese money, I think we are looking at ten years before microbivores are commercially available, and that's only if there are no unexpected problems. And think of what it will mean when they're available. It's going to revolutionize the treatment of infectious disease, and think of cancer. It will be a nontoxic, targeted cure. No more need for chemotherapy or harmful radiation, which will be seen to be the equivalent of medieval medicine. And microbivores will most likely prevent and cure Alzheimer's disease. We're talking about a medical revolution."

"But at what cost?"

"At the cost you saw. As I said, I'm sure there's nothing going on at Nano that isn't going on at other research facilities around the world."

"I don't believe that."

"I know it to be a fact."

"You said that everyone who was at Nano was there voluntarily: all these subjects. Are you telling me these people volunteered to be vivisected?"

"Yes, I did say they were all volunteers, and I mean it. They were convicted of capital crimes in China. Every one of the subjects brought over to Nano was a condemned prisoner in China. The country executes, I don't know, three thousand people a year, which I'm not saying I personally agree with, since some of them are for things like fraud or embezzlement. A few were selected and asked if they wanted to take part in a medical trial."

"They were vivisected!"

"Those subjects you saw in the Nano aquariums had been subjects who had suffered irreversible, life-threatening consequences from the oxygen-caused hypermetabolic cardiac failure. They were brain dead before they were prepared to serve as physiological preparations. It was through their sacrifice that we were able to learn the proper concentrations needed for safety. They were not vivisected, as you suggest, at least not in a strict definition of the word. I know their deaths were regrettable but we never killed a healthy subject."

"Oh, good! Is that supposed to make me feel better? Where's that contract you had for me, I'll sign it right away."

Berman stared at Pia. He could feel his anger and frustration returning as her sarcasm was obvious, suggesting that he was not making the headway he had hoped and thought he was making only minutes earlier. He cleared his throat.

"Listen, these people in the tanks had to all intents and purposes died prior to their being placed there, and they were going to die anyway if they had not been allowed to come to Nano and participate in our work. Much sooner, in fact. Science has to find its way, and there have to be sacrifices. For centuries, people have died researching drugs. If we reach our goal with the microbivores even five years ahead of time, we could save a million lives, who knows?"

"That's not how it works and you know it. When the Nazis were brought to trial at the end of World War Two, it was specifically decreed that countries cannot experiment on prisoners. There is no way they can be considered legitimate volunteers."

"The U.S. government gave subjects syphilis after the end of the war . . ."

"Okay, but they're not doing it now. And the experiments you are alluding to have been totally discredited."

Berman was silent. This wasn't going how he had hoped, but he wasn't really surprised. Pia was unlikely to roll over at the first opportunity. If she was going to relent, it would take time, and Berman had thought she might be more receptive to the argument about sacrificing a few to save many than she seemed to be. He wasn't going to give up.

"We lost maybe ten subjects in the whole project for which we can save millions."

"How long has this respirocyte project been going on?"

"It's been going on four years," Berman said, encouraged that she was asking legitimate questions.

Pia let out a sigh and glanced up at Berman. He was looking down at her with an expression she couldn't read. Did he really think he could talk her around? That he could persuade her into believing that his sick way of looking at the world was justified? It was the darkening realization that Berman did believe he could convert her that was making Pia feel so downcast. She wondered what she could do to give herself a chance at getting away. Was she really somewhere in the United Kingdom? Was she capable of a charade, knowing that he knew she'd already had pulled it off not once but twice? What was going to happen to her if she didn't give in to the role he wanted her to play? Was he going to try to force her to have sex with him? Too many questions and no answers.

"I'll never sleep with you," said Pia.

"I'm not a monster, you might think that of me right now, but you should give some serious thought to what I have been saying. Think of the scientific opportunities there are for a woman like you when you have access to the best equipment and unlimited funds. Believe me, I would not have Mariel Spallek breathing down your neck if you came back for research. I know that's what you want to do, and I'm offering you a chance that most scientists would jump at."

"Not if they had to touch you, they wouldn't. Is this how you get all your girlfriends to sleep with you, by blackmailing them?"

"On the contrary. I told you about Whitney. She and I had some very spirited conversations before she converted to my point of view, and now she is my most loyal employee. You are fortunate that I did not leave you in her hands in Boulder. We certainly wouldn't be having this talk if I had."

"Paul Caldwell will find me."

"I very much doubt it. Your friend George is with him now. They went to my house. Then they went to Nano, where they were kind enough to hand over their IDs. They've been to your apartment a few times. Now, they're just sitting around Paul's apartment wringing their hands. Perhaps they're holding hands, I know Paul would enjoy that."

"He's ten times the man you are."

"Well, chances are we'll never know."

"They'll go to the police."

"Yes, I'm sure they will. But I can't imagine they are going to get much satisfaction telling the police their concerns about your well-being. You remember how helpful the cops were the last time you saw them."

Pia did. Clearly, at least some members of the Boulder PD were on Berman's payroll. Perhaps Berman was bluffing about Paul and George, but Pia wouldn't be surprised if Berman didn't have Paul's apartment under surveillance. She had to stay strong and resist.

"My arm is hurting," said Pia. "Is there a doctor here?" She wanted to see another face; anyone but Berman.

Berman nodded. "I'm glad you asked me that." He thought the fact that Pia was requesting a doctor was a positive sign, reflecting that she was able to think beyond her offended morality. And for Berman, it was important that Pia get better. He wanted desperately to have her physically, as she expected, but not when she was injured like this. He did have standards to maintain.

Berman turned and rapped twice on the door. It opened and admitted a Chinese man, about sixty, in a white lab coat. Berman tapped his own arm where Pia had her break, and the man nodded. He stepped over to Pia and bid her to stand up before he started examining her upper left arm and the cast on her wrist.

"There's something I forgot to tell you," said Berman. "It might influence your thinking. If somehow your two men friends talk some judge into issuing a search warrant for Nano, perhaps looking for you or whatever, I want to tell you that the human preparations you happened to see have all been replaced with dogs. The humans served their purpose and have all been removed and their ashes will be appropriately sent back to China to be given to their families."

With that, Berman turned around and rapped on the door to be let out.

52.

Paul and George rode to the Boulder police station, arriving a little after eight in the morning. For a few minutes, they sat in the car and discussed the best approach to take. George Wilson was very impatient; he had been ever since he arrived back in Colorado, and he looked the part with mismatched clothing and a two day's growth of beard. He felt there must be something more they could be doing after checking out Berman's house and trying to get into Nano, while Paul counseled patience. Paul had worked his shift at the ER the previous evening and would work again that night. He had tried to get some time off, but Paul's private practice that had the contract to run the ER was already down to two doctors, all the others were out on family summer vacations. Consequently Paul would have to keep working while they looked for Pia. George, on the other hand, had a lot of free time. Before he left L.A., he had managed to arrange for a two-week vacation on an emergency basis. The powers that be had looked kindly on his request as he had not taken any vacation since starting the residency program, and they had been encouraging him to do so.

George had done his best to get Paul to do something more, but in Paul's estimation, George's ideas—breaking into Berman's house and breaking into Nano—were ridiculous and would be counterproductive. Under the surface he was as frantic as George, but he didn't show it. He was certain there was no sense in racing off and getting arrested: they had to go to the police first and play it by the book, and they would do it that morning if they hadn't heard from Pia, and they hadn't.

The upshot of the strategizing was that Paul insisted on doing the talking with the police. Actually he would have preferred to go in alone, but George was having none of that, although he did acquiesce to the idea of letting Paul be the point man. Paul had told George it was he who knew the situation better, it was he who had last seen Pia and to whom she was due to return. In reality, Paul was worried George was likely to fly off the handle and make wild accusations against Berman and Nano that he couldn't substantiate. They had to be calm and businesslike, and that was Paul's department.

But meeting with the police wasn't quite as easy as they had envisioned. After a half hour of waiting in unforgiving plastic chairs in the lobby of the building with what looked to be a half dozen other derelicts, some even less presentable than George, even Paul's patience was wearing thin. By then George was pacing around like a caged animal, checking his phone and sighing loudly.

"Come on!" muttered George, more to himself than Paul. "Isn't anyone going to help us?"

Finally an officer came out, called out their names, and led them to a desk, still in the public area of the facility.

"Aren't we going inside the station?" asked George. He'd seen enough police procedurals to expect such treatment.

The young uniformed officer, whose badge read Gomez, looked at George. "This is where we conduct first interviews, sir."

"Of course, thank you," said Paul, glaring at George. Paul found himself remembering a saying that you know you're getting old when the police officers start looking young, but Paul felt he was too young himself for such a sentiment. But still, Officer Gomez looked to be about sixteen. They all sat down. Paul then outlined the story to her including what he and George had done but leaving out the parts in which Pia had drugged her boss and that she had essentially broken into her former place of work. He could feel George shifting in his seat as he talked. After a while, Gomez put down her pen and pad and faced the two men.

"Sir, you understand it's not against the law for someone over the age of eighteen to leave their home without warning. And they are entitled to their privacy. Even if she showed up in Denver, and we found her, if she said she didn't want to be contacted by certain individuals, we couldn't tell them we knew where she was."

"Listen, I understand. I'm an ER doctor. We see domestic violence cases all the time. For all you know I could be an abusive partner looking for my girlfriend to beat up."

"Paul, that's ridiculous," said George. "Officer Gomez, Pia Grazdani has been kidnapped. I'm sure of it. Not in the usual ransom sense, but more to get rid of her and shut her up. My friend isn't saying all this because he's afraid we won't be taken seriously, but I'm convinced that's the case."

Paul sighed and looked at George with a combination of irritation and frustration. Officer Gomez stiffened in her seat. As Paul feared, she was now looking at George, unshaven and shabby, in a different light.

"Officer Gomez," said Paul, using his calming, official doctor voice. "My friend is agitated. Before Pia disappeared, we know she had entered her place of work using a borrowed ID." Paul didn't elaborate on his euphemistic description of Pia's elaborate foiling of Nano's iris security system and flouting a specific order to stay away from her lab.

"She implied to me that she had stumbled on something illegal going on at Nano," Paul continued in an even, calm tone. "I know you're obliged to act if there is evidence that the person was abducted or is in danger, and I believe she is in great danger. The last time she saw me in the wee hours of Monday morning, after she had made the disturbing discovery, which she said she would explain later, she told me she would be coming directly back to my apartment. Sometime later she texted she was on her way but never showed up."

"You're essentially saying she got into the Nano complex illegally?" said Gomez. "This is the same Nano Institute up in the foothills that makes such effort on security to avoid, should we say, industrial espionage?"

"Yes," said George, answering the question that had been directed at Paul.

"Wait here!" said Gomez, who got up and left.

"Great, George. You were supposed to let me do the talking. Now Pia's gone from a missing-person's case to a fleeing fugitive."

"So what?" said George. "Which do you think they'd spend more time looking for?"

Thirty minutes later, Gomez reemerged, accompanied by a man in a suit who looked every inch the veteran detective that he was, with an outdated haircut, gray mustache, overweight, and an old-fashioned suit.

"Detective Samuels," he said, shaking Paul's hand and then George's. "Okay, we called your friend's place of employment, and they say she's on paid leave and as far as they are concerned, there have been no irregularities or problems with unauthorized visitations. I also talked with Nano security who corroborated that there have been no reports of any break-ins or lost IDs that could be used to gain illegal entry. They did say you two gentlemen showed up there yesterday trying to get in and were turned away."

Paul snuck a quick look at George.

"We're worried about our friend," said Paul. "She was very upset by something she found at work."

"Did she say what it was?"

"No, as I mentioned to Officer Gomez, but I could guess it had something to do with a Chinese runner . . ."

"A Chinese runner? Okay," said Samuels skeptically, "Officer Gomez filled me in on what you gentlemen have told her. Seems that your stories, or at least your interpretation of the situation, is somewhat different. You, Dr. Caldwell, feel that she was very upset and failed to come to your apartment in the wee hours of the morning after having illegally broken into the Nano facility. And you, Mr. Wilson, are convinced that this woman, who is on medical leave, was kidnapped?"

"I know she was," said George.

"You went to her apartment," said Samuels, reading from Gomez's notes, "and you found a Web page with driving directions to a place in New Jersey . . ."

"Someone else called up that page!" George was raising his voice. "Pia would never stop to look for directions, she'd just start driving. She's very headstrong . . ."

"Someone who'd break into a place, headstrong in that way?" said Samuels.

"But no one reported it, did they," said George.

"And you also say you received a text from her phone that you don't believe she sent." Samuels let that piece of information hang in the air. "Has it occurred to you guys that she's stringing you along? I don't see any evidence she's been kidnapped. We'll take those pictures you brought in. I wouldn't mind asking her about this illegal entry she was talking about. I know a lot of those security guys who work at Nano. They are a very professional group and justly concerned about industrial security involving proprietary secrets and any and all episodes of illegal entry. I will take everything you have told us under advisement, and we will be back to you gentlemen. Thank you for coming in."

"Are you implying that's what Pia Grazdani was doing? Stealing secrets from her workplace?"

"I'm not saying anything, Mr. Wilson," said Samuels. "Okay, I think we're done here. Again, thanks for coming to see us today. Come on, Officer Gomez! We have work to do on this matter."

Samuels and Gomez walked away.

"Don't say it," said George.

"I have to," Paul said. "When someone over eighteen disappears, there has to be hard evidence of foul play, and the only known crime here was committed by Pia herself."

"But we know she's been taken," said George.

"Sure, but look at it from their point of view," said Paul.

"You heard the guy," said George, who started to walk out of the building. Paul followed. "He's pals with the security at Nano. I know Pia can be paranoid, but that looks mighty cozy, don't you think? I wonder if Nano recruited from the local law enforcement for their security team. What about the FBI? I think we should go and talk to them. I doubt there's any former Feds at Nano."

"You think the FBI is going to say anything different? They have the same standards of evidence, and they're sure to knock it back to the police."

"So it's up to us, is that what you're saying?" said George. "Should we just try to file a run-of-the-mill missing-person's complaint?"

"I think that's what we just tried to do."

"I suppose you are right. This is the kind of situation where Pia's isolation works against her. But we can't just do nothing."

"I don't know what we can do. Listen, George, I'm willing to help you, of course I am, but I don't see how breaking into Berman's house or anything else along those lines is going to help, if that's what you're thinking."

"I know if I could only get into Nano. . . ."

"Then what, George? The place is tight as a drum with security. Remember what Pia did last, and she worked there, remember?"

"What about Pia's boss, Mariel? Mariel whatever her name is.

She's a piece of work, but who knows? We could start there, talk to her, see if she'll tell us anything."

"I suppose. If we can figure out how to get in touch with her. I assume she'll be at work on a Wednesday."

"My sense is that work is all she has," said George. "It might be hard to contact her, but we have to do something. Maybe it would be helpful to find out where she lives." He winked at Paul.

Paul shrugged, but didn't say anything. At least it was better than trying to break into Berman's castlelike house or Nano.

53.

Pia had spent the day mostly sleeping in bed, a real bed, not the filthy mattress on the floor of the dungeon where she had talked to Berman. After being examined by the doctor, two men wearing fatigues and surgical masks had moved her to a small, utilitarian bedroom up some cement steps leading out of the basement and along a corridor with the lowest ceiling Pia had ever seen. Even she had had to hunch down while she walked. There was one unadorned lightbulb in the middle of the featureless ceiling.

Pia felt groggy and out of it. She had lost track of time and was unsure of where she was until her mind cleared. Halfway along the route from the basement cell there had been a small window, and Pia had caught a glimpse of some trees and a garden. It had been raining outside, and it looked gray. At the time she had questioned where it could have been. Could it be Colorado? But the trees looked wrong. And it was too green. Berman had said something about being in London. *Is that where I am?* she wondered.

The two men had shackled Pia to the metal-frame bed in the room. There was no furniture or windows, and the door was of heavy steel. This was another cell, only less humid than the cellar. Pia was livid with Berman for putting her in this position. She saw there was a bedpan she was going to have to use. She felt humiliation along with her anger. She was being kept like an animal.

After a few minutes of being awake, the door opened, and the Chinese doctor came back.

"Do you speak English?" she asked. The man looked at her with a blank expression. He was indeterminately middle-aged, with a puffy, doughy, expressionless face.

"If you're a doctor, whatever happened to 'Do no harm'? Tell me that."

The doctor looked down, and Pia imagined she was about to be injected again with whatever they had been using to knock her out. He grasped her arm.

"No, you don't!" she screamed. "I don't want to be drugged again. Leave me alone, you asshole." Pia squirmed out of the man's grasp and screamed and shouted at him. He didn't try to restrain her nor say anything, he simply rapped on the door and stood aside as two Chinese guards came into the room.

"Leave me alone! I demand that you tell me where I am. Where's Berman? I want to talk to him."

Pia cried out in pain and one of the guards grabbed her roughly by her bad arm. In the confined quarters of her small room, it took only seconds for Pia to be thoroughly restrained.

The doctor held his hands out to show he wasn't carrying a needle, and examined Pia's arm.

"You're another Nazi experimenter, like Berman. I know you can understand me. You are not going to get away with this. They're going to get you, too." The doctor gazed at Pia without a single facial muscle contracting. She couldn't even tell if he blinked. Without a word, he left, along with the guards.

54.

Paul Caldwell used a friendly 411 dispatcher to find Mariel Spallek's address on the city system when it turned out she wasn't listed in any of the public records. She lived in an affluent town adjacent to Boulder, in a single-story rental building that was one of four attached units. The dispatcher had told Paul there were no other occupants listed at that specific address, a revelation that didn't surprise Paul in the slightest.

"So now we're here, what are we going to do?" said Paul, who parked fifty yards down the road, just in case. "Are you going to walk up to the front door and ring the bell?"

"Why not?"

"Didn't you say you've met her? What are you going to do, say you just moved in next door and want a cup of sugar? Say you've joined the police department?"

"I don't think I'm dressed for that." George had gone to the store, but only added a pair of cheap sneakers to his frat-boy outfit of sweatpants and a T-shirt.

"I don't know, I'll think of something," said George.

"According to Pia, she's a pistol, George. You're going to have to think of something good."

"Let's face it, Paul, at this time of day, she's going to be at work. I'm counting on that."

Before Paul could respond, George hopped out of Paul's car and walked down the street and up to the door of Mariel's apartment. The entrance was shielded from the neighbors by wooden fencing. He rang the bell three times and waited. There was no reply, and no barking dog to worry about. George then went next door to the apartment on the end of the row and rang that bell also, and again got no reply. If he had to bet, these apartments were all rented by single people. They had one-car garages, and the gardens were neat enough but untidy. There were no kids' toys lying around and only one small garbage can in each entryway.

With calm that surprised him, George walked around the back of the building and saw that the yards were separated by fences that extended only as far as a wooded area in back, and were not closed off. *No one has a dog*, thought George. *Good!* He approached and clambered around the fence and into Mariel's yard, then went to her back door, tried the handle, and when that didn't open, he took a rock from the garden, smashed the glass above the handle and carefully let himself in. *That was easy*, he thought.

George looked for the alarm box a resident would use to switch the system off or on, but there wasn't any. He then walked to the front door, opened it, and peered down the street, gesturing to Paul to come in. When Paul didn't move, George jogged down the road to the driver's side of Paul's car.

"Are you crazy?" said Paul.

"Probably. Do you have any surgical gloves in the car? I'm going to wipe down what I touched already."

"George, what about the neighbors? And an alarm?"

"There's no alarm and I'd bet my last dollar there are no neighbors at this time of day. Come on, get the gloves, you're wasting time. And come in and help."

"I don't believe you," said Paul. "I'll do anything to help, but it's

got to be within the law, George. You're on your own on this one."
He got a pair of sterile surgical gloves and handed the package to
George. He kept them in his car along with other medical equip-
ment for roadside emergencies.

"Okay," said George. "Keep a lookout. If she comes back, call me,
or honk the horn, or something."

ERIC MCKENZIE and Chad Wells were three hours into their shift,
tasked with following the Subaru with the distinctive roof racks and
the two guys who'd shown up at Nano the previous day. At the
briefing at Nano, the head of security said the men weren't dangerous, and they weren't to be approached. Just follow them and don't
get noticed.

The admonition to remain incognito was what struck Chad when
they saw the Subaru turn into the entrance gate of a well-to-do sub-
division after having been parked for more than an hour at their old
stomping ground at police HQ.

"Why did you stop?" said Eric after Chad pulled over. The Subaru
had gone ahead out of sight.

"Look at this place. Rows and rows of houses, no traffic. They're
going to spot us right away."

"So what?"

"So the boss told us not to get spotted, dumbass. We're not paid
to think, which is a damn good thing in your case. It would be hard
to live on six dollars a week."

"Very funny."

"So you better start walking," said Chad.

"What?"

"Get in there and see if you can see them. I've been here before.
This is the only entrance. I'll radio base and tell them where they
went, see if they can figure out who they might be visiting."

"The radio still works if the car's moving, you know," said Eric.

"Out!"

"Goddamn this job," said Eric out loud ten minutes later. "Who'd live out here anyways? Streets all the same, no one around. Half these places look empty." Of the Subaru, there was no sign, which was little surprise, given the size of the development. But McKenzie walked on, overheating in the afternoon sun. He cursed having to wear his sport coat in the heat of the day, too, so that the pistol he wore wouldn't be visible.

His radio connected to an earpiece crackled to life.

"Eric, where are you?"

"Dunno, I'm on a street that looks the same as the last one."

"Well, find a cross street and tell me what it's called. The geniuses back at HQ have figured out who these knuckleheads are here to see."

"Okay, I'm at Franklin and Jackson."

"Okay, don't move. See you in five."

WEARING THE LATEX GLOVES, George went through Mariel's apartment methodically. He found some files in an unlocked drawer, but they were all personal, one for the car, one for the washer-dryer, and so on. George's phone rang and he dropped the file.

"Find anything?" said Paul.

"Is she coming?" said George.

"No, no one's coming, I'm just checking in."

"Well, don't. I nearly jumped out of my skin. I'm still looking." George ended the call.

ERIC STOPPED THE CAR down the street as far from Mariel's house as the doctor's car, which was parked on the other side. Through his binoculars, he could see someone sitting in the Subaru.

"There's one in the car, so I guess the other one's in the house.

Must have got in. They said these guys were doctors or something. I didn't think doctors did break-ins."

"So why did you stop down here?" said Chad. "Let's just grab the guy." He was always ready for a fight.

"Hold your horses," said Eric. "I'm going to call it in to Nano."

"How boring is that?" said Chad, who fidgeted in his seat while Eric had a quick conversation with the head of security.

"We're going to call the police," he told Chad after finishing the call. "Those are our instructions. The boss said there's nothing incriminating at this house—the woman is too careful to bring anything important home with her. So the guy can stay in there and search as long as he wants, he won't find anything. If the police catch them, they'll be arrested, and that should stop them playing amateur detective. If we go in there and sort them out, it'll just make them look harder. If they have the balls. These guys really have no idea what they're doing."

"Well, that's disappointing."

"Sure, I know. If they don't give up, then it's our turn to have a word next, so don't sulk about it. Now, call your pal in the department and give them the details. This is the address."

Chad handed Eric a piece of paper.

PAUL LOOKED AT his watch and shifted in his seat, George had been inside about twenty-five minutes. Paul checked his mirror— there was a car parked down the street that hadn't been there a minute earlier, which stood out since there had not been any traffic whatsoever. How long had it been there? Paul strained to see if anyone was sitting in the car. He thought he could see at least one figure in the car. He called George again.

"George, a car pulled up down the street behind me and parked. Actually I didn't see it come. Just noticed it now."

"In front of here?"

"No, but I think there are two men in the car. I think. Actually I can only see one for sure. But it seems a little worrisome."

"But they're not moving?"

"No."

"There has to be something in here," said George. "This woman is involved in it up to her armpits."

"George, get out of there. You've been in there too long."

"One more minute," George said, and clicked off.

Paul was beside himself. The one minute stretched to two, then three, then five. Paul was perspiring heavily. He turned on the engine to get the air conditioner going. He thought he could hear the car down the street follow suit. Paul was fixated on watching the other car in his rearview mirror. Then, in the distance, he could see another vehicle approaching. Paul had a sinking sensation in the pit of his stomach. He knew it—it was a police car. He quickly speed dialed George again.

George was stretched out on the floor, his arm extended way out, reaching under the couch. His phone rang again and he was exasperated—Paul was being a real pain. He stood up and glanced out of the window and saw movement. As he walked toward the front of the room, he saw the police cruiser pull up right in front of Mariel's walkway out to the street.

"Oh, shit," he said, and raced back toward the kitchen door, moving as if his life depended on it, running down the yard and out into the wooded area behind Spallek's house. Despite the undergrowth and young trees, he tore along, making good progress. After a couple of minutes, he stopped and looked back the way he had come. He called Paul.

WHEN GEORGE DIDN'T ANSWER his last call and two uniformed police officers got out of the car and walked up toward Mariel's front door, Paul pulled away from the curb very slowly. He looked back, and the Malibu that had been parked behind him followed at a distance. Paul expected sirens to blare and to be pulled over, but it didn't happen. He now thought the Malibu was an unmarked police car. He was holding the phone in his hand when it went off.

"George!"

"I'm out back in the woods. What's going on?" George was out of breath.

"The cops went in the house and I'm being followed by that car that showed up. But they can't be cops, because they'd have stopped me."

"Just drive toward home. They must be Nano security."

"Why do you say that?"

"Who else could it be? Look, I need to keep walking." George terminated the call. He pushed through the undergrowth for another ten minutes before reaching a minor road. He followed the sun and after twenty minutes of walking in the shadows came to a junction. He called Paul again, who answered, using his hands-free device.

"I'm at a road," said George. "No one's coming for me, it doesn't look like."

"Thank God!"

"Are you still being followed?"

"I don't know, George. I don't see that car. This is making me feel totally sick. And I'm supposed to be at work in an hour."

"You go," said George. "I can get my coordinates from the phone. I'll call a cab and see you later."

"You're very calm about all this," said Paul.

"I think we learned a lot just now. Someone is following us, right? It has to be Nano. If Pia wasn't right about there being a conspiracy going on there, why would they bother?"

"So you have a plan for what we should do next?"

"No. But we need help."

"Obviously. But who's going to help us?"

"I don't know, Paul, I really don't."

55.

Pia felt as if she were swimming in molasses. Without another seda-
tive injection, it had taken her an age to fall asleep, but once she did,
she fell hard. It was obvious to her that she still had some of the drug
on board. As she slowly awoke, Pia wondered how much time she
had lost. She hadn't seen Berman since he had left her in the underground cell after making his big speech about nanotechnology. It
was impossible to keep track of time. She had been denied the usual
diurnal cycle; the light in the room was always on. When was it that
she saw Berman? Yesterday? Last week? It might have been last year,
for all she knew. Pia's head was throbbing and her vision was blurry.
She felt terrible, but she had to try to focus on what was happening
to her.

However much time had passed, Pia hadn't had much of an opportunity to think about her situation because of the drugs she'd
been given, but now, as she passed through her mind whatever details she could recall, she came to an understanding. Berman had
told her too much for her release to be a viable proposition. Her
position was extremely precarious. She'd have to submit to Berman
or face the consequences.

It took only seconds for Pia to look around her room. An IV ran to a bag that hung on a plastic drip stand for hydration. There was nothing else she could use as a weapon, even if she could reach it, as she was still loosely restrained.

As Pia tried to clear her head a little, a slot in the door that she hadn't noticed opened, and then closed quickly. The lock on the door was activated and the doctor came back in. Pia sat up, ready to fight him again.

"I come to look at your arm. They want you healthy." The man avoided making eye contact with Pia.

"So you do speak English. They want me healthy for what? What do they plan to do with me? And who are 'they'? If you are a doctor, you have an obligation to help me."

The door swung open and a powerful-looking guard came in, closed the door, and silently faced forward, an intimidating presence.

"Where is Berman, the American . . . ?"

"You cannot talk, miss."

The doctor took hold of Pia's bad arm. In addition to her muddy brain, her arm was hurting. Pia knew enough about bone fractures to understand that ideally she should have been holding her arm in the sling to maintain the proper alignment for it to heal. But she had been spending most of her time prone, and she may even have been lying on the arm, she didn't know. However much she hated the doctor, she let him manipulate her arm gently. She didn't want a non-union, meaning the shaft of the humerus would not reconnect to itself, or a misalignment if they connected but did not line up properly. Both situations would require operations to rectify.

"How does this feel?"

"It feels okay. I mean, there is some tenderness but it's not overwhelming."

"You know this could be a problem if you do not look after it."

"I'm being held prisoner somewhere shackled to a bed. It's not like I have a lot of say in the matter. You're too much, telling me it is my responsibility."

"If it doesn't heal, your arm may be bad forever."

"Like that is the worst of my problems." Pia realized she was not in the best of shape, and she wondered if that was the reason Berman hadn't forced himself on her. "I'm rather vulnerable on a lot of fronts," she added.

The man said nothing.

"Maybe being infirm has its advantages. Maybe that's why I haven't been taken advantage of by the wealthy American." No sooner had the comment escaped her lips, than a dreadful thought crossed her mind.

"Unless he has. He hasn't, has he?" Pia thought not, but when she was awake she couldn't remember much, and when she was out of it, she wouldn't know, as heavily as she'd been sedated. But she'd feel something, and Berman would have bragged about it. Wouldn't he?

"You know what kind of man you are working for, don't you?" she said to the doctor.

The doctor did not respond, but scribbled some notes in a small book, pocketed it, and left the room. A moment later he came back with a bowl and a bottle of water. He had a manila folder tucked under his arm.

"This is soup. You should eat. And water. The American boss man wants you to read this."

The man left the soup on the floor, where Pia could reach it, and left. The folder contained a document about ten pages long. It was stamped CONFIDENTIAL in red and had a serial number printed like a watermark on each page. Pia skimmed through before tossing the document on the floor in the corner of the room. It was a business prospectus for potential investors outlining plans for Nano's expansion through the year 2020. *He's trying to impress me*, she thought.

And a prospectus is supposed to prove that he's a legitimate business-man. Do legitimate businessmen do this? she asked herself holding up a shackled arm. Pia's head hurt too much for her to read what she was sure was Berman's self-aggrandizing BS.

"If you want me to read this crap, let me out of here," she yelled at the door.

Pia lay back on her bed and stared at the ceiling. She didn't feel well but didn't want to sleep anymore. Some time passed and Pia remembered the soup the man had left her. She sat up, which made her head pound anew. After a minute her head cleared a little and she ate the cold soup. With her foot she pulled the prospectus to where she could pick it up. Out of sheer boredom, she read through it.

According to what Pia read, nanotechnology was going to change medicine forever. *Tell me something I don't know*, thought Pia. Nano-bots could eat plaque and fix clogged arteries. They could consume even the most rapacious of cancers and infection. They could attack the sites of inflammation; seal wounds; clean teeth, even.

One application was given more prominence in the document than any other. Nanobots could have an impact on the buildup of proteins in the brain of a patient with early-stage Alzheimer's; they might even have prophylactic properties that would ensure a person at risk of the disease could be treated before the onset of any symptoms. Berman had told Pia about his mother suffering from the disease while she lived out her life in an assisted-living facility near Nano.

Of course, thought Pia in a moment of clarity, *this is why Berman is taking so many chances, cutting so many corners. This is why he was desperate to get a ten-year march on his competition.* Berman was how old? Late forties? If he was susceptible himself, the first changes may already be taking place in his brain. In ten years, they might be ir-reversible. Pia felt sure she was right. But what could she do with this information?

Pia thought about Berman's motivation. Working to cure Alzheimer's was a legitimate reason to pursue research. It could be vitally important, even noble work, but not when it was carried out as Berman was doing it. Pia finished her meal and drank some water. She knew there was nothing she could do until she saw Berman again.

56.

Jimmy Yan never ceased to amaze Zach Berman. Berman was barely able to keep his eyes open while Jimmy sat in the VIP area of this expensive nightclub in Mayfair, deep in conversation with a stunningly beautiful Chinese woman who was at least six inches taller than he. The other woman, who had sat down next to Berman when they arrived, had lost interest and wandered off a half hour previously. The club throbbed with beat-heavy music and was thronged with young, attractive men and women. Try as he might to join in, Berman just wanted to go to bed.

"You are not enjoying yourself?" asked Jimmy, shouting to be heard above the noise.

"I can hardly hear you," said Berman, cupping a hand to his ear.

"But you like places like this. We went to places much like this in Milan."

"I know. But it's late, and I'm tired."

What Berman truly wanted was to have Pia there by his side. Try as he might he couldn't get her out of his mind, knowing she was back at the vicarage wasting away. He had fully expected to have heard through the Chinese doctor that she wanted to see him, but it hadn't happened. Berman had asked the doctor directly, but he had insisted that Pia had not said anything of the kind. It was, in Berman's mind, a kind of Mexican standoff, both accustomed to getting their way. He cursed her doggedness while recognizing it was part of her allure.

Berman yawned, and he covered his mouth to try to conceal it. There was no doubt he was tired. He and Jimmy had been on the go all day. The difference was that Jimmy still looked as bright as he had that morning. They had driven in an official car from the vicarage in Chenies to the Olympic site in east London where the international championships were taking place, a journey of forty miles that should have taken an hour but took three in nightmarish traffic, which was bad by local standards.

Jimmy Yan took Berman to the apartment where the marathoner Yao Hong-Xiau was staying. Berman had been pestering Jimmy relentlessly to be allowed to see the man who carried his future on the soles of his size-eight shoes. Lying on the bed in his small apartment room, Yao seemed calm and well prepared. He didn't go out much, he told Zachary and Jimmy, there were too many distractions, and he was sticking to his light training schedule and resting.

Later, Berman told Jimmy that Yao was right about the distractions. London was in full summer mode. Jimmy had abandoned the car with its driver in Stratford, where the championships were taking place, and had taken Berman on the Underground—the London subway, something Berman hadn't done since he was an undergraduate at Yale on the grand tour—back into the center of the city. The small subway cars were packed with people. Berman heard a multitude of tongues, and two-thirds of the occupants appeared to be tourists. A busker started singing a Sinatra song, badly, and was shouted down by a gaggle of Australians clutching beer cans.

The narrow sidewalks of central London were bursting with tourists and Londoners. Groups of armed police stood on major intersections, and local cops tried to keep the pedestrians out of the street. Rock music blared from storefronts, and the aromas of a hun-

dred cuisines filled the air. It was a hot and sunny day, and Berman
wondered what had happened to the famously bad English weather.

"Jimmy, what are we doing here?"

"This is Leicester Square, in the middle of London. It is fun, no?"

"No. I've never seen more people in my life."

"I am Chinese, at home I see more people every day. Come on."

Jimmy grabbed Berman's arm and steered him through narrow
side streets to a doorway. A small sign, in Chinese, hung above the
door and Jimmy pushed Berman through.

"We are in Chinatown. Best Chinese food in Europe right here.
These people are from my province."

Jimmy obviously knew the proprietor, who bowed three or four
times. The food, when it came, was incredibly spicy, and unlike any
Chinese food Berman had tasted.

"Is it too hot? I asked them to tone it down, for a Westerner."

"It's good," said Berman, chewing a piece of fiery meat. "But it
is spicy."

"I want to take your mind off that woman. She is not going to
come around, you know."

Why did Jimmy think that? The rooms at the vicarage were probably bugged, Berman realized, and Jimmy probably knew of Pia's
response to his entreaties.

"She will come around," Berman said. "She has to. Look, Jimmy,
I appreciate your being discreet about her, with your bosses."

"Who says I haven't told them?"

"I trust you haven't. Nothing has happened to this point to jeopardize our enterprise. The only fallout from snatching her out of
Boulder is a couple of guys who went to the Boulder police and asked
a couple of questions. They are not getting anywhere. In fact, they're
the ones who may be in trouble, not us. As far as anyone knows, Pia's
in the wind."

Jimmy shrugged. Berman knew Pia meant nothing to Jimmy. But
while the deal was in the balance, she could remain as his guest. The

marathon wasn't for another two weeks, so there was ample time for Berman to wear her down. He'd never failed before.

Now, many hours after lunch, with more sightseeing and an endless dinner, Berman was calling it a night,

"As you wish," said Jimmy. "The car is outside if you want to go back. My friend and I were discussing Chinese agricultural policy. Seriously. I'll come back later."

Jimmy turned back to his new companion. *Good for you*, thought Berman, *but I'm done*. He wondered how much of what he was feeling was because of Pia or if it was because it was half past two in the morning. Berman had a sense that his feelings for Pia were not just carnal, otherwise he would have made sure he could possess her as soon as they had reached the vicarage. He wanted her recognition that he was a pioneer and that they could build this company together, with Berman at the helm and talented scientists like her alongside. The Chinese phase would be over soon, and there would be no more need for clandestine experimentation. It had been necessary to jump-start the program, to get the capital funding, but now everything was going to be aboveboard. Pia could take the NIH on a tour of Nano herself if that would placate her.

A new rhythm thudded its way into Berman's head as the disc jockey started a new set. Berman could see that Jimmy wasn't about to leave anytime soon, so he got up from the leather couch, thanked the man for the enjoyable day, and made his way through the crowd of pretty people toward the exit.

57.

Paul and George disagreed over whether they were likely to receive a visit from the police after their jaunt to Mariel Spallek's home, and Paul took no pleasure in being proved correct. George had not dismissed Paul's opinion out of hand, so the two men were able to agree on their story before Detective Samuels came around the evening following with a colleague he introduced as Detective Ibbotson. The four men got situated in Paul's living room, with Paul and George on the couch and the two investigators on kitchen chairs facing them. The atmosphere was strained. Samuels started in.

"We can talk here, or we can talk more formally at the station tomorrow," Samuels said. He was looking at Paul as the host, but George answered.

"We're happy to talk here."

"So where did you go after we talked yesterday?"

"We drove around, figuring what to do. I mean, we were worried about our friend and didn't get much satisfaction from our visit to the police."

"Sorry you feel that way, but we are still looking into the situation. Where did you drive to?"

"About one-thirty, we went out to Niwot. We found out that Pia Grazdani's boss at Nano, Mariel Spallek, lived out there. We thought maybe she might be home and willing to answer some questions about Pia. We're really kind of lost about what to do. But Mariel Spallek was not at home, so we went away, thinking we might return some evening."

"You were out there around one-thirty," said Samuels.

"Around then, yes," said George, and offered no more. They had been at Niwot, but by one-thirty, he was in a cab on his way home.

"And you can confirm this," Samuels said to Paul.

"Yes. I know the time, because I had to get to the hospital. I was late."

"He drove in, I took a taxi. From Niwot." George knew that if they checked, they would find that he had taken a taxi, but from a location that might require some explanation.

"Why did you take a taxi?"

"Paul had to get to work. I took a taxi from there rather than from the hospital. I was on my way back here."

Samuels regarded the two men. He guessed they were being less than truthful, but in the grand scheme of things, did it matter that much. "So you rang the bell at Miss Spallek's, and no one answered?"

"That's right," said George.

"Did you see anyone? Anyone that you might have thought didn't belong in the neighborhood?"

"There was a car parked suspiciously on the same street."

"Suspiciously how?"

"Well, not parked suspiciously, but parked in the street with two men sitting in it. It was just down the road from Mariel's house. There were no other cars or people. It looked suspicious to us, and we talked about it."

Paul nodded.

"Can you describe the car?"

"Dark blue," said Paul. "Full-size sedan. American. Buick or something like that. I actually assumed it was a police car. It was kind of drab like that. No offense."

Samuels looked at Paul, then at George. *Very clever*, he thought, and closed his notebook. This whole situation wasn't worth his time. He knew that the police had gotten the tip from Nano, suggesting that Nano had had them under surveillance, possibly because they had tried and failed to get into their facility. Samuels had the gut sense that there was some weird romantic aspect to this story, but at that point he wasn't going to speculate. The facts of the case were that someone, maybe the two sitting in front of him, had broken into Mariel Spallek's apartment, but nothing had been stolen or damaged save for a pane of glass in a back door. More important, Mariel Spallek specifically declined to take the matter further when contacted, and the responding police officers hadn't actually seen anyone, despite the clear evidence of a break-in.

"Detective Ibbotson, how about you head out to the car. I'll be right out," said Samuels. His partner nodded and left.

"I don't know what's going on here," he said, "but my sense is that you guys need to cut out playing detective before you get yourselves in trouble. I know those security people at Nano, and they're no fools. Next time you try a stunt like this, I hope they don't get to you first."

"That sounds like a threat," said George.

"Actually, it isn't. It's a piece of friendly advice. Your girlfriend will come back, provided she wants to. That's what happens in ninety-nine point nine percent of cases like this. If she doesn't, then she won't. But we have the facts as they exist, and we will continue to follow up on the case. We are in direct contact with the Nano human resources department. We have the woman's description and photo. There was evidence that she had returned to her apartment after sending the text to you, Dr. Caldwell, along with the suggestion that she had driven east. We, of course, will be following up on that. So, fellows, cool it before you get arrested or hurt."

Samuels got up and left.

"Funny they should know to come right after my shift finished," said Paul after Samuels had walked out.

"Paul, I've been thinking. It's pretty apparent we're being followed by Nano, and the police are onto us, and we're getting nowhere finding Pia. She's gone, I'm sure of it. I don't believe she drove east for a second. I think someone took her. I think it was Berman. And we don't have the resources to find her."

"So what the hell do we do? The authorities obviously aren't listening to us."

"When Pia was in trouble before, her father saved her. I think I have to ask for his help. I hate to do it, because he's basically a gangster of the worst kind."

"Her father? I didn't know Pia had any family."

"He's a higher-up in the Albanian mafia organization in the New York metropolitan area. I have no reason to think he'll even help, but he did the last time Pia got into this kind of trouble, which, I have to say, is remarkably similar in many respects to what's going on now. She was kidnapped then, too. God, it's as if she is a magnet for disaster."

"Albanian mafia. Good lord! I think I saw a movie about them. Extremely violent."

"The worst."

"What's the father's name?"

"Burim Graziani or something like that."

"Not Grazdani, like Pia."

"He had to change his name for some reason."

"How did he save her?"

"She'd been kidnapped by a rival Albania mafia clan who were under contract by some financial types to kill her. They didn't because of her last name, which they knew was Albanian. The father, being a connected man, was contacted, and he proved she was family. The Albanians are a bit like the Italian mafia with family and their own idiosyncratic ideas of honor above all else."

"Mafia or no mafia, I think you should give this Burim a try. Why do you think he might not be willing to help?"

"After he did manage to save her from the rival Albanian group, he tried to resurrect some sort of relationship with her, but she wouldn't have any part of it. She wouldn't even talk to him. When she was around six he had abandoned her to the New York City foster care system, where she had been psychologically tortured. He actually called me at that point, which is why I have his cell number. He asked me to try to intervene and get Pia to call him. Stupidly I tried to help, but Pia went ballistic, accusing me of interfering in her life. That was the last I saw her until I popped out here in April."

Paul shrugged. "This father sounds less than charming, but I don't think we have a lot of choice. Unfortunately it's pretty clear the Boulder police are not going to do anything unless some sort of direct proof surfaces of her being snatched. My sense is that she is not here in Boulder."

"That's my thought, too."

"I do have a contact out at the airport. Maybe as a starter I can find out if the Nano jet is around, and if it isn't, where it might have gone. I don't know if that is common information or not, but pilots do have to file flight plans."

"It wouldn't hurt," George said. "Shit. I don't like the idea of talking with the likes of Burim Graziani. He's very hard-core, but I'm at my wit's end. I don't see any alternative."

"I guess you'd better call him," said Paul.

"Actually, I already did. Of course there was no answer. I had to leave my name and number."

THE CALL GEORGE had been hoping to get came an hour later. As soon as George started to talk, the caller, who admitted he was not Burim, said that he wanted to hear no details over the phone. If George wanted to talk to Burim, it had to be in person in a public place, meaning George had to travel east. The caller then warned George that he better not be wasting anyone's time. The invitation, grudging though it might be, was what George needed to hear, but the question then arose of how to get away from Boulder without being seen. Neither George nor Paul thought it a good idea to advertise where George was going as long as Nano had them under surveillance.

George booked a ticket on the 8:37 A.M. United flight to Newark, and then he and Paul strategized a way for George to get to the Denver airport without being detected. Which was why Paul sat in his Subaru at four in the morning in the car park of his apartment building with the engine running.

"HEY, ERIC, they're on the move."

Having failed to get Caldwell and Wilson arrested at Mariel Spallek's house, Chad Wells and Eric McKenzie pulled the Nano security detail's night shift. They had parked down the street from Paul Caldwell's apartment building in a spot that afforded them a view of the parking lot. Chad was lucky—he had fallen asleep, as had Eric, but awoke in time to notice Caldwell's car's lights on and the engine running and see the men sitting in the vehicle.

"Are they both in the car?" said Eric trying to get his eyes to function. "What the fuck time is it, for chrissake?"

"It's around four."

"What the hell are they doing up at this time? Where the hell could they be going?"

"I think that's what we have to find out. Remember, they are doctors. Maybe they got called on an emergency."

"It looks like they are both in the car."

"That's my take," said Chad, but he didn't know for sure as far away as they were. But it seemed safer to sound definite than admit he couldn't be sure. Besides, it was a good bet both of them were there, as the two of them had done everything together up to this point. Besides, he didn't want to stand out in the damn cold if Eric suggested he do so.

"Okay, let's follow. But stay well back, okay?"

"Got it."

AFTER FIVE MINUTES, Paul started to move, and he drove very deliberately out of the parking lot making sure his headlights strafed the car he assumed was the surveillance vehicle. The idea was for him to drive out toward Berman's house, hang out for a time, and then and loop back via the hospital. It would take at least an hour, by which time George would have the opportunity to walk out of the back entrance of the apartment building and be met by a prearranged car service at a gas station a half mile down the road in the other direction. Both Paul and George doubted there would be more than one car involved in any surveillance, and even if a man were to be left behind at the apartment complex, he wouldn't be able to see George leaving out the back. Or so they hoped.

GEORGE WATCHED PAUL LEAVE and then let the curtain fall back into place. After waiting fifteen minutes, he followed the plan and left Paul's apartment, making his way out the rear door, and walked down the road quickly without looking back. He had borrowed one of Paul's sports coats and a pair of dress pants that fit him well enough. For some reason, he wanted to dress up for the meeting he'd arranged for four o'clock that same afternoon. Just thinking about it gave him an uneasy, queasy feeling that made his pulse race. George knew he was not a risk-taker by nature, but he knew he had to do it and do it soon. As he approached the gas station, he saw a town car sitting on the forecourt and knew it had to be his ride.

Now George essayed a glance over his shoulder and saw he was quite alone. He'd made it.

58.

George Wilson sat at the back of the Roy Rogers restaurant. It reminded him of long family trips he had taken as a child, and of sitting in places like this. His family had always bought their own food, buying only beverages, and George used to sit eating homemade egg sandwiches while other kids gorged on hamburgers. He guessed that was why he'd ordered a hamburger today, but he'd taken one bite and couldn't eat any more. He nursed his jumbo Diet Coke and waited.

Twenty minutes later, and thirty-five minutes late, his meeting arrived.

"You're still here," said Burim Graziani, née Grazdani, surprising George, who hadn't noticed him walk in. He was accompanied by another man with whom he could have been related. Burim was just as George remembered him. A slight man of medium height, seemingly in his fifties, dark-complected in all respects, with piercing eyes as black as coal. His mouth pulled up slightly in the left corner in a kind of sneer from a scar. In George's eyes he was the stereotypical hoodlum with a demeanor that suggested he was incapable of remorse. He was dressed in an ill-fitting black leather jacket and black turtleneck. He sat down, keeping both hands under the table.

George imagined he was armed. The other, larger man stood where he was with his arms folded, eyeing George like a cat might eye a motionless mouse.

"Of course, I'm still here," George croaked. He cleared his throat. "I wanted to see you."

"I can't say the same. We met before but it was a waste of my time. I asked for you to help me, but you fucked up and made it worse. I saved my daughter's ass almost two years ago and all I asked for my trouble was some kind of . . ." He struggled for the right word.

"Détente?" George suggested.

"Don't be a smart-ass," Burim snapped and regarded George for a moment with narrowed eyes. "But, yeah, something like that. All I wanted to do was get to know her a little bit, but she's too high and mighty to have anything to do with me, being a doctor and all."

"She's in terrible danger."

"That's how it's to be, huh? Every time she's in danger I have to see you?"

"Listen, her boss in Colorado—"

Burim held up his hand.

"Stop right there. You need to go with my guy here. He has to search you."

"Search me why?"

"You don't like it, our conversation is over. You understand what I'm saying?"

George did as he was told. The thuggish-looking man with Burim took George outside and into the back of a blue panel van. Another man patted George down roughly and very thoroughly. As he ran his fingers through George's hair for some reason, he winked. Was this the uncle Pia had told him about? When he got back to the table, George didn't ask. Burim had finished his soda.

"Okay, college boy. Tell me the story." He pointed to the chair George had vacated.

George laid out the whole tale, as much as he knew, emphasizing that Pia's boss, Zachary Berman, had come on to Pia sexually. He explained that Pia had become convinced that something weird was going on where she worked at a research company called Nano, and had put herself in danger by trying to find out what it was. The only thing she knew was that it somehow involved the Chinese because she, and the other doctor friend, had had a run-in with a stricken Chinese jogger who was also associated with Nano. Then when she apparently found out what it was, she had disappeared. "She texted a friend to say she was on her way to his apartment to explain what she learned, but never showed up. Since then no one has seen her. Myself and this other doctor friend are convinced she'd been kidnapped by her boss."

"When did all this take place?"

"A few days ago. Monday morning to be precise."

Burim glanced up at his colleague. "Sounds like the same thing as two years ago. Jesus Christ, the girl is impossible." The colleague nodded. Burim looked back at George. "My daughter reminds me of my wife. She was a firebrand, too. And that is not a good thing. She pissed me off big time when I was struggling to get started. Neither of them showed me no respect."

"Pia's had a hard life. She was in those foster homes . . ."

"Careful, college boy."

George swallowed hard but continued. "Those places made it very hard for her to connect with people. She doesn't trust anyone, including me. She doesn't have many friends; in fact I only know of two, myself and this other gay doctor."

"Oh, please!" Burim said, raising his hands above the table. "I don't want to hear about that."

"The point that I'm trying to make is that besides myself and this other doctor, there is no one else to sound the alarm about Pia disappearing. Listen, if you are truly interested in getting to know her, it's going to take years. If that's what you want, it's not going to be

easy. It was never going to happen overnight like you wanted. You'll
have to be patient."

"Why should I bother?"

"Because she's your flesh and blood. She's family. That's why you
went to save her last time. That was a pain in the ass, too, I expect,
but you did it. Pia's not the kind of person to bow down and say
thank you in a situation like that. She has a lot of pride; that must
mean something to you. She wouldn't speak to me or see me for
almost two years after I tried to help you."

"Is that right?"

"Absolutely."

Burim nodded. "Flesh and blood. She looks just like her mother,
you know."

"Your wife must have been a very beautiful woman when you
met her."

Burim looked at George and narrowed his eyes.

"You still in medical training?

"Yes."

"You becoming a shrink?"

"Hardly. No, I'm becoming a radiologist."

"Then how do you know all this crap about Pia?"

"You don't have to be a professional to appreciate what she had
gone through growing up. The fact of the matter is she's had a
hard life, but she's a remarkable person: intelligent to beat the band
and beautiful. A lot of men are attracted to her, including myself, if
you want to know. I'm really worried about her. I and this other doctor tried to get the Boulder police involved, but they are content to
sit on their asses. There is no specific evidence that Pia was kidnapped. In fact they think they have evidence that Pia drove away,
heading east, perhaps in a nonrequited funk, which is ridiculous.
But the bottom line is that they are content to wait it out, saying
that in most instances like this, the woman reappears. But I'm tell-

ing you, she is not going to reappear. This guy Berman took advantage of her, I'm convinced. I'm sure he kidnapped her. He may have molested her. Raped her. He may have *killed* her. This is Pia we're talking about. Your daughter."

George paused—he hoped to hell he wasn't pushing too hard.

"If this Berman guy did kidnap her, where would he take her? Do you have any idea?"

"Not specifically. But the other doctor I mentioned has a friend who works out at the Boulder airport. Through him we found out that the Nano jet, presumably with Berman aboard, took off the morning Pia disappeared."

"Where did it go?"

"The flight plan was to Italy. One of Milan's airports."

Burim stared out of the window a good minute.

"Flesh and blood," Burim said quietly. "You wait here."

Ten minutes passed, and George started to think Burim had walked out on him. Then he was back.

"What makes you think she has been killed?" he asked. "Or put another way, what do you think are the chances she's already been killed?"

"I don't think she has been killed. I think she is being held prisoner someplace, I guess in Italy."

"The trouble is there are no Albanian clans in Denver. But that's not a major problem."

"What about in Italy?" George asked.

"No problem in Italy. I even lived there for a time on my way here to the States. It's where I met and married my wife. We have a lot of people in Italy. Hell, it's only fifty miles between Italy and Albania."

"I hope to God you can find her and quick enough to save her."

"Shit! I already did this once," Burim said. "I guess I'm gonna have to do it again. But she better show a bit more gratitude this time, because there is not going to be a third." His thin-lipped mouth managed a ragged smile.

AT 11:10 THAT EVENING, Burim Grazdani sat in his premium economy seat in a British Airways Airbus bound for London Heathrow and looked at his watch again. His flight had been scheduled to leave five minutes before, but the flight attendants were still walking around checking passengers' safety belts. Next to his house and car, this plane ticket was the most expensive item he had ever purchased legitimately, or semi-legitimately, since the name on the passport was not his own. Despite the price, he had been told by the booking agent he was very lucky to get even this ticket at three hours' notice. There had just been a cancellation of a group booking and stand-by passengers had taken every spare seat but one. Burim booked the flight without even listening to the price.

George Wilson had sat with him in the restaurant at the Vince Lombardi Service Area on the New Jersey Turnpike for another half hour. Burim told George he had done the right thing. The police weren't going to help; and George couldn't. He needed professional assistance with the resources of the Albanian mafia. Burim hadn't used the word *mafia*. Instead he had said family, but George knew what he meant.

Burim asked George to relay the story to him a second time to be sure of the details. He took no notes, but absorbed the information easily—there really wasn't much to go on. Burim asked George more about this Berman guy. George said he knew he was truly rich—he had a yacht, or access to a yacht, and, of course, the plane.

That was enough information for Burim. He dropped George at the railway station in Paramus, as George said he wanted to go into Manhattan to check on the condition of Will McKinley. Burim Grazdani made no more comments about the events from two years before in which he had been intimately involved, and which had led to McKinley's injury. He had rescued Pia once, and he was prepared to try to do it again.

Burim drove back to his boss Berti Ristani's place in Weehawken.
Burim's value as a trusted lieutenant to Berti had only increased
over the years, and Berti was happy to help his friend. This was family, after all. On Burim's behalf, Berti had made a call. In the world
of organized crime, Albanian style, it always made Berti proud when
he realized how far the tentacles of the beast now extended. As
usual on a strictly business call, making even one phone call meant
an elaborate charade. The Albanians had been burned by the FBI
one too many times. Berti used a burner phone to call another one-
use cell phone, which eventually led to a call back to a third phone,
which Berti would use once, then throw, along with the first phone,
into the nearby Hudson River.

Berti told Burim that he learned from his contact at a friendly
family in L.A. that another family had numerous aviation interests
around the country, particularly in general aviation at municipal airports and at the FAA. If you wanted to get something or someone
into or out of the United States quickly, you could try to use a major
hub, or go through a smaller link, like Teterboro in New Jersey, or
Boulder Airport.

This was another area where civilians like George Wilson were
fatally limited. They were incapable of thinking like a criminal.
Burim had no doubt this rich creep had taken Pia out of the country.
As Pia had done before, she'd stumbled across someone doing something he shouldn't, and made a nuisance of herself. This guy Berman
fancied himself as some kind of playboy, or so Burim quickly learned.
Burim could imagine Pia resisting him, and the guy taking her away
somewhere. He felt that familiar rage. When that happened, someone was always going to have to pay.

Then Berti had made another call, to someone outside the Albanian family, but with a connection, and with a favor to repay. Burim
sat in Berti Ristani's office for an hour, waiting for another dispos-
able phone to ring. Berti constantly drank water and chewed gum.
After a health scare six months before, Ristani had announced he

was going to lose weight, and to his crew's astonishment he had dropped fifty pounds and he was loving life.

"You know, if we was the police, the jails would be full," said Berti. "We can find out shit fifty times faster than the cops can or the FBI."

"Because we know all the criminals," said Burim.

"That's right! Perhaps I should go straight and run the CIA. Serve my country." Berti smiled. "Having said that, I hope these assholes aren't gonna let me down."

"Berti, if I need to take some time over this . . ."

"Burim, don't worry 'bout nothing. Anything you need. Hold on. This must be them."

Berti took the call. It had to be the contact out west—no one else in the world had the number to this phone. Berti said nothing to the caller, but he spoke to Burim with his hand over the bottom of the phone.

"Yes, the plane belonging to Berman left Boulder that night, it's confirmed. He was heading for Milan, Italy. That was the flight plan."

Burim stood up.

"Wait, there's more." Berti listened.

"They know from a contact who was sitting in the tower when they were leaving. The pilot asked about another flight plan, for Stansted, wherever that is. Okay," said Berti into the phone. "And thanks." Berti ended the call.

"The pilot talked about a second flight plan they were going to file. He said they were going to turn right around and fly from Italy to Stansted, which is near London, England. That was the final destination."

"Thanks, Berti," said Burim. "Listen, I owe you."

"Hey, it's nothing," said Berti. "We know people in London. There's lots of family in London, and they can help you when you get there. I'll make another call. I'll have someone meet your plane with a sign that you'll recognize. Just come back here safe, you're valuable to me, you know that. And sort out the scumbag who took your daughter."

FINALLY THE JETWAY retracted from Burim's plane and the plane was pushed off from the concourse at Newark, with Berti's helpful words resonating in his head.

59.

Pia couldn't keep track of the days but she knew she hadn't seen Berman in a long time. The only people she did see were the doctor and the same guard who never looked her in the eye. The slot in the door had been pulled back once and she could swear it was Whitney Jones standing out there, but she never came into the room. Pia's arm was doing a little better, but she felt very dulled and listless. How long was Berman going to torture her this way? Her muscles felt flabby from lack of use.

It was on the sixth day since his last visit that Berman returned.

"What do you want?" she said. She thought she detected a slight smile on his lips, which just angered her that much more.

"How about a walk?" he asked as if this were the most normal thing in the world for the two of them to consider.

"If it'll get me out of this room, sure," said Pia. She had tried to keep flexing her arms and legs in basic Pilates moves but she knew she would be stiff if she walked any distance.

The guard undid the shackles that attached Pia to the bed and bade her to stand. She felt terribly weak, and her head throbbed, but she was able to remain upright if she placed her hand against the wall. The guard helped her to the door as Berman stood outside,

where a walker was waiting for her. Pia felt better—perhaps half
human, as she grabbed hold of the walker and shuffled after Berman.

"I am truly sorry about this, Pia. I only wish you had been more
cooperative. You must realize I am laying a lot on the line keeping
you here like this."

Pia was alarmed—Berman seemed to be talking with a grave
finality.

"Where are you taking me?"

"For a walk, I told you."

A heavy door opened from outside and they walked out into the
back garden of the vicarage. It was fifty yards long and shaded all
around by thick woodland. A high wooden fence corralled the lawn,
which was encircled by a path, with benches at all four corners.

"I want you to get your strength back," said Berman. "Have you
thought about our conversation? Did you read the material I left
for you?"

"Of course I thought about our conversation. And I read the material. Sure, it's very impressive. Nano in 2020 will be the biggest
medical researcher in the world. But you're neglecting some important aspects of your less than glorious past."

"Pia, I implore you to look beyond that. The bodies you saw, those
people were going to die anyway—pointless, anonymous deaths. I
think of them now as pioneers of a kind. Because of their sacrifice,
we will be able to make these incredible medical advances."

"That's ridiculous and you know it. It's not a sacrifice if you're
made to do it." It felt good to be walking, so Pia pressed on. She
wanted to keep this conversation going. Berman spoke again.

"Do you remember how excited you were when you first came to
work at Nano? The enthusiasm with which you talked about your
work was truly infectious. When you came over for dinner with that
boy, you and I talked about the possibilities of what we are doing.
And this is a whole new world of possibilities. A new frontier for
medicine. It's going to open up treatments and cures for thousands

of maladies. And you know something else: it is going to save money. Nano is about to enter a new era. I'm done with respirocytes and athletes. We can move on to legitimate experimentation and development using animal models first and then humans. Can you imagine injecting a few cc's of respirocytes into a drowning victim? Or what about people with debilitating COPD who can't breathe enough to climb a single flight of stairs. They'll be cured with respirocytes. The good we are going to do in the future will be a thousand times greater than any harm we did in the past. Ten thousand times more! We have no need for the kind of experimentation that was required to develop respirocytes fast enough for our Chinese backers. And to tell you the truth, on some level I now regret it."

Pia glared at Berman.

"Bullshit. You'll still do whatever it takes."

"I see that you may not believe me, but it's true."

"You wanted to take shortcuts so you could save yourself."

"What do you mean?"

"You told me about your mother, who's living with Alzheimer's. The literature you gave me focuses a lot on Alzheimer's. You're terrified you're going to see signs of it in yourself and you'll do anything to find a cure."

"It's not guaranteed that I'll get the disease, but, yes, the chances are high. Both my parents struggled with it, and it was tragic to see my father go as he did. Now my mother is going downhill quickly. And I do have the gene associated with an increased risk, meaning I'm facing a double whammy. So, yes, I'm focused on Alzheimer's research as well as infectious disease. Is that such a bad thing?"

"So you admit it. Of course it's a bad thing, when you're killing people in order to do it."

"Ten people, perhaps, and they were criminals, convicted felons who were scheduled for execution. They would have died anyway if our program had not existed. And we didn't intend them to die, that was not the goal. In reality all we affected was the date of death."

Pia had promised herself that she would adopt a more concilia-
tory tone with Berman if she got another chance to talk to him. She
had to give in, she saw that, or who knew what would happen to her?
If she didn't agree to Berman's terms, there was no chance of her
making it back to the United States. She even knew there was a
deadline—the marathon at the athletics championships. But when it
came to it, she couldn't help herself. She found herself saying things
she knew she shouldn't. It was a bad habit, to say the least.

Pia suddenly felt physically exhausted but she wanted to keep
walking. It had been almost a week since she had gone to see Berman
at his house, as near as she could figure. It felt like ten years. Pia
wondered: if she pretended to relent to Berman, would he take her
home. Perhaps she could promise him the physical favors he so
craved once they were back on American soil, but knowing him as
she did, she doubted it very much. She knew she was powerless to do
anything while she remained a prisoner here.

"How much longer are you going to keep me here like this?"

"How much longer are you going to resist the inevitable?"

"Perhaps forever."

"I have said the consequences for you would be disastrous."

"Can you at least get me a cell with a real bathroom? Or is that
how your mother is, soiling herself in a diaper? You like the women
in your life to be degraded, is that it, Berman?"

Pia steeled herself, ready for Berman to strike her. But he didn't.
Instead, he stopped walking. Pia looked at him and his face was
thunder.

"You're lucky you're so pathetic yourself. I'm sure you are aware
that I could have had my way with you if that had been my only
intent. The fact of the matter is that I'm protecting you from our
hosts, taking a risk, I might add, that their patience might run out.
But that doesn't mean I have to protect you forever. Think about
your situation again. What are you going to do, climb that wall over
there?"

Pia looked at the enclosure surrounding the garden. It was an impossibly huge fence, especially in her weakened condition. Even if Berman said to go climb, she wouldn't be able to do it. Pia knew Berman was right. She was trapped with little hope of rescue. The only person who might guess that she had been abducted was Paul, and what could he do, especially since there was no way he could know for sure what had happened to her?

60.

"You like watching this, Burim?"

"Under different circumstances," Burim said. He was trying to be a good guest, but he'd been sitting here for hours watching the TV. Now the men were watching what looked like billiards. Burim could barely watch, and after his third beer, he turned down their offer of more. He needed to keep a clear head.

Burim knew what good fortune he'd enjoyed to this point. He had arrived at Heathrow, tired and disoriented, and was met by an unmistakably Albanian man holding a sign that read BERTY'S FRIEND. The sign was as redundant as it was misspelled—this unshaven, raven-haired thug was obviously the right man. He introduced himself as Billy and said he was going to look after Burim. Billy told Burim that Berti had called to say that the car Pia was using had been found in Iowa, but the police still weren't treating her disappearance as suspicious. Burim said there was no way Pia was in Iowa. She had been on that plane to London from Italy. He was convinced.

After that, the men drove in silence to this terraced house in a run-down but functioning neighborhood in North London. Burim was bursting with questions, but he followed his driver's lead and kept quiet.

Billy let Burim into the narrow home with lurid wallpaper and the smell of damp, and introduced Harry, a slightly older and better-dressed man.

"Billy and Harry?" said Burim in their common tongue.

"I know," said Harry, "but the less we know about each other, the better, yes?"

"Agreed."

"We have a room upstairs. It's small, but you won't be here long. Take a shower if you want. The water pressure is low, and don't use all the hot water. You'll need some clothes."

"I'm fine. What are we doing about locating my daughter?"

"Of course. That's why we're all here. We have the picture that was forwarded, and the description. She is a lovely young woman. Which makes our job easier. The picture has been distributed to all our friends and associates. Who have their own friends and associates. They know there is a reward available. There is a reward available, yes?"

Burim nodded. He knew that question would arise, and he would pay. He just didn't know how much. Burim struck that thought and moved on. "What about the Chinese? The plane that arrived at Stansted that fit the description was listed as a Chinese diplomatic flight."

"It was," said Harry. "Which makes us think that the contact in America may have been mistaken. We're checking other airports."

"But I know there was a Chinese connection with the case my daughter was investigating."

"That's right. But the reality is, if it was a Chinese government flight, our job is much more difficult. There are certain countries that are very hard to take on, and China is one of them. The triads here in London are a real problem—very powerful and impossible to infiltrate. So we're hoping to find the plane in another location."

"So what can I do?"

"Nothing. You have to stay with us while our people do their work. You don't know London. It's a huge city and you'll only get in trouble. There are Albanian factions that we are not friendly with who we need to avoid. You know how it is. I'm sure it's the same with you."

Burim nodded. There was always a certain amount of factional warfare going on among rival Albanian clans.

"Have a beer and try to watch the snooker. It's a cool game."

Harry smiled and Burim shrugged. He'd play along, for now.

61.

George Wilson was amazed by Paul Caldwell's ability to compart-
mentalize his life. Paul was going to work, doing night shifts, putting
in long hours. Every couple of hours he'd call George to check in, but
George never had anything to report. The police hadn't called him
back; Nano wasn't responding to his emails. He still couldn't find a
phone number for Zach Berman, and Burim Grazdani had not been
in contact, either.

George found that he was unable to concentrate on anything.
After returning from a quick visit to Will McKinley in New York,
where there had been no change, George came back to Boulder,
where he spent his time pacing about Paul's apartment. He had never
been so depressed or frustrated in his life; he knew there was nothing
he could do, and it was driving him crazy.

This day, he had checked in again with the Boulder police, who
now were shunting his calls to a civilian liaison. Paul had come home
and switched his attention to trying to find Whitney Jones and was
working his way through the phone book in an attempt to locate a
relative of hers. The same 411 operator that had come up with Mariel
Spallek's apartment had given him an address, but he quickly dis-
cerned it was the postal address for Nano, LLC. Perhaps the woman

did actually live in the office. All the while, he cursed Whitney for being a Jones and not a Johansson or any other less popular name.

Then, as George was about to make a call himself, his phone rang. A stream of numbers appeared on the screen. More than the usual ten. An international call. *It's Pia*, he thought hopefully, *she's safe*. He picked up.

"Pia?"

"No names, remember." It was a man's voice, gruff and terse. It took George a second, then he placed it. Burim.

"Have you found her?"

"No."

Burim was calling from a public place—George could hear voices in the background, and a public-address system sounded in the distance.

"Where are you?" George asked.

"Have you heard from her? If she shows up, or you find out something, you let me know, right?"

"Of course. Should I use the original mobile number I have for you?"

"Yes, but don't say anything. I'll call you back when I see you have called. So you haven't heard anything at all?"

"Nothing, we've had no word."

"Okay. In that case, I want you to get your ass over here," Burim said.

"What?" said George. "Why?"

"Because I'm doing a lot of legwork, and you're sitting on your butt in a place where we know she isn't, okay?"

"You want me to help you?"

"Don't get excited, college boy, I'm not offering you a job. This is busy work. But we should make the most of what we have. I know you'd be able to recognize her if we come across her. Now, get over here and I'll call you in twenty-four hours, okay?"

"Where are you? Milan?"

"London? Come to London and contact me, and I'll call you back." Burim hung up the pay phone.

THE SEARCH FOR PIA had yielded nothing in London. Harry confirmed to Burim that, yes, the flight that came in from Milan via Colorado was an official Chinese government plane. Harry told Burim that no one he knew had any links to the Chinese crime syndicates, let alone the Chinese government itself. It was clear to Burim that he had received all the help he was going to get from the Albanians. The Chinese connection was like a metaphorical stone wall. But he knew he was welcome to stay as he continued the search himself.

Burim had taken to traveling around central London, looking in flophouses and cheap hotels, whorehouses and gentlemen's clubs, showing Pia's photograph around so much it had become dog-eared and stained by the dirt of a thousand hands. As attractive as Pia was, he thought she could be worth something in a drugged state, like a lot of other Eastern European girls and women. But he was worried that his hopes of finding Pia were fading at the same rate as her picture when his Albanian connections came up with zilch. When the picture became unrecognizable, he would know he had lost her. But his determination was strong. He would help her if she was in danger; he just needed something to go by besides the Chinese association, which had turned out to be a bust.

62.

When Berman came to fetch Pia, she was sitting on her bed, reading. There was also a night table with a small lamp. Berman had acceded to Pia's request and got her a better room with a proper toilet. There was a single, small leaded-glass window less than a foot square high on one wall. When Pia had brought over the night table and had stood on it, she'd been able to see green trees and pastures. Best of all the window afforded Pia a chance to adjust her diurnal schedule. She now knew when it was day and when it was night. The shackles were gone but there was still a stout locked door and a twenty-four-hour guard stationed outside. Berman had found some old paperbacks for her to read, and he had made sure she was allowed to walk around the garden for an hour a day on a leash like a dog with the guard following her around. *Carrots and sticks*, thought Berman.

Pia felt strong and was coiled like a watch spring ready to unravel. But she maintained a cool and slightly pathetic demeanor and hoped that what Berman felt as concern for her well-being would not morph back to the lechery she knew he was capable of.

Berman sat down next to Pia. She stiffened as he placed a hand on her knee.

"How are you feeling?"

"I feel great," said Pia sarcastically.

"You do have the books I gave you, and a bathroom. And you're looking better. Much better."

"I'm just about ready for the runway at the fashion show." She was wearing a simple black T-shirt and black shorts with which she'd been provided.

Berman's hand traveled up Pia's thigh and she brushed it off.

"You don't want to go there," Pia said. "So please take your goddamned hand off my leg, you pervert." Pia looked daggers at Berman, but he pressed his leg harder against hers. Pia squirmed and batted at Berman with her good hand. She restrained herself from giving him a sharp martial arts–style chop on the side of his neck with her good hand that might have brought him to his knees. The trouble was she thought it probably would also put her back in the basement. "Is this your new way of trying to talk me around? Well, forget it. It's not going to work."

Berman's hand was on her thigh again, rising higher. Pia again slapped it away.

"Just leave me alone," Pia yelled at the top of her lungs. The sudden, unexpected scream startled Berman, and he stood up.

"Okay, okay. That got my attention. I was just teasing you to see how you would react."

"Well, now you know."

"Actually I came here to tell you I have arranged a little treat. You and I will be taking dinner together in the kitchen."

"How romantic," Pia commented sarcastically. She had been receiving simple meals in her room now that the IV had been discontinued. "If you poison my dinner, I promise to eat it."

Berman laughed. "I thought I'd stop by to give you proper warning. Perhaps you'd like to freshen up. I'll be back in a half hour or so."

True to his word, Berman returned when he said, and then led

Pia out of her bedroom. She noticed the guard by the door, it was the one with the expressionless face: the one she had seen the most often. He followed after them. Otherwise they didn't see another person in the large dwelling. The kitchen was below ground level and was dominated by a massive iron stove on which were several covered pots and pans. Pleasing aromas of cooking wafted through the room. A butcher block table fit in one end, and there were three chairs and three place settings at the table. The guard came into the room and stood to the side.

"Are we expecting someone else? Who is it—let me guess. Whitney Jones?"

"Not Whitney, she is busy. Another colleague said he might join us." Berman busied himself by the stove. Pia looked at him while he worked. A few days ago she would have refused to sit at the table under any circumstances. Now it was apparent to her that she had to concede a little in order to survive, and she had to stop herself from making her customary sarcastic and insulting outbursts at Berman. Pia thought Berman was truly deluded. What a bizarre situation. He was fixing dinner as if the two of them were on a date.

"You're probably fed up with soup," he said. "So I made us a salad to begin." Berman presented a plate on which sat a fresh-looking summer salad. "Some fresh bread?" he asked.

"Can I have a long, sharp butcher's knife for the butter?"

"Alas, no. I'll butter the bread for you. Come on, Pia! I'm making an effort here. I'm trying to establish a dialogue with you in a pleasant setting."

Pia ate. The food was good despite the circumstances being so grotesque.

"I like to cook," Berman said, trying to be conversational. "I don't know if I ever told you that. I made some fish—trout. With almonds. I've practiced a couple of times this week as a break from the Chinese fare that's the usual aroud here, and the dish isn't bad. I'm eager to get your opinion."

"Whatever," said Pia. She was feeling dizzy again, and her patience with this charade was wearing thin. *Dialogue, my ass*, she thought but kept her opinion to herself.

"You want some wine?" said Berman.

"Why not," Pia said trying to suppress the sarcasm in her voice.

Berman went to the fridge to fetch a chilled bottle of Chablis.

The door opened and a man entered. Pia noticed the guard stiffen and hold himself taller. It was obvious to her that whoever this person was, he was important. He was Chinese, about Berman's age, Pia thought, maybe younger, but she couldn't be certain. She knew she had trouble gauging Asian age with both men and women. The man had a pleasant, relaxed expression. He was wearing an expensive-appearing T-shirt, possibly made of silk, and stylish jeans. He sported a fashionable, Western-style haircut.

"Hello," Jimmy said to Pia casually. He merely nodded to Berman. He didn't introduce himself to Pia. Earlier he had told Berman not to use any names if he showed up at dinner.

Berman slammed the door to the refrigerator and then busied himself opening the wine.

From Pia's perspective it seemed that Berman was demonstrably unhappy to see the man there, apparently wanting to be alone with Pia for the so-called dialogue he had in mind. She was glad to see the man whoever he was.

"Who are you?" asked Pia. What did this mean? Berman continued to be abrupt, with his throwing away the cork and slamming the cabinet door. He came over to the table and thumped the wine down on the table. Pia looked from Berman back to the sudden visitor. There was a tenseness in the air. If Berman was this man's superior, he would have ordered him out, or so Pia surmised. One thing was for sure: she had to play this carefully.

"Ah, I see you are about to have dinner," the man said. "I don't want to interrupt."

"You're not interrupting," said Pia. "Mr. Berman here is playing happy family, and I haven't talked to anyone else for weeks. We have an extra place, so sit down. So who are you, if you don't mind my asking?"

"Of course I don't mind your asking. And you won't mind if I don't tell you." Jimmy smiled. He looked at Berman, who was exceedingly uncomfortable.

"Of course this is a very unusual situation," said Jimmy, looking at Berman. "And one that we have to resolve."

"Who is 'we'?" said Pia. "And by the way, I'm sitting right here. If you want to talk about me, that is. You could include me in the conversation. What I'd say to you is that I'm being held here against my will and I demand to be released. I'm losing interest in this nanotechnology stuff by the day, so I'll be happy to go back to working on salmonella someplace else. What do you two say?"

Jimmy was impressed; she showed no fear at all. He sensed her tenacity.

Pia looked at him. Her head was pounding again, but she was trying to look resolute.

"Well, all that notwithstanding, Mr. Berman and I have to resolve the situation."

"We are resolving it," said Berman to Jimmy. "*I* am resolving it. We have plenty of time."

"Plenty of time for what?" said Pia.

"For us to prove that you and I can work together, Pia. Your scientific promise will be invaluable to Nano as we move into our next stage. I know you realize that in your heart of hearts. Perhaps you just haven't admitted it to yourself."

Berman smiled at Pia and she looked back at him. What Jimmy saw in that moment of time spoke volumes to him. She was a beautiful woman, in that Berman was not deluding himself, but there was a hardness there that went beyond tenacity of purpose that Berman clearly hadn't accounted for properly. Berman could only see the woman and overlooked the tigress.

"Well, we shall see. Mr. Berman, I wanted to let you know that we are going to watch some competition tomorrow, at the Olympic Stadium."

"We?" said Berman.

"You and Miss Jones and me. Miss Grazdani will have to stay here, I'm afraid. But you and I are going to have a fascinating day, I can promise you. We're going to travel by boat—the river is the only way to travel, with traffic the way it has been the last few days. The athletics competition is starting. It's going to be fun. We're leaving at eight."

"I had some plans for my day here, but if that is what you wish."

"It is."

"I don't have any plans," said Pia, looking at Jimmy. "Why don't you bring me along? It can be a party."

Jimmy smiled even more broadly at Pia. He could tell that she was a remarkable woman in many respects, and dangerous. "Enjoy your dinner."

"Why don't you stay and eat with us," said Pia. "I would enjoy it."

"Miss Grazdani," he said simply, and left the room.

"So who is he, Berman?" said Pia after a pause. "Your money guy? Your liaison with the Chinese government? The guy who sends you the future cadavers from Chinese jails? His English is perfect, by the way—is he Chinese American?"

Berman didn't answer. The room might be wired; the guard might speak English—probably both.

"Let me check on the trout," Berman said.

JIMMY YAN WENT BACK to his room on the third floor of the vicarage. He had confirmed what he thought about Pia, which meant tomorrow would be an even busier day than he'd already had planned. On his cell phone he made the first of a number of calls, he needed to make.

"Hello, yes, it's me. The plan we talked about, we need to execute it tomorrow. But the timing is crucial. I'll call you later with the exact schedule."

63.

Burim showed the color Xerox of the photograph of Pia to yet another young girl who was living on the streets. By now he must have
shown that picture to ten thousand strays and runaways. He had
been offered girls like that, if such was his fancy, or perhaps a younger
girl? He had been told many times that he could have the address of
the girl in the picture for twenty or fifty or a hundred pounds. But
no one had seen Pia. Burim knew it was useless, but he pressed on.
It was better than sitting around doing nothing, and he felt progressively desperate. In reality he knew that the only way he would ever
hear anything was if the London Albanian crime network picked up
some word. Burim took the cell phone that Harry had lent him the
day before, and called the house in Tottenham. No, Harry hadn't
heard anything. And what was Burim thinking, calling at this time
of the morning?

Burim ended the call. He wondered if George was having any
luck or if Burim had just replicated his own futility in bringing him
here. Of course part of the reason for getting him to London was
just for Burim to give vent to his anger at George for getting him
involved in such a futile wild-goose chase.

The man who had been following Burim for the past three hours noted the time of Burim's call, and emailed what he had observed to his boss. This was what he had been asked to look for, and finally, he had witnessed it.

GEORGE HAD FOUND BURIM late on Thursday morning. Burim had decided even before he got there that it was probably smart not to let the local Albanians know he had brought the kid over, so he had told George to find himself a room in a different part of town from him. He had handed George a sheaf of banknotes and told him to get himself a cell phone. Then he gave George a few copies of the picture of Pia and told him to keep his cell phone on. He never knew when the call might be coming. George was dutifully doing as Burim asked, visiting the major Underground, train, and bus stations with the pictures of Pia, and like Burim, he was seeing a different side to London than most American visitors ever saw.

JIMMY YAN HAD BEEN asleep only two hours when his alarm woke him on Friday morning. Still, he wasn't tempted to try to grab another few minutes—it was not his habit to do so, and today it was important that everything run on time. Jimmy had stayed up most of the night to finalize the elaborate preparations, finishing with a long call on the secure line to his superior in Beijing, going over every detail of the plan, especially the piece that catered to their unexpected houseguest.

He knew Zach Berman and Whitney Jones had been woken early, and he called his associate to gather the party in front of the vicarage after a light breakfast.

"Good morning, Whitney, I haven't seen you in a while," said Berman when he came out of the house.

"I've been busy," said Whitney Jones, irritably, looking at her boss. "It's hard to run a business in Colorado from rural England."

The barb went over Berman's head. He expected Whitney to do her job whether there was a seven-hour time difference or not.

Jimmy then joined Berman and Whitney. He motioned for them to join him in the second of two cars.

"We are taking the scenic route to Windsor," said Jimmy. He was in a buoyant mood as usual. He had learned early in life that it was best not to play one's hand. "Little Chalfont . . . Amersham . . . Beaconsfield."

Jimmy was an enthusiastic tour guide. As they drove up a steep hill out of the small town of Amersham, Jimmy said this was called Gore Hill, named for an ancient battle with Vikings, after which blood ran down the incline and back into the town.

Berman and Whitney had dutifully looked out and nodded. Neither was all that interested.

"That way is John Milton's house, in Chalfont St. Giles," said Jimmy, indicating a road even smaller than the one they were on. "But it is too far out of our way. Perhaps we'll check it out next time we're in the countryside."

Thirty minutes later they were aboard a speedy riverboat, headed east down the Thames. Whitney Jones was enjoying her freedom from the confines of the dingy room she had been working in for days; Berman looked completely distracted. Jimmy checked his smartphone every couple of minutes. A flurry of texts kept him apprised of developments. Everything was running according to plan.

As Pia lay in bed in the still of the morning, she had heard the doors of two or three cars close and the sound of tires on gravel as they had driven away. She had assumed this was Berman and Whitney Jones leaving with the Chinese man she had met last night. Who

ROBIN COOK

was that man? Pia wondered. In the last few days she had looked forward to her walks around the garden, and she doubted she was going to be allowed out in Berman's absence. These recent days had been more bearable, with the food, the bathroom. Even the ridiculous dinner the night before had, in reality, been a welcome diversion from her general boredom.

Just as she had that thought, the door opened and the Chinese doctor entered the room, followed by a guard; a different man, for once. The doctor walked straight over to Pia and grabbed her good arm.

"Hey, what's this?" she demanded, trying to pull away.

The doctor was avoided her gaze, and Pia knew that was a bad sign.

"What are you doing to me?" she demanded, as the guard put his hands on her shoulders and forced her back supine on the bed.

In the next instant, she felt a stab in her arm, followed by a stinging sensation, and then a kind of spinning blackness settle over her like the slow-motion closing of an old-fashioned camera's shutter.

BURIM'S BORROWED cell phone rang once, and before it could sound again, he answered the call.

"Yes?"

"It's Harry. We heard something, from a reliable contact. She's in the Pipeline."

"The pipeline? What's that, for God's sake? Where is she?"

"We don't know where she is. Listen carefully! Remember these peoples' names, and go to a library and look them up on a computer. You'll find out what the Pipeline is."

Harry mentioned two Albanian names to Burim. Burim wrote them down.

"Do you have everything we gave you?"

Harry had given Burim the cell phone he was talking on, and a

SIG Sauer automatic pistol with a spare ammunition clip, which Burim had stuffed in a small backpack at the house in Tottenham. He carried it over his shoulder

"Yes, I have everything."

"Okay. Be ready. We may not hear anything more for hours. But you will have to respond quickly if there is any chance of success so stay alert."

Burim looked at his watch. It was two o'clock. He was at King's Cross railway station, a busy terminus, and within a couple of minutes he was on his way to the St. Pancras Library nearby.

ZACHARY BERMAN WAS BEMUSED to learn that the evening's athletics events did not begin until seven P.M. at the Olympic Stadium. Why had they left so early? Why did they have to sit around in this corporate suite hobnobbing with Chinese officials? In contrast Whitney Jones was seemingly having a fine time, or so Berman gathered from looking over at her.

Whitney was enjoying herself. This was the first time she had been able to relax since they'd come to England almost two weeks before. Even though the future of Nano was being decided at these championships, something she knew about intimately, there were still humdrum details to deal with. There were numerous experiments running in Boulder, as well as the day-to-day operation of the facilities. Staff had to be managed, along with all the other mundane tasks, and her boss had shown little interest in any of them, since he had Pia to worry about. So everything had all fallen on Whitney's capable shoulders.

Now Whitney sat in the Chinese delegation's suite, sipping Champagne and talking with Jimmy Yan, whom she found delightfully intriguing. Jimmy was such a breath of fresh air compared with Berman, and Whitney couldn't help but complain about her boss a little.

"Yes, he does seem to be preoccupied," said Jimmy. "And I agree, that woman is not healthy for him. But we are businessmen. Or businesspeople, Miss Jones. As long as Mr. Berman can deliver what he has promised to us, we are happy. We all have our foibles. I just hope that the big picture has been adequately taken care of."

"I can assure you that everything is ready," said Whitney. "The Web sites are prepared and just need to be accessed."

"I am very confident that everything will run smoothly. As smoothly as the athletes this evening. London has done a good job with these games, as they did with the Olympics. They weren't as spectacular as Beijing, of course, but the English have been interested in involving their citizenry, which was less of an issue for us."

"They have to allow the taxpayers access," said Whitney. "That's the way democracies are supposed to work."

"Indeed," said Jimmy. "But not in here, not right now. Would you like more Champagne?"

"I notice you are not drinking."

"Not yet. I want to toast a Chinese victory. I see we have a women's hundred-meter race up first. Sprinting has not proved to be a strong point for us like it is for the Jamaicans, so perhaps I will have to wait for our success in the long-distance, endurance events."

BURIM SAT IN FRONT of the computer monitor in the St. Pancras Library. The homeless man he had elbowed off the terminal had said he was going to find "the management," and Burim hurried, in case the man actually persuaded someone to come see what he was complaining about. Burim found the search engine and typed in the two names he had been given. What he eventually found didn't make for pretty reading.

The men were key figures of an Albanian sex ring that specialized in smuggling Eastern European girls to the Far East or North Africa or the Arab states of the Middle East. The ring was not averse to taking vulnerable girls off the streets of London or Manchester or Edinburgh, or any other European capital. The girls were often teenage runaways unable to find adequate work in Prague, Budapest, or Bratslavia and were often rather attractive in the current paradigm of the fashion world: youthful, slim yet curvaceous with sculpted facial features. Such a young women of exceptional beauty could fetch up to £500,000 in the Arab market. Burim read quickly to the end of the article. "The Pipeline" was what they termed the chain along which the captured girls were passed, usually forced to take heavy doses of illegal drugs. Once someone was in the Pipeline, the piece read, it was almost impossible for them to be traced. It was the equivalent of being sucked into a black hole. They all but disappeared.

Burim hurried out of the library and called Harry, but there was no reply. Then he called George.

"Any luck?" he said.

"Not a thing. There are so many runaways. I had the wrong idea about London," said George.

"Keep working but keep your phone handy," Burim said, and hung up. He didn't think George would cope well with hearing about the Pipeline, but he wanted him available.

To conserve battery power, Burim resisted trying to call Harry. Otherwise he merely walked the London streets as the day wore on; he couldn't sit still. What he wished was that all this was taking place in New York, where he had real power and connections, not London.

JIMMY YAN HAD TO force Berman to come sit in the front of the box to watch the evening's last event, the women's 10,000-meter final. Berman had continued to brood, and had drunk more gin and tonics than he should have. There was a Briton in the race, and the possibility of her winning the medal had the regular Brits in the crowd cheering her name and chanting in unison.

"This race will be a good one, I can feel it," said Jimmy.

After five laps, a pack of four women—two of them Kenyans, with the Briton and an American—were leading and pulling away from the field. The Kenyans took turns in the lead and pushed the pace of the race. Whitney cheered for the American by name, and Jimmy chided her jokingly.

"Well, the Chinese runner is way back," said Whitney.

"Give her time," said Jimmy. "She's a slow starter."

Berman saw the Chinese runner, Wei, make her move with four laps to go. It was as if she had engaged another gear, and she picked up speed smoothly and effortlessly. From near the back of the field she overtook the women one by one, until with two laps to go only the Kenyans and the American were in her way. The crowd saw her coming, and as the British runner tired, they cheered Wei's heroic charge. On a large TV set in the suite, Berman could see Wei was running with marvelous economy. He looked across at Jimmy Yan. As the Chinese officials around him hollered and screamed, Jimmy was impassive, as if unsurprised. Jimmy looked over and caught Berman's eye. He nodded and smiled and pointed to the track.

"Look at her go!" shouted Whitney. On the last lap, Wei caught the Kenyans and ran on their shoulder as they raced two abreast, trying to hold her at bay and block her passage to the front. Wei was undaunted. She steered a wide course around the duo on the final curve, so wide it looked as though she were running herself out of contention, but she managed to find yet another gear. First she was at their shoulder, then she overtook the Kenyans with apparent ease, and as she coasted to the win and the world championship she waved her arms over her head in joy.

Inside the box, it was pandemonium. Amid the din, the men around him clapped each other on the back. They were delirious.

Feeling like the odd man out, Berman went back and used the facilities. The suite had a small powder room in the rear. After using the toilet, he flushed it, then stared at himself in the mirror. He knew he had drunk too much, but his mind was functioning fine. What was bothering him was the way the woman won the race. It had seemed too staged, too planned, too improbable considering the level of competition involving several preeminent athletes, including the holder of the world record. Something didn't feel right. Berman washed his hands absentmindedly, then returned to the box.

"What's the matter?"

It was Jimmy, who had come up behind Berman, a hand clamped a little too hard on his shoulder.

"You tell me, Jimmy. There's something about the way that woman won the race."

"Come with me, and we can talk about it."

"Why can't you tell me here?" asked Berman.

"Come with me," said Jimmy. "I have to insist."

64.

Two of Jimmy's security men walked Berman to a small conference room at the back of the large suite across from the powder room. Berman was surprised to see that Whitney Jones was already seated at the table with another guard at her back. On the table in front of her were two powered up computers. There were several other Chinese men at the table in business suits. Each had their own laptop in front of them.

Jimmy closed the door behind him and bid Zachary Berman to sit down next to Whitney. When he didn't, the two guards forced him into a chair.

"Get your hands off me!" Berman yelled. His voice was thick from drink.

"Relax, Zachary. I realize I owe you an explanation," said Jimmy.

"You sure do." Berman was steamed, especially since he had been manhandled by Jimmy Yan's security. Jimmy was his friend; they were business partners, and Berman didn't appreciate being touched. The whole day had taken an ugly turn.

"Zachary, I assure you that nothing has changed in our relationship."

"You could have fooled me. What was going on out there? If I didn't know better, I would say that the winner was running with respirocytes in her system, and you say nothing has changed? The only place in the world where respirocytes are made is Nano."

"I said nothing has changed. Well, maybe the timetable we're on has been altered slightly."

"What does that mean? And who *was* that woman? I swear I never saw her before in my life."

"She is China's new heroine and world champion. She deserves to be congratulated. And you should be congratulated, too, Zachary. And you, Miss Jones."

"What does her victory have to do with me?" said Berman.

"Wei had been given a dose according to the newest protocol of respirocytes in a secret training location in China."

"What!" Berman shot out of his seat, only to be thrust back down into it by the guards. "That is outrageous! That is not how it was to be. We have our agreement! The technology is hardly finished, and you've stolen it already."

"I wouldn't say we have stolen it. We borrowed some respirocytes, as a loan against the sum—the huge sum, I might add—we are about to pay for the ability to share proprietary information and manufacture the nanorobots in China. And we are sitting here to complete our end of the deal. So really no harm has been done."

Jimmy turned and spoke to one of the associates at the table.

"What is he saying?" Berman asked Whitney. "Did you know anything about this?"

"No! Of course not. He is asking for the wire transfer to be prepared."

"I don't have the decryption key for the Web sites with the technological specs," said Berman. "I didn't imagine I'd need them today."

"I took the liberty of bringing your machine with me," said Jimmy, and handed Berman his laptop.

"Why are you doing this? Why are we not waiting for the marathon, as we agreed?"

"We decided we didn't have to wait. My superiors added more conditions to the deal, and they insisted I not share them with you. We had to replicate your anticipated success at the championships with a winning runner of our own. As the men's marathon is the last event, that presented us with a problem."

"How did you get hold of the respirocytes? Do you have spies in my company? Who are they? I'll find out if you don't tell me, and there'll be hell to pay."

"Zachary, please do not get agitated about any of this. You are wasting your energy. We are fully committed to nanotechnology and our partnership, and this money is the sign of our commitment. Miss Jones, please look at these details on the screen. Tell me if they look good to you."

Jimmy slid the two laptops over to Whitney, and she read the information. The amount of money, the huge amount, was correct. The bank was right; she had memorized the account number, and that was good, too.

"It looks fine to me," she said. "Everything seems to be in order."

"How can I ever trust you again?" Berman was staring at Jimmy. His voice wavered.

"That is not for me to answer, Zachary." Jimmy said. "Understand that the situation was out of my control. You have to believe me. Now please, if you could pass me the codes, we will access the Web site."

"And then what?"

"What do you mean?"

"What happens after I do that?"

"The money goes to Nano's account," said Jimmy. "As we agreed. And we have access to the company's technical specifications. Officially. Then we can begin to make nanorobots and share with you in the future research."

"And then we go back to the vicarage?"

"Unfortunately, that will not be possible."

"But . . . Pia . . ." said Berman, stumbling over his words. And the worst part of what had just happened suddenly occurred to him.

THE MORE TIME that passed without a call from Harry, the nearer Burim Graziani was to the end of his rope. He had gone to Piccadilly Circus, the station on the underground that seemed best situated for access to anywhere in London. Burim figured the Underground was the way to go if he was in a hurry, as the Friday-night traffic in the center part of the city was impossible. It was almost eleven o'clock, and he had heard nothing for hours. If there was a fate worse than death, Burim had read about it that afternoon. He knew about the sex traffickers, and what the girls these men took were subjected to. He could barely contain his fury. Someone was going down for this and that someone was going to be Zachary Berman.

"YOU BASTARD."

"Zachary, I am saving you from yourself. You have been useless these past two weeks. Miss Jones has been running Nano single-handedly while you have been monomaniacally obsessed with this Pia woman. You have spent your days and nights mooning over her. And I saw last night that she will never give herself to you voluntarily. As we have discussed, it is okay to have a weakness, but this woman is a fatal flaw in you. You're like a character in a Greek tragedy."

"I will see to it that you—"

"You will see to nothing. Yell and scream all you want. You have your money; we have the proprietary information. We have made arrangements for you to leave. Your plane is scheduled to depart from Stansted in ninety minutes to take you back to Boulder. By the time you get home, you will have seen the reason for what we have done and understand it."

"But where is Pia?"

"Obviously I am not going to tell you anything. In fact, I don't know where she is. In order to retain our . . . standing . . . we used an intermediary to tidy up your mess. I couldn't tell you where she was if I wanted to. Now you will leave. Voluntarily or otherwise, it is all the same to me. Go home, Zachary! Go back to that castle of yours, and find another diversion. You deserve a rest."

"I know I have been distracted," said Berman. "But I beg you to reconsider what you are doing. I know that Pia will come around by the time of the marathon. That was our agreement. She told me herself she was changing her mind. Damn you, you bastard."

Jimmy shrugged and told his men to make sure Berman got in the car downstairs without incident. He would follow them as they drove out to Stansted Airport.

WHEN BURIM'S PHONE RANG, he could hardly hear it over the noise of the crowd. There must have been a hundred kids with guitars, all sitting in the center of the square, all playing the same stupid song.

"Is this Burim?" said a voice Burim didn't recognize.

"Who is this?" Burim jammed a finger in his other ear and walked as fast as he could away from the din.

"I know where your daughter is being held."

"If you do anything to her, I will kill you," said Burim.

"I'm not holding her; there are two men," said the voice. Burim was trying to place the accent. Not Albanian for sure, not European at all.

"Just tell me where she is."

"Wimbledon."

"The tennis place? Give me the address."

The man gave Burim the details, which he memorized. Then the man asked "Where are you?"

"Central London."

"You'd better be fast."

Burim memorized what the man told him and started thumbing through the *London A–Z* guide he had bought for just this eventuality. When he found it, he phoned Harry and told him about the call.

"That's weird," said Harry. "Who do you think it was?"

"I have no idea, and I don't care. Can you guys meet me or not? I've got to get the fuck over there. The caller warned me to be fast."

"Okay, we'll come, but Wimbledon is clear across London. It's going to take us a while."

"Well, get there as soon as you can. I might need backup."

Burim hung up. Then, as he hurried toward the entrance to the Underground, he called George.

"Where are you?"

"Hammersmith," said George. "You heard something, I can tell."

"You have to meet me right now. It's a place in Wimbledon. I will give you the details. Pia is there, I hope. Grab a cab and and wait for me, but don't do anything until I'm there. Even if you happen to see her, don't interfere, just follow. Got it?"

"Okay, okay. Oh, my God. Just tell me where to go."

Burim gave him the address and repeated the admonition not to do anything before he arrived. He added that it could be dangerous for him and for Pia. As he started down the stairs he cursed the fact that he might have to rely on a goddamned stupid college kid like George.

JIMMY FELT A TWINGE of compassion for Zachary Berman, then discarded it. He was a weak man, after all. He had succeeded so well in life, yet had failed to control himself when it mattered. It had been easy for Jimmy to gain access to Nano's secrets, but still, it all could have turned out differently if Berman had been more of a man. Jimmy was so sick of Berman's whining that he rode in a separate car. After Berman had climbed into his, Jimmy had guided Whitney Jones into the second car and got in after her.

"You should have come to me earlier," said Whitney. "I would have talked to him. It might have worked out differently."

"I know you would have talked to him. But I think he was always going to be besotted with this woman. But his feelings will pass, and he will stop hating me. Or he won't. It's all the same to me." Jimmy smiled.

"Nano will be fine," said Whitney.

"I know," said Jimmy. "Mostly thanks to you." He looked at his watch. Everything was running like clockwork. They were already close to the airport, and it was important that Berman was safely in the air before the last act played out.

"Midnight," said Jimmy. And he sat back in his seat.

ALTHOUGH HE MADE his connection quickly at South Kensington station where he had momentarily considered exiting from the Underground and finding a taxi, Burim strained every sinew willing the Underground train to go faster. Why was the train so slow? Why did the stations need to be so close together? Burim found a passenger who was alighting at Wimbledon, and he found out from her that he needed to be at the front of the District Line train to make the fastest exit. He barged from car to car through the happy and mostly drunken Friday-night crowd, who all took one look at the man and gave him leeway without complaint, realizing he shouldn't be messed with.

Burim knew that Hammersmith was closer to Wimbledon than Piccadilly, and he had told George to hail a taxi, meaning he was bound to get there faster. Burim hoped to hell George could contain himself and wait for him. His job was to make sure Pia wasn't moved anywhere before Burim arrived.

Finally, the train arrived and Burim burst out of the car. It was about a mile to the home whose address he had and there were no taxis in sight. Burim busted a gut running there. He knew the route from the guidebook, and as he approached the address, he could see George Wilson standing in the street, and he ran toward him. This was a quiet residential street, a richer part of town than the one where he had been staying. The houses were all four stories tall.

"Have you seen anything?" Burim managed. He was totally out of breath gasping for air.

"Nothing," George said, offering no greeting. "I think it's the top flat, second house from the end. The one with the lights on. What are we going to do?"

Burim didn't answer but rather took out his handgun and cocked it, putting a bullet into the chamber before tucking the gun into this belt. With one more glance up to the lighted apartment, he ran across the street toward the building's front door.

For a second, George hesitated. The sight of the gun had unnerved him. But then, without really thinking about what he was doing, he took off after Burim. Burim was at the door, pulling a short-handled crowbar from the backpack he'd taken off his shoulder.

Wedging the crowbar into the doorjamb, Burim leaned into it, and the door gave way easily. He rushed through and charged up the stairs to the top level. George followed suit. On the top level, Burim raced to the appropriate door, 4A. Using both hands, he wedged the crowbar between the door and the jamb just above the lock. Then pulling out the gun from his belt with his right hand, he pushed the crowbar with his left, putting all his weight onto it. The door was dead-bolted and had a chain, but Burim was like a man possessed— his strength splintered the door and yanked it off its hinges.

A heartbeat later Burim was in the apartment, now holding his gun in front of him in both hands. Inside were two men on a couch, moving now, guns on the table, lines of cocaine. . . . Burim squeezed off two shots in the direction of each man aiming at their surprised faces—the first went down, but as the second reached for his gun, Burim fired again, with truer aim.

George pushed into the room and felt immediately sick. The

two men were obviously mortally wounded. Both were lying in grotesque positions: one was moaning, the other gurgling. Burim's aim
was good—both had been hit in the head, sending bits of bone and
brain splattering on the wall behind the couch. A TV was on and a
late-night host was still chatting with his guest as if nothing had
happened. On the coffee table with the guns and cocaine was a large
brick of 100-euro notes.

"Jesus," said George.

Still holding his gun out in front of him, Burim searched the
apartment, first looking into the kitchen area. It was a mess, with
dirty dishes piled on the countertops and in the sink. Wasting no
time, Burim dashed to the back of the living room. There were two
closed doors that led, he assumed, to bedrooms. Burim held the
handle to the first, clutching his gun in his other hand. He opened
the door quickly, and rolled around the door into the room, ready to
fire again. There was an unmade double bed, an open wardrobe and
not much else. Burim checked a small bathroom. It was empty.

Burim went to the second door off the living room. He ignored
George who was frozen in place two steps into the apartment.
Burim grasped the doorknob of the final door, holding this pistol at
the ready alongside his head. He then yanked open the door.

JIMMY YAN YAWNED. It had been a hell of a day. But Zach Berman's
plane was now ready to head back to Boulder, and in a few minutes,
Jimmy's car would be roaring on the motorway up the spine of England to Manchester and another airport, and a plane that would
take him home and to a powerful new life of his own.

Jimmy moved over to the base of the airstairs leading up to Berman's plane. Berman was standing on the tarmac off to the side, and
looked crushed and a little drunk. Jimmy nodded that it was time,
and the guards let Berman go. Berman walked unsteadily toward

the stairs. Jimmy held out his hand to shake if Berman was so inclined, but he wasn't. He stopped for a moment, glared at Jimmy for a beat, then climbed the stairs. At the top, he didn't look back.

Berman turned to the right and sank into one of the leather swivel chairs. He leaned back and closed his eyes. The pilots were going through their last preflight checks. A few moments later as the door to the Gulfstream banged shut, Berman opened his eyes and nodded to the cabin attendant. It was only then that he made a point to turn and look into the depth of the plane. He was surprised. He was the only passenger. Whitney Jones had never got on.

Berman leaned over to the large oval window, which was a hallmark of the Gulfstream design. He craned his neck to see what he could. He made out Jimmy's figure, and, yes, there was Whitney Jones, standing right next to him. Berman leaned back into his seat. *I have my money,* he thought, *but why does it feel like I've lost everything?*

"You feel okay?" Jimmy said to Whitney.

"I feel fine," Whitney said. "Better than fine. I'm flabbergasted at what you have been able to do. Nano will be far better with you at the helm."

"With your help," Jimmy said. "You'll be supplying the needed continuity."

"Thank you for the recognition," Whitney responded. "Actually, I deserve it, after how hard I had to work these last months trying to hold the place together. But you are the one who deserves the recognition."

"I'm pleased you have been so supportive of our little coup."

"Like I said, if you'd come to me sooner, I'd have helped. Berman was ignoring the business with his stupid, adolescent obsession. Nano will be much safer with you. What you did was so damn clever."

With Whitney Jones sitting next to him back at the stadium, Berman had looked at the transaction page on the computer and suspected nothing. At the time neither did Whitney. It was a dummy page that only looked like the real thing. There had been no money transfer. Berman thought Jimmy had stolen some respirocytes, but the truth was far worse. The proprietary secrets that comprised Nano's real worth, besides the highly mortgaged physical plant, was all in Chinese hands. In a few days, a Chinese buyout would complete what was already a de facto truth—Nano belonged to China. Jimmy knew all of Nano's research secrets, and by now Chinese researchers were well ahead of Nano's. Jimmy was going home to run the company with Whitney as his newly installed number two. For the foreseeable future China was to dominate medical nanotechnology.

"I'm glad you feel as you do," said Jimmy. "I'm happy."

Jimmy was feeling very pleased with himself. Nano was taken care of, and the girl was gone, too. When he learned, thanks to the UK-based Chinese Triads, that Burim Graziani was in London searching for Pia Grazdani, Jimmy decided he could use the Albanian to clean up after him. Burim was on Chinese intelligence's radar in the United States, recognized as an up-and-coming gangster and as such potentially a useful person in the New York area. Jimmy thought that using an Albanian team to get rid of Pia, and then sending in Burim to remove any evidence of the men who had done away with Pia, was a very neat way indeed to end the whole sordid affair.

WHERE THE HELL had Harry and Billy gotten to? Burim had called Harry and had told him they had missed the action, thank you very much, but that now his party were desperate for a pickup. When Burim had called, he was huddled in the shadows a few hundred yards down the street from the Wimbledon house that was now swarming with police. He knew they had to get out of the area and fast. When Burim's phone buzzed, it was Harry calling to fix their exact location.

"Where the hell are you? We're trapped and we need to get out of here now."

"Okay. We can see the cops from where we parked. We'll come around the other way real slow. Okay?"

"There's two of us," said Burim.

"I know. You got the girl."

There was a long pause before Burim spoke.

"No, I didn't," said Burim, reliving the event in his mind. "She wasn't there. The apartment was empty. We were too late. It's just me and an accomplice."

EPILOGUE

Within thirty minutes of the plane taking off, Zachary Berman was even more drunk than he had been earlier. Pia was gone, and what the hell was Whitney Jones doing? Had she fallen for that Chinese toad? Such a betrayal after all he had done for her. He was inconsolable, even though he had gotten his long-sought-after capital financing. His respirocytes had worked and China had its gold medal. Their athlete would probably win the marathon, too. Berman had seen the transaction go through and he had all the money he would need for his research, but this was the definition of a Pyrrhic victory. The personal price he had to pay was enormous. The loss of face alone was galling. Berman would get revenge, somehow, sometime.

Pia was too much for him. She was such a hard ass and couldn't be trusted. She'd never submit to him. She would work tirelessly to destroy him. That bastard Jimmy Yan had said all those things, but Berman knew that Jimmy didn't really know her. She was coming around, he was sure of it. If Berman had been given the time he was promised, she would have turned, and she would become as trusted a lieutenant as Whitney or Mariel had been, he knew it. When he thought about Whitney, he laughed ruefully.

"Look how that ended up!" he said out loud. There was no one in the back of the plane to answer him.

Such were Berman's constant thoughts as the plane pushed on toward home.

THE FIRST SIGN that something was amiss with Berman's flight was when its copilot failed to make his planned check in at four A.M. The control tower in Ireland that had been following the flight couldn't raise Berman's plane, and when authorities in Newfoundland, Canada, reported that they couldn't establish contact with the Gulfstream, either, the alert was sounded. But the force of the explosion that tore the plane apart was such that no identifiable wreckage of Zachary Berman's Gulfstream was ever found in the cold, deep waters of the North Atlantic.

extracts reading groups
competitions books new
discounts extracts
competitions
books
new
events books
extracts
new titles reading groups
interviews
discounts
new books events
events new
discounts extracts discounts
www.panmacmillan.com
extracts events reading groups
competitions books extracts new